The armchair philosophers may still quibble over what the cascade point images "really" are, but those of us who fly the small ships figured it out long ago. The Colloton field puts us into a different type of space, possibly an entire universe worth of it—that much is established fact. Somehow this space links us into a set of alternate realities, universes that might have been if things had gone differently . . . and what I was therefore seeing around me were images of what I would be doing in each of those universes.

It was no great feat to locate the images I particularly needed to see: the white-and-gold liner captain's uniforms stood out brilliantly among the more dingy jumpsuits and coveralls on either side. Liner captain. In charge of a fully equipped, fully modernized ship; treated with the respect and admiration such a position brought. It could have been—*should* have been. And to make things worse, I knew the precise decision that had lost it to me.

—From "Cascade Point"

Baen Books by Timothy Zahn

COBRA
A COMING OF AGE
SPINNERET
COBRA STRIKE

TIMOTHY ZAHN

CASCADE POINT

For Mick —
Renewed best wishes,

Tim Zahn
8/15/87

BAEN BOOKS

CASCADE POINT

This is a work of fiction. All the characters and events portrayed in this book are fictional, and any resemblance to real people or incidents is purely coincidental.

A Baen Book

Baen Publishing Enterprises
260 Fifth Avenue
New York, N.Y. 10001

First Baen printing, April 1987

ISBN: 0-671-65633-3

Cover art by Doug Beekman

Printed in the United States of America

Distributed by
SIMON & SCHUSTER
1230 Avenue of the Americas
New York, N.Y. 10020

Contents

Acknowledgments

"The Giftie Gie Us" was first published in *Analog*, July, 1981 issue. Copyright © 1981 by Timothy Zahn.

"The Dreamsender" was first published in *Analog*, July, 1980 issue. Copyright © 1980 by Timothy Zahn.

"The Energy Crisis of 2215" was first published in *Amazing Stories*, March, 1981 issue. Copyright © 1981 by Timothy Zahn.

"Return to the Fold" was first published in in *Analog*, September, 1984 issue. Copyright © 1984 by Timothy Zahn.

"The Shadows of Evening" was first published in *The Magazine of Fantasy and Science Fiction*, March, 1983 issue. Copyright © 1983 by Timothy Zahn.

"The Challenge" was first published in *Space Gamer*, December, 1980 issue. Copyright © 1980 by Timothy Zahn.

"The Cassandra" was first published in *Analog*, November, 1983 issue. Copyright © 1983 by Timothy Zahn.

"Dragon Pax" was first published in *Rigel Science Fiction*, Fall, 1982 issue. Copyright © 1982 by Timothy Zahn.

"Job Inaction" was first published in *Analog*, November, 1981 issue. Copyright © 1981 by Timothy Zahn.

"Teamwork" was first published in *Analog*, April, 1984 issue. Copyright © 1984 by Timothy Zahn.

"The Final Report on the Lifeline Experiment" was first published in *Analog*, May, 1983 issue. Copyright © 1983 by Timothy Zahn.

"Cascade Point" was first published in *Analog*, mid-December, 1983 issue. Copyright © 1983 by Timothy Zahn.

The Giftie Gie Us

The sun was barely up as I left the cabin that morning, but it was already promising to be a beautiful day. Some freak of nature had blown away the usual cloud cover and was treating the world—or at least the middle Appalachians—to an absolutely clear blue sky, the first I'd seen in months. I admired the sky and the budding April greenery around me as I made my way down the wooded slope, long practice enabling me to avoid trees and other obstructions with minimal effort. It was finally spring, I decided, smiling my half-smile at the blazing sun which was already starting to drive the chill from the morning air. Had it not been for the oppressive silence in the forest, it would almost be possible to convince myself that the Last War had been only a bad dream. But the absence of birds, which for some reason had been particularly hard hit by the Soviet nuke bac barrage, was a continual reminder to me. I had hoped that, by now, nearly five years after the holocaust, they would have made a comeback. Clearly, they had not, and I could only hope that enough had survived the missiles to eventually repopulate the continent. Somehow, it seemed the height of injustice for birds to die in a war over oil.

I had reached the weed-overgrown gravel road that lay southwest of my cabin and had started to cross it when a bit of color caught my eye. About fifty yards down the road, off to the side, was something that looked like a pile of old laundry. But I knew better; no one threw away clothes these days. Almost undoubtedly it was a body.

I regarded it, feeling my jaw tightening. I'd looked at far too many bodies in my lifetime, and my natural impulse was to continue across the road and forget what I'd seen. But someone had to check this out—find out whether it was a stranger or someone local, find out whether it had been a natural death or otherwise—and that someone might just as well be me. Aside from anything else, if there was a murderer running around loose, I wanted to know about it. I took a step toward the form, and as I did so my foot hit a small pile of gravel, scattering it noisily.

The "body" twitched and sat up abruptly, and I suddenly found myself looking at a strikingly lovely woman wrapped up to her chin in a blanket. "Who's there?" she called timidly, staring in my direction.

I froze in panic, waiting for her inevitable reaction to my face, and silently cursed myself for being so careless. It was far too late to run or even turn my head; she was looking straight at me.

But the expected look of horror never materialized. "Who's there?" she repeated, and only then did I notice that her gaze was actually a little to my right. Then I understood.

She was blind.

It says a lot for my sense of priorities that my first reaction was one of relief that she couldn't see me. Only then did it occur to me how cruelly rough postwar life must be for her with such a handicap. "It's all right," I called out, starting forward again. "I won't hurt you."

She turned slightly so that she was facing me—keying on my voice and footsteps, I presume—and waited until I had reached her before speaking again. "Can you tell me where I am? I'm trying to find a town called Hemlock."

"You've got another five miles to go," I told her. Up

close, she wasn't as beautiful as I'd first thought. Her nose was a little too long and her face too angular; her figure—what I could see of it beneath the blanket and mismatched clothing—was thin instead of slender. But she was still nice-looking, and I felt emotions stirring within me which I thought had died years ago.

"Are there any doctors there?"

"Only a vet, but he does reasonably well with people, too." I frowned, studying the fatigue in her face, something I'd assumed was just from her journey. Now I wasn't so sure. "Do you feel sick?"

"A little, maybe. But I mostly need the doctor for a friend who's up the road a few miles. We were traveling from Chilhowie and he came down with something." A chill shook her body and she tightened her grip on the blanket.

I touched her forehead. She felt a little warm. "What were his symptoms?"

"Headache, fever, and a little nausea at first. That lasted about a day. Then his muscles started to hurt and he began to get dizzy spells. It wasn't more than an hour before he couldn't even stand up anymore. He told me to keep on going and see if I could find a doctor in Hemlock."

"When did you leave him?"

"Yesterday afternoon. I walked most of the night, I think."

I nodded grimly. "I'm afraid your friend is probably dead by now. I'm sorry."

She looked stricken. "How do you know?"

"It sounds like a variant of one of the bacterial diseases the Russians hit us with in the war. It's kind of rare now, but it's still possible to catch it. And it works fast."

Her whole body seemed to sag, and she closed her eyes. "I have to be sure. You might be wrong."

"I'll go and check on him after we get you settled," I assured her. "Come on."

She let me help her to her feet, draping the blanket sari-style around her head and torso and retrieving the small satchel that seemed to be her only luggage. "Where are you taking me?"

That was a very good question, come to think of it. She wasn't going to make it to Hemlock without a lot more rest, and I sure wasn't going to carry her there. Besides, if she was carrying a Russian bug, I didn't want her going into the town anyway. Theoretically, she could wipe the place out. That left me exactly one alternative. "My cabin."

"I see."

I had never realized that two words, spoken in such a neutral tone, could hold that much information. "It's not what you think," I assured her hastily, feeling an irrational urge to explain my motives. "If you're contagious, I can't let you go into town."

"What about you?"

"I've already been exposed to you, so I've got nothing to lose. But I'm probably not in danger anyway—I've been immunized against a lot of these diseases."

"Very handy. How'd you manage it?"

"I was in the second wave into Iran," I explained, gently pulling her toward the slope leading to my cabin. She came passively. "They had us pretty well doped up against the stuff the Russians had hit the first wave with."

We reached the edge of the road and started up. "Is it uphill all the way?" she asked tiredly.

"It's only a quarter mile," I told her. "You can make it."

We did, but just barely, and I had to half-carry her the last few yards. I put her on the old couch in the living room and then went and got the medical kit I'd taken when I cleared out of Atlanta just hours before the missiles started falling. She had a slight fever and a rapid pulse, but I couldn't tell whether or not that was from our climb. But if she'd really been exposed to one of those Sidewinder strains, I couldn't take any chances, so I gave her one of my last few broad-spectrum pills and told her to get some rest. She was obviously more fatigued than I'd realized, and was asleep almost before the pill reached her stomach.

I covered her with her blanket and then stood there looking at her for a moment, wondering why I was doing all this. I had long ago made the decision to isolate myself as much as possible from what was left of humanity, and up till now I'd done a pretty good job of it. I wasn't about to change that policy, either. This was only a temporary aberration, I told myself firmly; get her well and then send her to Hemlock where she could get a job. Picking up the medical kit, I went quietly out.

It was late afternoon when I returned with the single rabbit my assorted snares had caught. The girl was still asleep, but as I passed her on my way to the kitchen she stirred. "Hello?"

"It's just me," I called back to her. I tossed the rabbit on the kitchen counter and returned through the swinging door to the living room. "How do you feel?"

"Very tired," she said. "I woke up a couple of times while you were gone, but fell asleep again."

"Any muscle aches or dizziness?"

"My leg muscles hurt some, but that's not surprising. Nothing else feels bad." She sat up and shook her head experimentally. "I'm not dizzy, either."

"Good. The tiredness is just a side effect of the medicine I gave you." I sat down next to her, glad to get off my feet. "I think that you're going to be all right."

She inhaled sharply. "Don! I almost forgot—did you get to him in time?"

I shook my head, forgetting how useless that gesture was. "I'm sorry. He was already dead when I found him. I buried him at the side of the road."

Her sightless eyes closed, and a tear welled up under each eyelid. I wanted to put my arm around her and comfort her, but a part of me was still too nervous to try that. So I contented myself with resting my hand gently on her arm. "Was he your husband?" I asked after a moment.

She sniffed and shook her head. "He'd been my friend for the last three years. Sort of a protector and employer. I'll miss him." She swallowed and took a deep, shuddering breath. "I'll be okay. Can I help you with anything?"

"No. All I want you to do right now is rest. I'll get dinner ready—I hope you like rabbit. Uh, by the way, my name's Neil Cameron."

"I'm Heather Davis."

"Nice to meet you. Look, why don't you lie down again. I'll call you when dinner's ready."

Supper was a short, quiet affair. Heather was too groggy and depressed to say or eat much, and I was far too out of practice at dinner conversation to make up for it. So we ate roast rabbit and a couple of carrots from last summer's crop, and then, as the sun disappeared behind the Appalachians, I led her to my bedroom. She sat on the edge of the bed, a puzzled and wary look on her face, as I rummaged in my footlocker for another blanket. "You'll be more comfortable here," I told her.

"I don't mind the couch," she murmured in that neutral tone she'd used on me before.

"I insist." I found the blanket and turned to face her. She was still sitting on the bed, her hands exploring the size and feel of the queen-size mattress. There was plenty of room there for two, and for a moment I was tempted. Instead, I took a step toward the door. "I've got another hour's worth of work to do," I said. "Uh, the bathroom's out the door to the left—the faucets and toilet work, but easy on the water and don't flush unless it's necessary. If you need me tonight, just call. I'll be on the couch."

Her face was lifted toward mine, and for a second I had the weird feeling she was studing my face. An illusion, of course. But whatever she heard in my voice apparently satisfied her, because she nodded wearily and climbed under the blanket.

Leaving the bedroom door open so I could hear her, I headed for the kitchen, tossing my blanket onto the couch as I passed it. I lit a candle against the growing darkness and, using the water from the solar-heated tank sparingly, I began to clean up the dinner dishes. And as I worked, not surprisingly, I thought about Heather Davis.

All the standard questions went through my mind—who was she, where did she come from, how had she survived for five years—but none of them was really uppermost in my mind. Five years of primitive hardship and self-imposed solitude should have pretty well wiped out my sex urge, or so I would have thought. But it was all coming back in a rush, and as my lust grew my thoughts became increasingly turbulent. I knew she would accept me into her bed—if not willingly, at least passively. In her position, she couldn't risk refusing me. Besides, I'd given her food and shelter and maybe saved her life. She owed me.

And then I glanced up, and all the passion left me like someone had pulled a plug. Reflecting dimly back at me from the kitchen window, framed by the bars I'd installed for security, was my face. I'd lived with it for over five years now, ever since the Soviet nerve gas barrage near Abadan that had somehow seeped through my mask, but it still made me shudder. The reactions of other people were even worse, ranging from wide-eyed stares to gasps of horror, the latter especially common among women and children. Frozen by some trick of the gas into a tortured grimace, the left side of my face looked more like a fright mask than like anything human; the right side, normal except for three parallel scars from a mortar fragment, only made the other half look worse. My hair and beard followed the same pattern: a normal chestnut brown on the right, pure white on the left. And if all that weren't enough, there was my left eye; mobile and still with perfect vision, it had turned from brown to a pale yellow, and sometimes seemed to glow in the dark.

I stared at my reflection for a long minute before returning to my work. No, I couldn't take advantage of Heather's blindness that way. It would be unfair of me to go to bed with her when she couldn't tell how horrible I looked. Somewhere in the back of my mind, I was aware that this was the same argument, in reverse, that I used to avoid approaching any of the sighted girls in Hemlock, but that was irrelevant. The discussion was closed.

I finished the dishes in a subdued frame of mind and then headed toward the front door. As I reached it, I heard a muffled sound from the bedroom and tiptoed in to investigate.

Curled into a fetal position under the blanket, her back to the door, Heather was crying. I stood irresolutely for a moment, then went in and sat down by her on the bed. She flinched as I touched her shoulder. "It's all right," I whispered to her. "You're safe now. It's all right. I won't hurt you."

Eventually, the sobs ceased and the tenseness went out of her body, and a few minutes later the rhythm of her breathing changed as she fell asleep. Careful not to wake her, I got up and went back to the doorway. There I stopped and looked at her for a moment, ashamed of my earlier thoughts. Heather wasn't just a warm female body put here for my amusement. She was another human being, and whether she stayed here an hour or a week she was entitled to courtesy and respect. It was the least I could do for her in the face of the barbarism out there. For that matter, it was the least I could do for *me*. There were enough savages in the world today; I had no desire to add to their number.

I closed the bedroom door halfway as a gesture to her privacy and went to finish my chores.

I stayed close to the cabin for the next couple of days, tending my garden and doing needed repairs and odd jobs. Heather's fever disappeared, and she recovered quickly from the effects of her journey and the medicine I'd given her. By the third morning after her arrival, I felt it was safe to leave her and go check on my snares. They were empty; but after a few hours of hunting with my bow and arrows I bagged a small squirrel, so at least we wouldn't go hungry. I swung by my "refrigerator" to pick up some vegetables and then returned to the cabin. Once there, I went straight to the bedroom to check on Heather.

She was gone.

I stood there for a moment, dumbfounded. The damn girl had cleared out, sure enough—and probably helped herself to everything she could get her hands on. I'd been a naïve fool to leave her here alone. "Heather!" I barked, the name tasting like a curse.

"I'm back here," a voice called faintly.

I started, and after a second I went outside and made my way to the rear of the cabin. Sleeves rolled up, Heather was standing by the hand pump that brought water from the nearby stream and sent it into the storage tank on the roof. She smiled in the direction of my footsteps, her face glistening with sweat. "Hi," she said. "I was just taking a break. How was the hunting?"

"Fair; we've got squirrel for supper," I told her, trying to keep my voice casual—hard to do when you're feeling like a jerk. "Also brought some corn. Why aren't you in bed?"

She shrugged. "I've never liked being a professional freeloader. Besides, you forgot to pump any water last night."

I hadn't forgotten—I'd just been too lazy—but I hadn't expected her to notice. The tank usually held enough water for three or four days, though I tried to keep it full. "Well, thanks very much. I appreciate it."

"No charge. You said you had some corn? Where did you get that?"

I started to point north, remembered in time the gesture would be wasted. "About a mile upstream there's a hollow right behind a small waterfall. The creek comes from underground at that point and stays pretty cold even in the summer. I use the hollow as my refrigerator. In winter, of course, it's more like a freezer."

"That's a good idea," Heather nodded, "although it's kind of far to go for a midnight snack. I'll bet it's fun keeping the animals out, too."

"It was, but I've pretty well got that problem solved." I suddenly realized I was still holding the squirrel and corn. "Come on, let's go inside. You look tired."

"Okay." She seemed to hesitate just a second, then stepped up to me and took my arm, letting me lead her back into the cabin.

Another surprise awaited me in the living room. Heather had neatly folded my blanket and laid it at one end of the couch; her satchel, some of its contents strewn around it, sat at the other end. In the middle lay a shirt I'd torn just that morning, neatly mended.

"I'll be darned," I exclaimed in delight, unaware of the pun until after I'd said it. "How did you know that shirt needed sewing?"

She shrugged. "I heard you getting dressed this morning, and right in the middle of it I heard something tear. You muttered under your breath and threw whatever it was onto the couch. When I got up I found the shirt and used a needle and thread from my sewing kit to mend it. I hope the thread doesn't look too bad there—I had no idea what colors I was working with."

I opened my mouth, but closed it again and instead reached for the shirt, my cheerful mood suddenly overshadowed by an uncomfortable feeling creeping up my backbone. Dimly, I remembered the sequence of events Heather had described, but it seemed too incredible that she should have pieced such subtle clues together that easily. Was it possible she wasn't quite blind?

There was a way to check. Still holding the shirt, I walked over to the window, loosening my belt with one hand until the big brass army buckle was free. The sun had come out from behind the clouds and light was streaming brightly through the glass. I turned slightly so that I was facing Heather and twisted my buckle, sending a healthy chuck of that sunlight straight at her eyes.

Nothing. She didn't flinch or even blink. Feeling a little silly, I let the loosened buckle flop back down against my leg and held up the shirt for a close examination, trying to pretend that that had been my reason for moving into the light in the first place. The seam was strong and reasonably straight, though the material bunched a little in places and the white thread was in sharp contrast with the brown plaid. "It looks fine," I told Heather. "It's exactly what I needed. Thank you for doing it for me."

Her face, which had been looking a little apprehensive, broke into a tentative smile. "I'm glad it's all right," she said, and I wondered that I had ever doubted her handicap. Only a blind woman could ever face me and still smile like that. And even though I knew how undeserved that smile was, I rather liked it.

I cleared my throat. "I guess I'd better go skin the squirrel and start cooking it."

"Okay. First, though, come on back and show me how to tell when the water tank's full. I want to finish that pumping before dinner."

It was pretty clear that Heather was completely healed from whatever she had caught, but I decided to keep her at the cabin for a few more days anyway. My official reason was that it would be best to keep her under observation for a bit longer, but this was at least eighty percent rationalization, if not outright lie: the simple fact was that I found her very nice to have around. I had never before had the chance to find out how much easier primitive life could be with an extra pair of hands to help with the work. Despite her blindness, Heather pitched in with skill and determination, and if I somehow failed to give her enough to do she would seek out work on her own. One morning, for example, as I was weeding the garden, she came to me with a pile of dirty clothes and insisted that I lead her down to the stream and find a place where she could wash them.

But most of all, I enjoyed just being able to relax in the company of another human being. That sounds almost trite, I suppose, but it was something I hadn't been able to do for five years. And, while I'd buried my need for companionship as deeply as I could, I hadn't killed it, a fact my infrequent trips to Hemlock usually only emphasized. The people of that tiny community were helpful enough— their assistance and willingness to teach me the necessary backwoods survival skills had probably saved my life the first year after the war—but I couldn't relax in their presence, any more than they could in mine. My face was a barrier as strong as the Berlin Wall.

But with Heather the problem didn't exist. We talked a great deal together, usually as we worked, our conversation ranging from trivia to philosophy to the practical details of postwar life. Heather's knowledge of music, literature, and household tasks was far superior to mine, while I held an edge in politics, hunting, and trapping. Her sense of humor, while a little dry, meshed well with mine, and a lot of our moral values were similar. Under different circumstances I would have been happy to keep her here just as long as I possibly could. But I knew that wouldn't be fair to her.

My conscience finally caught up with me late one evening after dinner as we sat together on the couch. Heather was continuing her assault on the pile of mending I'd accumulated over the years; I was trying to carve a new ax handle. My heart wasn't really in it, though, and my thoughts and gaze kept drifting to Heather. Her sewing skill had increased since that first shirt she'd mended for me; her fingers moved swiftly, surely, and the seam was straight and clean. Bathed in the soft light of a nearby candle, the warmth of which she enjoyed, she was a pleasure to watch. I wondered how I was going to broach the subject.

She gave me the opening herself. "You're very quiet tonight, Neil," she said after a particularly long lull in the conversation. "What are you thinking about?"

I gritted my teeth and plunged in. "I've been thinking it's about time to take you to Hemlock, introduce you around, and see if we can get you a job or something with one of the families there."

The nimble fingers faltered for a moment. "I see," she said at last. "Are you sure I'm not contagious anymore? I wouldn't want to get anyone sick."

"No, I'm certain you're completely recovered. I'm not even sure you had a deadly bug, anyway."

"Okay. But I wonder if it might be better if I stick around for another week or two, until the garden's going a little better and you don't have to spend so much time on it."

I frowned. This was going all wrong—she was supposed to be jumping at the chance to get back to humanity again, not making excuses to stay here. "Thanks for the offer, but I can manage. You've been a lot of help, though, and I wish I could repay you more than . . ." I let the sentence trail off. Heather's face and body had gone rigid, and she was no longer sewing. "What's the matter? Would you rather go somewhere else instead of Hemlock? I'll help you get to anywhere you want."

Heather shook her head and sighed. "No, it's not that. I just . . . don't want to leave you."

I stared at her, feeling sandbagged. "Why?"

"I like being here. I like working with you. You don't— you don't care that I'm blind. You accept me as a person."

There was a whole truckload of irony in there somewhere but I couldn't be bothered with it at the moment. "Listen, Heather, don't get the idea I'm all noble or anything, because I'm not. If you knew more about me you'd realize that."

"Perhaps." Her tone said she didn't believe it.

There was no way out of it. Up till now I'd been pretty successful at keeping my appearance a secret from her, but I couldn't hide the truth any longer. I would have to tell her about my face. "If you weren't blind, Heather, you wouldn't have wanted to stay here ten minutes. I'm . . . my face is pretty badly disfigured."

She nodded casual acceptance of the information. Maybe she didn't believe it, either. "How did it happen?"

"I was a captain in the army during the Iranian segment of the Last War; you know, the Soviet drive toward the oil fields. They were using lots of elaborate nerve gases on us, and one of them found its way into the left side of my gas mask." I kept my voice even; I was just reciting facts. "None of it got into the nosepiece or respirator, so it didn't kill me, but it left one side of my face paralyzed. I won't trouble you with any details, but the net effect is pretty hideous."

"I thought something must have happened to you in the war," she murmured. "You never speak of your life during that time. . . . Is that why you were here when the missiles came?"

"Yes. I was in a hospital in Atlanta, undergoing tests to see if my condition could be reversed. They hadn't made any progess when I saw the handwriting on the wall and decided it was time to pull out. A friend of mine had told me about his cabin in the Appalachians, so I loaded some supplies in a Jeep and came here. I beat the missiles by about three hours."

"Oh, so this place wasn't originally yours. And I'd been thinking all along how terribly clever and foresighted you'd been to have built a cabin out here in case the world blew itself up."

"Sorry. Major Frank Matheson was the one with all the foresight. He was also one of the best friends I ever had." That sounded too much like an epitaph for my taste; I was still hoping he'd show up here someday. But he and his wife had been in Washington when the missiles started falling. . . . I shook my head to clear it. "Anyway, we're getting off the subject. The point is that I'm taking advantage of you by keeping you here. I think you'd be better off living in a community with other people."

"Yes, I suppose you would think that." Heather's lip curled, and for the first time since I'd met her I heard bitterness in her voice. "You probably think it's been beer and skittles for me. Well, it hasn't." She glowered at some unknown memory; but even as I groped for something to say, her anger turned to sadness, and when she spoke again her voice was quiet. "I went blind almost a year before the war; two weeks after my eighteenth birthday. I had a small brain tumor in the back of my head and was taking an experimental interferon derivative. Somehow, something went wrong with the batch they were giving me, and at about the same time I caught some kind of viral infection. The combination nearly killed me—they told me afterwards that I had delirium, high fever, and an absolutely crazy EEG trace for nearly forty hours. When I recovered, the tumor was shrinking and I was blind. That first morning, when I woke up . . . I thought I was either dead or insane." Her eyes closed, and she shivered violently. After a moment she continued. "People hate me, Neil. Either hate me or are afraid of me, especially now that civilization's becoming a thing of the past."

"Why would people hate you?" I asked. "I mean, that's a pretty drastic reaction."

She hesitated, and a series of unreadable expressions flashed across her face. The moment passed, and she shrugged. "I guess it's because I'm blind. It makes me an oddball and—well, something of a parasite."

I snorted. "You're no parasite."

"You're very kind, Neil. But I know better."

I shook my head, thinking of all the work she did around here. To me it was perfectly obvious that she was pulling her own weight, if not a little more. I wondered why she couldn't see that; and, in response, a fragment from a half-forgotten poem swam up from my subconscious. "'O wad some Pow'r the giftie gie us / To see oursels as others see us . . .'" I murmured, trailing off as the rest of the piece drifted from my grasp.

Surprisingly, Heather picked up where I'd left off: "'It wad frae mony a blunder free us.

"'And foolish notion:

"'What airs in dress an' gait wad lea'e us,

"'And ev'n devotion!'"

She paused for a moment, as if listening to the last echoes from her words. "I've always liked Robert Burns," she said quietly.

"That's the only thing of his I know," I confessed. "My father used to quote it at us whenever our views of life were at odds with his. Despite your own estimation, Heather, the fact is that you're a very talented and hardworking woman and no one in his right mind is going to care whether you're blind or not. People won't think any less of you because of that."

A wry smile touched her lips. "You're not being consistent, Neil dear. That's exactly what you seem to think people are doing to you. If they can judge you by your face, why can't they judge me by my blindness?"

She had me there. I wanted to tell her that was different, but it was obvious she wouldn't buy any explanation like that—her blindness made it impossible for her to realize just how strongly my appearance affected everyone who saw it. I tried to think up some other reasoning I could use . . . and suddenly it dawned on me what I was doing. Here I was, sitting next to a lovely woman who was very possibly the last person on Earth who could endure my company—and I was trying to send her away from me!

Insanity has never run in my family, unless you count our military traditions. I'd tried being noble and honest, and my conscience was clear. If she wanted to think I was doing her a favor, that was up to her. "All right, Heather. If you're really sure you want to stay, I'll be more than happy to have you here. I have to admit that the thought of you leaving was pretty hard. But I had to—you know."

She reached over and touched my arm. "Yes. Thank you for being honest. And for letting me stay."

"Sure. Look, it's getting late, and we've got to get up by dawn. Let's get some rest."

"Okay." She paused. "Neil, were you ever married?"

I blinked at the abrupt change of subject. "Once, for a couple of years, when I was twenty-one. It ended in divorce. Why?"

She turned her head half away from me as if she didn't want me to see her face. "I was just wondering why you were still . . . sleeping on the couch instead of . . . with me."

The evening was rapidly taking on a feeling of unreality for me. I hadn't felt this strangely nervous since my first date in high school, and I opened my mouth twice before I got any words to come out. "I didn't want to impose on you." Damn, that sounded stupid! I tried again. "I mean, it wouldn't be fair for me to take advantage of you like that. You might just do it because you felt you owed it to me. I don't want it that way. I figured that if you ever wanted me like that you'd let me know somehow."

She nodded, her face still averted, and swallowed. "Neil . . . will you come to bed with me?"

I looked at her, my eyes sweeping her body, and for the first time I noticed that her hands were trembling. And suddenly I realized that she was not just offering an altruistic favor to a lonely hermit. In many ways Heather was an outcast, too, and she needed this as much as I did.

Never having been the romantic type, I didn't know the right words to say. So, instead, I blew out the candles, took Heather by the arm, and led her to the bedroom.

Afterwards she fell asleep next to me, one arm across my chest with her hand resting against my good right cheek. I watched the moonlight throwing shadows on the bedroom wall for a few minutes longer before drifting off myself, and I slept more restfully that night than I had in months.

The weeks went by, spring turning into summer with astonishing speed. Heather continued to take on a good deal of the day-to-day work of running our cabin, leaving me free to hunt, trap, and carry out repairs and maintenance that I'd been putting off for lack of time. We had our share of disagreements and misunderstandings, but as we got to know each other's moods and thoughts we began to mesh together, to the point where it sometimes seemed to me that we were becoming two parts of a single, well-oiled machine. Within the first four months I felt I knew this woman better than I'd known anyone else in my entire life. And, although I refused to use the word even to myself, I was quickly learning to love her.

And yet, there was something about Heather that bothered me, something so subtle that it was a long time before I could even put my finger on it. It wasn't anything big, and it didn't happen with any regularity, but sometimes Heather just seemed to know too much about what was going on around her.

I brooded about it off and on for several weeks, trying to remember everything Heather had ever said about her blindness. From her explanation I assumed her eyes and optic nerves were still healthy, that only the sight center of her brain had been affected, and for a while I wondered if her blindness was either incomplete or possibly intermittent. But neither explanation was satisfactory: if she was blind enough that she couldn't make out my face, she was too blind for any practical purpose; and if she occasionally regained her vision, her first reaction to my appearance would have been impossible for me to miss. Besides, there was no reason why she would keep such a thing secret, especially since she was so open about every other aspect of her life.

Eventually I gave up thinking about it and chalked up her abilities to the enhanced senses blind people are reputed to have. It really wasn't important, after all, and Heather and I had come too far for me to start wondering if she was hiding something from me. Having overcome the problems of my face and her blindness, I wasn't about to let a figment of my imagination become a barrier between us.

So we worked and sweated, laughed and occasionally loafed, and generally got by pretty well. As the crops in our garden grew large enough that Heather could take over some of the weeding duties, I began to expand the network of handmade traps and snares that I had set up in the wooded hills around our cabin. I took the job seriously—I was after enough meat and furs for two people this year— and I ranged farther than usual in search of good sites.

It was on one of these trips that I stumbled across the freshly killed man.

I stood—or, rather, crouched—by the still form lying face downwards in the rotting leaves, my bow and arrow half-drawn and ready as my eyes raked the woods for signs of a possible attacker. Nothing moved, and after a moment I put down the bow and began to examine the body. He was a middle-aged man whom I vaguely remembered as living in a shack some six miles west of Hemlock and a couple of miles southwest of my cabin. He seemed to have run and crawled here under his own steam before dying, probably no more than a few hours ago. The cause of death was obvious; a homemade knife hilt still protruded from his back just above the right kidney.

I rose slowly to my feet. The dead man couldn't have made it all the way here from his shack with that wound. He must have been either in the woods or on the road, which was only a quarter mile or so away from here, when he ran into . . . who? Who would murder a harmless old man like this? On a hunch, I knelt down and checked the pockets in the faded overalls. Empty. No pocketknife, snare wire, fishhooks, or any of the other things he was likely to have been carrying. So the crime had probably started out as a robbery, perhaps turning into murder when the victim tried to escape. Not a local, I decided; more likely a wandering vagrant, who was probably long gone by now. Unless, of course, he'd gone down into Hemlock.

Or had found my cabin.

My heart skipped a beat, and before my fears were even completely formed I was racing through the woods as fast as I dared, heading for home. The cabin was not easy to see, even from higher spots on the surrounding hills, but it wasn't invisible, and there'd been only so much I'd been able to do to disguise the old drive leading up to it from the road. If anything happened to Heather . . . I refused to think about it, forcing myself instead to greater speed. Maybe I could beat him there.

I was too late. Out of breath, I had slowed to a walk as I approached the cabin, and as I started the last hundred yards I heard male voices. Cursing inwardly, I nocked an arrow and made my way silently forward.

There were six young men standing casually around the front of our cabin, chatting more or less amicably with Heather, who was leaning back against the closed front door. The visitors were all of the same type: thin and hungry-looking, with hard-bitten faces that had long ago forgotten about compassion or comfort. Their transport—six well-worn bicycles—stood a little further from the cabin. In another age the men would have fit easily into any motorcycle gang in the country; the image of them pedaling along on bicycles was faintly ludicrous. But there was nothing funny about the sheath knives they were wearing.

I raised my bow and started to draw it, aiming for the man nearest Heather . . . and hesitated. I had no proof that they had killed the man I'd found, and until I did I couldn't shoot them down in cold blood. Besides, there were too many of them. I couldn't get all six before one of them got to Heather and used her as a shield.

Lowering the bow again, I tried to think. The smart thing to do would be to triple-time it down to Hemlock and recruit some help. But I didn't dare leave Heather alone. From the bits of conversation I could hear I gathered that Heather had told them I would be returning soon, and it was clear that they had decided to behave themselves until I showed up. But they wouldn't wait forever, and if they came to the conclusion she was lying things could turn ugly very quickly.

There were really no choices left to me. I would have to go on in and confront them, playing things by ear. If I bluffed well, or played stupid enough, there was a chance that they would take whatever food we offered them and leave without causing trouble. Even at six-to-one odds murder could be a tricky business; hopefully, I could convince them we weren't worth the risk.

One thing I was *not* going to do, though, was provide them with more weapons. Backing a few yards further into the woods, I found a pile of leaves and hid my bow and quiver beneath it. My big bowie knife went into concealment in my right boot. I then made a wide quarter-circle around the cabin so as to approach from a different direction. Taking a deep breath, I strode forward.

I deliberately made no attempt to be quiet, with the result that, as I broke from the woods, all eyes were turned in my direction. I hesitated just an instant, as if startled by their presence, and then walked calmly up to them.

Heather must have recognized my footsteps. "Is that you, Neil? Hello, dear—we have some visitors."

"I see that," I replied. I'd been wondering how I could tip Heather off that there could be trouble here, but I saw now that that wouldn't be necessary. Her voice was cheery enough, but her smile was too brittle and there were lines in her face that I knew didn't belong there. She already knew something was wrong. "Welcome, gentlemen; it isn't often that we get this much company."

Their apparent leader—who looked to be all of twenty-five—recovered first from the shock of my face. "Uh, howdy," he said. "My name's Duke. We were wondering if maybe you could spare some food."

"We haven't got much ourselves, but I guess we've got a little extra," I told him, studying the six as unobtrusively as possible. They were all younger than I was, by twenty years in some cases, which probably gave them a slight edge in speed and maybe stamina. All were armed with knives, and two of them also sported club-sized lengths of metal pipe. On the plus side, I was much better fed than they were and had had a good deal of combat training and experience. If I'd been alone with them, I would have judged the odds as roughly equal. But Heather's presence put me at a dangerous disadvantage.

I would have to remedy that, and while I still had the initiative was the best time to try. "Heather," I said, turning to face her, "why don't you see how much rabbit meat is left from last night."

"Okay," she breathed and started to open the door behind her.

But Duke was smarter than I thought. "Colby," he called to one of the boys nearest Heather, "go with her and give her a hand."

"That's not necessary," I said, as Heather hesitated and Colby moved to her side. "She's perfectly capable."

"Sure, man, but she *is* blind," Duke soothed. "Hey, Colby won't take nothing."

"Yeah," Colby agreed. "C'mon, kid, let's go in."

"No!" I barked, taking a step toward him. I knew instantly that I had overreacted, but I couldn't help it. Attached to Colby's belt were two sheaths, one of which was empty. From the other protruded a hilt whose workmanship I recognized.

Perhaps Colby saw me looking at his empty sheath, or maybe it was something in my voice that tipped him off. Whichever, when I raised my eyes to his face I found him staring at me with a mixture of anger and fear. "He knows!" he croaked, and reached for his remaining knife.

He never got a chance to use it. Even before the words

were out of his mouth I had taken the single long stride that put me within range; and as the knifetip cleared the sheath, I snapped a savage kick to his belly. He doubled over, and I had barely enough time to regain my balance and turn around before I found myself surrounded. Out of the corner of my eye I saw Heather disappear into the cabin, one of the boys in hot pursuit, but I had no chance to go to her aid. Knives glinting, they moved in.

I didn't wait for them to get within range, but charged the closest one. He probably hadn't been attacked by an unarmed man in years, and the shock seemed to throw his timing off. I deflected his knife hand easily and gave him an elbow across the face as I passed him. The others, yelling obscenities, ran forward, trying to encircle me again. One came too close and got his knife kicked from his hand. He backpedaled fast enough to avoid my next kick and drew the metal pipe from his belt. Clearly surprised by my unexpected resistance, my attackers hesitated, and I used the breathing space to pull my bowie knife from my boot.

For a second we stood facing each other. "All right," I said in the deadliest voice I could manage, "I'll give you punks just one chance. Drop your weapons or I'll carve you into fertilizer."

I'd never fought with a knife in actual combat, but the training was there, and it must have showed in my stance and grip. "Duke . . . ?" the boy I'd elbowed began.

"Shut up, Al," Duke said, but without too much conviction.

A sound from the cabin door caught my attention. Heather, struggling against an arm across her throat, was being forced outside by the punk who'd been chasing her earlier. "Not so fast, you son of a bitch," he called at me, panting slightly.

"Attaboy, Jackson," Duke crowed. He turned back to me, eyes smoldering. "Now you drop *your* knife, pal. Or else your broad gets it."

"Don't listen to him, Neil!" Heather shouted, her sentence ending with a little gasp of pain.

"Leave her alone!" I took a half step toward the door—and heard the faint sound of cloth against skin behind me.

Heather shrieked even as I started to turn, my left arm rising to block. But I was too late. The whistling iron pipe, intended for my head, landed across my shoulder instead, still hard enough to stun. I felt my legs turn to rubber, and as I hit the ground the world exploded in front of me and then went black.

I must have been out only a few seconds, because when my head cleared I was lying on my back with Duke and two of his pack standing over me. I wondered what they were waiting for, and gradually realized Heather was shouting at them. "Don't kill him! I'll make a deal with you!"

"You don't have nothing to offer that we can't take by ourselves," Duke said flatly, his glare still on me.

"That's not strictly true," Heather shot back, her voice tinted with both horror and determination. "Rape isn't nearly as enjoyable as sex with a willing woman. But I'm not talking about that. I can tell you where there's a big cache of food and furs."

That got Duke's attention, but good. He looked up at her, eyes narrowed. "Where?"

"It's well hidden. You'll never find it if you hurt either of us."

"Willy! Zac! What've we got?" Duke called.

I turned my head slowly toward the cabin as two of the boys came out the door. Heather, I saw, was no longer being held, though Jackson stood close by her with his knife drawn.

"Not too much in here," one of the two called back. "A couple days' worth of food, maybe, and some other stuff we can use."

Duke looked back down at me. "Okay, lady, it's a deal. Zac, go see if you can find some rope."

"You gonna tie him up out here?" Al asked. "Someone might find him."

"Naw, we're gonna take them inside. But I want his hands tied before he gets up." Duke grinned down at me.

"You've got a good place here to hole up. We almost missed it."

I didn't bother to reply. A moment later Zac brought out most of my last coil of nylon rope, and in two minutes my hands were tied tightly behind my back. I was then dragged to my feet and marched at knifepoint into the cabin. Heather was already inside, her hands similarly tied.

"Let's put 'em in the kitchen," Willy suggested. "We can tie 'em to chairs there."

We were taken in and made to sit down, but they ran short of rope and only I was actually tied to my chair. Al suggested instead that Heather and I be roped to each other, but Duke decided against it. "She can't get into any trouble," he scoffed. Stepping over to me, he inspected my ropes and then drew his knife, resting its tip against my Adam's apple. "Okay, girl, I got my knife at your friend's throat. Give."

She gave them directions to my upstream "refrigerator" hollow. "You'll probably need to walk—there's too much undergrowth for bikes," she concluded.

"Okay, we'll go take a look." Duke sheathed his knife and glanced at the others. "Jackson, you and Colby stay here and keep an eye on things. And keep your paws off the food—hear?"

"Gotcha," Jackson said. Colby, mobile but still hunched over from my kick, nodded weakly.

Willy caught Duke's eye, glanced meaningfully in my direction. "Why bother with guards?"

"'Cause if she's lying we want him in good shape, so we can take him apart for her," he said calmly. "Let's get started."

They left. Jackson and Colby hung around a little longer, until the sounds of conversation from the others faded into the distance, and then went into the living room where they'd be more comfortable. The swinging door closed behind them and we were alone.

I looked at Heather, wishing I had something encouraging to say. "Did they hurt you?" I whispered instead.

"No." She paused. "They're going to kill us, aren't they?"

There was no point in lying to her. "Probably. I blew it, Heather." The words made my throat ache.

"Maybe not. They took the four kitchen knives out of the drawers earlier. But they didn't find your bayonet."

I stared at her, hope and surprise fighting for supremacy in my mind. I'd long ago told Heather of the weapon and its hiding place, of course: it had been put on top of the wall cabinet over the kitchen sink precisely for a circumstance like this. There was only a three-inch-high gap between the cabinet and ceiling, an easy spot to overlook in a quick search. But how did Heather know Duke's punks had missed it?

For the moment, though, the answer was unimportant. Carefully, I tested the ropes that held me to the chair. It was a complete waste of time—the boys hadn't taken any chances. "There's no way for me to get over to it," I admitted to Heather at last.

"I know." Her face was very pale, but her mouth was set in grim lines. Swaying slightly, she stood up from her chair. Her feet were tied at the ankles, but by swiveling alternately on heels and toes she was able to inch across the floor. Turning her back to the counter that adjoined the sink, she used her tied hands to help push herself into a sitting position on top of it. The counter was, for a change, clear of dishes and other obstacles, and by twisting around Heather was able to rise into a kneeling posture. Positioning herself carefully, she bowed forward at the waist and stretched her hands upwards toward the bayonet.

She couldn't reach it.

"Damn, damn, damn," she whispered bitterly. She tried again, straining an inch or two higher this time, but she was still nearly a foot too short. Standing up would help, but there was no way, tied as she was, for her to get the needed leverage to manage such a move.

She seemed to realize that, and for a moment she knelt motionlessly. I could see tears of frustration in her eyes. "It's all right, Heather—" I began.

"Shut up, Neil." She thought for another minute and I could see her come to some decision. Moving cautiously, she turned so that she was leaning over the sink in a precarious-looking position. Then, taking a deep breath, she hit the window sharply with her elbow. It shattered with a loud crash.

I bit back my involuntary exclamation. Jackson and Colby stormed in, knives at the ready. "What the hell's goin' on?" Jackson demanded. He glanced at me to confirm that my ropes were still intact, then strode to the counter and roughly hauled Heather down. "What the hell were you trying to pull, bitch?"

She shook her head defiantly. He slapped her, hard, and turned to me. "What was she tryin' to do?"

A damn good question, especially as I hadn't the slightest idea. "She didn't say, but I think she was trying to get out," I said, hoping I was way off the mark. "I guess she forgot about the security bars."

He looked back at Heather, who was now looking sullen. From the doorway, Colby spoke up. "I'll bet she was looking for something. Let's check those cupboards."

Jackson dragged Heather back to her chair and then returned to the cabinet. I watched in helpless silence as he searched all the cabinet shelves and then, almost as an afterthought, climbed onto the counter and looked on top of it. With a triumphant war whoop, he pulled out the bayonet. "Trying to get out, huh?" he sneered at me. "Hot damn! Wait'll Duke sees this."

"Jackson," Heather said, speaking to him for the first time, "won't you let us go? Please? We can't hurt you anymore—you'll all be long gone before we could do anything."

"Screw you, sister." He looked at her a moment, as if wondering whether she should be punished for her escape attempt, then apparently decided against it. Swinging the bayonet idly, he nodded at Colby. "Let's get back to the cards. I don't think we'll have any more trouble from these two."

I squeezed my eyes shut, feeling crushed. The bayonet had been, at best, a very long shot, but somehow it had helped just to know it was there if I was ever able to get to it. Now that last chance was gone; and all because I hadn't had a convincing lie ready when it had been needed. I'd blown it for us twice.

A faint scraping sound made me open my eyes. Heather had stood up again and was once more inching her way toward the sink. "Heather—?"

"Shh!" she hissed. Her face held concentration, and not even a touch of the despair I was feeling. What was she up to?

I soon found out. Again she hoisted herself to a sitting position, on the edge of the sink itself this time. Instead of getting up on her knees, though, she extended her hands back toward the jagged spikes of glass in the broken window. Without hesitation—and without touching anything else—her fingers zeroed in on a particularly loose fragment. She tugged, breaking it free with only the slightest *snap*, and I finally realized what her plan had been. Hopping down with her prize, she started back toward me.

But we were still a long way from freedom. We now had something to cut the ropes with, but with my hands half-numbed from loss of circulation I knew I could never cut Heather's bonds without severing a vein in the process. Her hands were probably in the same condition, and even with her enhanced sense of touch she wouldn't do much better on my ropes. Still, it was our only hope.

Heather, however, seemed to have an entirely different idea. "Open your legs an inch," she whispered as she reached me. I started to object, but she seemed to know what she was doing, so I shut up and did as I was told. Turning so that her back was to me, she stooped down and placed the piece of glass directly between my knees. "Close 'em," she said.

"Wait a second, Heather, this is too dangerous," I objected, suddenly realizing what she had in mind. "Why don't you go around and cut my ropes instead?"

She ignored the suggestion. "Close your knees and hold it tight," she hissed furiously.

I did so. I was terrified for her hands, and my stomach was knotted at the thought of what was probably going to happen, but we were running out of time. If we did nothing before Duke returned, we were dead. Heather crouched a bit more, placed one of her bonds gingerly against the glass, and began to rub.

After all my fears it was like watching a minor miracle happen. Quickly, accurately, and with no wasted motion, Heather attacked the ropes around her wrists. Even with her hands undoubtedly numb she always seemed to know exactly where the ropes and glass were relative to her skin, almost as if she had eyes in the back of her head. Only once did she so much as scratch herself, and that was due to a momentary loss of balance that made her sway a little.

Seconds later her hands were free. Sitting down on the floor, she took the glass from between my knees and set to work on her ankle ropes. They were off almost immediately. For another few seconds she remained where she was, grimacing as the blood flowed back into her hands and feet. Then she stood up and walked around behind me, and I felt her fingers tugging and probing at the ropes on my wrists. "Come on, hurry up," I muttered impatiently.

"Just a minute," she whispered back, her voice strangely tense. Her examination finally over, she began to cut my ropes, moving much more slowly than she had earlier. Despite her caution, though, she nicked me twice and once even managed to cut her own finger. However she had worked her earlier miracle, things unfortunately seemed to be back to normal now.

But finally I was free, and as I rubbed life back into my tingling hands Heather cut the ropes on my feet and those tying me to the chair. Standing up carefully, I tiptoed over to the cupboard and utensil drawers to arm myself. A large pan lid and carving fork went into my left hand, the fork extending a couple of inches past the lid's rim; a one-piece wooden rolling pin, the housewife's traditional weapon, went into my right. I handed Heather a small metal frying pan and positioned her by the swinging door. "I'll announce myself before I come back in," I told her. "If anyone else comes through, clobber him."

"All right." She paused. "They're both still sitting on the couch playing cards. The bayonet is on the floor in front of Jackson."

I nodded. I still didn't understand Heather's strangely capricious radar, but for the moment the *how* and *why* were irrelevant. She seemed to know how it worked and when it could be trusted, and that was what mattered right now. "Good. This should only take a minute."

"Be careful, Neil," she said, moving next to me for a quick hug.

I kissed her. "You bet, honey." Facing the door, I settled my nerves for combat. I'd nearly blown it for us twice now. This time was going to be different.

And it was.

The rest of the incident, though not without some danger, was straightforward and almost not worth mentioning. Jackson and Colby, taken completely by surprise, were easy to overpower and tie up. By the time Duke and the others came trooping back, Heather and the two prisoners were safely locked in the cabin and I was outside with my bow and arrows and lots of cover. The boys put up some resistance, but they had no real chance, and after two of them collected arrows in the shoulder they finally gave up. I marched the whole group to Hemlock, confirming my story by taking the town leaders to the body in the woods. Frontier justice being what it is, the boys were found guilty of murder and hanged that evening.

The stars were shining through gaps in the cloud cover when I returned to the cabin. Heather had left a candle burning in the window and was waiting for me on the couch. "How did it go?" she asked quietly.

"They were convicted. I'm giving their bikes to the town; some of the men will come by tomorrow to pick them up."

She nodded. "I'm almost sorry for them . . . but I don't suppose we could have let them go."

"No. If it bothers you too much, try thinking about their victim." I sat down next to her. "Heather, we have to talk. I need to know how you were able to do the things you did today. I think you know what I mean."

"Yes." Her smile was bittersweet, with traces of fear and weariness, and I suddenly realized this wasn't the first time she'd had this discussion. "You're wondering if I'm really blind or somehow faking it." She nodded heavily. "Yes, I am completely and totally blind. My eyes are useless. But the . . . disease, accident, whatever . . . that blinded me did something strange to my brain's optic center. Somehow, I'm able to pick up the images that all nearby people are getting. In other words, I *can* see—sort of—but only through other people's eyes."

I nodded slowly as all sorts of pieces finally fell into place. "That was one possibility that never occurred to me," I said. "A lot of things make sense now, though. What sort of range do you have?"

"Oh, thirty or forty feet." She sounded vaguely surprised. I wondered why, and then realized that the usual reaction was probably one of shock or revulsion. I wasn't following the pattern.

"It must have been rough for you," I said gently, taking her hand in mine.

She shrugged, too casually. "A little. I haven't told very many people. They usually . . . aren't sympathetic."

"I can imagine. I'm glad you told me, though."

"I couldn't hardly keep it a secret after all that stuff with the ropes," she smiled faintly. Then she turned serious again, and when she spoke her voice was low and just a little apprehensive. "Do you want me to leave?"

"Don't be silly. My gosh, Heather, is that why you held out on me this long? You thought I would toss you out?"

"Well . . ." She squeezed my hand. "No, not really; not after the first two months. By then I knew you cared for me and wouldn't treat me like a freak or something worse. But . . ." Her voice trailed off.

But she couldn't override her own defenses, I decided. Not really surprising—a good set of defenses would be vital to protect her from both external and internal assaults. I thought of what it must have been like, waking up that first time to see your body from someone else's point of view. No wonder she'd almost gone insane.

And a horrible thought hit me like a sledgehammer.

Heather must have sensed my tension, for she gripped my hand tightly. "Neil! What is it?"

It took me two tries to get the words out through my suddenly dry mouth. "Those hoodlums. If you could see through them . . . you saw my face."

She sighed. "Neil, I've known what you look like since the first night you brought me here. I saw your reflection in the kitchen window while you were washing the dinner dishes."

I stared at her, my head spinning. No wonder she'd cried herself to sleep that night! "But if you knew—?"

"Then why did I stay? I explained that to you months ago. Because you're a warm, generous man and I like being with you."

"But my face—"

"Damn your face!" she flared. "That thing has become an obsession with you!" She closed her eyes, and after a moment the anger drained from her expression, leaving weariness in its place. "Neil," she said, her quiet voice brimming with emotion, "I've wanted to tell you about my . . . ability . . . for a long, long time. But I couldn't, because I was afraid that you'd never believe I could care for you if I knew what you looked like. I was afraid you'd make me leave you."

Letting go of Heather's hand, I put my arm around her and held her close. All around me, I could feel reality going *tilt*. "I get the distinct feeling I've been acting like a jerk," I told her humbly. "I'm a little old to start changing all of my preconceived ideas around, though. I'll probably need a lot of help. You'll stick around and give me a hand, won't you?"

She took my free hand in both of hers and rested her head on my shoulder. "I'll stay as long as you want me here."

"I'm glad." I paused. "Heather, I think I love you."

Eyes glistening with tears, she treated me to the happiest smile I'd ever seen. Then she chuckled. "You mean you're just finding that out? My darling Neil, sometimes I think you're blinder than I am."

I denied that, of course. But now, after fifteen years with her, I sometimes wonder if she was right.

Afterword

This story gave me my first genuine head-on collision with the First Law of Science Fiction: There are few, if any, truly "new" ideas. For a beginning writer it was a bit traumatic, but as it turned out I got off with only minor fender damage and no ticket at all.

I'd just sent off the manuscript to Stan Schmidt at *Analog*, and was still congratulating myself on such a neat concept as a blind woman who saw through other people's eyes, when my copy of the July 1980 *Analog* appeared in my mailbox. Which contained the first part of Dean Ing's "Anasazi" . . . which featured a blind woman who saw through other people's eyes.

I walked around in a permanent wince for six weeks, awaiting with dread the caustic comments that must surely be on their way. But—surprise!—when Stan sent the story back he made no mention whatsoever of the unintentional overlap, merely saying that he liked the story but was too overbooked with novelettes to buy it right away. He must have been sincere, because when I ran it by him again five months later he bought it, again making no mention of "Anasazi."

Which was, I suppose, my introduction to the Second Law of Science Fiction: What you actually *do* with the idea is the truly important thing.

The Dreamsender

It was always a great day for me when my tiny office was graced by the presence of a paying client, so when I got two jobs in the same day it was cause for a quiet celebration. Riding up the thirty floors between my office and apartment I decided to splurge and cook myself the steak I'd tucked away in the freezer for a special occasion. It was a shame I couldn't have a bottle of wine with it as well, but that was one of the ironies of this job: the only times I could afford to buy good liquor I couldn't afford to drink it. I learned long ago what alcohol did to my performance.

I had just finished changing into more comfortable clothes and was hunting for that steak when the doorbell buzzed. Frowning a bit—I wasn't expecting anyone—I glanced through the peephole. The woman I saw was short, dark, rather plain-looking, and a complete stranger to me. I opened the door.

"Mr. Jefferson Morgan?" she asked without preamble. "The Dreamsender?"

"Yes," I admitted. "What can I do for you, Miss, ah—"

"May I come in?" I stood aside and she brushed past me,

moving quickly as if afraid someone would happen by and see her here. I motioned her toward the couch and closed the door.

"My name is Louise Holst," she said as we sat down. "Please forgive me for bothering you at home like this, but I was afraid to come to your office. I didn't want your secretary to hear what I have to tell you."

"As it happens, Miss—ah, Mrs. Holst," I amended, noticing her rings for the first time, "I don't have a secretary. I prefer to meet my clients personally." I didn't add that I couldn't afford a secretary even if I'd wanted one. "What seems to be the trouble?"

She took a deep breath. "Let me start at the beginning. My husband, Captain Lawrence Holst, is in the middle of a six-month tour of duty at the army's base in Krieger Crater, on the moon. The day before yesterday was our anniversary, and he had promised he would call me then. He's never broken a promise like that before, so I waited until this morning and then called him. Or, rather, I tried to. The operator at Krieger said he couldn't put me through to Larry, that he was off the base for a few weeks on special duty. When I asked what kind of duty, he got vague and mumbled something about surface mining operations."

I shrugged. "They do a lot of that at Krieger, or so I hear. Lots of heavy metals up there."

"Yes, but Larry isn't a miner. He's in the Signal Corps. But the thing that really worries me is this. I'm afraid I made something of a scene over the phone, ending up threatening to call every hour until he got in. About a half hour later someone else—a lieutenant colonel, I think—called me back. He said he was in charge of Larry's expedition and that they were patching him through from some Farside mining area. He told me that Larry was okay and that I should stop worrying, that they would be back at Krieger in a month or so and Larry could call me then."

"And you don't believe him?" That much was obvious.

"No. He sounded—well, *stiff*, as if he was watching every word. And he sounded worried and tense. *And* that was no patch; I've talked over those before, and the reception is terrible. This wasn't like that."

She ran out of words, or breath, or both. I said, "So you think something is wrong with your husband? What?"

"That's what I want you to find out. I'd like to hire you to—to contact him tonight."

Much as I wanted another job, I knew I had to be honest with her. "Mrs. Holst, I'm afraid you have a slight misconception of just what a Dreamsender can do. Basically, dreamsending is—"

"I know all that," she interrupted my standard lecture. "Dreamsending is a limited form of telepathy where the sender appears in a dream of the recipient and delivers a short message. But surely the communication is two-way, isn't it?"

"Of course, but how do I know whether what I'm seeing is truth or fiction?" She looked rather blank, so I went on, "Look, from all I've ever been able to tell, dreams are largely made up of random bits from the memory, perhaps focusing on some current problem or wish. People aren't trained to—well, to *think* in a dream. Sure, I can tell whether a person I've contacted has gotten the message, and usually whether he really believes that I wasn't just a normal dream. But that's more of an emotional response than a rational one. If I asked a specific question I wouldn't have any idea how much of the answer I could believe. If any of it."

She was silent for a long minute. "I'd like you to try anyway," she said at last. "If you will."

I shrugged. "I'd be happy to."

She reached into her purse and withdrew a photo and an envelope. "Here's your hundred-dollar fee, and this is a picture of Larry."

Captain Holst was young and serious-looking, with wavy hair and large ears. "May I keep this for tonight? I may have to refer to it again later."

"Certainly." She stood up, looking maybe a shade less worried. "When can I find out the results?"

"Come in any time tomorrow or phone. You know where my office is?"

"Yes. But so soon? What if you can't catch Larry in one of his dreaming stages tonight?"

"I don't have to. As long as he's asleep he'll start dreaming when I contact him."

"Oh. Then I'll be in tomorrow, Mr. Morgan. Good night, and thank you."

She left, and I tossed my steak into the micro to cook. Then I sprawled on the couch and mulled over my new job. I myself doubted that there was anything seriously wrong with Holst, though it might be a problem convincing his wife of that. But at least this job made a change from my usual missing persons or runaway assignments. I picked up Holst's picture and studied it. The unique advantage of dreamsending over other communications was that the Dreamsender didn't need anything but the recipient's name and a fairly recent picture of him. Approximate location was useful, but by no means necessary, and even a wrong location didn't seem to hurt too much. No one knew why; but then again, no one had the slightest idea how *any* aspect of dreamsending worked. Even though I was having trouble making a living with my talent, it gave me a certain kick to know how thoroughly a score of Dreamsenders were confounding the entire scientific community.

In the kitchen the micro pinged. Tossing the photo onto the couch, I headed for the kitchen, feeling better than I had in weeks. Three clients in one day! Maybe this business was finally going to start paying off.

Joanna Smith was dreaming about an apartment that was somehow attached to—and a part of—an elevator. Only one of the other people in the elevator had a distinct face; probably one of her real-life friends, I decided. Stepping up to Joanna, I said, "Miss Smith?"

"Yes?"

"My name is Jefferson Morgan. I'm a Dreamsender in New York. I have a message for you from your parents."

There's always an emotional tremor as the recipient

realizes this isn't the way dreams normally go. Joanna decided to be scared, and she started running. But people don't really go anywhere in dreams and I had no trouble staying alongside her as the scenery flew past us. "Don't be afraid, Miss Smith. I won't hurt you, but I have a very important message to give you."

Curiosity was beginning to overcome her fear. I waited, knowing better than to try and deliver my message before she was ready to hear it. Finally she gave in. "What is it?"

"Your uncle Glenn has had a stroke. The doctors aren't sure whether he'll live or not. Your parents knew you would want to see him, but you didn't leave an itinerary for your camping trip and they couldn't find you."

She was wavering now, unsure whether to believe me or to defend herself against emotional shock by declaring this dream to be an ordinary nightmare. Images, emotional bursts, and random words were starting to pop up all over the place. "Please believe me," I said quickly. "Your uncle very much wants to see you. Call your parents to confirm this message or, if you prefer, call the toll-free Dreamsenders number in the phone book. I won't even be offended if you want to consider this some sort of occult clairvoyance— which it isn't—and me some figment of your imagination— which I'm not. But *do* believe my message. Your parents paid a great deal of money for it and I would hate to see that money wasted."

It was a long speech for a dreaming person to hear, but it did the trick. She was finally convinced. I said good-bye and broke the contact, knowing that as I did so she would wake up.

I awoke myself with the slightly disoriented feeling that I always get after sending a dream. Turning on my bedside light, I blinked at the ceiling for a minute, and then reached to the nightstand for Larry Holst's picture. Two down, one to go. As I marshaled my thoughts concerning this message, it occurred to me that I was about to make Dreamsender history: to the best of my knowledge no one had ever before tried dreamsending to the moon. Maybe I would rate a footnote in a history book someday. Snapping off the light, I rolled over and went back to sleep.

Sometime—probably about an hour later—I was in the half-conscious, half-dreaming state that I need to make contact. With a slight effort I formed an image of Captain Holst in my mind. Slowly, an unfamiliar scene appeared around me, and from a mist at the edge of my vision a figure emerged. It was Larry Holst.

I moved toward him with a strange buoyancy I'd never felt before, almost as if I were myself in the moon's lower gravity. "Captain Holst?" I said. "My name is Jefferson Morgan—"

"It won't work," he interrupted wildly. "He can't get away with it."

"Sir, I'm here to help you," I said. "I'm Jefferson Morgan, a Dreamsender."

Images were flashing by, and I realized he wasn't really paying any attention to me. I opened my mouth to try again, then thought better of it. Maybe he would settle down in a few minutes; surely he couldn't maintain this emotional level for long. Meanwhile, I'd watch his dream images and try to figure out why he was so upset.

It was something like trying to simultaneously watch five movies, all of which are on high-speed settings. Pictures popped up all over the place, sometimes out of nowhere, sometimes generated by preceding thoughts. Often a given image would start its own series, as well. Some of the images and thoughts were familiar—a series of craters, for example: Tycho, Krieger, Mairan, Foucault, Aristoteles, and more—while others I could only guess at. Circuit diagrams, sunlit lunar landscapes, scenes that must have been from science-fiction movies—all of it snarling together into an absolute mess of image, sound, and emotional coloring.

Enough was enough. This wasn't getting me anywhere. "Captain Holst!" I shouted over the din. "You must listen to me. Your wife is worried about you."

Everything slowed down as he realized I was still there. "Who are you?"

"I'm Jefferson Morgan, a Dreamsender. Your wife asked me to contact you, to see if you were all right."

Holst's emotional tremor was much gentler than Joanna Smith's had been. Maybe the idea of receiving a dream didn't scare him much, or maybe he was just running out of emotional energy. "Where are you, sir? Are you all right?" I asked when he was listening again.

"Krieger D barracks," he said and suddenly there were bars around us.

"Are you in jail there?" I asked, startled by the image.

"All of us were sequestered by the Colonel." I got a picture of Holst tinkering with a machine—circuit diagrams flashed again—near something that looked like surface-mining equipment. Several other men appeared nearby, and the cage around us expanded to include them.

"A mine?" I guessed, trying to make sense out of the images that were going by. "Where? What kind?"

"New one, north. Iridium vein, very rich."

"And you were all sequestered? Why?"

His answer, if he gave one, was lost in a new explosion of pictures: more movielike scenes in the background, while nearby a colonel was struggling to stuff something into a sack. A group of snakes appeared and Holst began to argue with them for permission to reassure his wife. Thoughts of her seemed to agitate him; the bars around us turned thicker and darker, and again his dream began to resemble a high-speed kaleidoscope. For the first time in my experience I felt myself being caught up in the emotional current. "I'll talk to you later. Good-bye," I said hurriedly and broke the contact.

I woke up covered with sweat. Rolling out of bed, I went into the kitchen to make myself some hot chocolate. Never before had a contact hit me that hard. I still didn't know what was going on up at Krieger, but *something* sure as taxes was worrying the stuffing out of Captain Lawrence Holst.

It was another two hours before I felt calm enough to go back to sleep. I spent most of that time going over that last contact, trying to recall as much detail as possible, and as I did so several elements of the dream began to stand out. The imagery was going to be tricky, though, and before trying to decipher it I decided to wait until I could consult with the local expert on Larry Holst's mind.

Louise Holst was at my office door at nine sharp. I sat her down, gave her a cup of coffee, and took a seat across from her. She was obviously eager for my report, but had the self-control to wait until we were settled.

"Did you contact my husband last night, Mr. Morgan?" she asked.

"Yes, I did." I hesitated. "I'm afraid your suspicions were correct. Something is definitely going on up there. Nothing obviously harmful to your husband," I added, seeing her stricken look.

"Then what is it?"

I shook my head. "I don't know for sure. There were a lot of images in his dream that made no sense at all to me. I hoped you could help me interpret them."

I proceeded to describe the contact to her. She asked occasional questions, but generally listened quietly to my account.

"I wish I could help you," she said when I had finished, "but I don't understand most of those symbols myself. All I can suggest is that Larry often refers to sneaky people as 'snakes.' I guess I don't know him as well as I thought I did."

"Don't let it worry you. I doubt that he understands much of his dream imagery himself," I told her. "I've been thinking about your husband's dream, Mrs. Holst, and I think I can take at least a stab at what he was trying to say. The outstanding elements are the new iridium mine, his own presence there, and the sequestering of everyone there by the colonel. Do you know this colonel, by the way?"

She nodded quickly. "Colonel Avram Stark is the commander of Krieger Base. He reports directly to General Blaine at the Pentagon."

"So Stark is completely in charge on the moon, eh?" I

drummed my fingers on the chair arm. "Can you think of any reason he'd lock up everyone who had been at a new mine?"

"A bad accident, maybe? Something they didn't want publicity about?"

"I wonder. Stark was trying to put something in a sack in your husband's dream. Do you happen to know if he gets a percentage or bonus on new mineral wealth?"

She looked astonished. "In the *army*?"

"I didn't think so. This is a wild idea, but do you suppose Stark is trying to take the iridium in that mine for himself?"

"How would he get it off the moon?"

"I haven't the foggiest. I've never given much thought to interplanetary smuggling. I imagine it's possible, though." We both considered this.

"If you're right," she said slowly, "then Larry is in real danger. Stark couldn't let word of the mine leak out, and he can't hold those men forever. He'd have to—to kill them." She turned suddenly widened eyes on me. "You have to help me, Mr. Morgan."

"How? I doubt if I can get any more information than I already have from here."

"You could go to the moon and get proof. You could get it to the newsmen, or the Pentagon, or someone—"

"Just a second, Mrs. Holst. I'm afraid you've got the wrong guy for this job. First of all, I can't get to the moon— I haven't got the money for a commercial flight, and there's an eight-month waiting list, anyway. Secondly, this isn't my field. You'd be better off hiring a private eye. And thirdly, our theory may be completely wrong, and if it is I'd be sticking my nose deeply into army business, a practice the Pentagon takes a very dim view of. I'm a Dreamsender, not a professional kamikaze. I've done my part here."

She looked at me with an expression that was scared, tired, and cold, all at once. "All right, Mr. Morgan. Thank you for your help in contacting my husband. I'll do the rest alone."

"How?"

"I have a military pass that entitles me to get an

immediate seat on a commercial lunar flight. I think our savings can cover a round-trip ticket." She stood up. "I'll get to Larry somehow."

"Sit down, Louise." She did so, not batting an eye at my use of her first name, and waited. I stared out the window for a half minute or so, wishing I weren't so softheaded. But I had little choice. It was a cinch she could never get close enough to find out anything—she was probably known on the base, and Stark knew she had tried to talk to her husband. He'd be watching for her to show up. And if he *was* up to something illegal, he might decide that he couldn't let her live, either. She'd just be saving him the trouble of coming down here and getting her. "All right, Louise. *If* you can pay for the ticket and *if* we can figure out a way to get me aboard a flight with your pass, I'll take a crack at it."

She didn't throw her arms around me or roll her eyes heavenward or do any of the standard grade-B-movie things. She just sat there with melting eyes and said, "Thank you, Mr. Morgan."

"Call me Jeff," I said. "Let's get to work."

Besides, I'd always wanted to visit the moon.

"Last call, Flight 126 for Collins Space Station and Prinz Crater, Luna."

That was my cue. Picking up my carry-on bag, I trotted around a corner and went to the check-in desk. "Larry Holst," I told the man, handing him the ticket Louise had purchased a few hours previously with her priority pass. I hoped he wouldn't look carefully at it.

He did. "Uh, sir? This ticket is made out to *Ms*. L. Holst."

I craned my neck to look. "You're right," I agreed with what I hoped was the proper touch of amused surprise in my voice. "I never even noticed."

"I'm sorry, but I'll have to see some identification, sir."

"Sure." This was the touchy part, but Louise and I had planned for this and if I'd timed it correctly it should work. Pulling out a thick wallet, I began rummaging through it.

Tossing a couple of Larry Holst's credit cards on the desk, I commented, "My driver's license is in here somewhere."

The clerk glanced at the name on the credit cards, then at his watch. "Never mind, Mr. Holst, this will do. You'll have to hurry now, they'll be sealing the ship in two minutes. Right through that door there, sir, and have a good flight."

I made it with a minute to spare and sank into my seat thankfully. So far, so good, and for the next few days I was in the clear. Louise had given me the code numbers that went with Larry's credit cards, so I could charge my room and meals on Collins without raising any suspicions anywhere. But Collins and Prinz Crater were purely civilian stations, after all, and as long as I wasn't using stolen cards no one really cared whether I was Larry Holst or not. The real problem would be trying to get in touch with Larry at Krieger without getting caught.

Well, one crisis at a time. Right now I needed to give my attention to the stewardess as she explained how to use the emergency oxygen masks. Fastening my seat belts, I decided to sit back and try to make myself relax.

Prinz Crater, located at the south of the Harbinger Mountain range, was fairly unusual in that it was only a partial crater, its rim forming a semicircle that opened to the south. The colony had been built just outside the crater, nestled into the shadow of the northern rim, and consisted of a half-dozen domed buildings connected by underground passages. My room at the Prinz Hilton seemed rather Spartan—especially considering the price— but a careful look at the clientele suggested that luxury would have been wasted anyway. Prinz seemed to be the major spaceport for both civilian traffic to Krieger Base and scientific parties bound for the diggings in the Schroter's Valley region, and I doubted whether either group cared much what the Hilton's rooms looked like. Ordinary tourists seemed a little scarce, but there were enough around to keep me from feeling too conspicuous.

I spent my first day on the moon in and near the hotel,

learning about the spacesuits and other rental gear, and studying maps of the region. After dinner that evening I discovered that the Hilton had a colorful pamphlet on lunar history. Taking a copy back to my room, I sprawled across the bed and read it through carefully. Of special interest was a section on the army's military bases, a section that included a sketch of the nonclassified areas of Krieger Base, Krieger "D" barracks, Larry had said; only there was no "D" barracks listed on the map.

I stared at the page for several minutes, pondering this unexpected problem. Louise and I had worked out a way for me to get in touch with Larry, but I needed to know at least approximately where he was being kept. Obviously, I had misread the information during that first confused contact; just as obviously, there was nothing for me to do except try it again. I wasn't crazy about the idea, but it was that or catch a flight back to Earth. Besides, he was bound to have calmed down somewhat by now.

My first attempt that night failed—Larry was apparently not yet asleep—but I made it on the second try. The scenery around Larry this time seemed relatively quiet, though there were rumblings like thunder in the distance. "Captain Holst?" I called. "This is Jefferson Morgan again."

He turned from the circuit he had been working on and faced me. "What do you want?"

"I'm here to help you," I told him, trying to ignore the unfriendly look he was giving me. "Where are you?"

"Special Duty Barracks, Krieger D. Why are you here?"

"Your wife asked me to help you, remember? She—"

"You leave Louise out of this!" he shouted, unfriendliness turning to outright hostility in an instant. The whole dream reflected the change; thunder crashed nearby and a strong wind began to blow. Louise appeared to one side and Larry sprang over to stand between us. Protecting her from me? "Go away!" he yelled, shaking his fists at me. "Leave me alone, do you hear? Leave both of us alone!"

"Okay, okay, I'm leaving," I said. Struck by a thought, I added, "Don't worry, Stark won't hear about this from me."

That got me a reaction, all right, but it was so fast and multifaceted that I couldn't read anything at all from it. I gave up and broke the contact.

I lay in bed for a few minutes afterwards, thinking about what I'd seen and felt. At least I now knew where he was, more or less: not Krieger "D" barracks but a barracks in Krieger D. The latter, I remembered from the maps, was a small crater about twenty kilometers from the main base. It was only about three kilometers across, so I should have no trouble finding the barracks itself.

And I *was* going to find it. Larry had been angry, hostile, and threatening, but behind all of that I had been able to sense another emotion: fear. Larry Holst was still afraid of something, and more than ever I wanted to know what. I had undertaken this job mainly from a lopsided sense of duty, but my own native curiosity was starting to take a keen interest in things.

There was still one chore to do before I could close shop for the night. I contacted Louise, assured her Larry was all right, and told her I would try to contact him directly the next afternoon. It still bothered my scientific intuition that dreamsending from the moon felt no different than if Louise was across the street, but I had too many other things on my mind to worry about it. Later, maybe, when all this was over, I'd write a letter to some journal somewhere. For the moment, I was just glad that this time all I had to do was *send* information, and not try to receive any.

Finally, message complete, I set the alarm for seven o'clock and settled down for a good night's sleep. Tomorrow was going to be a busy day.

"Good morning," I said briskly to the clerk at the rental counter. "I'd like to check out a suit and buggy for the day."

"For a long trip, sir?"

"Probably. I want to go exploring a little around the Aristarchus Rille area. Pick up some rocks, get a few pictures, that sort of thing."

He consulted his list, confirmed I'd been checked out on the equipment yesterday by one of the staff. "I can let you have one of the Selenes, Mr. Holst; number eight. Is that satisfactory?"

"Fine." The solar-augmented batteries of a Selene, I had been told, gave the buggy an almost unlimited range. Even with the decoy run I would have to make, the round trip to Krieger should be easily less than three hundred kilometers.

The suit and Selene were delivered in ten minutes, one of the hotel staff then taking another thirty to help me double-check everything, but within an hour I was tooling northwest along the sun-lit lunar landscape at the rip-roaring speed of forty kilometers an hour. The terrain was pretty hilly for a while, until I had crossed Prinz Rille I, but then it generally settled down, and I was able to devote less of my already busy mind to the chore of driving.

It took me a bit over an hour to reach Aristarchus Rille V. Finding a close-set pair of hills, I parked the Selene between them and set to work with the buggy's toolkit. What I was doing now was not only illegal but was the act of a suicidal idiot as well, and I could feel sweat gathering on my forehead. Carefully removing the self-contained radio beacon from its hiding place under the seat, I took it outside and left it beside a recognizable rock formation. The beacon was, naturally, designed so that it couldn't be turned off and was continually monitored from Prinz. To those observers, I would simply have left my vehicle parked while I went exploring on foot, and my side trip north to Krieger would go completely unnoticed. But, by the same token, if something happened to me, I couldn't be found by a rescue team. That one I tried not to think about.

It was only another fifty kilometers to Krieger D, but I took the time to give the entire Krieger crater system a wide berth. Swinging east, I circled Krieger D at a distance of about ten kilometers and made my cautious approach from the northeast. I reached the rim without incident and, after parking the Selene in a convenient depression, I began setting up my apparatus.

Among its equipment the Selene carried a very fine tripod-mounted monocular adapted for spacesuit use. Setting this up, I scanned the shadows at the south end of the crater, the likeliest place for the barracks to be. I wasn't disappointed. There it was, a squat building with a row of porthole-type windows near the ground, looking sort of like a cross between a cliff dwelling and a Quonset hut. Jumping the monocular's power, I took a look through all the windows I could see from my position, hoping fervently Larry was in an outside room. If he wasn't, the plan Louise and I had cooked up would be useless. But again I was lucky: neatly framed in the third porthole from the end was Larry Holst, writing busily at a foldaway desk.

So far, so good. Now came the hard part. I obviously couldn't use a radio to contact him, even if he had a transceiver, which I doubted. No sentries were in sight, but there had to be *some* security measures in force around the building, so going up and knocking on Larry's window was out, too.

However . . .

A few years ago the number of scientific parties poking around remote areas of the moon had grown so great that some method of good communication had become essential. A series of satellites had been the answer, satellites that would accept modulated laser beams from the surface and relay such messages to a central switching station. Austere though the Hilton's rooms had been, the management knew better than to scrimp on any safety equipment, and my Selene was equipped with a beautiful laser transmitter. It would make a bright red spot on Larry's wall, a spot I could flick on and off in Morse code. Larry should be able to come up with something to make his own dots and dashes with, and with the monocular I would be able to see whatever he used.

I was just about to go get the laser when a motion in the room caught my eye. Another soldier had entered and was talking with Larry. The conversation was brief, though. Larry stood up and disappeared from my view; he returned a moment later buckling a gunbelt around his waist. Then, together, they left the room.

I thought about that for all of three seconds. Then I got up, stowed the monocular, and took off just as fast as the Selene would take me. Granted all I don't know about military procedure, I *do* know prisoners are *not* issued weapons. Larry was very clearly no longer a prisoner, and the obvious conclusion followed immediately: He had thrown in with Colonel Stark.

The trip back to Prinz was uneventful, which was a good thing as I wasn't paying much attention to my driving. Over and over again I shuffled the facts, lined them up, and added them together, and each time I came up with the same answer. Somehow Stark had gotten to Larry, either through bribes or threats—the latter, perhaps, directed at Louise. That would explain Larry's protectiveness toward her last night, as well as the fear I had sensed. If Stark got caught now, Larry would be run through the percolator along with the colonel, and he knew it. No wonder he had tried to throw me out of his dream.

For me, it all boiled down to the fact that my sole information source had dried up. I had counted heavily on a direct contact with Larry, on the solid data that he would have provided; without it I was effectively stalemated.

I lost an extra hour getting home by nearly forgetting to go back for the radio beacon I'd left at Aristarchus Rille V. I finally made it in around seven-thirty, itching all over from eleven hours in a spacesuit. First on my priority list was a bath, after which I had a late dinner. Returning then to my room, I stood in front of the porthole and glowered at the landscape.

There had to be a way to figure out what was going on at Krieger D. I couldn't go back to Louise and tell her she'd used half of her savings to send me to the moon for nothing. Larry might not yet be in so deeply that he couldn't be saved, especially if Stark was using threats to keep him in line. The right facts in the right hands might do it, but I needed facts first.

The really aggravating thing was that, down deep, I knew everything I needed had been in that first confused contact with Larry. I still remembered most of the images and words from that dream, but a good ninety percent of them had to be extraneous, and there was no way for me to separate the facts from the garbage.

Unless . . .

Unless I could correlate Larry's dream images with someone else's, someone who also knew what was going on. I leaped over to my nightstand—very literally; I'd forgotten about lunar gravity—and picked up the pamphlet I'd studied earlier, turning to the first page of the military-history section. Sure enough, right below the picture of General Conrad Blaine was a photo of Colonel Avram Stark. I took the time to memorize both faces, even though I just needed Stark's at the moment. Blaine, as Pentagon honcho in charge of the moon, would be the man to contact once I had some facts.

With one last look at Stark's photo, I snapped off the light and slid into bed.

The overall tone of Stark's dream was a curious mixture of anxiety, frantic activity, and icy calmness. I stayed near the edge of the scenery for several minutes, watching for anything that looked familiar, but either Stark didn't use any of the same symbols as Larry or else he just wasn't dreaming about the mine tonight.

Perhaps a nudge would help. "Colonel," I called, "where are you?"

Stark turned at the sound of my voice as a burst of symbols, including several sets of latitude and longitude, went by too fast to catch completely. Two words—Krieger and Mairan—were visible for just a second. Between the two craters? Or was one name superfluous? I gambled and tried one more question. "Where is your irridium mine?"

"Forty, due east," he said, his eyes boring into mine with an intensity I didn't at all care for. I was just thinking about making a graceful exit when all hell broke loose.

"You're a Dreamsender!" Stark shouted as weapons appeared beside him and began blasting ineffectually at me. "How much do you know, damn you? Who else have you told?"

I should have stayed and tried to bluff my way out, to convince him I was only a dream image. But I panicked. I backed away and got out of there, knowing even as I did so that he would wake up with a vivid memory of the dream.

But at least I now had some idea where the iridium mine was. The name of Mairan Crater, some four hundred twenty kilometers north of Krieger, had showed up in both Larry's and Stark's dreams, in the latter case as an answer to a direct question. "Forty due east," Stark had said: forty kilometers east of Mairan? Larry had said the mine was "north," which would be approximately the right direction from Krieger D.

It was finally time, I decided, for me to blow the whistle. Stark's violent reaction, combined with Larry's earlier comment that "he can't get away with it," left me no further doubt that something illegal was going on at that mine. Admittedly, nothing I had so far could be considered hard evidence, but I should at least be able to spark an investigation by the Pentagon. And the sooner I started, the better.

Rolling over, I went back to sleep. An hour or so later I stepped through a misty barrier and came within sight of General Conrad Blaine himself.

His dream seemed to be a replay of some military crisis from his past. Shells and rockets whizzed about us, and he was dressed in full combat garb. I made my way toward him easily, but somewhere in the back of my mind something felt wrong, and for a moment I hesitated. Something in the scene around me? I couldn't tell. Nuts to it, though. I had a job to do.

"General Blaine? I'm Jefferson Morgan, a Dreamsender. I'm speaking to you from the moon with an urgent message."

Blaine's emotional tremor nearly knocked me off the

map. I hung on and waited for it to subside before continuing. "There is something going on at your Krieger Crater Base that you should know about. Colonel Stark is up to something regarding a secret iridium mine near Mairan Crater—"

Blaine had been settling down, but the mention of Mairan set him off again. I waited for the emotional swirl to die down, but more than ever I felt something was wrong with this contact.

"Who are you?" Blaine asked. "How do you know this?"

"My name is Jefferson Morgan. I've been in contact with Captain Lawrence Holst, one of Stark's men at Krieger Base."

"What did he tell you?" Blaine took a step toward me, bouncing slightly.

Bouncing? *Bouncing?*

My thoughts froze in midsentence as the reason for my uneasiness hit me like a sledgehammer. I felt *light*—the same feeling I'd had when sending dreams to Larry, but *not* when I'd contacted Louise, even when I myself was here. It was a feeling that seemed to go with the recipient's location.

General Blaine was here on the moon.

I didn't even bother to say good-bye, but broke the contact just as fast as I could, and was pulling on my clothes almost before I was completely awake. Blaine on the moon and reacting violently to the name of Mairan could mean only one thing: He was in this thing with Stark, in it up to his neck. And speaking of necks, mine was now in serious trouble. I'd given Blaine both my name and Larry's and told him I was on the moon, and it would be trivial for him to track me down. I had to get out of here, and fast, or I would end up in the Krieger Base stockade. Or worse.

I needed a new plan of action, and one possibility began to take shape in my mind as I finished dressing. I would have to go to the mine now and get hard, photographic evidence of the plot. Once I had that, I could hole up somewhere and send dreams to every reporter and government official I could find. Lunar spacesuits were designed for long-term use, I knew, and with a Selene's supply of emergency oxygen tanks I could survive for a week or so away from civilization, long enough for someone to check on my story and blow the whistle on Stark and Blaine. I would have the photos to exchange for a government guarantee of safe-conduct back to Earth. It wasn't the best plan in the world, but it was all I could come up with. Whatever I did, I at least had the considerable advantage that no one could cut off my communication with the outside world.

Taking my camera and a few other things, I headed for the Hilton's lobby and rental counter, forcing myself to walk casually. This was no time to look like a fugitive. Blaine couldn't have gotten the word out this fast.

"I'd like to take a Selene out for a few hours," I said through dry lips.

The clerk looked at his list. "You're up pretty early, Mr. Holst," he commented. "You came in yesterday at 1930, and it's only 0400 now. We like our guests to rest at least twelve hours between trips outside, sir. It's safer that way."

"But I don't sleep much anyway," I told him, "and I can loaf around back on Earth. I came here to see the moon, not sit around a hotel."

He peered at me carefully. I don't know how I looked, but God knows I felt alert enough to drive that buggy all the way to Tycho. I was just wondering if I should offer him a bribe when he nodded. "All right, I guess it'll be okay. Suit fourteen, Selene five; sign here, please."

The usual procedure included a half-hour equipment check, but I had no intention of hanging around that long. I gave everything a cursory once-over, made sure oxygen, power, and ration indicators showed full, and was rolling eastward within fifteen minutes. Ten minutes later I was out of sight of the Prinz Crater colony. Pausing only long enough to pull the radio beacon out of the buggy, I turned north and headed for Mairan.

Four hundred twenty kilometers north of Krieger D, the

map said. That put it about five hundred from my present position, and at forty kilometers per hour it would take over twelve hours to get there, not counting any cautious skulking I might have to do. The adrenaline-fed energy I had felt back at the hotel was ebbing fast, and my current lack of sleep was making itself felt throughout my entire body. For a moment I was tempted to find a convenient hiding place about halfway to Mairan where I could take a nap. But only for a moment. The sooner I got to the mine, the better chance I'd have of getting through whatever security Stark had set up there. Given enough time, they could button the place up so tight I'd never get near it.

So I gritted my teeth, kept my foot on the accelerator, and kept myself awake by making a mental list of the newsmen I was going to send dreams to as soon as I was safely holed up.

My eyelids felt like lead by the time I completed my wide circle of the Mairan region and parked the Selene a few kilometers north of where I estimated the mine to be. The subterfuge was probably so much wasted effort—they were bound to be guarding the northern edge as well as they did the southern part—but somehow I felt safer approaching from this direction. I had spent a lot of my trip here trying to recall the latitude and longitude figures I'd seen in Stark's dream, figures that seemed to match with the rough idea I had of the mine's location. If I was right, I knew to within a kilometer or so where my target was. If not, it could be a very long search.

I don't know how long I walked. The whole area was hilly and littered with rocks, and I was feeling pretty groggy as well, but I didn't fall over too often, and I always had the energy to get back up again. Still, my reflexes weren't as bad off as I feared, because when I topped that last rise and saw the spacesuited figures not more than half a kilometer away, I managed to crouch down into a shadow without standing in plain sight for more than a couple of seconds.

There were four of them that I could see from my

position. They didn't seem to have any mining equipment, but rather were poking at the ground with spades and long probes. I frowned to myself. Stark's men looking for new veins of ore? Or had I stumbled onto the wrong party completely?

There was no point in taking chances. I edged off to the left, intending to circle the group. With most of my attention on the others, it was not particularly surprising that I never saw the metal plate sticking out of the ground until I had tripped over it.

It says a lot for my mental state that I had rolled over and levered myself into a sitting position before it occurred to me to wonder what a metal plate was doing half-buried on the moon. Looking closer, I saw that the corner I had stumbled over was smooth-faced and was coppery silver in color. Only about thirty centimeters of the plate was visible, the rest being under the loose soil, and the edges I could see were ragged, as if the plate had been torn away from something else. Just at the corner was a mark of some kind etched into the surface. An identifying mark, perhaps, except it was like no letter or symbol I had ever seen.

Curiosity overcame my caution. Getting a good grip on the plate, I pried it upwards. It was a good four or five square meters in area, but the gravelly soil was loose and offered little resistance. I never got a real look at the underside of the plate, though, because something underneath it caught my eye. Something light yellow in color, about a meter long; with four arms, two legs, and an incredibly alien face . . .

"Okay, buddy, lift 'em."

I was halfway through my backward jump before I realized the voice had come through my headphones and not from the alien figure in front of me. Raising my arms, I slowly turned to face the figure striding toward me. His spacesuit held the insignia of a Marine sergeant major, and his gun was holding very steadily on my middle. He gave me an appraising look, glanced at the alien I had uncovered, and nodded inside his helmet. "This is Conlin," his voice said in my ears. "I've got a snooper up on Hill Ten; I'm bringing him in. And we've got another body up here, too."

The major at field HQ decided to wait for higher authority to arrive before questioning me, and so I had to sit for an hour in a tiny office with two taciturn guards. They very obviously considered me a spy—my single attempt to ask a question made that quite clear—and I was almost relieved when my interrogators finally came. There were two of them: General Blaine and a grim-looking Colonel Stark. The latter nodded to the guards and waited until they were gone before speaking.

"Well, Morgan, just what in hell are you doing here?"

"What was that thing I saw on the hill?" I asked, ignoring his question.

"Look, mister, you're in enough trouble already," Stark gritted. "Answer my question."

I was too tired to fight him. "I thought you were trying to pull a fast one with the new iridium mine. I was trying to stop you."

"Iridium mine?" Blaine spoke up.

"There was a vein of ore opened up just before we found the wreckage, sir, but we haven't had time to work it at all. It's in my report."

"Oh, yes. Go on, Mr. Morgan."

I told them the whole story, from Louise Holst's first visit, through my contacts with Larry and Stark, to my panicky trip to the Mairan area. When I finished, Blaine turned to Stark.

"I think we'd better get Mrs. Holst up here as soon as possible," he said. "No telling who else she might go to with her fears."

Stark nodded. "I agree, sir." He glared at me. "No telling what kind of nut might listen to her, either."

"That's unfair, Colonel," I complained. "I told you the facts I had. What sort of conclusion did you expect me to come to?"

"No one asked you to draw *any* conclusions, as I recall," he snapped back. "But you just had to play private eye and stick your nose where it didn't belong. Now we've got to figure out what to do with you."

I didn't like the implications behind that, but curiosity was overriding all considerations of good sense. "You could start maybe by telling me what's going on out there."

"Forget it," Stark said darkly. "You know too much already."

"Look, Colonel, you can't leave me with half an answer like this. Lock me up, threaten me, *shoot* me if you have to, but tell me what the hell that thing was."

"It was part of the wreckage of an alien spaceship," Blaine said quietly. Stark looked at him in astonishment, but the general shrugged. "He's right, Avram. He has to know the whole story now. It's not like we can lock him away from everyone." To me he continued, "Colonel Stark's men ran across part of the ship and one of the alien bodies near the iridium vein you mentioned. Everyone who was near the site, whether he had actually seen it or not, was immediately sequestered and a security seal was slapped over everything and everyone involved. So far all we've found are bits and pieces that seem to be from the ship's hull and *very* small chunks of machinery and maybe electronics. Plus some bodies, as you already know."

"So why was Captain Holst so upset when I first contacted him?" I asked. "I remember distinctly the phrase 'he can't get away with it.'"

"Holst was violently opposed to the security measures we were taking," Stark said, clearly not happy at telling me all this but apparently willing to follow Blaine's lead. "He thought more damage would be caused by a cover-up than by spilling all of it right away."

"I think he's right," I told him.

"Then think again," Stark shot back. Suddenly, through all his anger, I saw how worried he was. "You don't seem to realize how big a bomb we're sitting on here. If we don't announce this properly we could rip civilization apart. The whole world system has been balanced on a knife edge for the last century, and this is more than enough to bring it down. We simply *cannot* afford to let even a hint of this get out. Not yet."

"Nuts," I said. "Civilization isn't all *that* fragile. People aren't going to curl up and die just because you've found some chunks of metal and alien bodies. . . ." I trailed off as an uncomfortable thought struck me. "You *did* say that's all you found, didn't you?"

Blaine nodded. "You see our problem now. The cultural effects will be bad enough, but the political ones will be even worse. So far we've found nothing that even *looks* like an alien weapon, let alone one that might still work. But will everyone believe that? I don't think so. And all it would take would be a single doubter, a single preemptive attack, to spark off a major war. Coupled with an unpredictable reaction from the general public over the discovery, that war might become this civilization's last."

It was an overly dramatic speech, but I hardly noticed. What he said made uncomfortable sense.

Blaine continued, "This is why we're asking for your cooperation. We have no idea yet where this ship came from, what it was doing here, or even how it crashed, and we need those answers long before we can start preparing the public—and foreign governments—for this shock. I might point out that Captain Holst came to this same conclusion once he had thought things through."

"We'll have your cooperation, too," Stark added. "Willing or otherwise."

"Avram, your threats aren't going to work this time," Blaine said, looking suddenly tired and very old. "Mr. Morgan is a Dreamsender. You can't lock him away in Leavenworth and keep him from talking to anyone. If he won't go along, we've lost the war."

"Not necessarily, sir. There are many ways of destroying a man's memory. Or we could put him into a long-term coma if necessary."

"Save your breath, Colonel," I said. "I do have a working

conscience, you know. No one will ever hear about this from me." The last statement was only probably true, of course. I still wasn't really happy with the whole idea of a cover-up, but there didn't seem to be a better alternative at this point and I was willing to go along with it for now. Whether the army would be a responsible guardian of the secret, though, was something else again, especially if they turned up anything of real military value. But now that I knew how much useful information could be gleaned from another's dreams, I felt sure I could keep tabs on major developments up here, and if someone got too far out of line I could always blow the whistle. But I obviously couldn't even hint at such threats. As long as I was a prisoner my bargaining power was just a fraction above absolute zero.

Either Stark read something in my face or he was just naturally distrustful. "I don't think we can afford to believe him, General. Once he's out of here there's nothing to stop him from calling anyone on Earth and spilling the whole story." He squared his shoulders. "I'm willing to take responsibility for his treatment, sir."

"Not so fast, Avram. Mr. Morgan could be of considerable service to us." Blaine was giving me a very speculative look. "Mr. Morgan, you said you sent a dream from here back to Earth, correct? Was there anything unusual about that contact?"

I shrugged, wondering what he was getting at. "No, not really. It wasn't harder to make or maintain contact, if that's what you mean."

"Any unusual time delay between question and answer?"

"No. Not that I noticed, anyway."

Stark frowned. "But Earth's one and a quarter light-seconds away from here. That means a two-and-a-half-second delay, round trip."

"It wasn't there," I told him.

"Which means dreamsending is very possibly instantaneous," Blaine said. "And distance didn't seem to affect it."

Stark and I both stared at him. Then slowly, Stark

nodded. "I think I understand, sir. But we'd need a name and face, wouldn't we?"

"I don't know. We're talking about a whole race, not a specific individual. It may be possible to get someone at random just by knowing what they look like generally."

"It's worth a try, certainly," Stark agreed.

"If it's not too much trouble," I cut in irritably, "would one of you mind telling me what you're talking about?"

They just looked at me . . . and suddenly I understood. "Oh, no. No. Forget it. I won't do it."

"Come now, Mr. Morgan," the general said soothingly, "we can at least discuss it, can't we?"

And in the end I gave in.

It's been nearly a year now, and I really have no complaints. I would have preferred being on Earth, but Blaine wanted everyone involved with the project kept isolated at the new base in Mairan Crater, himself the single exception. Still, my quarters are quite comfortable and I'm treated with the courtesy due me as the chief—and only member, so far—of the new Office of Alien Communication, so I suppose I'm doing pretty well.

My Seipaic contact, Garun'Sutt, has finally gotten over her original terror at my alien presence in her dreams and is beginning to consider our relationship something of an adventure. I suspect this is partly due to her government's interest in her communication with me and the resulting attention she gets from her people. It's not everyone, after all, who can talk to an alien who's at least—we estimate—fifty light-years away. But whatever the reason, I'm not complaining. I'm still not sure why I always get her when I send out these dreams, though I suspect her face is just very similar to that of the first dead Seipai I saw. Since she seems to be my only contact I'm glad she's calming down.

We've started exchanging factual data about our respective races, and are trying to figure out a way to locate each other's planet. Blaine isn't absolutely sure that's a good idea, but I think that by the time we solve the problem I'll know

Garun'Sutt and her people well enough to know if we can trust them. In fact, I'm secretly hoping the Seipai can get a ship here to visit us within my lifetime. The way Stark and his PR men are pussyfooting around the whole issue, I figure there's an even chance Earth won't hear about the Seipai until they actually drop anchor here.

And I'd love to be around to see the headlines that day.

Afterword

To answer the standard question "Where do you get your ideas?" I got this one, appropriately enough, from a dream. Visiting my sister in California, I dreamed of a friend back home and tried to ask her a question. I woke up before she could answer, and dreamsending as a profession was born.

"The Dreamsender" was a bittersweet turning point in my life. It was my second sale and therefore proof that I wasn't just a single-shot writer; but the word of its acceptance came the same July 1979 day that I learned my thesis adviser had suddenly died. The combination of these two events led, five months later, to my leaving physics entirely and striking out toward the quixotic goal of becoming a professional, living-wage-earning writer.

How much the fields of physics and science fiction have benefited from that decision I can't say. I *do* know, however, that *I've* certainly gained from the deal.

The Energy Crisis of 2215

Its birth had been in the fiery turbulence of the primordial explosion, and for the billions of years since then the tiny black hole had drifted quietly through the expanding universe. Not once in all that time had it found itself closer than half a light-year to any star, much less approaching to within a few million miles as it was doing now. But there is a first time for everything.

Never very large to begin with, the black hole had steadily been losing mass during its long lifetime, and its gravitational effects were virtually undetectable even tens of meters away. But the strange laws which governed its existence required that a decrease in mass be accompanied by an increase in effective temperature, and so the black hole was now radiating energy and particles as if it were at a quadrillion degrees. Without this power output it might have slipped unnoticed through the solar system; as things were, it hadn't a hope of doing so.

The black hole was just crossing the orbit of Saturn when it was first detected by a routine gamma-ray scan. Identification came soon afterwards; and on Earth, Luna, Ceres, Hestia, and the Space Colonies debates were soon raging as to what should be done about the intruder. A large body of opinion was for letting the black hole continue unmolested along its hyperbolic path, or possibly even assisting it on its way out of the system. But others saw a unique opportunity in the chance meeting, and their views eventually prevailed, though at the cost of bitter feelings and many broken friendships.

The preparations took even longer than the debates had, but finally all was ready, and on January 1, 2215, the first of four specially designed space tugs matched orbits with the black hole and began pouring protons into it. As the intruder's positive charge increased, the tugs used electric fields to nudge it from its original course and, eventually, into a stable orbit at one of the Earth-Luna Lagrangian points.

Project Firefly had begun.

Dr. Ray Carter, Director of the Firefly Project, ran his eyes over the bank of monitor screens that wrapped themselves around the main control board like a lucky horseshoe. The glance was pure reflex; everything had been ready for the past two hours and the only thing holding up the works now were the speeches still going on from the main auditorium. He felt no impatience, though; if turning Day One into a media event would help sell Firefly to the public, it had Carter's blessing. Glancing around the room, Carter noticed a familiar figure staring out the port into the blackness outside. Walking carefully in his Velcro shoes, he joined the other. "You can't see it from here, Senator," he remarked by way of greeting.

Senator Chou didn't turn. "I know," he said, his voice carefully neutral. Nodding toward the port, he continued, "It's two kilometers to the DeVega dipole accelerator platform, a hundred meters to the energy collector sphere, and another half kilometer to the black hole itself. And the whole thing a superbly engineered waste of money."

Carter winced slightly. Chou had always been one of the

strongest opponents of Firefly, and Carter knew better than to try to argue with him. Apparently even coming over to say hello had been a mistake. "If you'll excuse me . . . "

Chou turned to face him. "Sorry. No real point in screaming about it now. But it wasn't necessary, you know. Fusion plants and solar power are quite adequate for Earth's needs."

"For now, sure. But what about the future? Even at the present rate of increase we would have a hard time building enough fusion plants to supply our needs by the turn of the century."

"The sun will still be there."

"Sure will," Carter nodded. "And did you know you'd need a billion and a half square kilometers of solar collectors to generate as much power as Firefly will? That's about three times the Earth's surface area, I believe. Excuse me, please."

Carter went back to the control board, his annoyance at Chou evaporating quickly. Rossetti, chief operator, looked up. "The Secretary-General is just about finished, Doc," he said.

"Good. How are the collectors doing?"

"Seem to be okay. Firefly's throwing off a lot of particles, both charged and neutral, but most of them are being collected, or at least stopped. Efficiency for charges is hovering near eighty-five percent; heat exchangers about half that."

Carter nodded. Firefly—the black hole was almost universally called by the name of the project nowadays—was behaving as expected, losing its mass in a thermal spectrum that included both photons and subatomic particles. The fast-moving charged particles were no problem; a set of electromagnetic fields at the collector sphere slowed them down to safe speeds, simultaneously converting their kinetic energy into electric current. The X rays and neutral particles were captured by a special multicomponent liquid blanket, their energy absorbed as heat to be changed into electricity by more indirect means. And for the ultra-high-energy gamma rays that passed through the collectors as if they were tissue paper, there were ten meters of shielding.

Pity we can't use the neutrinos, too, Carter thought wryly. Firefly's temperature, he noted, was still increasing, and he hoped the Secretary-General's speech wouldn't take much longer.

A yellow light flashed twice. They were ready in the auditorium. "Okay, Rossetti. Fire when ready."

"Aye, aye, Admiral." Rossetti's hands moved over the controls as Carter watched the indicators. Kilometers away, the three massive DeVega accelerators came to life, sending narrow beams of neutrons directly into the tiny black hole. Firefly's radiation levels jumped as the gravitational energy of the falling neutrons began to reach the collectors. Rossetti carefully adjusted the flux levels and Firefly's temperature began to stabilize.

"That's it, Doc," Rossetti said at last. "Total neutron flux about ten to the twenty-eighth per second; total Firefly luminosity one point six times ten to the eighteenth watts. Temperature holding near ten to the fifteenth degrees Kelvin. We've got steady state and she's running like a champ."

A loud cheer erupted in the control room, echoed, no doubt, in the auditorium. Someplace a cork popped loudly, accompanied by the steady hum of video cameras. Carter smiled for the reporters, his first real smile in weeks. After months of argument and backbreaking work, the closest thing to a total matter converter that mankind was ever likely to have was finally operational.

There were still things to be done, of course, but most of them were routine. He would first have to give a statement to the assembled dignitaries and cameras in the auditorium. Then came a check of the maser banks that would be beaming the energy to Earth and Luna, a quick trip to each of the DeVega accelerators to personally congratulate the operation crews there, and spot checks of other parts of the complex.

Five hours later he was finished, and he made a last stop

back in the control room. "Any fluctuations in the plate potential?" he asked the dark-skinned man who had taken Rossetti's place at the main control board.

"No problems, Dr. Carter," Kapoor said, his gloomy face in marked contrast to the smiles worn by the rest of the Firefly Project staff today. "The black hole is holding position to a small fraction of a fermi, as nearly as we can tell."

Carter nodded satisfaction. The carefully shaped electric field of the main plates was all that held the positively charged black hole suspended in place at the focus of the three neutron beams. If it drifted even slightly the beams would miss the tiny object. "Anything else to report?"

"No, sir."

"Okay. Well, I'm off. See you in three weeks."

Kapoor glanced up. "You're going on vacation?"

"Theoretically, yes. Practically, it'll be one week of rest and two of speeches on Earth and Luna."

"It will be a nice change for you, anyway."

"Yes." Talking to Kapoor always depressed Carter a little. Something about the Indian's attitude seemed to indicate disapproval, although it was nothing you could put your finger on. As near as Carter could remember, Kapoor's geniality had evaporated during the Assembly's debates on a name for the project. It had come within a hair of being called *Shiva*, after the destroyer/regenerator of Hinduism, and Carter strongly suspected that Kapoor had considered even the suggestion to be sacrilegious. "Well, take care of the project, Kapoor," he said, a bit lamely, and left the room.

It could have been worse, Carter thought, walking down the hall. The Assembly had also considered the name *Lucifer*.

As things turned out, Carter was not away from Firefly for three weeks. He was gone for exactly fifty-eight hours, and the ship that returned him to the station was a big Patrol craft that made the trip in record time. No one aboard would tell him what was going on, but the message was painfully clear.

Something was terribly wrong at Firefly.

The entire senior staff was assembled in the conference room when Carter arrived and slid into his usual chair. Nodding to the group, he turned to the Deputy Director and asked, "What's happened, Paul?"

Dr. Paul Rurik looked like he was next in line for a one-way tumbril ride. "We may have a runaway on our hands, Ray."

Carter felt his hands tightening into fists under the table. "Fill me in."

Rurik touched a switch and a set of graphs appeared on one of the displays. "During last night's Owl shift Firefly's temperature started to rise. When we tried to restabilize this morning we discovered we couldn't do so. We tried everything we could think of and then sent the Patrol to get you."

"Who was the operator last night?"

"I was, Doctor," a young man spoke up, a slight quaver in his voice.

"It wasn't Galton's fault," Rurik said. "The temperatures were within the allowable range we've calculated."

Carter nodded heavily. An operator couldn't be expected to notice that the *rate* of temperature increase was not following the theoretical curve. Only one of the scientists like Rurik or himself would have had the necessary knowledge.

Rurik went on, "I suspect Firefly drifted a little out of place, causing one or more of the neutron beams to miss it."

"No." Carter pointed to a display. "If that had happened you'd have gotten a big energy jump in the heat exchanger directly across from the beam that's missing. Instead, that extra neutron flux is spread out over several exchangers; furthermore, it's happening for all three beams. The beams aren't missing—they're being deflected."

"How?"

Carter looked toward the voice in surprise. "What are you doing here, Senator?"

"I was still here at Firefly when the crisis occurred," Chou said. "It is my right to be kept informed. How are the neutrons being deflected, Doctor?"

"Firefly emits particles in a thermal spectrum," Carter explained. "That means there are some at every speed from zero to near lightspeed. The ones that are moving slowly tend to stay near the black hole, forming a sort of cloud around it, and it's this cloud that's deflecting the beams."

"Surely they can't change the beam directions very much," Chou argued.

"They don't have to," Rurik put in. "Firefly is much smaller than the neutrons themselves. But, Ray, we took that effect into account when we set our temperature limits."

"I know. All I can think of is that our subatomic particle theory must be wrong somehow. If there are some particles coming out of Firefly that we haven't taken into account, all of our temperature curve calculations will be off."

"Hell cubed," Rurik muttered under his breath. "I'll get the theory people on this right away. Maybe with the extra particle emission data Firefly's giving them they can figure out where we're going wrong."

"For the moment, that won't help us," Carter said. "What we have to do is get more mass into Firefly, and that as soon as possible. The hotter it gets, the denser that particle cloud becomes. Not much, since most of the particles emitted have high kinetic energies, but even a slight increase in the number of low-energy particles just makes things worse. What have we got that we can throw at the black hole?"

"We have a spare DeVega accelerator," Rossetti volunteered, "but I don't think that'll help any."

"Why not?" Senator Chou asked. "That would give you an extra neutron beam."

For an instant Carter had an overpowering urge to tell the Senator to shut up. None of them had the time to explain things to a layman. "DeVega dipole accelerators require very tricky and sensitive electromagnetic fields to function. On a ring the diameter of the accelerator platform we can place only three DeVegas, spaced one hundred twenty degrees apart. Any closer and their fields would interfere with each other."

"What about putting the extra accelerator farther out from the center?" Chou persisted.

"At the distance we'd need the beam would spread out too much to be useful. And before you ask, directly above and below Firefly are the charged plates that hold it in place, so we can't run a neutron beam through there. Paul, can we increase present flux any?"

"No way. We're already running them ten percent above spec maximum, though I don't know how long they can hold that. We may in fact have stopped the runaway—the temperature is changing so slowly now we can't tell if it's going up or down."

"Let's assume it's still going up," Carter said. "Anything else we can use?"

"We've got a few X-ray lasers," someone said. "They could be set up to fire at Firefly."

"I've already checked that," Rossetti said. "It won't give a significant mass increment, and might add an extra scattering component to the neutron beams."

"Sir?" Galton spoke up hesitantly. "I may have an idea."

"Spit it out, son," Rurik said brusquely. "This is no time to be shy."

Carter winced at the tone as Galton blushed slightly. The young man's reticence was clearly not shyness, but instead the result of guilt feelings over his part in this mess. Rurik had never been good at understanding human emotion, though. He had declared that the fault was not Galton's and, for him, that ended the subject. It would never occur to him that Galton might still be upset.

"Sir, the DeVegas will accelerate any neutral particle that has a reasonable dipole moment. If we used, say, iron atoms instead of neutrons, we might be able to reverse the runaway."

Rurik nodded slowly. "That might just work, Galton.

You'll probably get fewer hits on Firefly because of heightened beam self-interference diffusion, but the ones that go in are fifty-six times more massive. And they'll be deflected less by that particle cloud around Firefly." He looked at Carter inquiringly.

"It's worth a try," Carter agreed. "Anyone know how long it would take to switch beam materials?"

"I checked, sir," Galton said. "The beam would only have to be off for ten minutes. And there's enough spare iron around for about ten hours of operation."

"If we can't reverse the runaway in that time we'll have to try something else, anyway." But to have the beams off for even ten minutes might prove disastrous. Carter weighed the options briefly, painfully aware of the need for speed. "All right. Galton, get the DeVega crews together and brief them. We'll switch just one accelerator for now— make it Beta. If it helps, we'll do the other two a little later. Paul, I suggest you get the control room people ready for the switchover. The rest of you go to your Emergency posts—I want to be ready if any problems crop up. Get to it."

There was a mad scramble for the door, but as Carter turned to leave he found his way barred by Senator Chou. "Dr. Carter, a word with you, please."

"I'll be up in a minute," Carter called to Rurik over Chou's shoulder. Rurik nodded and glided from the room, not bothering to use his Velcro shoes. "What is it, Senator?" Carter said when the others had gone. "Make it fast, please. I'm in a hurry."

"What are our chances of stopping it, do you think?"

"Is that what you wanted? I have no idea. You'll just have to wait until the rest of us know."

"I can't wait for certainties—probabilities must do for now. I have a duty to the people of Earth. If anything goes wrong here we will have to begin taking steps to protect them, and the sooner we start the fewer will have to die."

Carter looked at Chou with new insight. For the past several months he had seen the Senator as simply an opponent, a cardboard cutout violently and irrationally opposed to the Firefly Project. Now, suddenly, Carter saw him as a human being. "You really care about Earth, don't you?" he said softly.

"It's my profession to care, Doctor. You may recall that I wanted the black hole placed a good distance further from Earth, where it would have been less of a danger to both the planet and the Space Colonies. I am not antitechnology, despite your side's efforts to paint me so, but I wished for a larger safety factor."

"Senator, there wasn't a decent safety factor available. If we can't stop the runaway, Earth has had it no matter where Firefly is."

"I don't understand."

Carter took a deep breath. "If we can't stabilize Firefly's temperature, it will keep getting hotter and hotter. The hotter it gets, the faster it radiates its mass as energy until it basically explodes. According to current theory, in the last tenth second of its existence it will radiate with one percent of the sun's total power output."

Chou's eyes were very wide. "Good Lord! And you allowed this—this *nova* to be placed in Earth orbit? You must be insane!"

"Senator, if Firefly lets go *anywhere* in the solar system Earth is finished. The sun will go crazy with all that extra radiation hitting it. If the extra solar heat doesn't sterilize the inner system, the extra radiation will. But we had no real choice in the matter. I don't think more than a handful of people realize this, but if we had just ignored the black hole from the very beginning the same thing probably would have happened. Firefly was already too close to blowing. We didn't deliberately put Earth in danger, Senator; we were trying very hard to save it. And we still are. Excuse me, but I have to get to the control room."

It was an hour later before Carter was satisfied that the DeVega accelerator crews had the technique down well enough to be able to switch beam materials in the shortest possible time. The Project's chief design engineer, Felix Mahler, floated by Carter's shoulder as the control-room personnel waited for word that the changeover had been completed.

"Santos and Trumbell are the best techs I've got," Mahler said into the brittle silence as the minutes ticked by. "If anyone can get the DeVegas going in ten minutes it's them. Matter of fact, Ray, I'll bet you they'll do it in nine."

The speaker crackled. "Beta station; Santos. We're ready here."

Rossetti, at the control board, didn't wait for Carter's nod. "Firing," he said.

"Eight and a half," Mahler muttered to no one in particular. "They're better than I thought."

Carter smiled slightly, but it was an automatic response. His full attention was on the meters that gave Firefly's luminosity and temperature, both of which had been running. The indicators jumped wildly, as always happened when a new beam was brought to strength, and Carter's heart rate jerked in sympathetic response.

"Beam's steadying down," Rossetti muttered.

"How's it look?"

"It's hard to say, Doc. We're getting extra power just from the gravitational energy effects—since the iron atoms are heavier than neutrons—and that's fouling all our calibrations." Rossetti stared hard at the temperature indicator. "If Firefly's cooling down I can't tell from this. Not yet, anyway."

"We could shift the feed on the other DeVegas," Mahler suggested. "That would make any temperature change more visible."

"I'd rather not risk shutting off the neutron beams for the time that would take," Carter said. "Not until we're sure it'll do us any good. Let's give this an hour or so and see what happens."

The results after two hours were very clear. Firefly's temperature was still increasing.

"Damn!" Carter muttered through clenched teeth. "It's got to work. Galton's numbers prove that. What's going wrong?"

He threw a glance around the room, a glare brimming with frustration that most of the others seemed to interpret as fury. "I've looked over Galton's work, Ray," Rurik spoke up with some hesitation. "I can only think of one effect that hasn't been taken into account."

"Well?"

"We're dealing with iron atoms here, much larger than neutrons, and with electron clouds at—relatively—great distances. As the atoms approach Firefly, the first things to be swallowed will be an electron or two, which will leave the atom with a net positive charge. Since the black hole is also positive, the atom—the ion, now—will be deflected slightly before the nucleus gets to Firefly."

"And some of the shots that would otherwise have hit don't make it in," Carter growled. "Makes sense. Unfortunately. Is it worth switching the other two beams, do you think?"

"I doubt it. We'd gain a little, maybe, but most of that would be offset by the losses while the DeVegas are being altered."

"Doc, would it help to run the beams faster?" Rossetti asked. "If the time interval between ionization and contact was smaller, the atoms wouldn't be deflected as far."

Carter looked at Mahler and raised his eyebrows. "Possible?"

"Sorry. These DeVegas were specially designed to deliver high-particle currents, and for technical reasons we can't boost the velocities any higher than they are now."

There was a moment of silence. Then Kapoor's soft voice broke into the others' thoughts. "Dr. Carter, are you going to switch back to a neutron beam?"

"Why? The iron atoms aren't doing any worse than the neutrons are and we'd just lose ten more minutes of beam during switchover."

"It seemed to me, sir, that if the black hole is absorbing one or two electrons from even those atoms which are deflected—"

Kapoor never got to finish his sentence. "My God!"

Rurik exploded. "He's right, Ray. We've got to change that beam, fast."

"Right." Carter had caught Kapoor's drift at the same time Rurik had, and his heart was pounding violently in his ears. "Felix, get your men on that beam, now."

Mahler was already talking urgently into his intercom.

"I don't understand, Dr. Carter," Senator Chou murmured from his left.

Carter turned to face him. "The only thing that keeps Firefly in place is the electric field from the main plates, and for that to work Firefly has to have a heavy positive charge. Each extra electron that goes in cancels one of those charges. If the charge goes down to zero, we'll have no way of holding Firefly in the neutron beams."

"You couldn't recapture it?"

"Not in time. Possibly not at all."

Mahler looked up. "Okay, Ray, Beta's down again. Santos and Trumbell will have it running with neutrons in a few minutes."

"And I've just talked to the control room," Rossetti added. "Firefly's still holding positive charge, well within safety limits."

Rurik leaned back in his chair. "We were lucky," he muttered to no one in particular.

"Yes," Carter agreed. He took a deep breath and let it out slowly before continuing. "Gentlemen, we still have a crisis on our hands. We have *got* to find a way to get more mass into Firefly. Suggestions?"

There was a long silence. "I don't suppose it would help to enclose Firefly in degenerate matter of some kind," Rossetti said hesitantly.

Rurik shook his head. "We'd need better than neutron star density to make any headway—and even if we could make material like that we'd never get it near Firefly. The thing's just too hot."

Mahler looked up from a tablet he'd been writing on. "Whatever we're going to do, we have to do it fast," he announced quietly. "At the current rate of temperature increase, Firefly's radiation pressure will soon match the driving force behind the neutron beams. When that happens the DeVegas are, for all practical purposes, useless."

Carter had to force the words out. "How long?"

"Sixty hours. Maybe sixty-five."

Someone muttered a shocked obscenity. Carter felt his stomach trying to curl up and die. Sixty hours! His eyes swept the room of their own volition, as if looking for a way out, and finally came to rest on Kapoor's abnormally pale face. The Indian had been right to be so gloomy, Carter thought, feeling strangely light-headed. It had been sheer folly to suppose mankind could tame even a tiny black hole. They might as well have tried to hitch a tiger to a plow. . . .

With a physical effort Carter shook the vertigo from his mind. He couldn't afford to go to pieces. "All right," he said. "You all know what that means. I want some ideas and some solutions. For starters"—he looked at Mahler—"I want the spare DeVega set up as close to the accelerator ring as possible." He raised a hand as the other started to object. "I know, at that distance it won't help much. But we need anything we can get, and it may at least buy us some time. Punch some holes in the shielding and collector sphere to let the beam through."

"Right." Mahler scribbled a note. "I'll get a crew on it right now." Sliding his chair back, the engineer launched himself through the door.

"I'm calling a recess," Carter said to the others. "We'll meet back here in an hour."

Carter remained in his chair until the others had left, staring at the table as he gently kneaded his temples with his fingertips.

"You look tired. You'd better get some sleep."

Carter looked up in surprise. "I thought you'd left with the others, Senator."

Chou shook his head, his eyes never leaving Carter's face. "I meant what I said about sleep, Doctor."

"Can't afford the time." He smiled wanly. "Why the sudden solicitude? I thought you didn't like me."

"My likes or dislikes are of complete unimportance,"

Chou replied. "If anyone can come up with the solution we need, it will probably be you, and we can't afford to let your intellect break down from fatigue."

Even to himself, Carter's laugh sounded hollow. "Some intellect. I wasted several badly needed hours with the iron atom fiasco, and damn near lost our control of Firefly in the bargain. I tell you, Senator, if we're relying on me, we might as well quit now."

Chou was silent for a moment. "If we can't stop this, how long do we have?"

"Until the explosion? A year, probably. If our theory is right, that is; if it isn't I have no idea. Of course, Firefly will be far too hot to approach long before that."

"Dr. Carter . . . *can* we stop Firefly?"

Carter shook his head slowly. "I can't see any way to do it. No way at all. My God, Senator, what's going to happen to all those people?"

"We won't be able to evacuate them in time. Besides, where would they go? Ceres and Hestia can't absorb any excess population. Maybe we can tow the Space Colonies out of Earth orbit into the asteroid belt; they should be able to survive out there." Chou shook his head, his face a mirror of horror and pain. "But Earth has no chance."

"No."

Chou looked up. Carter avoided his eyes. "The blame is not yours, Doctor," the Senator said. "We—mankind's leaders—made the final decision on Firefly. Ours is the responsibility. Not that laying blame helps any." He sighed. "Ironic, isn't it? For the past three centuries we have been continually worried about running out of energy, but now the final crisis arrives in the form of too *much* energy."

Something brushed the edge of Carter's mind. "Say that last again, will you?"

"What? I just said our final crisis was too much energy, whereas in the past—"

"Too much. Too much." Suddenly the fatigue was gone, dislodged from his mind by a maelstrom of new thoughts and ideas. Fumbling out his intercom, he keyed for general 'cast. "This is Carter. All senior staff, report to conference immediately."

"Dr. Carter . . . ?"

Carter glanced up and smiled slightly at the Senator's uneasy expression. "Don't worry, I haven't crossed my circuits; at least, not yet. You just reminded me that there are two sides to this problem and we've been ignoring one of them. Excuse me now, I have to think."

He was still scribbling on a pad when the others arrived and took their places. "All right," he said. "First of all, has anyone else come up with anything?"

No one spoke, but Carter could feel the drop in tension throughout the room as they realized there was a hidden promise in his question. "I don't guarantee this," he warned them, "but see what you think. So far we've been concentrating on getting more mass into Firefly. Maybe we can hit the problem from the other direction; namely, to decrease the density of the particle cloud that's keeping the neutrons out in the first place."

"But it's not like a real, stationary cloud," Rurik objected. "It's self-regenerating, more on the order of a bathtub with a faucet at one end and a drain at the other."

"Exactly. So we're going to enlarge the drain. What is the cloud composed of, gentlemen?"

"Subatomic particles," Galton said. "Positive and neutral, mostly."

"Right," Carter agreed. "Why no negative ones? Because the positive plates that hold Firefly itself in place rip away any negatives as soon as they're formed. Conversely, the plates tend to keep the positives near Firefly. The neutrals don't care either way." He handed a sketch to Mahler. "Felix, I propose setting up a pair of negatively charged plates a few meters from Firefly and where they won't block the neutron beams. What I want is to set up an extra electric field that will pull the positive particles away from Firefly without risking moving the black hole itself. Can it be done?"

Mahler frowned at the sketch for a moment. "It'll be tricky," he said. "Any extra charge near Firefly will change the field of the main plates. What we need is stable equilibrium right at Firefly's position and a small nonzero field a few angstroms away. We'll probably need curved electrodes of some kind; the computer can figure the shape for us."

"But be damn careful with that field," Rurik spoke up. "The black hole has got to be at a stable equilibrium point or we'll lose it."

"I'll set up the programming myself," Mahler said, making notes beside Carter's sketch.

"Doc, what about the neutral particles?" Rossetti asked.

"I think we're stuck with them," Carter admitted. "But if we can decrease the density of positives even a little it may be enough." The excitement he had felt a few minutes before was wearing off and fatigue was beginning to pull at him. It was an effort to continue speaking. "If there are no further questions let's get to work. Felix, get those plates designed and built as soon as possible. The rest of you assist him or stay out of his way. That's all, then. Paul, I'll meet you in the control room in a few minutes."

Carter had intended only to rest his eyes for a moment before rejoining the others. It was with some shock, therefore, that he dragged himself from a nightmarish dream two hours later to find himself still sitting at the deserted conference-room table. Blinking the sleep from his eyes, he pulled out his intercom. "Carter to control room," he said thickly.

"Rurik here, Ray."

"What's going on up there? Why did you let me sleep this long?"

"We thought you needed the rest. The new electrodes have been made and tested, and Galton and Telemann have just about got them in place. There's nothing you need to do for at least a couple of more hours. Why don't you go back to sleep?"

"In a minute." Sleep was beginning to fog his brain again, but what he had to say was vital. "Paul, when they're finished out there I want you to set up those X-ray lasers to fire at Firefly."

"But the photons don't carry enough mass to make any real difference. Remember?"

"Don't care about the mass. The X-ray photons will get trapped into orbits around Firefly, either spiraling in or being absorbed by particles in the cloud. Most of those particles will be neutrals, since we're pulling away the others. Any particle that absorbs a photon will gain its kinetic energy and momentum."

"I understand," Rurik nodded excitedly. "The neutrals will tend to move away from the black hole faster. Just like heating up a gas and making it expand, really."

"Right. I admit it'll be a small effect—Firefly's own X-ray output is heating up that particle cloud far more than our lasers could ever hope to—but it may be worth doing, anyway."

"Agreed. We'll get on that right away."

Deep in Carter's subconscious the decision was made that he had done all that he could and that Firefly's fate was now in the hands of the universe. He barely managed to turn off his intercom before he was once more deeply asleep.

It was another four hours before he again awoke. This time he had the strength to go to the control room. One look at the meters was enough. "We did it," he murmured, half to himself.

Rurik swiveled in his seat at the main board. "You're awake," he said unnecessarily. "Yes, thanks to you. Firefly's temperature is dropping steadily. We've already cut the DeVegas back to safe flux levels, and will probably be able to shut off that extra field soon. Just as well, since the two electrodes are in pretty bad shape already from radiation damage."

"That reminds me. Did you tell me Galton was helping to install the new plates?"

Rurik lowered his eyes. "He insisted on going. I think he felt—well, responsible for the runaway."

"He's an operator, not a tech," Carter growled. "He had

no business going out there." He looked around the room. "Where is he, anyway?"

There was a long moment of silence. Then Rossetti spoke up quietly. "He and Telemann are both in intensive care, Doc. Severe radiation burns. They're not sure either will make it."

Carter stared at him, a cold fist squeezing his heart. "Oh, God. I never even thought of that."

"They knew the risk," Rurik said. "They also knew it had to be done."

"A high price to pay, but it bought the lives of Earth's billions," Senator Chou added.

Carter turned to face him, anguish turning to unreasoning fury. "And I guess that's what matters to you, isn't it? That and closing down the Firefly Project. Well, you've got plenty of new ammunition now, don't you? So go ahead— tell the Council, hold your news conference, and get everyone screaming for the Project to be shut down. Then what are you going to do, demand we put as much mass as we can into Firefly and try to push it out of the system before it blows?—never mind that that's more dangerous than keeping it here."

He stopped, out of breath. In a quiet voice the Senator said, "The Council must be told, certainly. But there will be no news conference. The people of Earth must never know what almost happened."

The anger and frustration rising within Carter vanished at the unexpected answer. He stared hard at Chou, a dozen questions swarming through his mind. Only one got out: "Why?"

"Because you were right, Doctor. I've spent some time in the last few hours studying the figures. Without Firefly Earth would spend nearly eight percent of its resources over the next four decades in building new energy supplies, and we just can't afford that. There are too many problems that will take our full attention to solve. Like it or not, we need Firefly." He waved toward the control board. "Oh, I will push strongly for more safety precautions— running Firefly at a lower temperature, for example. But you have proved that the black hole can be handled, with the right man in charge." He must have seen something in Carter's face, for his eyes narrowed slightly. "You *do* want to stay, don't you?"

Carter turned toward the port, looking through it as if he could see through the shielding and collectors at the impossibly brilliant pinprick in space that was Firefly. Once he had seen it as a servant, even a friend. But it had turned on him once, and he would never again be able to look upon it without knowing the acrid taste of fear.

He took a deep breath. "I'll have to think about it," he said.

Afterword

This one grew out of a series of five lectures on black holes given at the University of Illinois by a visiting astrophysicist in the spring of 1979. After filling a notebook with more facts, figures, numbers, and equations on black holes than any sane layman could possibly want or need, I figured the least I could do was to get a story out of it. Maybe more than one—I'll have to check those notes one of these days and see what else is lurking in there.

As a matter of historical interest, the black hole Firefly was originally named Shiva. Elinor Mavor, then editor of *Amazing,* asked me to change it to avoid comparisons (or confusion) with the Gregory Benford/William Rotsler novel *Shiva Descending.* I've never felt Firefly was as aesthetically pleasing a name as Shiva, but it was the best of the twenty-odd alternatives I came up with. Writing, like politics, is often the art of compromise.

Return to the Fold

The tiny spaceship was very definitely in trouble. Six enemy defiants were bearing down on it in a loose net pattern that Tomo knew was far more effective than it looked. Choosing one of the defiants at random, he kept his eye on it, control rod gripped tightly in his palm . . . and as the blue globe zigged he twisted the rod hard over, sending his spaceship into a zag maneuver that ran it neatly up against the defiant's side. Up against it at the required zero delta vee, in fact, and Tomo smiled briefly as the defiant vanished and his own ship grew another size. One down, five to go, with his craft now a bigger and slower target.

"Tomo?"

"What is it, Max?" Tomo answered, his eyes still on the images darting around above his lounge chair.

"I've located a fault in my number-five close-approach antenna," the computer told him. "Nothing serious; just a bearing shell that needs replacing."

"And you want it done *now*, I suppose?" He sighed, the gesture more theatrical than serious. Max always waited until they were only days out from a spaceport before checking the *Goldenrod*'s docking equipment, and the ship's six mainters were well used to it by now. In theory, it could result in a mad rush if something major went bad, but in practice the odds against that were low enough to ignore. "All right. Freeze the game and give me a schematic. Flat will do."

The holographic game images froze in midair and then vanished as Tomo levered himself easily out of his chair. The *Goldenrod* was decelerating at about two-tenths gee, half of what he was used to. Setting his game stick down beside the main control ball, he watched as Max put a complex schematic onto the nearby viewer. The affected bearing flashed in red; tracing a curve on the control ball with his finger, Tomo had the view enlarge and rotate. He debated changing his mind and asking for a complete hologram, decided the bearing's orientation was clear enough from the flat. The data box beneath the schematic directed him to Level Four, access panel four-twenty-six. Stepping to the circular staircase, he picked up his tool belt from its holder and started down.

Level Four was an equipment deck, with the sort of floor plan that could only be approved by someone who'd never have to work there. It took Tomo three minutes to work his way back to panel twenty-six, two more to get the plate off, and two more after that to find a comfortable position to work in. "Has Maigre Port sent you our manifest and next destination yet?" he asked Max, prodding a bolt experimentally with his wrench.

"Yes," the computer answered. "The main items are bioelectronics and exotic foodstuffs; we'll be taking them to Canaan Under Vega."

"Tricky stuff, bioelectronics. Should be good for, what, a seven-day layover?"

"The port has scheduled us for eight point five. Is the number significant?"

"Well . . ." Tomo paused, wondering whether he ought to bring this up. It seemed like such a crazy idea, sometimes, even to him. Still, he was going to have to talk to *someone* about it, and Max at least wouldn't laugh at him. "Tell me about Maigre. What's it like?"

"The design is a common one: a rotating disk in equipoint orbit, with docking facilities—"

"No, not the spaceport," Tomo interrupted. "I mean Maigre the planet."

"I'm not sure I understand the question. Do you want physical or sociopolitical data or something else entirely?"

"Oh, never mind." Tomo picked up another tool and got back to work. "I just . . . Actually, I've been thinking about maybe—well, maybe going dirtside this layover. Just to see what life on a planet is really like."

There was a short pause. "I see," Max said in a surprisingly neutral tone. "Actually, I don't believe you'd like it. Conditions are vastly different than they are on the *Goldenrod*. There are large, open areas without walls or ceilings—"

"I know, I know—I've seen all the tapes. I just thought it might be . . . interesting . . . to see it for real."

"I see. How long have you been thinking about this?"

Tomo had the computer's tone pegged now. "Oh, no you don't," he shook his head, grinning. "That 'I see' opener is a dead giveaway you've tied in your psych program. You're not starting me on that silly motivation questionnaire just because I've been thinking about planets and people lately." With a gentle tug he removed the top half of the damaged bearing shell, the bottom half dropping neatly onto the grab-cloth he'd spread out beneath it.

"Lately?" Max persisted.

Tomo twisted his head to send a mock glare at the computer monitor. "Max—"

A beep from the pod-to-pod interrupted him. "Tomo?" a voice asked. "What's the word on that antenna?"

"No problem, Andra," Tomo assured him. "Just a fatigued bearing shell. Take me a couple of hours to replace it."

"Good. I don't like dockings even when Max has all six close-approach systems to work with. I'd hate to try it with one missing."

"Aw, come on—you'll have Max thinking you don't trust him."

"*Max* I trust. It's those rinks who're supposed to hold the port steady for us. They're all dirtsiders at heart, you know. Lunatics, every last one of them."

"Yeah." Tomo grinned, then sobered. "You've never actually been dirtside yourself, have you?"

Andra snorted. "What kind of crazy question is that? Of course not."

"Right. Stupid question," Tomo backtracked quickly, mentally eliminating Andra as a possible confidant on this. "Everything else checking out?"

"Far as I know. Max?"

"Everything is functioning properly except for the antenna Tomo is repairing," the computer replied.

"Good," Andra said. "I'll let you work in peace, Tomo. Signing off." A second beep signaled his departure from the voicelink.

"Doesn't sound like I should invite Andra to come down to Maigre with me, does it?" Tomo remarked, striving to keep his manner light.

"Tomo—" Max began, in neutral tone again.

"No, let's just drop it for now, okay?" Tomo interrupted. "It's just a random idea—it hasn't got any deep psychological significance or anything."

"As you wish."

"Good. Though I'd appreciate it if you'd keep all of this secret. Andra will be riding me all the way to Canaan Under Vega if he gets hold of it."

"I understand." There was just the barest of pauses. "I'll keep the conversation private."

"Thanks." Climbing to his feet, Tomo squinted at the inside of his bearing sphere half. "Now, how about looking up which locker we keep spare FST-938 bearings in?"

Dr. Alexei Ross was already in a foul mood when the station computer told him Director Halian wanted to see him in his office. "*In* his office?" Ross asked, not sure whether to be angry or astonished at the request. "Is something wrong with the intercom system?"

"The intercom is functioning normally," Iris replied. "Director Halian said to tell you that the sensitivity of the topic required a face-to-face meeting."

"Probably his exact words, too," Ross grunted. For a moment he considered refusing on the truthful grounds that he was too busy to go running all over Maigre Space Station just because Halian felt like being melodramatic. Parallax Industries might own most of the station, but as chief physician Ross was explicitly out of Halian's direct control. But even as he mentally considered sending back a borderline-nasty message, logic prevailed. If Halian wanted to discuss something without the risk of being overheard, he probably had a damn good reason for it. Possibly something new on the G- and H-deck thorascrine leaks that had put forty-five people in Ross's ward in the past twenty hours. "All right," he sighed. "Inform the director I'll be down as soon as I can."

"Yes, Doctor. Also, the bioscan data is in on Marc DeSabia now; my analysis indicates thorascrine concentrations in liver, kidneys, and thyroid gland."

"Okay." Ross spent a few minutes logging orders that weren't part of Iris's standard medical procedure programming and leaving contingency instructions for his staff. Then, still fuming a bit, he stalked to the elevator and rode down to W-deck and Parallax Industries' executive offices.

Director Jer Halian was staring out the oval porthole when Ross stomped in. "This better be important, Jer," the doctor said, stepping over to Halian's desk and sitting down in the plush guest chair. "I've got a wardful of people upstairs who still need all my attention."

Halian turned to face him, and Ross saw for the first time the other's expression. It wasn't an encouraging one. "Anyone died yet?" the director asked, his mind clearly on something else entirely.

"No, and I'd like to keep it that way." Ross rubbed at his forehead, grimaced at the perspiration oils there. "Another ten hours and this last batch should be out of danger."

"Good." Halian took a deep breath. "Because in about ninety-*five* hours we're going to have an even worse mess on our hands. One of the *Goldenrod*'s mainters apparently wants to visit Maigre during his layover."

Ross felt something prickly dock between his shoulder blades. "Holy drine. You sure?"

Halian picked up a cassette and rolled the slender cylinder across the desk. "The *Goldenrod*'s MX computer sent me this private report a half hour ago. The mainter refused to discuss it in depth, so all the MX could give us was his last general psych profile." He leaned forward a bit. "This *is* a problem, now, isn't it? I mean, this Tomo character *won't* be able to stand it for long down there, will he?"

Ross snorted. "It's even worse than that. He shouldn't even *want* to try mixing with other people, any more than you'd seriously consider spending your life in a starship pod. The very fact he's talking this way means he's already in serious trouble."

"Great," Halian said heavily. "Just what we needed."

A sudden, horrible thought occurred to Ross. "He's not *flying* the ship, is he?" Visions of the freighter ramming full-tilt into the station—

"Oh, no—no way he can take control away from the computer, either," Halian assured him. "*We're* not in any immediate danger."

"I'm sure that's a great comfort to the rest of the *Goldenrod*'s crew," Ross said dryly.

"They're not in danger, either, at least not at the moment. In fact, they don't even know anything's wrong."

"Handy. Sounds like one of your ideas."

Halian didn't seem to notice the barb. "It was the computer's, actually. But never mind that. I want you to start getting your people and programs ready right away."

Ross shook his head. "I'm afraid we're not equipped to handle anything like this. We're going to have to bring a psychoses expert up from Maigre. I'll go check the medical directory." He started to get up.

"Hold it—*hold* it," Halian snapped. "We can't let outsiders in on this—the company'll have our heads if bad publicity gets out. What about that therapy session you put Randoff through when he went all flutey last month?"

Ross sank wearily back into his chair. "Jer, we're talking about a *starship mainter* here—the most carefully circumscribed personality type that's ever existed. As far as I know, no mainter has *ever* gone out the sunward lock like this, and I'm not going to trust him to a computer that hasn't even got a decent data base to draw on."

Halian turned back to his porthole, and Ross saw the lines around his mouth tightening. "And there's no one on your staff who can handle it?"

"No." Ross shook his head. "Anyone who developed a problem this severe would be immediately shipped to a dirtside facility."

Halian grunted, and for a long moment the room was silent. Ross found himself staring at the model of a star freighter sitting on the corner of Halian's desk. Six long cylindrical pods, arranged hexagonally about the central drive cylinder, the whole thing tied together by a network of bracing struts . . . and each of those cargo pods someone's home for years at a time. The very thought of it made Ross's skin crawl.

"All right," Halian said, breaking Ross out of his uncomfortable reverie. "But get someone who can keep his mouth shut. And don't give him any more information than absolutely necessary. That goes for your staff, too."

"I'll do my best," Ross said, annoyed at the other's peremptory tone. Standing up, he snared the cassette with Tomo's psych profile and slid it into his pocket. "And in the meantime, you get *your* people on top of those thorascrine leaks. I can only handle one crisis at a time, and I want my ward empty when Tomo gets here."

Halian looked up at him with tired eyes. "Believe me, Doctor, no one wants those leaks stopped more than I do."

Ross felt his irritation with the other melting away. Halian was a solid company executive, but in spite of that he really wasn't a bad sort. "I know," he told the director. "I'll talk to you later."

* * *

A starship's natural environment, Tomo had always felt, was out in interstellar space, hundreds or thousands of kilometers from anything larger than an ice cube. Docking—actually bringing the ship into physical contact with a giant spinning disc—was thoroughly *un*natural and therefore the most nerve-racking part of every trip. But Max performed flawlessly as usual, matching motions and gliding smoothly into the docking berth like an off-center axle. The port's spin gave the *Goldenrod* an effective gravity similar in magnitude but different in direction to what Tomo was used to, and he grimaced slightly as his floating crash chair came to rest against what he usually considered a wall.

"The access tunnel is connected now, Tomo," Max informed him as he unstrapped and climbed a bit gingerly from the chair. "Whenever you're ready . . ."

The tunnel led from the pod to a short corridor in the port proper, and a door at the far end opened to a spacious five-room suite. Tomo gave himself a quick tour, and then returned to the living room area. "Not bad," he said aloud. "Better than that cubist's nightmare at Burnish, anyway—remember that horrible holosculp?"

There was no response, and Tomo snorted at his forgetfulness. Of course Max had no direct voicelink pickups *here*. Stepping to the desk, he located the "communications" section of the control ball there and traced the proper curve among the many alternatives. "Max? You there?"

"Of course," the computer's voice answered. "What is it?"

"Oh, nothing—I just wanted you around." He paused, eyes still studying the unfamiliar control ball. "Wait a second—can you tell me how I call up the port's computer on this thing?"

"I believe you'll need to interface through me for all computer functions."

"Oh?" A corner of Tomo's mind noted that such an arrangement seemed unnecessarily awkward; but these *were* port people, after all. "All right. Uh . . . would you call up a sky-to-ground shuttle schedule for me?"

"Very well."

The screen beside the control ball lit up with lines of numbers and words. Sitting down, Tomo leaned forward to study them . . . but he'd barely begun to decipher their meaning when the screen abruptly blanked and the face of a middle-aged man appeared. Startled, Tomo leaned back again.

"Welcome to Maigre Space Station, Tomo," the man said, smiling. "I'm Director Jer Halian, in charge of Parallax Industries' operations here. I hope you had a good voyage?"

"Quite nice, sir," Tomo managed, still feeling a bit off balance.

"And I trust your rooms are satisfactory?"

"Oh, certainly."

"Good. Well, we want you to be comfortable for the duration of your stay. Is there anything we can do for you? Something special, perhaps, that we haven't thought to provide?"

Tomo took a deep breath. *It's not an unreasonable request,* he told himself firmly. "As a matter of fact . . . would it be possible for me to visit Maigre while I'm here? I'd sort of like to see what dirtside life is like."

Halian's expression didn't change. "I'm sure something can be arranged. Uh—" His eyes flicked to the side. "Why don't you come down to my office and we can work out a schedule for you?"

"Come down . . . in person?" Tomo asked, faltering a bit. Somehow, his rather hazy plan hadn't included consequences quite this immediate. "Can't we do it from here?"

Halian shrugged fractionally. "Oh, we *could.* But I wouldn't think it'd be a problem for someone who wants to visit a planet full of people."

It was nothing Tomo could put his finger on, but suddenly he felt like he was at the far end of a microscope. Halian was watching him closely . . . too closely . . . as if this was some sort of test. . . . "You're right, of course," he told the director firmly. "How do I get to where you are?"

If Halian was surprised, he hid it well. "There are guidelights along the hallway walls; I'll have them set to lead you to my office. I—guess I'll see you in a few minutes. Good-bye."

"Signing off," Tomo nodded as the screen went blank. For a moment he sat there, working up his courage. Then, standing, he strode resolutely to the emergency door with its bold EXIT TO STATION inscription. Almost unwillingly, his hand reached out to touch the red plate, and with a gentle *whoosh* the door slid open. Licking his lips quickly, Tomo stepped through—

And jumped back inside, using a hand on the doorjamb to swing off to the side. Back flat against the wall, he mouthed a silent curse at the still-open door. Finally, it slid closed . . . but not before the two men he'd fled from had time to pass by.

He stood there for several seconds, slowly mastering the emotion of that near-contact. Unlocking his frozen joints, he peeled himself from the wall. He tried to step to the door again, but his feet seemed unable to take him that direction. The touch plate glared mockingly at him; turning away, he returned to the desk and gingerly sat down. "Max," he croaked.

"Yes, Tomo?"

He licked his lips, and this time they worked better. "Get me the director's office, will you?"

"Certainly. Are you all right? You sound agitated."

"Just make the call, huh?"

Max didn't answer, but a moment later Halian's face appeared on the screen. "Yes, Tomo, what is it?"

"Sir . . . would it be possible for *you* to come *here* instead?" Tomo asked. "At your convenience, of course, and if it's not too much trouble."

"No trouble at all. I'll be up in a few minutes. Is it all right if I bring a couple of colleagues with me?"

Tomo wanted very much to say no, but Halian had that microscope look again. "Uh . . . yeah, sure."

"Good. We'll see you soon, then. Good-bye."

The screen blanked and Tomo wilted a bit in his chair. *No trouble at all,* the director had said airily, as if taking a trip through a crowded port was the easiest thing in the universe.

Unbelievable!

Director Halian turned off the intercom, sent a glance at Dr. Ross, and then focused his attention on the newcomer. "Well, Dr. Scharn?" he invited.

Dreya Scharn shrugged, wondering what the flapdoodle secrecy was all about. To her, the whole thing seemed absurdly open-and-shut. "If it were anyone but a starship crewman I'd class him as a severe case of anthropophobia and start chemo-imbalance correction immediately. But surely you realize that after however-odd many years in space, any of us would be pretty weak in the social-contact areas. I'd suggest you give him a few days before you start getting worried."

She stopped, suddenly aware that their reactions didn't fit what she was saying. "Is something wrong?"

Halian cleared his throat, flashed an annoyed look at Ross. "I see Dr. Ross hasn't given you the whole story yet."

"Sorry, Jer," Ross said, with the brusque manner of someone on the defensive. "But I didn't want to say too much until Dr. Scharn arrived—and I was expecting Tomo to give us a little more time." He turned to Scharn. "You see, Doctor, it isn't exactly Tomo's fear of people that concerns us—as a matter of fact, that's a normal part of a starship mainter's personality. The problem—"

"Just a minute," Scharn interrupted. "Are you telling me Parallax Industries is using mentally disturbed people to fly its starships?"

"No, of course not," Halian said before Ross could answer. "The mainters are perfectly sane and well adjusted . . . within their own parameters."

"Mr. Halian, there's no way you can consider extreme fear of people to be within the bounds of normal sanity."

"I said 'within their parameters,'" Halian reminded her. "Mainters are specially chosen for loner characteristics."

Scharn cocked an eyebrow. "'Chosen'?"

Halian's eyes slipped just a bit from her gaze, but his nod was firm. "Yes."

Truth-bender, she labeled him silently. She considered pressing the point, decided to file it for later. "All right. Then if anthropophobia isn't Tomo's problem, what is?"

"The fact that he's talking about taking a trip dirtside," Ross said. "A mainter shouldn't even be *thinking* things like that, let alone seriously considering them."

"Why not?" Scharn frowned. "Maybe after—this is what, his third voyage? Maybe after twenty-odd years on a starship he wants to try something new."

"If one of your patients said he wanted to jump off a high rise without an air belt, would you say he just wanted to try something new?" Ross countered.

Scharn glared at him. "That's an absurd comparison and you know it. People can't fly, but even extreme loners can learn to deal with crowds."

Halian shook his head. "Mainters can't. That's the whole point."

For a moment Scharn stared at him, something cold starting to stir in her stomach. "Then we're not talking about people who've simply been *chosen* anymore," she said coldly. "What you're saying implies a great deal of mental conditioning, very likely illegal as well as unethical."

"I assure you, Doctor," Halian said, "that Parallax Industries is not engaged in any illegal activities. As for ethics, I think you'll find things aren't as simple as you might imagine."

"Oh?" Scharn gave him a hard smile. "Then perhaps it's time I found out how 'things' really are. And it'd better be a *complete* explanation."

"Not to change the subject," Ross interjected, "but before we get into anything lengthy, shouldn't we go upstairs and see Tomo? He *is* expecting us, remember."

Scharn kept her eyes on Halian. "I can't begin any kind of diagnosis until I know exactly what I'm up against."

"You'll get the complete explanation—I promise," the director said. "But Ross is right. Perhaps you can treat this as an orientation session or something."

Scharn hesitated, but this time she sensed Halian was telling the truth. "All right. Let's go, then."

The elevator trip was the oddest Scharn had ever experienced. She knew enough to be ready for the change in weight as they moved toward the station's rotation axis, but she'd forgotten about the Coriolis effect that nudged her sideways into the wall and held her there for the embarrassing seconds it took to get her feet back into position and lean into the pseudoforce. Halian and Ross ignored her clumsiness, but she knew they'd seen it. She was glad when the car finally slowed and came to a halt.

The corridors were another surprise, though a little reflection told her she should've expected this, too. Several decks above the station's living and business areas, there was no call for bright colors or cushiony carpeting here. Only cargo handlers and station mainters used this area, and they were more interested in utility than aesthetics.

The door Halian led them to was like all the others they'd passed, except that its ID label was lettered in bright red and cautioned the prospective entrant to check with the station computer to make sure no starship mainter was inside. The warning gave her momentary pause—was there something dangerous about starship mainters?—and she hastily searched her memory for anything she might have heard on the subject. But Halian showed no hesitation as he stepped to the door and pushed the hailer. Scharn heard a soft ping, and an even softer reply, and Halian fingered the touch plate. The door slid open and they walked in.

Tomo was standing behind a small desk across the room, his back solidly against the wall. His expression was one Scharn had seen before, on nervous lab animals.

"Hello, Tomo," Halian said. "I'm Jer Halian. Sorry we were delayed a bit."

Tomo nodded once, a quick up-down jerk of his head. "Hello," he said.

Scharn's peripheral vision picked up a couch to their left, a couple of meters farther from Tomo's position than they were now. "Couch," she murmured, nudging Halian.

For a wonder, he caught the hint and led them over there. They sank into it, and Halian gestured to the desk chair a meter in front of Tomo. "Won't you sit down, too?"

Tomo's eyes flicked to the chair, then back to his visitors. Gingerly, he pulled the seat back to rest against the wall beside him and sat down.

"Well," Ross said briskly. "Tomo, Director Halian tells us you'd like to take a trip down to the surface while you're here. We'd like to talk to you about that, if we may."

Some of the tension left Tomo's face, to be replaced by suspicion. "You sound like Max in his psychological mode. Are you a psychiatrist?"

"No, no—I'm Dr. Alexei Ross, chief physician of Maigre Space Station. You must understand that your safety— whether here or dirtside—is our responsibility, and we have to make sure you're properly fit before we can let you go. The gravity's twice what you're used to, for starters."

If Ross had hoped to distract Tomo from his original question, it didn't work. Shifting his gaze to Scharn, he asked. "How about you?"

"I'm Dr. Dreya Scharn," she began; but before she could go on, Halian jumped in.

"Dr. Scharn's from Maigre proper, Tomo," the director said. "We brought her here because she knows more about dirtside conditions than anyone aboard the station. She has some questions she needs to ask you before we can discuss your trip to the planet."

Scharn managed to keep her professional face in place, but it was a near thing. To half-lie about her profession and then drop the conversational burden directly into her lap was a double whammy she hadn't expected. But she was damned if she was going to let Halian's action throw her. Smiling at Tomo, she opened with the simplest time-buyer in her repertoire. "Why don't we start by getting to know you better, Tomo. What was your childhood like?"

"You mean my trainage?" Tomo asked, still looking wary. "Just like anyone else's. Lynn—that was the station's LNN Learning Computer—taught me how to inspect and repair all the machinery on board a starship. When I'd learned everything I was assigned to the *Goldenrod*."

"What were your parents like?" she asked.

A flicker of puzzlement crossed the mainter's face. "Parents?"

"He won't remember any human parents or nurses," Halian murmured in Scharn's ear. "He'd have been taken away from them when he was young."

"I see," she said, trying hard to keep her astonished horror from showing. Mental conditioning was a well-defined, if seldom used, psychological tool, but never had she heard of it being started so early in a subject's life. The legality of this whole thing was getting shakier and shakier. "Were you lonely as a boy?" she asked Tomo. "You had playmates, didn't you?"

"Of course. I already told you about Lynn."

"No, I mean other children. Did you play with any of the others at your station?"

Tomo shrugged fractionally. "I sometimes played with Orbin on the viewer. I liked playing alone or with Lynn better, though. Look, what does all this have to do with my fitness to go dirtside?"

A damn good question, Scharn thought. "We wanted some idea how much experience you've had interacting with other people," she improvised, hoping it sounded reasonable. "So after your training you went aboard the *Goldenrod*. Do you get along with the other mainters?"

"Well enough. We don't talk to each other much."

Scharn frowned. "You mean you're all together in the same ship for years at a time and don't do things together?"

"We're not really *together;* we've each got our own pod, you know. And there usually isn't any maintenance that requires two of us working in sync. Max flies the ship and tells me when there's work to do; the rest of the time I read or play music or fiddle with my electronics kits."

The starship model Scharn had seen on Halian's desk suddenly made sense. Six mainters, six mutually isolated pods . . . "So you really *are* all alone out there."

"Pretty much, except for Max."

"I see. How do you feel about being alone? Does it ever bother you?"

Tomo snorted. "Of course not. What kind of stupid question is that?" His eyes flicked between Scharn and the others. "What's going on here, anyway?"

Scharn raised her hands chest high, palms outward, in a soothing gesture she hoped Tomo would understand. "All right; let's get back to Maigre, then. Can you tell me exactly why you want to visit the planet?"

Irritation was beginning to replace the tension in Tomo's face. "Why is everyone making such a big deal about this?" he snapped. "I've never been dirtside before and I got curious about it. Haven't any of *you* ever wanted to try something new?"

"Of course we have," Ross put in. "It's just that dirtside conditions are *so* different from starship life that we wanted you to understand exactly what it would be like. On a planet, you see, you have wide, open-roofed spaces—"

"I know—Max already gave me the full list. I can get used to it."

"There are also people down there," Scharn reminded him. "*Lots* of people. It seems to me you're having trouble right now, with just three of us in the same room with you."

The tension flooded full force back into Tomo's expression, and Scharn had the sudden impression that he'd halfway convinced himself that his visitors were actually just images on a viewer screen. "I can manage," he ground out. "If you can get used to a port, I can get used to a planet."

"You're talking nonsense, Tomo," Halian said, his frustration evident in his tone. "You're a starship mainter—you don't belong on a planet."

"Do people belong on Charon's World?" Tomo retorted.

"Or Tau Ceti? Human beings can adapt to practically *anything*."

"Sure they can. Except that—"

Halian broke off abruptly; at the same time, Scharn sensed Ross jerk in reaction. She turned back and forth quickly, trying to catch the men's expressions before they could be covered up. She saw enough to decide it was time for a showdown. Turning back to Tomo, she said, "I think we'd better leave you for a while, Tomo. I need to discuss a few things with Director Halian before we talk any more about your trip to Maigre. In the meantime, though, I'm sure you could walk around the station if you'd like. It's not a planet, but it would give you some practice in getting used to other people."

She stood up, Ross and Halian following suit. The latter gripped Scharn's upper arm in a reaction that added fuel to her suspicions. "I'm not sure letting him run loose is a good idea," the director whispered.

"Good-bye," Scharn smiled at Tomo. She stepped past Ross, the movement forcing Halian to release his hold on her arm, and led the way out of the room. As the door closed she got a glimpse of Tomo sagging in obvious relief.

"Dr. Scharn," Halian said, again taking her arm, "he should *not* be allowed free access to the station—"

She shook off the hold and started down the corridor. "Let's go to your office, Mr. Halian," she called back over her shoulder. "We've got a lot of talking to do."

The return trip was made in chilly silence. Scharn held her fire until Halian was seated behind his desk again, and then let him have it.

"I don't know what you think about miracle cures and psychiatry," she bit out, "but I can assure you that I won't be able to do the job *you hired me for* unless I start getting some straight answers."

"I know," Halian said, waving her toward the seat she'd occupied earlier. "Sit down, Doctor."

She remained standing. "I mean *genuinely* straight answers. First Tomo was *chosen*, then he was *conditioned*, and now you've practically bitten your tongue off because he started talking about what humans can do. Now, either you give me the whole story or you schedule me a seat on the next shuttle back to Maigre."

Halian stared up at her in stony patience for a couple of heartbeats after she finished her speech, then once more indicated her chair. "Sit *down*, Doctor."

She hesitated, then obeyed, realizing with some chagrin that Halian was still in control of the situation. Psychological training, apparently, was no match for the experience gained in boardroom battles.

"You're right, of course," Halian said. "We should have told you everything right away. I suppose my only excuse is that you're an outsider, and that after a certain number of years keeping secrets away from outsiders becomes a very strong habit." He shifted his gaze to Ross. "Doctor? You know the details better than I do."

Ross pursed his lips briefly. "As I'm sure you know, Dr. Scharn, every human personality trait is a product of both heredity and environment, the genetic arrangement forming a sort of bedrock infrastructure of tendencies and aptitudes on which the individual personality is expressed." He paused. "What you may *not* know is that any of these genetic tendencies can be . . . *enhanced,* as it were, to a point where none of the subsequent environmental factors can really affect it. That's basically what's been done to Tomo."

She'd halfway been expecting this, but hadn't really wanted to believe it. "Are you saying," she said carefully, "that you've genetically engineered that entire corps of starship mainters to be *afraid* of people?"

"Not on purpose," Ross said. "The procedure was designed to make them able to tolerate—even enjoy— years of solitude at a time. Apparently the anthropophobia comes as an unavoidable part of the package."

"The *package?*" Scharn exploded. "My *God*—these are *human beings* you're talking about. *People* you've deliberately warped." She glared at Halian. "And it is most *certainly* illegal."

The director didn't flinch. "As a matter of fact, Parallax

Industries has a special exemption from the general laws on genetic engineering. And if it helps any, I was just as outraged as you are when I first found out about this."

"You've done a good job of silencing your conscience, then," Scharn said coldly. "Does Parallax pay *that* much?"

"It's not a matter of personal bribery. It's the simple fact that the benefits of interstellar trade vastly outweigh the costs."

"Oh, of course," she retorted. "The costs are negligible—unless you happen to be one of those people out there."

"I'd advise against hypocrisy, Doctor," Halian said, a touch of irritation showing through his executive mask. "You benefit as much from the trade as anyone else, and I doubt you've ever given two seconds' thought to the people who provide you the goods."

"Don't shift the burden to *us*," Scharn bit out. "If people knew you were using genetic slavery they'd give up their precious furs and exotic foods like a shot."

"And their last fifteen years of life, too?" Ross asked quietly.

Scharn turned to him. "What?"

"Fifteen years is the extra life expectancy that outsystem medicines have provided us," he amplified.

The first hint of uncertainty began to play around the edges of her anger. "Medicines can be synthesized, though, once the molecular structure's known," she pointed out. "Intersystem lasers can transfer the knowledge at that point."

"Usually," Ross nodded, "but not always. Have you ever heard of Willut's Chaser?"

Scharn frowned. "I think so. Isn't that that weird semiliving chemical that seeks out cancerous cells?"

"That's the one. Revolutionized the whole treatment procedure, made it possible for the first time to really root out an entire tumor without doing even a scrap of damage to the surrounding healthy tissue. And after sixty years we still can neither synthesize it nor successfully cultivate the Altairan nematoid strain that produces it."

There was a moment of silence. Scharn tried to whip up her righteous anger again, but her sister's face kept getting in the way. Maia, who had spent a couple of days in a hospital ten years ago for the routine treatment of brain cancer . . . "Why don't you build larger ships, then, so that you could use normal people running the ship as a group?" she asked. "Better yet, how about complete automation?"

"Because we'd need freighters the size of the original colony sleeper ships to give a normal crew the kind of room they'd need," Ross told her. "Anything smaller and you'd have violence and psychoses within the first five years, no matter how carefully you screened the crews." He hesitated. "Parallax tried that once; the records of those voyages aren't pretty."

"Then why not automate?" Scharn persisted. "Surely a powerstat TPL computer and its mobile units would be able to handle whatever maintenance a starship needs."

"The problem," Halian said, "is that a TPL, or any computer that powerful, requires an extremely high-density memory system, and high-density systems are notoriously vulnerable to radiation damage. On a powerstat that's not a problem because you can afford the weight of extra shielding and you have continuous error-weeding by ground-based systems. On a starship—well, the drive radiations aren't really dangerous to biological tissues, but your TPL would be out of commission in two years at the outside. Putting multiple units aboard would slow the process, but not enough."

"But . . ." Scharn raised a hand in a frustrated gesture, let it drop impotently to her chair arm. "It's still immoral to do that sort of thing to human beings."

Ross shrugged uncomfortably. "Would you rather we try putting normal people in what amounts to solitary confinement for ten years? Risk their going permanently insane or else drug them to their eyelids and never mind the physiological consequences? Don't forget, the mainters truly *like* what they're doing. They really *are* happy out there."

"All except Tomo," Scharn said.

Halian nodded grimly. "All except Tomo. He's an unknown, Dr. Scharn; and along with being worried I don't mind admitting I'm scared. What other supposedly impossible thoughts might he be having? Could he be going paranoid, too, or even homicidal?"

Scharn pursed her lips tightly. She still didn't like what had been done to Tomo . . . but her immediate responsibility was not for his past but for his present. And if he posed any danger to either himself or the station . . . "Do you have anything like a standard psych profile for the mainters as a group?" she asked.

Halian's response was to reach for his desk's control ball, fingering the classified-access section. "We've got both that and Tomo's own last profile."

"Good," Scharn said. "I'd also like any previous readings on Tomo that you might have."

Halian's screen lit up with lines of print, and he swiveled it to face her. "I'll have the *Goldenrod*'s computer send us up a complete dump. In the meantime, here's the general mainter profile."

Putting her feelings on standby, Scharn began to read.

It had been nearly an hour since the others had left him; long enough for Tomo's panic to have subsided into emotional fatigue and then resurface as restlessness. Scharn had said they would talk again later, a statement that could qualify as either a promise or a threat. Whichever, he wished they would hurry up and get on with it. Waiting like this was worse than docking—then, at least, Max could keep him informed as to what was happening. Here at the port, they were both in the dark.

Or were they? "Max?" he called impulsively, sliding into the desk chair.

"Yes, Tomo?"

Just as quickly, he recognized the absurdity of what he'd been about to ask. "Oh, never mind. Um . . . how's the unloading going?"

"Unloading and refurbishing operations are proceeding smoothly. Is there anything I can get for you?"

"No, no. I'm just—I'm fine."

"I see." Max paused. "Tomo, would you mind coming back aboard ship for a few minutes? There's no one in your pod at the moment."

Tomo frowned. "Why?"

"Your tone of voice indicates stress. My biosensors can't take readings outside the ship."

"I'm all *right*, Max," Tomo snapped. "Why is everybody so interested in me all of a sudden? The second I get here Halian calls me up, then he smothers me in doctors, and now *you*—"

He broke off abruptly, seeing for the first time the pattern there. But how . . . ? "Did you tell them that I was talking about going dirtside?" he asked suspiciously. The computer remained silent. "Max! Answer me!"

"Tomo, I had no choice. I cannot keep secret information that indicates you may be suffering physical or emotional dysfunction. Under such conditions I must report my findings in coded form to a company grade-one executive as soon as possible—"

"Wait a second. *What* physical or emotional dysfunction?"

There was a short pause. "Your thoughts about a planetward trip were judged to be four sigma outside normal range. A two-sigma deviation is considered—"

"Max, how many times do I have to tell you that there's *nothing significant about that?*" Tomo snarled, barely controlling his anger. This whole thing was becoming ridiculous. "Why are you making such a major operation out of it?"

Max's answer, when it finally came, was a complete surprise. "I'm sorry; I cannot continue this discussion."

Tomo's anger vanished into puzzlement and a slowly growing uneasiness. "What is it, something I'm not supposed to know?"

"My programming requires me to protect your emotional well-being. There are certain topics of discussion which

would unduly distress you, such as descriptions of warfare
or—"

"But this is something a lot more personal than warfare,
isn't it?" Tomo interrupted, blocking Max's attempt to
sidetrack the conversation. "Something having to do with
my physical or psychological makeup, right?"

"I'm sorry; I cannot continue this discussion."

Aha, Tomo thought. For a moment he gazed into space,
searching for a usable loophole. "All right. The information
might—*might*—bother me. Correct?"

"I'm sorry; I cannot—"

"Shut up! It *might* bother me—but now that I know
something's wrong with me, the uncertainty is *definitely*
bothering me." He paused, but Max remained silent. "The
tension alone—you know better than I do what prolonged
tension does to blood sugar and adrenaline levels. Did your
programmers anticipate this kind of situation?"

"They did," Max said in resignation. "Very well, then,
but the information must be kept secret from the *Goldenrod*'s other mainters."

"Agreed. So?"

"In order to endure the solitude of starship service, you
have undergone a kind of mental conditioning which has
made you less dependent than the average person on social
interaction."

For several heartbeats Tomo just sat there, attempting to
assimilate the right-angle turn his private universe had just
taken. *Egocentrism*, he thought through the numbness.
The assumption that you are basically the norm. He'd
known the people on planets and ports were different; but
somehow he'd never considered the possibility that *he* was
the odd one. And to have been deliberately *made* this
way . . . "How much less dependent?" he asked.

"It allows you to spend long periods of time alone, which
is necessary for your job." Max's voice was soothing, as if he
were doing his best to soften the shock. But his best wasn't
very good. "But it also makes it extremely difficult for you
to interact with others at close range."

"So because I wanted to do something you didn't think I

could do, you slapped a 'dysfunction' marker on me and yelled to the authorities." The mental numbness was fading now, anger once more rising to take its place. "Is that it?"

"It has nothing to do with what I personally think," Max protested. "Your conditioning places specific limitations on your actions, limitations as laser-cut and well defined as—"

"As your own programming?"

"I wouldn't have put it quite that way—"

"But that's what you were thinking, wasn't it? Well, I've got fresh input for you. *You* may be defined down to twelve decimals, but *I* am *not*. I'm a human being, and I can do anything any other human being can do."

"Tomo, your vocal stress levels are becoming—"

Tomo cut him off with a well-aimed slash at the control ball. Getting to his feet, he stomped over to the exit door. For a moment he stood there, anger battling common sense for supremacy. But the anger was far stronger. Slapping the touch plate, he stepped out into the port corridor. This time, no one was in sight. Picking a direction, he started off, determined to find his way to Halian's office. Halian, Scharn, Ross, even Max: he'd show *all* of them.

The deviation between the two curves was small—well within the one-sigma accepted tolerance—but with the advantages of hindsight it was obvious to Scharn that that was where it had begun. "Right there," she told Halian and Ross, tapping the spot on the screen. "You can see the slip starting to form as early as a year ago."

"Too small a change for the MX to key on," Ross muttered.

"I wasn't blaming the MX," Scharn said, leaning back in her chair. "And it brings up an interesting question. Is Tomo becoming mentally unbalanced, or is his genetic programming somehow unraveling and allowing his personality to drift more toward human norms?"

"How could it do *that*?" Halian asked. "A genetic effect like that should be permanent."

Scharn shrugged. "In theory, so should damage to a

section of mature brain. But stroke and accident victims routinely regain lost functions as the neural pathways restructure themselves. Perhaps some combination of hormones and neurotransmitters is acting to counteract the genetic bias here."

Halian harrumphed. "I don't buy that. Anyway, I can't see that it makes any practical difference—"

"Of course it makes a difference," Scharn shot back. "In the first case he's ill and can probably be treated with some form of chemo-imbalance correction. In the second, though, what we actually have is a rapid version of personality evolution, which is not only normal but could be dangerous to suppress artificially."

"I believe," Ross interjected quietly, "that Mr. Halian was referring to Tomo's continuing presence aboard the *Goldenrod*."

It took a moment for Scharn to pick up exactly what he meant. "You mean leaning toward sociability will make him less able to stand solitude? Um . . . Maybe, maybe not. It depends partly on whether—"

She stopped as a double ping sounded from Halian's desk, followed by Iris's cool voice. "Mr. Halian, *Goldenrod* Mainter Tomo has left his quarters and entered the station: moving spinward on corridor D-9. Do you have instructions?"

Scharn felt her stomach tighten. It had been her suggestion, but she hadn't really expected Tomo to act on it. Halian and Ross looked even more stunned.

"Full sector/level monitor until further notice," Halian instructed the computer. "Is anyone else in that immediate area?"

"Negative," Iris reported. "D-8, D-9, and D-1 are clear."

"All right." Halian looked at Ross as if for advice, but didn't seem to get any. "All right, just monitor Tomo's movements and keep me informed. I'll be on mobile. Oh, and better lock down all computer outlets and elevators in his vicinity, just in case."

He picked up a small rectangular clip-on from the side of

the viewer screen and stood up, the others following suit. "Let's get after him."

"Can't you seal him into that corridor?" Scharn asked.

"I could," Halian told her. "But it occurs to me that letting him run into a few people might be the best way to convince him that he can't handle that kind of social interaction."

Scharn's first reaction was that he was making an exceptionally poor joke. A half second later she realized he was serious. "And what if it merely drives him over the edge permanently?" she asked coldly. "Or don't you care about that?"

"He won't hit any heavily populated areas for quite some time without the elevators," Halian assured her. "If meeting with us didn't do anything permanent to him, neither will any situation he's likely to run into up there. Besides—" He hesitated. "The fewer people who know about this, the better. For *all* concerned."

Especially for you, Scharn thought bitterly. "I'm going for the sedation kit I left in my quarters," she said. "Will one of you wait here for me?"

"We both will," Ross said before Halian could respond.

There was something in his voice that made Scharn look hard at his face. But whatever was wrong was too well hidden for a quick interpretation, and she didn't have time for anything else. "All right," she said. "I'll be right back."

Ross waited until the door had closed solidly behind the psychiatrist before turning to Halian. The director returned his gaze steadily; and after a moment Ross realized the other was going to make him raise the subject. He cleared his throat, glancing at the desk to make sure Iris's monitor was off. "You realize, of course," he told Halian, "that Tomo will pass through the thorascrine leak area on G-deck if he stays in 9-sector on his way down."

"That area's been adequately cleaned up," Halian returned evenly. "You certified that yourself."

"For us, yes. But Tomo's been in a medium-radiation environment most of his life. There've been reports that

that can sensitize a man, make him much more susceptible to thorascrine poisoning." He paused, waiting for a reaction that didn't come. "But I see you already knew that, didn't you?"

"I may have heard of it somewhere. I don't remember."

"Sure." The sheer callousness of Halian's attitude was infuriating . . . and yet, even Ross could see the logic behind it. Legally, Tomo was less human than he was property, and Halian had both the right and responsibility of treating him as any other malfunctioning component. "Well," he said slowly, "I suppose it actually would make things a lot easier if Tomo got incapacitated somehow. The *Goldenrod* would leave on schedule without him and you wouldn't have to make a snap decision on his fitness for deep space. Scharn could take him dirtside and study him to her heart's content. The *Goldenrod* can manage with a missing mainter, can't it?"

"It can theoretically fly with even three of the six missing." Halian seemed to be having trouble meeting Ross's eyes. "The question then is what would happen to Tomo. If we take him off the *Goldenrod* he'll probably never be placed on another ship, even if he can be cured or whatever. So Scharn studies him for maybe a year or two . . . and then what? Starship mainting is all he knows how to do, and given his personality there's really nothing else he can be retrained for."

Ross felt his mouth go dry. To remove Tomo from his ship—by whatever means—was one thing. But *this*— "What you're talking now is way beyond an incapacitating injury," he said softly. "You're talking deliberate murder."

"I'm not talking *anything*," Halian said, his face unreadable. "I'm simply . . . thinking how an accident at this point would . . . simplify things."

This isn't happening, Ross thought as a sense of unreality seemed to darken the air between him and Halian. Premeditated murder . . . or was it? How human *was* Tomo, anyway? Form, intelligence—neither one was exclusive human property anymore. Genetic structure? Tomo's was no more human than that of any other biological construct. Surely there were legal guidlines, but Ross had no idea what they were. He could still raise a fuss, of course, and he could sense that Halian would back down at sun-grazer speeds if he did so, whether the director was in the legal right or not. But would that really do Tomo any favors? Because Halian was right—Tomo really *couldn't* do anything else. Unless Scharn's bafflegab about some so-called personality evolution came true with a vengeance . . . but no, that theory was equal parts absurdity and wishful thinking. Which left Ross exactly where he'd started, at dead center.

In front of him, the statue that was Halian came to life, raising the clip-on he still held and flipping it on. "Iris? Status report on Tomo."

"He's outside the D-13 stairway . . . He has now entered . . . moving downward."

"Damn," Halian muttered. "Well, at least that tells us something. If he can still charge on into the station after suffering through that interview with us, it means he's past simple curiosity. He's up to full-fledged obsession." He fastened the clip-on to his tunic collar, leaving it active. "Come on. We'll pick up Scharn on the way."

Ross followed him to the office door, still wondering what he was going to do. It wasn't until they were outside in the wide corridor that he realized the decision had already been made. Halian had given him the chance to object; his silence had been interpreted as tacit agreement. *But that can be changed*, he told himself. *I can still stop this*.

But before he could do that, he needed to decide whether he truly wanted to . . . and the time for that choice was running out fast.

A starship pod consisted of eighteen one-room levels connected together by spiral staircases in flight and by simple hatchways when port docking changed the normal directions of up and down. The passageways linking the pods to the central drive cylinder were seldom used, but even they were simple tubes: straight, short, and without stairways or cross-corridors. Never in his life had Tomo been anywhere nearly so confusing as Maigre Port.

He was almost afraid to admit it, but he was pretty sure he was lost.

The obvious solution, of course, was to ask for help; but so far he'd been unable to get any of the hall computer outlets to work. Until he found one that was live there was nothing to do but keep moving.

Ahead, still out of sight around the slight curve, he heard the sound of an opening door; and suddenly there were voices in the corridor.

Tomo's instinct was to freeze, but momentum and a sudden idea kept him moving. The voices were ahead and coming closer, but only a few meters in front of him was a cross-corridor he could duck into. If he hurried . . . Putting on a last-minute burst of speed, he rounded the corner—

And practically ran down the two men crouched there.

With a strangled gasp, Tomo hurled himself toward the cross-corridor's far wall, slamming back-first against it. He had just enough time to notice the open access panel and the scattered tools when the men charged him.

There was no chance for thought, no opportunity for anything but the most basic reflexive action. One of the attackers stepped in to block his continued passage down the corridor; slapping the outstretched arm aside with all his strength, Tomo ducked past and ran for it. Their shouts echoed weirdly behind him, partially drowned out by the thudding of his feet on the thin carpeting. He turned at the first opportunity and kept going. Three corridors and a stairway later he finally decided he'd lost his pursuers and slowed to catch his breath. Looking around, though, he could tell there was no use trying to fool himself any further.

He *was* lost now. Thoroughly.

"—and just crouched there looking scared. I went over to see if he was okay, and for no reason at all he hit my arm and took off like a meteor with fluorine afterburners. Till and I called for him to come back, but he just kept going."

Halian pursed his lips, glancing sideways to try and catch Scharn's reaction as they hurried down the corridor. Ross's reaction he could guess. "Either of you hurt?" he asked into his clip-on.

"No, sir," the answer came. "Maybe bruised a little."

"All right. Just get back to work; I'll handle this. Goodbye." He waited for the termination click, then said, "Iris? Where's Tomo now?"

"Corridor F-39," the computer replied.

"Those workers probably just got in his way and he panicked," Scharn spoke up. "Mr. Halian, we've *got* to close him off from the rest of the station."

Halian could feel Ross's eyes on him. "I suppose you're right. Iris, seal all routes between decks G and H. Are there any security personnel above H-deck?"

"There are four, all currently on E-deck."

"Alert them, and have them start moving toward F-9. They're to try and box him in there—" he hesitated a fraction of a second—"or on G-deck if he gets that far. They're to use minimal force."

Scharn leaned toward the clip-on. "And warn them he's not dangerous so much as he is terrified," she added.

"Right," Halian agreed. "If they can avoid contact until we get there, so much the better."

"Acknowledged. Security forces are on their way."

Halian took a deep breath, let it out as inconspicuously as possible. *Stay calm*, he told himself. *Just stay calm.* "The direct-access elevator's right up here," he said, pointing.

They were passing K-deck when the first security report came in: One of the guards had spotted Tomo in corridor G-9, forcing him to move into cross-corridor G-19B.

"Have the guard move just inside G-19B and wait there," Halian instructed Iris carefully. "Order the other three to approach from opposite directions along G-19, see if they can keep him from coming out there." He looked at Ross. "Ross . . . when we hit G-deck, I want you and Dr.

Scharn to go down G-29, try to intercept him if he gets to one of the other cross-corridors. I'll go up G-19B and try to cut him off there."

Ross's face was a sweat-plated mask as he gave a silent nod; but fortunately Scharn didn't seem to notice as she dug a hypo tube from her belt pouch. "In case you do," she said, handing the tube to Halian, "here's a sedative—you can inject it anywhere. It's already set for Tomo's weight."

A moment later, they arrived at G-deck.

The corridor they stepped out into was deserted and, aside from normal mechanical noises, silent. Ross passed up the final accusing gaze Halian had half-expected from him, taking Scharn's arm instead and heading away without a backward glance. Halian watched until they turned a corner, then permitted himself the luxury of a sigh. The die was now cast; Tomo's fate was in the hands of the universe. The thorascrine leak area was just one turn from the cross-corridor Tomo had entered. If Halian had guessed the mainter's probable movements correctly he would soon be in the proper position to send the other "accidentally" through the center of the contaminated region. If the universe had other plans for Tomo, it would have to guide the mainter elsewhere, and under such circumstances Halian would have no choice but to accept its ruling. The director was several generations beyond the spacers who had built Maigre Station, but he still possessed a little of their traditional belief in fate . . . except that he knew the strong and the clever could build their fate as they chose.

Halian believed in fate. He did not necessarily believe in justice.

Turning, he hurried down the corridor. Tomo would be coming by very soon.

Leaning against the wall, Tomo wiped the sweat off his forehead and tried to catch his breath. Safe again . . . but only for the moment. They were closing in on him now; drawing the walls of their box closer and closer— "They won't hurt me," he whispered aloud. "I don't need to be afraid of them. I *don't*."

It was so much wasted breath. He *was* afraid of them, and there was no way he could pretend otherwise. The thought of their approaching him, maybe even *touching* him . . . he shifted his shoulders uncomfortably beneath the sweat-soaked coverall. If he could only get back to his quarters before anyone reached him . . . but he might as well wish himself a child again.

From the corridor ahead and to his left came the sound of footsteps. Tomo tensed; but even as he pushed away from the wall something within him accepted the inevitable. Standing rigidly, legs trembling with their mindless urge to run, he waited as the other came into sight and stopped.

"Tomo?" Director Halian called gently. "I've come to take you back."

Tomo remained where he was, not acknowledging Halian's words but not running off, either. Licking his lips, the director lowered his voice. "Iris? Secure from surveillance mode. I have Tomo in sight."

"Acknowledged. Sector/level monitor disengaged."

Halian flicked the device off . . . and he and Tomo were alone. "Don't be afraid," the director told the mainter, aware of the irony of his words. "I'm Director Halian—remember? Let me show you the way back to your quarters. You don't have to come close, just follow me at a distance. You can do that, can't you?"

Tomo's mouth worked once, but no words came out. Eyes unblinkingly on Halian, he nodded.

"Good. Come on, then." Walking carefully, Halian backed into the corridor he'd emerged from. A moment later, Tomo followed. Step by step they went, separated by the ten meters or so Tomo seemed to find comfortable.

Halfway down the corridor, still walking backwards, Halian stepped over the fuzzy line onto the thorascrine-stained part of the carpet.

A few more steps, Halian told himself, his eyes on Tomo.

Once on the stain, his feet kicking up minute bits of the heavy dust, there would be no turning back. Whether enough remained to kill him or merely make him sick, the important result would be the same: The *Goldenrod* would leave for Canaan Under Vega without the risk of an insane man aboard. After that . . . Tomo's fate would be in the universe's hands.

And midway through a step, Halian abruptly stopped.

Tomo stopped, too, five meters from the edge of the thorascrine stain, his face rigid with wary tension at the director's unexpected move. Halian stared at him for a long, painful second . . . and slowly a new truth dawned on him.

It was one thing to discuss death as a necessary and even humane action. It was another thing entirely to face the person involved and personally carry out the proposal.

He couldn't do it. And he hated himself for his weakness.

He took a step toward Tomo . . . and another . . . and with the third, Tomo's look of stunned disbelief changed to terror. *"No!"* he yelled as he spun and disappeared back into the other corridor.

Halian made no effort to chase him. His knees were weak with reaction, frustration and anger a bitter and debilitating taste in his mouth. He started to turn back, to recross the thorascrine and lose himself in the maze of corridors until the others could make the capture . . . but he'd taken only a couple of steps in that direction when the most chilling scream he'd ever heard jerked him around again. A dozen quick strides took him around the corner—

A hundred meters away Tomo was thrashing like a fish in the grip of two security guards.

Halian got to the scene in record time; but even so, Scharn and Ross managed to beat him. Tomo's whimpering rose to a final scream as Scharn reached between the guards with her hypo, a terrified shriek that left a ringing in Halian's ears even after it faded into silence. A moment later the mainter's last twitchings ceased. Scharn said something Halian didn't catch, and the guards lifted the limp form and carried him toward the elevators.

"Well?" a soft voice asked at Halian's side.

The director jumped; he hadn't really noticed Ross come over. "No," he murmured bitterly. "I lost my nerve."

Ross said nothing, but gripped Halian's arm briefly before hurrying to catch up with the others. Halian followed more slowly. *All right, Doctor,* he thought at Scharn's receding back. *You've got your chance now. And you'd damn well better not mess it up like I did.*

It was a long way up from the starless pit of unconsciousness, but there was something soothing in the darkness that removed any possible terror from the disorientation. Tomo had plenty of time to think and remember; and when he finally opened his eyes it was with total lack of surprise that he found himself lying in the lounge chair in his portside quarters. Attached to his right upper arm was a wide band, and he puzzled over it a moment before deciding it must be some sort of biosensory telemeter.

"Hello, Tomo."

He jerked at the quiet voice . . . but Scharn was only present via the viewer on his desk. "Hello, Doctor," he said, relaxing again.

"Sorry if I startled you," she apologized. "I wanted to talk to you and thought this would be the best way. How are you feeling?"

Tomo sighed. "Tired, mostly." He locked eyes with her image. "It's true, isn't it, what Max said. I've been conditioned to be afraid of people."

Scharn's lip twitched minutely. "More or less. That part wasn't done on purpose, but I don't suppose that's any comfort."

"Not really." Tomo closed his eyes, feeling almost relieved that it was over. No uncertainties remained; only cold, hard truth. "So that's it, then. I'll never be able to be with other people."

"Does that bother you?"

He shrugged. "I don't know. How can I miss something

I've never experienced? It's just—" Something seemed to catch in his throat. "It's just that I know now that there's something normal people can do that I can't. It makes me . . . something less than human."

He opened his eyes in time to see Scharn catch her lower lip between her teeth. "There are a lot of things in this universe that some people can do that others can't," she said gently. "I could never spend years at a time alone on a starship—and even if I could, I wouldn't know the first thing about maintaining it. You can do both of those. It doesn't mean either of us is better or worse than the other; it just means we're different."

"Maybe." Tomo paused, steeling himself for the crucial question. "Are you going to let me go back to the *Goldenrod*?"

He saw her eyes shift left, and knew she was checking some of his physiological readouts: reading from his body's reactions the state of his mind. The thought of being laid open like that before her didn't bother him; briefly, he wondered if it should. "I don't think that'll be a problem," she said after a moment. "If it's what you want, of course."

"It is," he said. "It's where I belong. The only place I ever will belong."

"Some people spend all their lives trying to figure out where they belong," she pointed out softly. "At least you've got that much."

Tomo looked at her . . . and slowly it dawned on him that the gentleness in her voice was perhaps less professional technique than it was simply pity. "You don't need to feel sorry for me, Doctor," he told her. "I really *do* enjoy being in space . . . being who I am. It's just—well, I'd like to be *able* to face other people. Even if I never do it. You understand what I'm trying to say?"

"I think so," she nodded. "You're trying to expand the edges of your life, to push yourself as far as you can go."

He grimaced. "Looks like I'm already there, doesn't it?"

"Nonsense!" Scharn snorted with a vehemence that surprised him. "You're a human being, Tomo. No human being yet has ever found his own limits."

Echoes of his own words to Max, Tomo thought. He'd believed them then; now he wasn't so sure. "Um," he grunted noncommittally.

"I mean it. There'll always be new challenges for you—you'll see." Again her eyes shifted to the bio readouts, and when she spoke again her voice was back to its earlier quiet control. "I'm going to let you sleep now; give your body time to throw off the rest of the sedative. If you want to talk again later, I'll be available. If not, that's fine, too."

Fatigue was indeed tugging at Tomo's eyelids, but with an effort he forced them open again. There was one question he still wanted to ask. "Dr. Scharn? Would you tell me what it's like being dirtside?"

He caught just the briefest half-smile before his eyes closed again. "Mostly," Scharn said from the bottom of a long stairway, "it's very, very noisy."

Somehow, the answer seemed profound . . . but before Tomo could think about it, he was asleep.

Scharn turned off the viewer with a sigh, letting the professional calm evaporate from her face as the ache she really felt flooded in to take its place. Yes, Tomo would be able to return to his ship; a couple more days of biochemical analysis on him would conclusively prove what she already knew, that he wasn't drifting into psychosis. A small spurt of growth in his personality—true, in an unexpected direction—was really all that had happened, and in the controlled environment of starship travel there would be no stimuli to encourage further development. Like a teenager's grandiose dreams of his future, Tomo's thoughts of mingling with humanity would quietly fade and die. The mainter would be content with his world again; the company that owned him would be pleased and would return to business as usual.

Owned him. *Owned* him.

And something in Scharn snapped.

She thought about it for a long minute, and then traced a curve on the control ball. "Yes?" Iris answered.

"This is Dr. Scharn," the psychiatrist said firmly. "Get me the *Goldenrod*'s computer. I'd like to leave a private message for Tomo."

The *Goldenrod* launched on schedule, driving slightly out of the ecliptic plane and incidentally giving a grand view of Maigre in the rear viewer. "Well, that's it, Max," Tomo said, the deck feeling good beneath his feet. "Next stop, Canaan Under Vega. Docking equipment all secured?"

"Secured and shut down," the computer replied. "I'm running a check on deep-space functions, but so far everything registers normal."

"Good." Tomo watched the view of Maigre a moment longer, then picked up the cassette he'd earlier pulled out and placed by the control ball. He toyed with it, wondering if he really wanted to do this.

Max might have been reading his mind. "You don't have to try it yet, you know. Dr. Scharn made it clear this was to be strictly voluntary."

"I know," Tomo snapped, feeling the tension of this brand-new uncertainty and wishing Scharn had left things as they were. Almost wishing it, anyway . . . Abruptly, he jammed the cassette into the player and dropped into his lounge chair. "All right," he told Max, bracing himself. "Let's give it a try."

And suddenly there was someone else in the room with him.

Tomo stiffened as the stranger nodded pleasantly. "Hello, Tomo," he said . . . and from behind him a second man appeared . . . and a woman . . . and another man. . . .

They vanished as abruptly as they'd appeared, and Tomo slumped in his chair. He could feel the sweat on his forehead, and even over the roar of the drive his heartbeat was audible. "I think," he said when his breathing was finally back to normal, "that those are the most realistic holograms I've ever seen. Uh . . . how'd I do?"

"Quite well," Max said. "Six point eight seconds. I'm sure you could have managed another few seconds, but the programmed cutoffs are very specific."

"Six point eight, eh?" Tomo repeated, trying hard not to let his disappointment show. "Well, I suppose I have to start somewhere. You think there's a chance I'll be ready by the time we reach Canaan Under Vega?"

"I really don't know," was Max's diplomatic reply. "But we have ten point four years to find out."

Tomo smiled and resettled himself in the seat. "We sure do. Okay; let's try it again."

The dirtsiders at Canaan Under Vega were going to be very surprised.

Afterword

"Return to the Fold" (one of my *least* favorite titles, by the way) started life as a script for some friends who wanted to make an SF movie. We actually took the project pretty far—for amateurs with no budget to speak of, anyway—even testing some potential actors at the local cable-TV facility. But we were eventually put on indefinite hold by a lack of hallways and offices that could be dressed up (cheaply) to look like those aboard a ship and space station. With a script already in hand, I decided I might as well go ahead and turn it into a story. The story sold, was published, and even went on to become a Hugo nominee, which is certainly all one can expect from a humble little novelette. Still, sometimes I wish . . .

Anybody out there have a futuristic home you'd like to lend out for, say, about a week?

The Shadows
of Evening

The late-afternoon sun was sending fingers of chilly
darkness across the landscape as Turek topped the last
hill and came within sight of the village of Akkad. He stood
silently for a moment, looking down with mixed feelings at
the sprawl of adobe huts. The village's growth in the years
since he'd last been here was good, in a way; a sign that
Man's foothold on this uniquely hostile world was increasing. But on the other hand, the more people in an area, the
more trouble there generally was with Shadows. Not only
were man-made objects in greater abundance to begin
with, but there was always an idiot or two in a large village
who simply wouldn't learn—and such, Turek suspected,
was the case here. Tugging almost savagely on his blue
cloak to resettle it on his shoulders, he headed down the
hill.

The crowd around the jeweler's shop was something of a
surprise to him when he arrived there. The messages had
said the Shadow was a large one, but even large Shadows
weren't usually worth any particular attention by the

general populace. Pushing forward—no difficult task; the
crowd parted like the Red Sea for him—he came to the
inner edge of the ring and saw what they were looking at.

Sitting on the ground, gray face screwed up with pain
and nausea, was a middle-aged man in a jeweler's apron. A
plump woman knelt beside him, alternately fussing over
him and scolding him for some action she clearly considered stupid. In front of him lay a rock-wood slab and a
tray of tiny tools, some of which had spilled from their slots
onto the dusty ground. On a cloth nearby lay a neat pile of
delicate gold chains and sparkling gems.

Turek stood there silently for several seconds before the
man noticed him and, gasping with the exertion, scrambled
to his feet. Leaning on the woman, who'd also risen, he
gave a shallow bow.

"Master Turek, please accept my humble thanks for your
generous aid. It is an honor to stand in the presence of a
Shadow Warrior, defender of the people—"

Turek cut him off with a wave of his hand. He'd heard a
thousand welcoming speeches in the past twenty years and
was tired of them. And the gray-faced man was worse than
the average at it. "You are Merken the Jeweler?" he asked
shortly.

The man bobbed his head. "Yes, Master Turek," he said.
Already color was coming back into his wrinkled cheeks;
Turek must have arrived just as the jeweler had emerged
from the Shadow. For the second or third time, perhaps?

Turek nodded at the wooden slab and tools. "I told the
messenger I'd come. Didn't you believe me?"

"Of course, Master, of course," Merken said hastily. "I
just . . . well, in case you were delayed . . . I can't
work inside, and I thought . . ."

"Um." Turek gazed speculatively at the jewelry shop
doorway a dozen feet away. Shadows were invisible to
normal sight, of course, but Shadow Warriors had techniques. . . . Settling his mind into the proper pattern,
Turek closed his eyes and willed his pupils to dilate. Then,
for a brief second, he snapped them open, closing them
again as the sunlight triggered his blink reflex. Squeezing

his eyelids tightly, he studied the afterimage burned for a moment onto his retina.

The Shadow was very clear.

Turek opened his eyes, blinking as the pupils readjusted, and looked at Merken. "It fills the whole building, and extends a good six feet outside," he told the jeweler. "What have you got in there?"

Merken already looked as distressed as he could, but the plump woman still standing beside him whitened slightly. "I'm a jeweler, Master; I have need of many tools and instruments which draw Shadows—"

"I trust you don't consider me an idiot," Turek said coldly. "I'm well acquainted with jeweler's tools, and I know how fast Shadows grow around them. *That*"—he waved at the shop—"wasn't caused by any normal tool. What did you make?"

"Please have mercy, Master," the woman blurted suddenly. "It wasn't his fault—I asked him to make it for me—it was my idea—"

"You aren't to blame," Merken interrupted her, taking a half step to put himself between her and Turek. "I built it; it's *my* responsibility—"

"Cease!" Turek snapped, reducing them both to frightened silence. "I don't care a beggar's damn whose fault this is. You and your neighbors can thrash that out later. All *I* want to know is *what* it is."

"It's a foot-powered gem faceter," Merken mumbled, staring at the ground. "There's a small potter's wheel with adamant dust on it, with a treadle and a gearing system to keep the motion steady. I didn't mean any harm, Master—really. But Romneen here had to do it by hand, and it's hard, with her arthritis and all . . ." He trailed off.

Turek curled his lip. Always there was someone who seemed to believe the laws of the universe would graciously bend for his convenience. Glancing over his shoulder at the crowd, he raised his voice. "All right, you can all go back to your work now. There's nothing more to be seen here."

The people knew an order when they heard one. Within

minutes Turek was alone on the street with the jeweler and his wife. "Relax," he told them, trying to dredge up some of the sympathy that had once been a prominent part of his personality. The effort was only partially successful. "I'm really *not* here to mete out punishment to anyone. Show me where it is."

Merken still looked shaky, but he nodded and started toward the doorway. "Yes, Master; this way."

The first wisps of feeling began as Turek passed the invisible edge he'd seen earlier. As usual, it started as a vaguely uncomfortable feeling, a sort of exaggerated nervousness. But as they stepped into the shop and walked across the front room it increased, and Turek could feel sweat popping out as his skin began to creep uncomfortably. A feeling of nausea grew steadily in the pit of his stomach; his heart was already pounding loudly. His eyes felt like they were being squeezed into his skull. Firmly, he fought the Shadow's attack—and almost blundered into Merken as the jeweler stopped abruptly and pointed with a trembling hand at a door behind the service counter. "In there," he managed, gagging. Turning, he fled the building.

Turek snorted with contempt as he continued alone. Behind the door, under a high window, he found the device Merken had described.

He stood there a moment, swaying only slightly, as he studied the mechanism. The tapered gears were made entirely from wood, as was the potter's wheel and a device that appeared to be some sort of speed governor. Turek smiled grimly as he realized there wasn't a scrap of metal anywhere on the apparatus. The jeweler was apparently one of those who believed that something wasn't technology if it didn't make use of wrought metal. Any Shadow Warrior could have told him differently, of course—if he'd bothered to ask.

A touch of dizziness swept over Turek, reminding him he was wasting time in the most uncomfortable of places. Bracing himself against the doorjamb, he set his teeth and focused his mind; just so . . .

For a moment he felt nothing but the sickness in his body. Then, abruptly, something seemed to click.

And he was in union with the Shadow.

The darkness came like a wave, threatening to overwhelm him, to drag him into some nameless place where light never pierced. With practiced ease he deflected the assault and launched his counterattack. *Be destroyed! Scatter to the winds!*

It resisted his blow, and for an instant Turek seemed to hear something: like voices, but faint and wordless and inhuman. And then he felt the resistance break, and he was back in the jewelry shop.

Pushing off from the doorjamb, Turek headed back outside, walking as quickly as pride allowed. Clearly, the Shadow still existed; he hadn't expected to destroy it completely with a single assault. But his body told him it had reached its limit, and he knew better than to push Shadow-contact past that point. Besides, it would be easier to tell how much damage he'd done from outside.

He stepped from the building, and almost immediately felt the Shadow's effect disappear. A good sign; and when he'd regained some of his strength he checked it visually. Sure enough, the edge of the Shadow had receded almost four feet.

Merken and his wife were standing by the pile of jewelry and tools, looking nervous. "It's going to take several days, but I can do it," Turek told them.

"Several *days*?" Merken echoed, looking stricken.

"Yes, *days*," Turek snapped with a flash of anger. "And you're lucky I'm going to do it at all. Of all people, a craftsman like you should have known how fast Shadow collects around something that's obviously man-made."

"I'm sorry, Master, truly sorry," Merken said, cringing.

"Oh, forget it," Turek muttered, disgusted both with the jeweler and with himself. He shouldn't have gotten angry; the little fool had just been trying to make life a little bit easier for himself.

Even after ten generations, some realities were hard to accept.

A cool breeze found its way underneath Turek's cloak. He shivered, glancing upward to locate the sun. Only an hour or so until sunset; he'd been in there with the Shadow longer than he realized. "I can't do any more here today," he told Merken. "Is Persh's Inn still in business?"

"Yes, Master. Just down this street and turn—"

"I know where it is. I'll be back in the morning."

Turning on his heel, Turek headed down the street.

Persh's Inn was pretty much as Turek remembered it, though he'd only spent an afternoon there the last time he was in Akkad. He had barely seated himself at an empty table when the proprieter bustled up.

"Welcome back, Master Turek," Persh said, placing a carved-wood mug of lukewarm tarri in front of him. "How may I serve you?"

Turek smiled slightly. "Your memory for names is good. Do you remember how I like my tannu roast done?"

Persh's eyes defocused for an instant. "Lemon-seared rare, as I recall, Master. Served with salted green roll and plenty of hot tarri."

"Very good," Turek nodded. "I'll have the same now. Also, I'll need a room for the night."

"Yes, Master. Anything else you'd like?" The tone suggested *anything* meant exactly that.

For an instant Turek's gaze flickered past the innkeeper to the girl serving at the bar—Persh's daughter, probably. For a moment he was tempted. . . . "No, nothing else. Tell me, how are the Shadows around here? Any need clearing out?"

Persh shrugged. "Oh, a few are getting to a fairly uncomfortable size, but nothing is really critical. We're careful to keep our tools as primitive as possible, you know, while still being able to serve our customers. Of course, we'd surely appreciate it if you'd clear some of the Shadows out while you're here, but it's not like you *have* to for your—uh—"

"For my room and board?" Turek felt his expression hardening.

"Uh . . . yes, Master. Of *course* your stay here is without charge—we honor the old customs—"

"Just bring me my dinner," Turek interrupted him. "I'll clear out your Shadows later."

"Yes, Master; thank you, Master." Persh hurried away across the room.

Turek watched him go, his irritation melting into a mild depression. Fear; and an exaggerated deference that bordered on apotheosis. Simple friendship—the kind he'd had with people in his first few years as a Shadow Warrior— seemed to have all but vanished from his life. Only with other Shadow Warriors could he really be accepted just for who he was.

The other tables were filling up as the workday drew to a close and people stopped in for dinner or a quick drink. Frequent bursts of laughter began to punctuate the growing din of conversation; clearly, Akkad as a whole didn't seem unduly concerned by the presence of a large Shadow in their village. Turek listened silently to the noise, feeling more isolated than ever, and found himself watching the girl behind the bar. As recently as a couple of years ago he would've taken Persh up on his implied offer of feminine company. But that same fear had permeated that type of interaction, too, and the results were increasingly disappointing. Resolutely, he turned his gaze from the girl. No sense torturing himself.

Persh arrived a few moments later with a large plate heaped with food and set it down in front of Turek, snagging a pitcher of tarri from a passing waiter and refilling the Shadow Warrior's half-empty mug. Bowing nervously, he backed away, a trifle too hurriedly. Sighing, Turek picked up his flatware and began to eat.

The meal was something of a disappointment. The tannu, while juicy enough, lacked some of the subtle flavors he remembered from his last visit. The green roll, too, seemed to have been overcooked, leaving some of the vegetables on the tasteless side. Only the tarri tasted right, and even it was no better than the tarri a man could get anywhere.

Engrossed in his meal, Turek didn't notice the slight dip in conversation noise; didn't notice anything, in fact, until the bulky man settled into the chair opposite him.

Startled, Turek looked up—and smiled. "Weege! What're you doing here?"

The other man slid his blue Shadow Warrior's cloak off onto the chair back with a sigh that bespoke tiredness. "Oh, that feels good. Hello, Turek. What am I doing here? Eighty percent passing through; twenty percent looking for you."

"Oh, I'm flattered." Turek signaled, but he needn't have bothered; Persh was already hurrying over with a mug and pitcher. "What is it, trouble somewhere?"

"Not really." Weege nodded his thanks for the tarri as Persh poured, waving off the innkeeper's offer of dinner. "I'd hoped to catch you at Keilberg, but when I arrived they told me you'd come here. It was more or less on my way, so I thought I'd drop by with the current rumor." He took a sip from his steaming mug. "Tell me, have you ever heard of a guy named Javan? Comes from somewhere north of Lazuli."

"The self-proclaimed mystic? Sure. Claims to have a new way to destroy Shadows. Standard fruitcake."

"Maybe," Weege said, gazing into the depths of his mug. "But he's causing quite a stir. I hear he's got close on a hundred disciples and students now and is claiming a high success rate against Shadows."

Turek frowned. "A hundred students, eh? That's a good-sized army for a charlatan."

"Yeah. Some of us think it's time we challenged him, put him to a real test."

"Not our problem here, though. Lazuli's a long ways off."

"Javan isn't, though," came the dry response. "He's just a few hours' walk from here, up at Lander's Waste."

Turek sat up straighter. "Up by the old ship? What for?"

"Probably going to practice his technique. You can't find a bigger Shadow on the planet, you know."

"The kid sure thinks big," Turek growled. The old colony

ship that had brought mankind to Vesper hadn't been approached since the day it landed, the day when its seven hundred passengers and crew ran gasping from it and the Shadow which had begun to grow around it. For a while they'd feared the Shadow might grow forever, engulfing the whole planet in agony, but it had finally stopped. Legend had it that right by the ship itself the Shadow was dense enough to kill. "Maybe he'll try to walk to the ship. That would settle the whole thing right there."

"I doubt he's stupid enough to do *that*. No, he's probably doing this for the psychological value—you know, brave new Warrior camping on the doorstep of Shadow."

"Yeah." Turek gazed unseeing around the room, drumming his fingers thoughtfully on the table. "Maybe we *ought* to go up and challenge him. I'm on a job, but I could put it off a day."

"It's completely up to you," Weege said. "I can't go with you; like I said, I'm just passing through. Calneh's got a crisis situation on their hands, and they need my help. In fact, I can't even stay the night." He got to his feet, scooping his cloak with one hand and his mug with the other. Draining the latter, he dropped it back on the table and nodded at Turek. "We'll see you around, Turek. Give Javan a boot for me if you go."

"Sure. Safe trip to you."

Turek brooded for several minutes after Weege left, trying to decide what to do. The idea of facing down a hundred zealots did not especially appeal to him, even if they weren't far enough gone yet that they would actually attack a Shadow Warrior. But allowing a charlatan to operate unchallenged was a bad idea, too. Among other things, it tarnished the image of legitimate Shadow Warriors.

The decision actually came easily. Merken's shop would just have to wait an extra day. Turek couldn't feel particularly sorry about it—after all, the mess was the jeweler's own fault. Maybe next time he'd think before playing with advanced technology.

Flagging down Persh, Turek asked that a message be sent to Merken informing him there would be a short delay in the clearing out of his Shadow. Then he returned to his meal, discovering in the process that it wasn't any more palatable cold than it had been warm. He ate it, though, and downed two more mugs of tarri before calling it an evening.

And before going to bed, he spent an hour clearing Shadows from the inn's kitchen and toolroom.

He was up with the sun, and after a tolerable breakfast he set off for Lander's Waste.

It turned out to be a surprisingly refreshing walk. He was in no particular hurry for this confrontation, and as a result set a more comfortable pace than usual for himself. The meal Persh had packed at his request—Turek had no intention of breaking bread with Javan—rode easily on his shoulder, over his blue cloak. For the first time in months Turek found himself paying attention to the landscape around him, really *looking* at the multicolored plants dotting the gently rolling scrubland. Small animals darted around or sought cover as he passed; twice he spotted the double-wedge of migrating oriflammes, their red-gold plumage vivid against the deep blue of the sky. It was invigorating and strangely restful, as if he'd somehow been transported back to his youth, to the days before he became a Shadow Warrior. The blue cloak carries great weight, as the double-edged aphorism went, but even those who wore it seldom realized just how heavy the load was. To be free of the weight for even a few hours was an unexpected blessing.

An hour before noon, he reached Lander's Waste.

The term "waste" was somewhat misleading, since it looked no different than the area immediately surrounding it. Native Vesperian plants and animals thrived there, completely unaffected by the eight-mile diameter Shadow that had enveloped them for the past two hundred years. A ring of red granite boulders, laboriously moved there by the original colonists, marked the Shadow's edge. Just for practice, Turek used his afterimage technique and confirmed the edge was still where it always had been. No surprises there. Someday, he knew, the ship at the center would start to fall apart, its tools and machines collapsing back into dust—and when that finally happened, the Shadow would begin to shrink. Even as Turek began his circumference of the Waste, he shook his head in wonder. Two hundred years. Someone had really built that ship to last.

He'd gone less than a mile before he came upon Javan's camp, a sprawling tent city pushing nearly to the edge of the Shadow. A quick count showed Weege's estimate had been, if anything, conservative—there were easily enough accommodations here for a hundred and fifty people. A fair percentage of that number were visible around the area, doing various chores or sitting motionlessly just outside the boulder ring. Squaring his shoulders, Turek strode forward.

They saw him coming, of course, and a committee of five teenaged youths met him a hundred feet from the nearest tent. "Greeting to you, Master Shadow Warrior," their spokesman said formally in a voice that mixed friendliness, respect, and wariness. "I am Polyens. How may I serve you?"

"I am Turek," the Shadow Warrior told him. "I am here to see Javan."

"May I ask your business?"

Turek felt the first stirrings of anger. "My business is with Javan, not his gulls."

A low rumbling from the group cut off instantly at a signal from Polyens, and Turek revised upwards his estimate of the youth's position in the organization. Polyens' next words confirmed it. "I'm an aide to Javan, not merely one of his students. Do you pledge safety?"

Turek smiled sardonically. "In the middle of his own camp? Of course. Besides"—he raised the sides of his cloak away from his body—"you can see I'm unarmed."

"Very well. Please come with me."

Polyens led the way inward, the other four youths falling into step a few feet behind Turek. An untrusting lot, he thought, ignoring the covert looks others in the camp threw at him as he passed. Once more he was among people who feared—or even hated—him, and the youthful feeling of the early morning was gone without a trace. He was again a veteran Shadow Warrior, with all that that meant.

They came to a tent near the Shadow's edge, and Polyens disappeared inside. Almost immediately he emerged, accompanied by a cheerful-faced young man who couldn't be over twenty-five years old.

"Greeting to you, Master Turek," he said, bowing with what seemed to be genuine respect. "I am Javan; welcome to my school. May I offer you refreshment?"

Turek shook his head. "I'm not here as a friend, Javan. I've come to issue a challenge."

Polyens took a step toward Turek, his face thunderous, but Javan stopped him with a touch. "Peace. It's not a regular challenge; he's asking me to prove my abilities against Shadow."

Polyens relaxed. "Oh, I thought you were breaking your pledge," he explained, a little sheepishly.

Javan bailed him out. "Why don't you go get us some water?" he suggested. "Master Turek must be thirsty."

"At once." Looking relieved, Polyens hurried out.

"I've already said—" Turek began.

"I know," Javan interrupted him. "But you can surely drink water with me without commitment. Besides"—he smiled ingenuously—"it's been a long time since I've had the chance to talk with a Shadow Warrior. Won't you please indulge me?"

Turek shrugged. "Oh, all right." Ducking under the flap, he entered Javan's tent.

Given the size of his following, Turek had expected Javan would live in somewhat greater luxury than the tent's furnishings showed. The bed and straw-filled contour chairs were of the sort that any peasant might own, and aside from a simple candlestick to augment the light from the tent's windows, there wasn't anything "advanced" to be seen anywhere. Turek mentally added a point to his side: anyone who claimed power over Shadows shouldn't be afraid to own Shadow-drawing items.

"Your accent sounds mid-Southern," Javan commented as he gestured Turek to one of the contour chairs. "Are you from Paysan, by any chance?"

"Keilberg," Turek said shortly.

"Ah. I've never been there, but I've heard good things about it." Javan paused as Polyens appeared with a pitcher of water and two mugs. The youth poured in silence and left, and Javan raised his cup. "To your health," he said, drinking deeply and then setting aside the mug. "And now tell me, Master Turek—what are your thoughts concerning Shadow?"

Turek blinked once, caught off guard by the unexpected question. "What do you mean?"

"How do you visualize it when you battle it? As a natural phenomenon like rot, or as a living force?"

Turek sipped at his water, considering. He'd never thought about it in exactly those terms before. "I don't know. Sometimes I seem to hear voices when I'm fighting it. But on the other hand, it doesn't seem to learn or to focus its effect in any way, like you'd expect it to if it were trying to destroy us." He shrugged. "I'm not sure it makes any difference *what* it is. It grows; we clear it out."

"It *does* make a difference," Javan disagreed quickly. "If it's not alive, there may indeed be only one way to get rid of it, like cutting rot away from fruit. But if it *is* alive, there may be several ways to attack it."

Turek put his mug on the ground and crossed his arms across his chest. Now the conversation was going somewhere. "I already know one way to attack Shadow—and, in case you've forgotten, it took our ancestors five generations to develop it. So tell me about this new method you've got that everyone else has somehow missed."

"First of all, I should point out I'm also familiar with the standard way. I don't suppose you know, but I studied for three years to become a Shadow Warrior. And I didn't miss the cut," he added, correctly interpreting Turek's expression. "I left voluntarily."

"Why? Afraid you couldn't handle the Final Test?"

"Maybe partly. But mainly because of all the ones who *didn't* make the apprentice cut. It seemed such a waste of effort, on everyone's part."

"Fighting Shadows isn't easy. It takes strength of mind and a lot of stamina."

"Certainly, the way you do it. But I've found an easier way." Javan hunched forward earnestly. "You see, the usual method involves a sort of head-to-head confrontation where you have to basically *overpower* the Shadow—fight it with its own weapons, so to speak. The problem with this is that you have to go right into the Shadow, where it's strongest, and actually make contact with it. It's a terrific strain, which ages Shadow Warriors far before their time, and even seems to affect their personalities."

"Our personalities are not your concern," Turek said bluntly. "As for the rest of it, it's the price we pay to help the people of Vesper. And we pay it willingly."

"I'm sure you do. But it's not necessary. You don't need to outdarken the darkness, so to speak. You can use light."

"Light?" Turek had lost track of all the charlatans throughout history who had tried using light against Shadow.

"Yes—but not the kind you mean. It's an *inner* light, a sort of psychic glow."

"That's absurd."

Turek hadn't really intended the words to sound so harsh, but that was the way they came out. Javan reddened with anger. "So now you're going to give the verdict before the trial? Very convenient—saves time, I imagine."

"Don't worry; you're not going to get me into that old trap," Turek said grimly. "'Shadow Warrior persecution' is a standard charlatan excuse, and I'm going to make sure you can't use it."

"Charlatan!" Javan stood up abruptly, glaring down at Turek. For a moment the tent was filled with a brittle silence as Javan slowly regained a grip on his temper. "All right; enough talk, then. Name the test."

Turek closed his eyes, opened and closed them again. No good. Shadows eventually grew up around anything man-made, but with the primitive furnishings of Javan's tent the effect was much too slow to worry about. The Shadows blanketing the chairs and candlestick were thin enough that anyone with a modicum of Shadow Warrior training could handle them, and Turek had no intention of making things that easy for Javan. "Nothing worth doing in here. Let's go outside."

After the relative dimness of the tent the bright sunlight was dazzling, and Turek made use of it for two more afterimage searches. Again he was out of luck: no decent Shadows were visible anywhere. "You keep a clean camp," he grunted.

Javan shrugged. "The meditation required to learn my technique is hampered when a student is surrounded by lots of different Shadows. The learning comes quicker when there's just a single strong Shadow to work on."

A malicious smile tugged at the corners of Turek's mouth. "Thanks for reminding me. There *is* a decent-sized Shadow around for your test."

Javan seemed taken aback. "You can't mean Lander's Waste."

"Why not? Ordinary Shadow Warrior technique is useless against something that size. Ideal way to prove your stuff."

"That's completely unfair—" Javan began, but just then Polyens came around the corner of the tent.

"Excuse me, Javan, but there's a man here to see you about clearing out a Shadow," he said, his eyes flickering between his master and Turek. "He said it was important."

With one final glare at Turek, Javan deliberately turned to Polyens. "Bring him here."

Polyens looked toward the rear of the tent and nodded, and a middle-aged man came nervously into view.

It was Merken the Jeweler.

He froze in midstep as he recognized Turek, and the color drained from his face. "Master Turek!" he gasped.

Turek took a step toward him, fists clenched at his side, a sour taste in his mouth. "Yes, Merken, it's me. What's the matter, didn't you trust me to come back? You thought I was going to break my word?"

Merken was rapidly approaching a state of terror. "No, Master, no! But your message said you'd be delayed, and I didn't know how long, and I just thought—I mean, I've heard of Javan—and I thought maybe . . ." He ran out of words as he tried to burrow deeper into his cloak.

Turek took another step forward . . . and Javan was suddenly between him and Merken. "What seems to be the problem?" he asked calmly.

"Nothing!" Turek bit out. "Apparently the residents of Akkad don't trust Shadow Warriors. Fine; I'll see to it that no Shadow Warrior ever goes near the place again."

Turek had thought Merken's face as devoid of color as possible, but now he had the satisfaction of seeing the jeweler whiten still further. "Wait," he choked. "Please. It would destroy Akkad—no one could ever live there again."

"You should have thought of that before you decided I wasn't trustworthy." Turning his back, Turek began to walk away.

"Just a moment, Master Turek," Javan called.

Turek spun around, half-expecting to see Javan's minions approaching with fighting sticks drawn. But no one moved. "What?"

"It seems to me this would be a good opportunity for you to test my technique. I take it that this Shadow is one even a Shadow Warrior would have trouble with?"

"It'll take several attacks to get rid of it," Turek muttered, thoughts racing. It *would* be a good test, come to think of it—there was no way Javan could use Shadow Warrior methods against it without that being obvious. And there would be neutral witnesses there, enough to counter Javan's forces even if he brought his whole army along. "All right," he said at last. "The Shadow in Merken's shop—that's your test."

Javan nodded. "Good. We can leave immediately, if you're agreeable. Just let me get a few things for the trip."

Javan either had a great deal of confidence in himself or he shrewdly realized that descending on Akkad with a mob of his partisans would be ill-advised and unproductive. Thus, only four men left Lander's Waste a half hour later: Turek, Merken, Javan, and Polyens.

Turek walked in front, alone. His anger at Merken had cooled, leaving an undefinable ache in its place. Why he had reacted so violently before, he still didn't know, and it both irritated and worried him. After all, there was nothing like a contract between Merken and himself, and he *had* forgotten to mention in his message that he would probably not be gone more than a day. But logic didn't help, and the hurt remained.

If the others noticed his irritation, they didn't show it. Javan, especially, ignored him, preferring instead to keep up a more or less running conversation with Merken, asking about everything from the jeweler's family to the quality of life in Akkad. From his position ahead of them Turek couldn't help but hear every word, and he listened closely. But if Javan was just trying to swing Merken onto his side, he was doing a superb job of it. Nowhere in voice or questions could Turek detect anything but honest friendliness.

It was late afternoon when they reached Akkad. Merken's wife had clearly been on the lookout for them; she and a small crowd of neighbors were waiting at the shop when the four men arrived. Ignoring the uneasy looks the villagers were giving him, Turek stepped into the middle of the group. "In accordance with the laws and customs of Vesper, I hereby challenge the man Javan to prove his claimed power over Shadow," he announced, keeping his expression and voice neutral. "You are all called upon to be witnesses." Turning, he faced Javan and gestured toward the jewelry shop.

Javan walked forward slowly, stopping at the edge of the Shadow. For a moment he stood quietly, and Turek saw him use what seemed to be a slight modification of the Shadow Warrior afterimage technique. He raised his right hand, open palm just touching the Shadow, and the faint murmuring of the crowd cut off into an expectant silence. Turek watched him closely, every sense alert for whatever trickery he was about to use.

—And suddenly Javan blazed with light!

With a cry, Turek stepped back, instinctively throwing an arm over his face. But it was a useless gesture; the searing glare was in his mind, not his eyes. Desperately, he tried to fight it, to block it the way he'd blocked the thousands of Shadow attacks throughout the years. But for once it didn't work, and there was no time to make it work, for even as his defense cracked before the onslaught he felt himself falling. . . .

And the light vanished into a cool and welcome darkness.

The darkness lightened only slowly, and seemed somehow mixed with a cool wetness. As if from the bottom of a deep pond, Turek struggled upward and finally came awake.

He opened his eyes. He was lying on the floor of Merken's jewelry shop, his head pillowed on something soft. Beside him knelt Javan, his brow furrowed, wringing out a wet cloth into a small basin. "Never mind that," Turek said hoarsely.

Javan's head came around with obvious surprise. "You're awake," he said, dropping the cloth back into the basin. "How do you feel?"

"What do you care?" Turek glanced around the room, and for the first time noticed the lack of Shadow symptoms. "The Shadow?"

"Destroyed," Javan said. There was no trace of triumph in his voice. "Polyens and some of the others took Merken's device to the edge of town to break it up before the Shadow starts growing back."

Turek looked up at the youth, feeling his whole body sag. "You destroyed it," he said, the words tasting like ashes in his mouth. "You really did it—and with enough power left over to blast me, too."

Javan shook his head, his eyes full of concern. "That wasn't on purpose, Turek, believe me. I don't understand what happened to you. Most people can't see the light at all, much less be bothered by it—even I can just barely detect it. Merken's wife Romneen has gone for a doctor; maybe he can help."

"Never mind him—I'm all right. And it's probably never happened before because you've never had a Shadow Warrior present." Laboriously, Turek got to his feet, brushing off Javan's attempts to help him. "You said it yourself, this morning. Remember? Close contact with Shadows affects your personality." He wavered for a moment, as a brief touch of dizziness came and went. "I expect I've . . . absorbed . . . too much of Shadow into myself. However that light of yours burns up Shadow, it hit me, too."

"I'm sorry," Javan said in a low voice. "I had no idea."

"Forget it. It's not going to be a problem for you. Once the word is passed, the rest of the Shadow Warriors will stay out of your way." Turek's cloak and food bag stood on a nearby chair, the latter reminding him he'd skipped lunch and was ravenously hungry. No matter; he could eat once he was out of town. Picking up his things, he headed for the door.

"Where are you going?" Javan asked.

"I'm leaving Akkad, of course."

"Why?"

Turek paused to fasten his cloak. "Why not? I'm not needed here anymore."

He started forward again, but with a few quick strides Javan passed him and stood in the doorway. "Master Turek, I don't wish to part as enemies. Won't you please try to understand what I'm trying to do?"

Turek stopped. "I understand completely. You want to

clear all the Shadows from Vesper, to free mankind from
the drudgery of having to do everything by hand. Why do
you think *I* became a Shadow Warrior?"

"Then you have to realize what this new method means
for our people. It's easier to learn, takes much less effort for
the same results, and—most important of all—doesn't
require that constant penetration of Shadow that you've
had to go through. It'll free all of us up that much more,
you included. It'll be *good* for Vesper."

The youth was almost pleading, Turek realized—pleading for Turek's blessing, or at least his acceptance. But the
Shadow Warrior remained silent, and after a moment Javan
bowed his head slightly and stepped aside.

The sun was low in the sky as Turek set off for the edge of
town. It would be night long before he could reach
Keilberg, but he didn't care; anything was better than
staying in the same village with Javan.

He paused at the top of the first hill to tighten his cloak
and his gaze almost magnetically turned back toward
Akkad. Already it was too dark to see individuals unless
they carried candles, but in his mind's eye he could see
Javan and Polyens as they celebrated their victory over
Shadow . . . and over the Shadow Warriors.

Turek smiled humorlessly. Yes, he understood Javan
perfectly; that youthful idealism and desire to serve might
once have been Turek's own. And the new technique *would*
be beneficial . . . at least for Vesper as a whole.

But for the Shadow Warriors?

Turek had grappled with Shadow for half his life, had
sweated and suffered and gotten sick so that others could
maintain their precarious existence on this world. He'd
kept at it doggedly, long after the warm glow of youthful
enthusiasm had faded, even long after the multitude of
Shadow-contacts had begun to poison every facet of his
being, until only a dry sense of duty was left to keep him
going. A wife, a family, any kind of normal life—all had
been impossible for him to have.

He'd given his entire *life* to battle . . . but now Javan

had proved that the sacrifice hadn't been necessary, that an easier way was possible.

And Turek had wasted his life for nothing.

"It's not fair!" he shouted abruptly at the blood-red sunset. "Do you hear me? *It's not fair!*"

There was no answer, and after a moment Turek turned his back on Akkad and continued on into the growing darkness.

Afterword

It's been obvious since at least the Industrial Revolution that advances benefiting society as a whole can be pretty hard on segments of that same society. But unemployment aside, I think Turek's reaction illustrates a good part of the psychological resistance to change: the fear that doing things the hard way when an easier way exists somehow makes one a fool. The fact that that conclusion simply isn't true doesn't really matter—emotional reactions by definition lack logic.

If we could somehow eliminate this fear of looking foolish, would some of our resistance to change also disappear? *And,* given that not all change is beneficial, would losing that resistance be good or bad in the long run?

Not Always
To The Strong

The flat stone jutted up out of the log-and-thong vise like the gray tooth of some giant predator. Squinting along its surface, Turek set his cutter carefully against a small protrusion and hit it a sharp blow. A chip of the stone fell away, and for the hundredth time Turek ran his fingertips along the cutting edge. Almost done, he decided; by noon he should have a functioning hoe again. He spotted another flaw, and had just set his cutter again when the knock came at his door.

He paused, listening, wondering if he'd imagined it. Visitors these days were few and far between, especially since one of Javan's spanking new Mindlight Masters had taken up residence in Keilberg, eliminating the village's last real need for a Shadow Warrior's services. It was conceivable that someone from one of the farms to the west had come to ask his help, but even they seemed to prefer to walk the two extra miles into Keilberg. That it might be someone merely interested in Turek's company was unlikely in the extreme.

The knock came a second time, too loudly to be imagination. Putting down his tools, Turek got up and went to answer the door.

There were two of them; big men, both, dressed in gray cloaks and the dust of a long journey. The man in front was perhaps twenty-five, his companion a couple of years younger. "Master Turek, the Shadow Warrior?" the first man asked politely.

Turek studied him a moment before answering. From his coloring and accent Turek would guess him to be a northman, possibly from the Lazuli region . . . Javan's home territory, where his Mindlight school was centered. The old feelings, long buried, began to churn again within him. "I am Turek," he acknowledged coldly. "And you?"

The other didn't so much as move a single muscle—but Turek suddenly felt as if he'd tried to push over an eighty-year-old plains oak. The young man's aura of authority remained untouched by Turek's mild hostility; his eyes held a pride the Shadow Warrior had seen only rarely in his fifty years. Here was a man whose internal power bent to no one, and Turek's first suspicion vanished like dew under that steady gaze. Whoever he might be, he was emphatically no Mindlight Master.

"I am Krain," the man identified himself, "ruler of Masard, to the north. My aide, Pakstin. We'd like to talk with you, if you're free."

Something about his attitude suggested that he expected Turek to say no. But Turek had no interest in a battle of wills. Stepping to one side, he gestured them in.

The meeting area of the house was small and modestly furnished; Turek never entertained much. "Please sit down," he said, indicating the room's two chairs.

"Pakstin will stand," Krain said as he sank into one of the straw-filled contour chairs, his aide taking up position beside him.

Shrugging, Turek took the other seat. "What can I do for you?" he asked.

"Ask rather what we can do for each other," Krain

answered. "I've come here to offer you a permanent position in Masard."

"I see," Turek managed. It wasn't exactly the sort of response he'd been expecting. "To what do I owe this offer?"

"To my regret at seeing the noble brotherhood of Shadow Warriors in decline," the other said. "At Masard we are dedicated to improving the lives of our people by expanding the number and quality of tools available. Naturally, such attempts multiply the growth of Shadows in the region."

"Naturally." What the Shadows were and where they had come from was unknown, but the one absolute truth on Vesper was that everything made by man sooner or later grew a thick coating of Shadow. Invisible, intangible—but unpleasantly real. "And so naturally you need to hire more Shadow Warriors to deal with it. Right?"

"Of course."

Turek leaned back a bit more in his chair and favored the other with his most sardonic smile. "*Sure* you do. I don't know what kind of fool you take me for, Krain, but you're on the wrong road. In the first place, anything a Shadow Warrior can do for you one of Javan's swarm of eager young Mindlight Masters can do faster and easier—and Masard is practically next door to his Lazuli school. And in the second place, there must be dozens of Shadow Warriors closer to you than I am. Are you really going to try and persuade me that you had to come all the way down here—*personally*—to find one to hire?" He shook his head. "Try again."

"Very good." Krain's expression showed a pleased sort of satisfaction. "Very good indeed. You're quicker than most I've talked to. I'd begun to wonder if fighting Shadow diminished the mental faculties after a time. Tell me, would you like to be revenged on Javan?"

Turek stiffened. Memories flooded back. . . . "What would I want vengeance for?" he asked carefully.

"For destroying your livelihood, for starters." Krain's eyes swept the room carefully, his gaze lingering for a moment on the new hoe blade clearly visible through the open workroom door. "Ten years ago you would have had someone else making your tools and growing your food in exchange for your services against Shadow. You would have been the most valuable man in the entire Keilberg region. Javan's Mindlight technique ruined all that, usurping five generations of Shadow Warrior authority on Vesper."

"We never had any real *authority*," Turek disagreed quietly. "Nor did we desire any. Our desire was to *serve* the people, to help limit the Shadows that would otherwise force them to live like animals. Javan simply found a better and faster way to do that. Why shouldn't it replace our method?"

Krain shrugged, his eyes on Turek's face. "Yet I understand that your method eliminated Shadow at a high cost to your personal comfort and even, shall we say, to your long-term mental health. Why would you endure that if not for the prestige the blue cloak gave you?"

Turek shook his head; there was no answer he could give that would satisfy the other. "You spoke of revenge?"

"Yes." Krain leaned forward slightly. "As you stated, the power to destroy Shadow has shifted to Javan and his people, and with it has gone control over Vesper's technological growth. I submit that Javan is not qualified to make the decisions that such control will require."

The young northman stopped, but the message underlying his words was clear enough. "Passing up for the moment the question of whether or not your qualifications are better than his, what makes you think you can gain the influence you want anyway? Javan's probably got a couple of hundred students at any given time, and with all of them running around Lazuli destroying Shadows the village can probably support a population of over a thousand by now. Few of them are going to take kindly to interference or pressure from Masard."

"I won't be going to Lazuli alone," Krain said. "My army numbers nearly three hundred, and is well trained."

"So what? Fighting sticks are fighting sticks, no matter how expert your men are."

"True—but we have something a bit better than fighting

sticks." He gestured to Pakstin, still standing by his seat. In a single smooth motion the aide threw back his cloak, reached across to his left hip, and pulled out—

A three-foot-long sword.

Turek had seen swords before, of course; carved wooden things, usually, sometimes with sharp bits of stone embedded in their edges. Glorified clubs, really; but this one was different. Its handle was wooden, but its blade had the smooth sheen of pure metal, and even from several feet away it was clear that the point and edges were sharp. "Impressive," he murmured. "Probably draws Shadow like crazy, too."

"Why not check it for yourself?" Krain suggested.

Turek frowned, then shrugged. "All right. Hold it steady, Pakstin."

Closing his eyes, Turek set his mind into the proper pattern and dilated his pupils. He snapped them open for a second, then squeezed them shut again; and on the afterimage the Shadow was very clear. It was a good two feet in diameter, surrounding the sword like a black cocoon. Opening his eyes, Turek studied Pakstin's face briefly. Gripping the sword hilt, his hand in the middle of a Shadow of that size, the northman should be feeling a fair amount of discomfort—and, sure enough, the signs of tension were there. But just barely. Pakstin clearly had a good deal of self-control. If all of Krain's men were so well disciplined . . .

"How long would you estimate the Shadow has been growing?" Krain asked, breaking Turek's train of thought.

"Oh, six hours or so. Maybe twelve if the metal's not too well refined."

The other shook his head, a slight smile on his face. "We had a Mindlight Master clean it—and the blanket it was wrapped in at the time—in Paysan three days ago."

"Three *days*?" Turek hunched forward, interested in spite of himself. "What kind of metal *is* that?"

"First of all, it's an alloy, not a pure metal—a combination of copper and tin, actually—which should make it a little closer to a natural material. But the key, I think, is the fact that oriflamme bones are mixed into the molten metal during the alloying process. They don't seem to decrease the metal's strength appreciably, and the extra impurity dramatically decreases the rate of Shadow growth."

Turek nodded slowly as Pakstin sheathed his blade again. It made sense, he supposed—a metal loaded with impurities was certainly less advanced than a pure metal would be, and that seemed to be the only criterion Shadow cared about. But there was something else that was not quite right about this scheme, something he couldn't quite put his finger on. "So I presume what you're asking me to do is to come to Masard and keep Shadows off your weapons while you beat Lazuli into submission. Right?"

"Actually, I'm hoping there will be no fighting at all, that the village will recognize the futility of resistance," Krain said offhandedly. "But you're not just being hired for this single operation. You and the other three Shadow Warriors who've joined me will have honored positions in my realm, regaining the prestige you once held."

—And the missing piece fell into place. "These swords of yours," Turek said slowly, "you make them yourself?"

Krain nodded, the pleased look back on his face. "We have a group of smiths right in Masard turning out ten blades a day."

"With your new Shadow Warriors standing by to keep Shadows away from the final product," Turek nodded. "But you can't be making the metal itself, because to get an alloy strong enough for a sword blade you'd have to start with almost pure copper and tin. Three Shadow Warriors couldn't even begin to keep up with the Shadows *that* would grow—never mind the advanced smelters you'd also have to have." He gestured toward the hidden sword. "Someone in Lazuli developed this alloy, didn't they? Someone with a Mindlight Master or two standing over his shoulder. What did you do, sneak into the village and steal some of the metal?"

"More or less." If Krain felt any guilt over his action he hid it well. "But don't worry about that—we have enough to make all the swords we'll need to bring Javan to his knees. And after that we'll have both the smelter and the Mindlight Masters and can make all the weapons we'll ever need." The northman leaned back in his seat. "But I think you've heard enough to make your decision. What say you, Master Turek?"

Turek held the other's gaze for only a second. Then, almost of their own accord, his eyes shifted left to stare out the window as he remembered that day in Akkad—so long ago!—when Javan had once and for all proved his new technique . . . and had totally humiliated Turek in the process. He could still feel the stabbing pain of Javan's "psychic light"—the light which only Turek, because of his years as a Shadow Warrior, had been able to see . . . could still feel the shame of fainting in front of the crowd, and then awakening to discover the huge Shadow had been completely destroyed by that single blast. He'd hated Javan for a long time after that—and the knowledge that such feelings were unjustified had only made them worse. But of course the hatred had long since died . . . hadn't it?

And now he was being offered vengeance . . . and the chance to once more do something that would affect people's lives. Krain had been right—he missed the prestige of the blue cloak. Missed it more than he'd realized . . . perhaps more than was good for him. . . .

Krain was still watching him when Turek brought back his gaze. "Yes," the Shadow Warrior said firmly. "I'll come with you."

They left the next morning, picking up provisions in Keilberg on their way. It was a good ten-day trip to Masard; but though the two northmen were agreeable enough companions, Turek learned far less about them during the journey than he'd expected to. Krain, particularly, seemed unwilling to talk about his personal life and ambitions, and was adept at shifting the conversation whenever Turek tried to draw him out. Such reticence surprised the Shadow Warrior; he would have expected a would-be conqueror—especially one so young—to be more given to self-centered boasting. As a partial result, a great deal of their talk centered on Masard and the surrounding region, so that by the time they reached the village Turek felt almost as if he were coming home, even though he'd never before visited the area. Perhaps, he thought, that was the goal Krain had had in mind.

Masard was a huge village by Vesperian standards, its adobe buildings sprawling over several square miles and its population approaching the eleven-hundred mark. Krain's residence was on the northern edge, and as the three men walked through the village Turek kept his eyes open for signs of war preparations. Surprisingly, he saw none.

"Because the general population doesn't know about my plans," Krain said when Turek questioned him about it.

"How did you hide the conscription of three hundred men? Make up some story about a labor levy?"

"The core of my army is my personal guard. For the rest"—he shrugged—"I've hired men from Glasstone and the Fens."

Turek frowned. How did Krain expect to make any sort of permanent conquest if he wasn't even preparing his own people for the idea? And why keep the truth from them, anyway?

He found the answer to at least part of his question as they passed the next street. Two buildings down the avenue a young man was listening to an old fruit merchant near the latter's cart. Fastening the youth's ordinary brown cloak about his shoulders was a distinctive sun-shaped gold pin.

Turek paused, and apparently his blue cloak caught the youth's attention. For a moment they eyed each other across the gap, the Shadow Warrior and the Mindlight Master, as the old merchant prattled on, oblivious to the sudden tension in the air around him. Unconsciously tugging his cloak tighter, Turek turned away and moved on. Within seconds the youth was lost to view behind the next building.

"His name's Isserli—one of about six who live permanently in Masard," Krain murmured at Turek's side.

The Shadow Warrior nodded. Of course Krain hadn't told his people of his plans for Lazuli—aside from the fact that word would be bound to get back quickly to Javan, the people of Masard depended on the Mindlight Masters for the life of their village. Any threat to Javan would bring howls of protest and possibly a full-fledged insurrection.

"Once we have Lazuli and the Mindlight school, of course, there'll be no problem." Krain might have been reading Turek's mind. "Then we'll have all the Mindlight Masters we need and no one in Masard will have any cause to complain about my methods."

Or at least such protests would be few and far between. "When do you plan to move?" Turek asked.

"Very soon." Krain paused until they had passed a particularly crowded part of the street. "Already we have men watching the only road into Lazuli, watching to make sure they don't bring in more of the ores they would need to make their own weapons. In a week or less we'll seal the road completely and call on the village to surrender. If they refuse . . . we'll go in."

"I see." Turek strove to keep the surprise out of his face and voice; he hadn't realized the plan was that close to readiness. "What do you want me to do in preparation?"

"Pakstin will take you to the weapons shed to meet the other Shadow Warriors and the smiths," Krain told him. "They'll show you what needs to be done."

They walked in silence after that, and a few minutes later came in sight of a large but unpretentious house whose main distinctions seemed to be the wall surrounding it and the liveried guard at the main entrance. Krain said his farewells and headed for the house; Pakstin and Turek veered west and circled the wall. It turned out to be more extensive than Turek had realized, stretching back several hundred feet past the rear of the house itself. Set into it was another door, this one unguarded, at least on the outside. Stepping up to it, Pakstin knocked twice and spoke quietly through the peephole that opened in response. The door swung wide; beckoning to Turek, Pakstin led the way inside.

The area looked as if it had once been a formal garden-orchard of the imposing type Turek would have expected someone like Krain to own. But most of the flowers and bushes in the center had vanished, and the circle of trees now ringed a swordsman-training area. Twenty or thirty men were engaged in drills as Pakstin and Turek skirted the area, and the sunlight flashing from so many swords was an awesome sight. From somewhere to the south, the sound of gentle hammering was audible.

"The smithy is back this way," Pakstin said as they threaded their way through a group of medium-sized tents and headed toward the sound. The tent material was a fairly advanced type Turek had seen before: cloth impregnated with tree resins for waterproofing purposes. The resins, he remembered, had the unfortunate side effect of being flammable, but as long as one was careful the benefits usually outweighed the risks. Turek hoped Krain hadn't neglected that aspect of his men's training.

A moment later they had arrived at the smithy, an open-air sort of thing where four muscular men were carefully hammering the edges of embryonic sword blades, while other strips of the metal softened over a nearby fire. Standing off to one side, well away from the heat, were three old men in blue cloaks.

Pakstin made the introductions. "Rusten, Spard, and Brisher; this is Turek, who's just joined us. Perhaps you can fill him in on whatever Shadows need to be cleared out?"

"Yes, we'll take charge of him," Brisher rumbled. "You can go back inside and play with your maps and stones."

Pakstin's smile was tolerant and just a little bit condescending. "Maps of the area around Lazuli and markers indicating our men," he explained to Turek. "We use them to plan our strategy. I'll leave you to get acquainted."

For a moment after he left the Shadow Warriors eyed one another in silence. Turek had never met these particular three men before, but *had* heard of them, and was a little surprised they had lent their services to this endeavor. Older and more experienced than he was—Brisher, the youngest, couldn't have been less than sixty

years old—they should have been among the most willing
to step down when Javan's technique began to take root.
But even as he studied their lined faces and tired eyes,
Turek realized they were no more paragons of nobility than
he was . . . and they had fought Shadow longer than he
had before seeing their quiet sacrifices rendered unnecessary and unnoticed by the people of Vesper. No wonder
Krain had spoken so much of revenge; that approach
seemed to have already proved its effectiveness. Feeling
vaguely embarrassed, Turek shifted his gaze from them and
turned instead toward the smithy. Closing his eyes, he did
his afterimage trick. Forges and their associated tools grew
Shadows fairly quickly, but this one seemed reasonably
clean. "You're doing a good job with the Shadows here," he
commented, just for something to say.

"That's what we were hired to do," Rusten said, a bit
tartly. Turek's reaction to his tone must have been visible,
because his next words were a degree more civil. "Sorry—
didn't mean to jump all over you. You're from Keilberg,
aren't you? I seem to remember hearing your name some
years back."

Turek nodded. "You've got a good memory for trivia. I've
heard of all of you, of course. You were considered among
the best Shadow Warriors on Vesper when I was an
apprentice."

Spard smiled thinly. "'Were' is the proper word," he
said.

"Yes." Feeling awkward, Turek hunted for a less painful
topic of conversation. "Tell me, what do you think Krain's
chances are?"

Spard shrugged and glanced at his fellows. "Pretty good,
I suppose. Considering that no one's ever tried warfare on
this scale before, Krain seems to have the details worked
out reasonably well."

"His chances are excellent," Brisher growled, fingering
his beard restlessly. "Lazuli's built with its back against
sheer cliffs to the north and east, and a narrow but very fast
whiteriver to the west. Even with only three hundred men

he can easily control the village's exit, and can therefore starve them into submission."

Turek nodded; he'd already come to more or less the same conclusion. Lazuli's unusually sheltered location, he remembered hearing, had been an experiment to see if cliffs and rapids hindered Shadow formation in any way. It hadn't worked, of course.

"Krain's not going to bother with something like that," Rusten disagreed. "He can't afford to spend that much time without control of Javan's school—all of us will be needed to clear Shadows from the weapons and there's no guarantee he'll be able to keep Isserli and his friends working in Masard."

"Speaking of weapons," Turek put in, "could I see the swords Krain has ready? I'd like to test the Shadow growing there."

"It's no different than the Shadow around a single one, except in degree," Spard said. "But they're piled over through there if you really want to see them." He pointed past the smithy. "Don't worry about the guards; they'll have been told about you by now."

"Thanks." Turek moved off as the discussion continued in a halfhearted sort of way behind him. Just another group of hirelings, he thought with mixed pity and contempt—hirelings submitting to Krain's ambition. He wondered if they realized how far they'd fallen.

Only later did he wonder if they saw him the same way.

The swords were stored in a thick-walled adobe shed, whose single door was flanked by two of the biggest men Turek had ever seen. Big, able-looking—and somewhat fidgety. A quick check showed why; the Shadow around the swords was already extending several feet outside the shed.

Sighing, Turek squared his shoulders and moved forward. A Shadow that size would take at least two assaults, and he might as well get started now. Besides, it would give him the chance to look at the swords. Nodding to the guards, he pulled open the shed door and stepped inside.

It wasn't as bad as it might have been. Shadows around the most advanced man-made objects not only grew larger

and faster than average, but also were "denser" in their
effect. Before Turek had even entered the shed he'd felt the
first uncomfortably nervous sensation; once inside, it got
quickly worse as his skin began to creep and nausea grew
like poisonous fire in his stomach. But he could fight it
somewhat—and he could walk right up to the neatly
stacked swords without feeling any of the muscular
twitches which could incapacitate a man if allowed to grow
large enough. Turek had heard of only one man who'd ever
gone that far into Shadow, down at Lander's Waste where
the old starship lay. He'd died for his audacity, the legend
said. Presumably in agony.

But such thoughts wasted time. Gritting his teeth, Turek
focused his mind against the Shadow . . . and after a time
he felt its resistance break . . .

Shaking his head to clear it, he stepped a bit unsteadily
to the wall. The sensations vanished just as he reached it,
showing him where the Shadow's new edge lay. A half
hour's rest, and he'd be able to clear the rest of it out. But
first—

He glanced out the door, confirmed that both guards
were facing away from him. Moving quietly, he walked
back to the Shadow's center. The sword he picked up was
heavier than he had expected, but not unreasonably so.
And fastened securely to his waist sash, hidden under his
cloak, it would be invisible. Outside, off among the trees,
he could take the time to destroy the Shadow that still
clung to it.

Leaving the shed, he set off in search of privacy.

Turek had half-expected one of the other Shadow
Warriors to finish the job he'd started at the weapons shed,
but to the best of his knowledge none of them even
bothered to go over and check on the Shadow there. Turek
wound up clearing out the entire Shadow himself, and after
that he spent a couple of hours tackling smaller Shadows
both in the training area and in the house itself. It was a bit
surprising to him that there *were* so many about, and he
wondered if perhaps the older Shadow Warriors simply

ignored them until they grew large enough to spark a complaint.

By dinnertime he was feeling exhausted, but a short nap in the room assigned to him revived him sufficiently to bathe and to join Krain's swordsmen for a good meal in the house's dining room. Their leader himself was not there—still planning strategy, Turek supposed—and the other three Shadow Warriors were similarly absent. Eating in their own rooms, someone explained when he asked about the latter. Apparently the Shadow Warriors didn't care much for the company of Krain's men—and, judging from the looks occasionally coming his way, the feeling was somewhat mutual. Finishing his meal quickly, Turek returned to his room.

But he didn't stay there long. Retrieving the sword he'd hidden under his straw-filled mattress, he again belted it securely under his cloak. Into the pack he'd brought from Keilberg went a blanket and a coil of rope he'd borrowed from one of Krain's craftsmen. Then, slipping out through a side door, he headed west . . . toward Lazuli.

The rapids and waterfall of the whiteriver bordering Lazuli were audible long before the village itself could be seen; that, plus the way the rising hills forced the road's direction, made the place impossible to miss. By the time the stars were beginning to appear overhead, Turek had arrived. For just a moment he paused, struck by the number of bright lights visible between the cliffs and the rapids, and then continued on, moving with the tired gait of a footsore man. He hadn't seen any of the watchers Krain had claimed were present, but had no doubt they were there and didn't want to draw any special attention to himself. With the blanket hiding his blue cloak and his rope-filled pack riding on his shoulder he should look like just another anonymous traveler.

A pair of strange lights flanked the road at Lazuli's edge. Turek glanced at them as he passed but didn't stop—wonders were bound to be common in a village where Shadows could be destroyed with ease, and he would perhaps have the chance later to study them. For the moment his main problem was how to locate Javan.

He'd taken barely ten more steps before the problem found its own solution. From alcoves on both sides of the street three youths materialized, fighting sticks held ready in their hands.

"Greetings, stranger," one of them said in a neutral tone. "What brings you to Lazuli after dark?"

"I can't change the time the sun sets," Turek answered mildly, studying the three. None wore the usual sun-shaped pin, but Turek didn't need such obvious clues. The air of naive idealism around them was almost thick enough to smell. "And where I was raised young men are more polite to their elders."

His challenger scowled. "Then you weren't raised near a band of thieves. Please state your business."

"I'm here to see Javan the Mindlight Master."

The others moved fractionally closer; their fighting sticks shifted a few inches toward defense stance. Turek kept his eyes on the spokesman and his hands at his sides. "Are you a friend of his?" the other asked.

Turek permitted the ghost of a smile to briefly touch his lips. "Not especially—but neither am I especially his enemy. Tell him Turek is here; he may remember me."

For a long moment the youth searched Turek's face. Then he nodded curtly. "All right. Come with me."

The other two guards faded back into their alcoves as the leader pointed Turek ahead and they set off down the street. For all of the boy's obvious idealism, Turek had to admit he wasn't stupid: he stayed a few feet to the side and slightly behind the Shadow Warrior the whole way.

Their path led to an inn, through the bustling and brightly lit common room, and to a small guest room at the building's rear. "I'll be back soon; don't try to leave," were his guide's last words as the door closed behind him.

And now would come the long wait. Sighing, Turek looked around him. Even in Lazuli straw-filled beds and contour chairs hadn't yet given way to something more advanced. But on the candle shelf jutting from one wall was something that looked like a smaller version of the streetlights. Sliding his pack onto the floor, he walked over to the odd device.

He had not yet figured out exactly how it worked when the door opened again behind him and three men stepped into the room. Two were youths of the type Turek had already met, and they looked wary. The third was Javan.

"Good evening," Javan said as he took a couple of steps into the room and stopped. "You wished to see me?"

Turek moved away from the light and faced the other. "Yes." He paused, studying Javan's face. Twelve years had put a lot of lines there, and already his brown hair was beginning to gray at the temples; but he still had the clear eyes appropriate to a self-appointed deliverer of mankind.

"What about?" one of the youths put in, suspicion in his voice.

Turek kept his eyes on Javan. "You don't recognize me, do you?" he said. "Perhaps this will help." Moving his hands slowly, he dropped the blanket from his shoulders.

Javan's reaction to the blue cloak was disappointing: no gasps or widened eyes, but only a faint smile as recognition came. "Ah, yes. Master Turek. It's been a long time since your challenge at Akkad."

"Twelve years. What I have to say is private."

Javan's eyes were coolly measuring. "Very well. Rensh, Streen—wait for me outside, please."

Neither of the youths looked happy at leaving their leader alone, but they left without argument or even comment. Javan indicated the chairs. "Shall we sit down?"

"Go ahead. I prefer to stand." Actually, Turek had little choice in the matter; the sword belted tightly to his side made sitting impossible. "This won't take long."

"Then I'll stand, too," Javan said agreeably. "What was so important that you came all the way from Keilberg to talk to me?"

"I haven't come from Keilberg, exactly. For the time being I'm living in Masard."

Javan's eyes narrowed slightly. "So Krain's hired you, has

he? I'd heard that he was trying to enlist Shadow Warriors for some unknown purpose."

"You don't know his plan, then?"

"Only that it's probably directed against Lazuli—and that it involves midnight thefts of our metals."

Turek was a bit taken aback at the touch of bitterness in Javan's voice. It told him something about how precious the metal was—and, hence, how hard it must be to make. "It involves your metal, all right," he told the Mindlight Master. "Krain plans to attack Lazuli with weapons made from it."

For a moment Javan was silent, a look of disbelief on his face. Krain, Turek reflected, had kept his secret well. "I don't believe it," Javan said at last. "You're talking about actual *warfare*. Why? What would he gain?"

"Lazuli's more advanced technology, for one thing—"

"It would be useless to him. The things we make draw Shadow far too quickly for him to use them, even if he's hired twenty Shadow Warriors."

"You're not thinking. Once he has Lazuli he'll also have *you*—plus all your young Mindlight Masters."

"We won't work for him." Javan's disbelief had become a cold anger. "We'll let Shadow swallow Lazuli forever before we'll work for a warmaker."

"Indeed. And if Krain threatens to kill you all, one by one? Or holds your families as guarantees of your cooperation?" Turek shook his head. "No, you'll work for him. Enough of you will, anyway, if he takes Lazuli."

"Then he must not be allowed to do so. How many men does he have?"

"Three hundred, armed with—"

"*Three* hundred? *Three?*" The relief in Javan's voice was unmistakable. "Master Turek, Lazuli can easily raise five hundred men to oppose him—possibly six hundred."

"That's nice. But it's not enough. Perhaps you'd like to see what you'll be fighting?" Without waiting for an answer, Turek threw back his cloak and slid his sword from concealment. Its blade flashed eerily in the candleless light.

Turek had half-expected Javan to shout for his waiting guards, or at least make a run for the door. But he'd underestimated either the other's courage or his trust. Javan didn't even take a step backwards; his eyes, watching the blade, were unreadable. Reversing the sword, Turek proffered the hilt. "Here—examine it yourself."

Gingerly, Javan took the weapon. He tested the edge, ran his fingers along the blade, and took a couple of practice swings. Then, his expression cold, he looked at Turek. "And you freely work for a man like that—a man who makes *these*?"

Turek shrugged, hiding his sudden uneasiness. The sword tip was pointed at his stomach, and Javan's knuckles showed white. "None of this is *my* fault, Javan. Your Mindlight technique and fancy metal are what made it possible. Don't blame me for trying to earn a living in the progressive age you've ushered in."

Slowly, the sword dipped until it pointed at the floor. Then, with a sigh, Javan held it out. Turek took the hilt and again fastened the weapon at his side. "I think you understand the threat a bit better now," the Shadow Warrior said as he resettled his cloak.

"Why did you come here tonight?" Javan's voice was flat, and for a moment Turek felt sorry for him. To recognize that you yourself had started the series of events that pointed to your own destruction . . . Turek knew how painful that could be. "Are you supposed to convince me to surrender?"

Turek shook his head. "I'm not 'supposed' to do anything. I'm here on my own initiative, to show you what you're up against and to show you the only way out." He pointed in the direction of the road. "Leave. Now. Pack up your school and students and get out of Lazuli before Krain blockades the village."

"And leave the residents to face him alone? I can't do that."

"Sure you can. You said yourself that Lazuli's technology would be useless without you. If you leave, attacking Lazuli would be a waste of effort."

"You don't know that. There are old rivalries between Lazuli and Masard—Krain may find sufficient motivation in that. Besides"—he smiled wryly—"do you really imagine he would go to all the effort to raise and equip an army and not use it *somewhere*? His authority could never survive such a humiliation."

Turek hadn't thought of that. "It's still your best chance," he muttered.

"Perhaps. But there's a higher principle to consider. Lazuli risked a great deal to let us set up our school here before we were generally accepted. If we pull out and leave in time of danger, who would take us in again?"

Turek snorted. "What's the matter—is a more nomadic life too much like the way we used to live?"

Javan didn't take offense. "The number of students would grow too slowly. You see, Master Turek, the only way Vesper will ever truly advance will be if almost *everyone* has at least *some* ability to destroy Shadow. The Mindlight technique is relatively easy to learn—but we have to become an established part of Vesperian society to attract that many people to our classes. We can't do that if we're dispersed or off in our own community somewhere. No. We'll stay in Lazuli and fight."

For a moment the two men gazed at each other in silence. Then Turek stooped down and retrieved his blanket, draping it again over his shoulders, and picked up his pack. "I didn't expect you to be reasonable," he said tiredly, "but I had to try. I'd appreciate it if you and your friends outside would keep quiet about my visit. Krain might not be happy with me if he found out."

"You're going back to him?"

"Of course—he's hired me. Besides, he's got enough Shadow Warriors to handle things even if I left." Turek gestured toward the light. "Before I go, would you mind telling me how that works?"

"There's an absorbent wick that rests in a pool of something called *alcohol*, which we can get from plant leaves and stems. It burns cleaner than candles and has other advantages, too."

"Progress." Turek nodded. "A good thing . . . usually."
He tapped the sword beneath his cloak. "Perhaps it's time
you and your people started considering the disadvantages,
too."

Javan stepped to the door and grasped the handle.
"Thank you for coming, Master Turek. I'll walk you back to
the road."

"Don't bother; I can find my own way. You've got more
important things to do with the time you have left."
Brushing past him, Turek pushed open the door and strode
out into the noise of the inn.

Outside, he started back toward the road—but only long
enough to make sure he wasn't being followed. Changing
direction, he made for the river, moving upstream toward
the cliff face that formed Lazuli's northern edge. His task
there took only a few minutes.

Two hours later he was back in his room in Krain's house,
sleeping like a dead man. Around the stolen sword, hidden
once more under his mattress, new Shadows formed,
troubling Turek's dreams.

The next few days were hectic ones for Krain's soldiers
and planners, but for Turek they were relatively uneventful. His time was spent clearing out Shadows from the
traning area, the smithy, and the stored swords. The latter,
especially, seemed to have wound up as his own personal
chore; Brisher and the others never seemed to go near the
shed anymore. Clearly, at least one of them must have been
clearing the Shadows from it before Turek arrived, and he
could only speculate that perhaps they had acquired so
much distaste for the weapons that they were perfectly
willing to dump as much of the burden onto the newcomer
as he was willing to take. Whatever the reason, the
situation suited Turek just fine, giving him that many more
chances to study the weaponry.

At first he was surprised to find that his earlier theft
seemed to have gone unnoticed; but on second thought it
seemed less than remarkable. After all, no one would be
periodically counting the weapons while they were all

under guard together. The loss would be discovered eventually, of course, but Turek wasn't worried about it.

Krain had said it would take a week to finish his preparations, but his estimate turned out to have been on the cautious side. Less than four days after Turek's arrival at Masard the last sword was finished.

And at dawn on the fifth day the residents of Lazuli awoke to find an army encamped against them.

The setting sun was throwing long shadows across the camp as Turek made his way up the low hill to where Krain's command tent had been set up. Behind him the hum of conversation and laughter was dying down as most of the army prepared for sleep; beyond the camp, if Turek cared to look, were twin picket lines stretched between river and cliffs to guard against a sortie; and a quarter mile beyond that were barricades Lazuli had erected. Even an untrained fighter like Turek could see the barricades wouldn't do much good.

Krain and Pakstin were sitting outside the command tent, talking quietly, when Turek arrived. "You wanted to see me?" the Shadow Warrior asked.

"Yes." Krain gave him a cool look. "Will the weapons be ready by dawn tomorrow?"

"No problem." Except for the swords the twenty men on picket and guard duty were carrying, all the weapons were stored together in a tent at the center of camp. "Brisher, Spard, and I will be clearing out the Shadow every hour or two throughout the night, and Rusten will do it again one final time right before you attack. The men will be able to fight for hours after that before the Shadows grow large enough to affect them significantly."

"So you say. Tell me, did you by any chance walk off with one of the swords while they were back in Masard?"

Turek nodded. "Yes. Why?"

His casual admission seemed to surprise the other. But he recovered quickly. "Why did you take it?"

"To study, and to defend myself with if necessary. Or

hadn't it occurred to you that Javan could ruin your plan instantly simply by killing the four of us?"

Judging from Krain's expression, the thought hadn't occurred to him. "Well . . . you should be safe enough in camp."

"At least until dawn. You *are* attacking then, aren't you?"

"The village has refused to surrender." Pakstin shrugged. "It's on their own heads."

"True." Turek looked at Krain. "Was there anything else?"

"No, I suppose not. Just make sure the swords are ready an hour before dawn."

"They will be." Nodding, Turek left, heading back downhill and into the camp.

But he didn't stay long. As soon as the darkness was complete he discarded his cloak and changed into dark, close-fitting clothing. Several large wicker baskets of the type used for carrying grain were lying empty by the storage tent; picking one up, he stole between the silent tents toward the river.

The cataracts and rapids that turned the river into a boiling torrent at Lazuli vanished a short distance south of the village, leaving a current that was swift but passable. Four small boats, evidently used by Lazulian fishermen, were drawn up on the grass a short way below the encampment. Taking a few minutes first to clear away the Shadow that had gathered around it, Turek got into one of the craft and began to paddle.

He arrived on the opposite bank a good deal farther downstream, and for what seemed like a short eternity he waded shin-deep in the icy water, towing the boat toward Lazuli. The current got progressively stronger, and it was with aching arms that he finally beached the craft, pulling it ashore at the base of the rocks where the rapids ended. Moving cautiously on the moss-slick stones bordering the river, he proceeded uphill, basket clutched awkwardly in one hand. It was hazardous going, and more than once he nearly fell into the water, where a reasonably certain death would have awaited him. But he made it, and at last stood just below the northern cliff face, looking across the river at Lazuli's northern end.

A thin cloud cover was obscuring the stars, leaving him only the dim light of Lazuli's lamps; but even so, it took him only a few minutes to find the fist-sized rock he'd thrown across when he'd visited the village several nights earlier. Untying the rope from around it, he pulled carefully on the line, hoping its long immersion among the rocks hadn't snagged it on anything. Luck was with him; not only did the rope come easily free, but a cautious tug showed that the other end was still secure around the boulder where he'd tied it. When he'd first set up this backdoor approach into Lazuli, Turek had had only the vaguest idea what he would use it for; now everything depended on this thin, waterlogged line. Stepping a few feet downhill, he pulled the line taut and, after first running it through the handles on his basket, fastened it to a thick tree root. Taking a deep breath, he grasped the rope and stepped carefully into the river.

He got three steps before the current knocked his feet out from under him, plunging him up to his chest in the icy water. Gasping with the shock, he nevertheless managed to hang onto the rope, and after a couple of false starts he managed to stand up again. He slipped twice in the next ten feet, but after that he seemed to get the hang of it and only fell once more before staggering up the opposite bank. For a moment he lay among the rocks, getting his breath back. Then, shivering violently in the night wind, he moved down toward Lazuli.

The afterimage method for locating Shadows was useless in such dim light, but even so Turek had no trouble locating the metalworking center at the village's northeast corner. The psychic light of Javan's Mindlight technique was visible to him from there, flashing every few minutes in a faint glow that indicated Turek's old sensitivity to it had faded somewhat. At least he hoped it had. . . . Loosening the sword in his sash, he moved silently toward the glow.

Clearly, no one in Lazuli was expecting any trouble at the metalworking area. There were no guards on duty, but only a single Mindlight Master—a boy half Turek's age—walking a lonely path among the machines, kilns, and alcohol lamps. Turek had half-expected to find a crowd of smiths frantically fashioning swords, but the village leaders had evidently decided that such last-minute efforts were futile. The decision was undoubtedly correct, and it made Turek's job much easier. Skulking around outside the circle of light, he quickly located what he had come for: the bins holding pure, refined metals.

Even with only one other man present, the area was too small for Turek to sneak over to the metals without being caught. Biding his time, he waited until the youth was facing the bins, his back to the Shadow Warrior . . . and as the glow of Mindlight dazzled Turek's mind, he stepped from concealment and slapped the other's head as hard as he could with the flat of his blade.

The boy sprawled to the ground with scarcely a sound. Replacing the weapon at his side, Turek hurried over to the bins. A small wooden bucket sat by each of them; grabbing one, he dipped it deeply into the nearly empty bin marked COPPER and came up with a load of fine, shiny dust. He debated taking a second bucketful, decided against it. A sudden thought struck him, and he lugged his bucket to an adobe structure that looked like a storage shed. Inside, he quickly located a large waterskin whose contents smelled like the alcohol lamps outside. With the waterskin in one hand and the bucket in the other, he headed back toward his rope.

The copper dust was astonishing, and more than a little frightening. Barely five minutes after scooping it out of the bin the effects of the Shadow growing around it were becoming painful; within ten Turek was forced to stop and clear the Shadow away. Never before in his life had he seen a Shadow grow so quickly, and for a long moment he wondered if he would ever be able to get the dust back to Krain's encampment. But he really had no other choice. Gritting his teeth, he picked up the bucket and kept moving.

The trip back would forever afterwards remain a blur in

Turek's memory; a blur of fatigue, Shadow-pain, and an endless series of battles, each one seemingly longer and less effective than the one before. He reached his rope guideline, loaded the copper and waterskin into his basket, crossed the rapids—a hell of water and cold that rivaled the usual image of brimstone—and stumbled down the stones toward his boat. The river current seemed twice as strong as before . . . and the Shadow made the trip seem to last forever.

Somehow, he made it.

"I don't understand," the older of the two guards said, his face puckered with confusion as his eyes flicked uncertainly over Turek's disheveled appearance.

"I didn't *ask* you to understand." Turek kept his voice low, his anger in tight check. Wet, cold, and deathly ill with fatigue, he was in no mood to be blocked *here*, ten feet short of his goal, by two fools. "I told you once: The picket line captain needs you up at post five immediately. Period. Now get moving."

"But our orders—"

"I'm giving you new orders. I'm a Shadow Warrior, one of Krain's personal servants. You'll do as I say."

There was something in his voice and eyes, Turek knew—he could tell from the way the guard seemed to shrink slightly within his own skin. The Shadow Warriors had commanded awe and not a little fear in their day . . . and this man was old enough to remember that. His gaze shifted to the sword at Turek's side, as if seeking proof of the Shadow Warrior's claimed status. "Very well," he said uncomfortably. Motioning to his companion, he eased gingerly past Turek and the two men left, disappearing into the gloom beyond the sputtering torchlight.

Turek watched until they were gone. Then, gritting his teeth against its growing Shadow, he retrieved his basket from behind a nearby tent and started forward—and as he did so a blue-cloaked figure stepped from the tent entrance and stood in his path.

It was Brisher. "So now you're Krain's *personal* servant,

are you?" the old Shadow Warrior growled. "What did he promise you, Javan's head and half of Lazuli?"

"Don't sound so virtuous—you're working for him too."

"I had no choice," the other muttered, dropping his eyes. "There was no other way for me to earn my livelihood anymore, and I'm too old to survive out on my own. But *you* don't have that excuse." He nodded at the basket. "What's that?"

The Shadow was growing painful again. "Step aside," Turek ordered.

"What is it?" the other repeated.

"Copper dust from Lazuli. Now step aside."

Brisher's eyes raked Turek's face. "What are you going to do?" he demanded. "Remember, our duty is to Krain now."

Turek's arms were beginning to tremble. If Brisher tried to stop him he would have to fight the older man. "We have a higher duty than that," he said, sudden weariness breaking through his tension. He was tired of fighting. "I'm going to do what I have to—what *you* should have done long ago."

For a long moment Brisher stood motionless, the resolve draining from his face and leaving him an eternity older. Bowing his head slightly, he moved away from the tent. Without looking at him, Turek stepped through the entrance.

Inside was unrelieved darkness; but Turek needed no light for what he was going to do. Dropping the waterskin by his foot, he raised the basket chest-high and, with a single convulsive movement, flung its contents over the neatly stacked swords. The basket he tossed to one side; picking up the waterskin, he went back outside. Brisher had vanished, and a quick look showed no one else in sight. Opening the waterskin, Turek doused the tent with the alcohol, concentrating on the middle of the roof. When the skin was empty, he threw it back inside.

And so all was finally ready. Stepping back, he pulled up one of the torches stuck in the ground. With a sigh more of fatigue than of relief, he flung it onto the tent.

The cloth ignited with a roar and a fireball that singed Turek's eyebrows. He stepped back hastily as sounds of confusion erupted suddenly from the camp around him and half-dressed men staggered from their tents. By the time they had a bucket brigade organized the waterproofing resins in the tent cloth were beginning to melt and burn, and strangely colored flames were leaping toward the clouds.

No one paid any attention as Turek left the scene and returned to his tent to wait.

The fire was nearly out when they came for him: Krain and two of his men, each with a sword that had clearly not been in the weapons tent. Turek emerged at Krain's command, once more clad in his blue cloak. For a moment the air was thick with tension; and then Krain broke the silence. "The Shadow around my swords is fifteen feet across and still growing," he said softly, the venom in his voice all the more intense because of that. "What did you do?"

"I ended your war of conquest," Turek told him, countering the other's rage with quiet firmness. Despite his fatigue, he stood straight and tall, with all the dignity he could muster. There was death in Krain's eyes, and Turek was determined not to show even the appearance of fear or cowering before it. "There's pure copper dust on your swords now, a fair amount of it glued there by drops of resin from the tent fire. Even if your Shadow Warriors—your other Shadow Warriors—can clear enough Shadow away to go in and untangle the swords from that sticky mess, you won't be able to use them until someone scrapes all the copper off—and you'll need a Shadow Warrior standing by while all *that's* being done, too."

"I can do that," Krain gritted—but there was uncertainty in his voice. "All your treachery has done is postpone things a couple of days. I'll still have Lazuli."

"Only if Lazuli is stupid." Turek waved toward the village's barricades. "They've seen the fire, and they'll know soon enough that I took some copper dust tonight.

And when morning comes they'll be able to see the Shadow. They'll figure it out—and they outnumber your army two to one."

"Then we'll pull back—"

"Pull back where? Your whole strategy depended on your being in control of the Mindlight school before Masard had time to react to the risk you were taking, the risk that they would lose all protection from Javan's people. By now they surely know what you've done—or, rather, *haven't* succeeded in doing—and are going to be getting nervous. If you prolong this insanity much longer you're going to have a revolt on your hands." A wave of dizziness swept over him; with an effort, he fought it back. "But don't take my word for it. Get your other Shadow Warriors and go ahead and try."

Krain exhaled a long breath, and somehow he seemed to slump slightly. "They're not here anymore," he muttered. "They all deserted during the fire."

Turek permitted himself a faint smile. "So they finally realized where their duty lay. Good."

"Their duty was to *me!*" Krain shouted abruptly. "*I* hired them, fed them, gave them back their self-respect and their power. And then they—and *you*—turn around and betray me!" Clenching his sword tightly, he took a step forward.

"Self-respect?" Turek's voice was still calm, but as cold as Lazuli's river. "No. All you offered them was escape from the lonely, ignominious death they were afraid was coming to them. Why else do you think none of the younger Shadow Warriors accepted your offer? That alone should have told you something was wrong."

"So your loyalty is only to yourselves," Krain spat contemptuously. "I understand, finally. How much is Javan paying you?"

Turek shook his head, too weary to feel anger at the insult. "Javan can't buy us, any more than you can. If you were older—if you'd known more Shadow Warriors—you might understand. We weren't in this for any personal gain.

We *served* the people of Vesper; served them with our sweat and pain and, ultimately, our lives. Our 'loyalty,' as you insist on calling it, was burned into us as part of our training; and it was to nothing more or less than the dream of a better existence for everyone. For *everyone*, not just our friends or our home villages. A lot of people misunderstood our refusal to pass judgments or take sides, but it helped us balance the more advanced technology our work permitted; helped keep people from misusing it. Do you see now why it was foolish to think we'd freely help you start a war?"

Hatred smoldered in Krain's eyes. "I can kill you. You know that, don't you?"

"Yes." Though he'd known this moment was inevitable, Turek's mouth was still dry. "But whether you do so or not, your war is still over."

For a long moment no one moved. Then, abruptly, Krain turned away and, without a backward glance, disappeared into the night. His two men eyed Turek uncertainly, exchanged glances, and followed their leader.

Turek let his shoulders slump. It was over, and he'd won. Not the war, of course, but certainly the battle he'd set out to win. As for the war itself . . . that burden was no longer his.

Reaching into his tent, he pulled out the pack he'd prepared and slipped it onto his shoulders. Deathly tired though he was, he still wanted to put some distance between himself and Krain before sleeping; the young ruler might yet decide to seek revenge. For a moment Turek looked toward Lazuli, tempted by the thought of its warm food and beds. But he didn't want to see Javan again, and there was no real point to such a meeting, anyway. The Mindlight Master had just had a lesson in the potential dangers of progress; nothing Turek could say would improve on that. And as for the responsibility for guiding this next stage of Vesper's growth . . . Turek wished them the best of luck. The Shadow Warriors had found a method that had worked for their more exclusive group; how Javan would do it, with his dream of giving control over Shadow to everyone, Turek couldn't begin to guess.

Keilberg and home lay to the southwest. Turek had taken only a few steps in that direction when he paused and, as an afterthought, returned to his tent. The sword lay just inside the entrance; picking it up, he once more fastened it to his side. It wasn't very heavy, and it might come in handy back home. His hoe, after all, still needed a new blade.

Afterword

And so, with something of a lurch, Vesper has started on the road to a—for them, at least—highly technological society. I'd originally planned a complete series of these stories, exploring both Vesper's growing pains and the nature of Shadow itself; but when the second story failed to sell, the whole thing went to the far back burner. (Ed Ferman at F&SF was too overstocked with series stories at the time, and it's usually hard to sell a sequel to a magazine that didn't publish the original.)

But now, after a fresh reading, I find my interest piqued once more. Perhaps I'll return to Vesper again, see how Javan's coping with the Pandora's box he's manhandled the lid off of. Or at least stay long enough to find out what the heck Shadow really is.

The Challenge

The clock radio went off at six-fifteen, as usual, and for a moment Elliot Burke hovered in that disoriented state between sleep and full consciousness. Then his brain cleared and he smiled at the ceiling.

This was the big day!

Leaning over, he typed *N153* on his keyboard and watched as the front page of the New York *Daily International* appeared in the center of the one-meter-square screen. More from a vague sense of duty than any real interest he scanned the headlines. Nothing much was new. The Antarctic Core Tap was bogged down with cost overruns, the Skyhome space colony was still processing applications for the third group of one hundred colonists, North Iran was rattling its sabers at both Russia and South Iran, and the President had announced he would run for reelection.

Impatiently, Elliot flipped the pages until he reached "Sports and Games"; and in the middle of the fifth page he found it:

Fans of the *Deathworld* series on channel G29 will want to be tuned in tonight to watch as the immovable object meets the irresistible force. The Orion Nomad, the highest-ranked *Deathworld* gamer still in active competition, will take on Doomheim IV, Lon Thorndyke's most recent world. In its four-month existence, Doomheim IV has not yet been conquered, though over fifty top-ranked gamers have tried it. The Nomad will be landing at 7:30 EST this evening to try his hand. Don't miss it!

Elliot smiled. He was the Orion Nomad.

Moving with a grace that seemed incongruous in so large a craft, the Sirrachat ship flew at mountaintop-height over the lunar surface, seeking the source of the subspace emanations which had attracted his attention. Nestled in the shadows at the base of a short ridge, he found another starcraft, one even larger than the Sirrachat's but of a totally different design. It was showing no lights.

The Sirrachat settled to the surface a few hundred meters away; and as he did so a laser beam flashed out from the other ship. Not an attack, but an invitation to communicate. In a moment they had contact.

"I am called Sirrachat."

"I greet you, Sirrachat," the other replied. "I am Drymnu."

"I greet you." The Sirrachat had heard of the Drymnu— a fairly young hive race from this region of space, in only its first millennium of star travel. "Are you in need?"

The Drymnu seemed to hesitate. "First I must ask, are you one?"

The collective intelligence that was the Sirrachat smiled tolerantly. "Certainly. All starfaring races are as you and I. Did you not know?"

"I knew that that is said, but I fear it may not be so for long. I am in great need of your counsel, Sirrachat."

"Speak on."

The Drymnu paused, as if collecting his thoughts. "It is said by all those we have encountered that fragmented races cannot attain the stars. The argument is that the self-

destructive competition common to these races will destroy them before they reach the necessary technological level. But I have now been studying the fragmented race on the planet below for twenty-nine of its years, and I see no evidence of imminent destruction. Indeed, it is already taking its first steps into space. Five permanent bases exist on this satellite, an orbiting space colony has been built, and expeditions to the second and fourth planets have been carried out."

"An interesting situation," the Sirrachat agreed. "Most fragmented races never get that far. However, I doubt that there is any cause for alarm."

"But it is a violent race, each member putting his own desires above all else. If it should escape its system it would bring ruin on us all—"

"Please—before you become overly worried," the Sirrachat interrupted. "I don't doubt the race's violent nature, but you are overlooking several basic forces which are likely to exist here. May I have access to your stored information on this race?"

"Certainly," the Drymnu said, already sounding more at ease.

Elliot strode through the door of his apartment and tossed his coat at the hook, turning toward the kitchen before it hit and slid to the floor. Another boring and frustrating workday, topped off by his biweekly run-in with Mr. Franklin over the possibilities of Elliot's advancement to Design and Development. Franklin's argument—that with only a B.S. in electrical engineering Elliot couldn't be promoted to D and D—made an unfortunate kind of sense, considering the glut of Ph.D.'s on the market. On the other hand, Elliot *knew* he could do the job, and spending his days checking other people's schematics for errors was driving him crazy.

For tonight, though, Franklin could go jump. Elliot's troubles vanished like leaves in a hurricane in the face of his excitement. Tonight he had a chance to do something no one else had ever done: to beat Doomheim IV.

By seven o'clock he was ready. Seating himself before the TV screen, the keyboard before him on an ancient typing table, he called up the proper channel. The *Deathworld* logo appeared on the screen. He typed his "game name"— Orion Nomad—and his secret code word. Then he named his destination: Doomheim IV. Somewhere in North America, the computers that handled the gaming functions of the vast Bell Info/Comm Net pulled the Orion Nomad's personal data file from storage and prepared the program that was Doomheim IV. The software that would handle the simulation of Elliot's journey was among the most sophisticated in the free world, and with good reason: the revenues from the multitude of games was the major financial base for the whole Net.

Elliot's screen began filling up with words—the basic information and rules for Doomheim. The planet, he was informed, had an Earth-like atmosphere and a temperate climate. Gravity was one point two gee and a wide variety of flora and fauna were present. A shuttle-bubble would land him at any point ten kilometers or more from the lifter that was his goal. None of this was new—Elliot had read it several times as he watched other gamers try their luck on Doomheim—so he skimmed it quickly and then moved on to choose his equipment. As he did so a line of words began to appear at the bottom of his screen:

Good luck, Orion Nomad. I'll be rooting for you.— The Adrian

Elliot grinned. The Adrian was one of his most loyal fans; only a so-so gamer himself, but an avid spectator of most of the SF games. Elliot had had several long conversations with him via the Net and had been astonished by the lists of players, scores, and standings he could reel off. It was apparently a family tradition; the Adrian's grandfather had done the same thing with football and baseball statistics. Or so he said.

But Elliot had no time for chitchat now. Turning his attention back to the equipment list, he began to type out his selections: medium-thickness body armor with respirator; extra heavy leatherite-steelmesh boots and gauntlets; two thermite torches; one laser armgun—more powerful than a pistol but still a one-handed weapon; three knives—one hunting, two throwing; fifteen grenades—seven blast, six concussion, two fragmentation; binoculars; compass; radio direction finder; and finally, a balloon lifter pack. The latter was a simple backpack with inflatable balloons and two small tanks of compressed helium, plus steering jets. It was lighter and less bulky than a full jet pack and, while not nearly as easy to maneuver with, it also did not attract predators as often. Its main disadvantage was that it was slow, taking up to thirty seconds to inflate completely.

Thoughtfully, Elliot scanned the list. A little light, perhaps. On the other hand, the Orion Nomad was quite fast and agile, and Elliot had often been able to outrun the creatures he would otherwise have had to fight. And several heavily armed, solidly armored adventurers had already gone to their deaths on Doomheim IV. Elliot would try it this way.

And it was time to go. From here on it was just the Orion Nomad against Doomheim—with maybe a thousand spectators electronically watching over his shoulder. Well, they wouldn't be disappointed; Elliot would make sure of that. Taking a last deep breath, he pressed the "start" key.

The TV screen split into nine sections. Five of them were full-color views of Doomheim's lower atmosphere as the Orion Nomad, descending in the shuttle-bubble, could see it; front view, left, right, above, and beneath, arranged in a convenient plus-shaped pattern. The four corner sections held data that he would normally have on a real planet, but which the TV's sight and sound alone couldn't provide.

As he had expected, nothing he could see was doing him any good. Below his bubble, the landscape was obscured by low-lying stratus clouds, a trick that Thorndyke almost always used on the worlds he created. Elliot took just a moment to confirm there were no breaks in the clouds and then checked his compass and direction finder, displayed on one of the screen sections. The needles were nearly in line; Elliot was coming down almost due south of the lifter. He changed the bubble's course slightly—

LAND BUBBLE R=10KM, 180 DEG

—so that he would be exactly south of his goal. Now, if anything happened to his direction finder, he could use the compass to find his way.

The bubble passed through the clouds, and for a brief minute Elliot could see the surface of Doomheim. Between himself and the lifter he could see bluish plains, at least one range of rocky-looking hills, and a patch of darker blue that he tentatively labeled a lake. And then he was down, a few hundred meters south of the hills, in a vast plain.

He stepped out—

LEAVE BUBBLE, STOP/TURN

—and looked around. The "grass" of this prairie looked much like ankle-high cattails with broad blue leaves extending horizontally. In many places the ground was completely obscured; he'd have to watch for concealed snakes and insects. There was no time to investigate the flora now, however—from his left two animals were loping toward him.

Elliot turned—

TURN LEFT, RH=ARMGUN,
AIM AT L ANIMAL

—and raised his laser. He was well prepared for this moment; one or more of these small tyrannosaurs had attacked every other landing he'd watched and he had expected them. They could be killed, he knew, by a one-second head shot . . . but there might be an easier way. The fact that they *always* showed up so soon implied they

had seen him coming. Maybe it was the bubble that
attracted them.

BUBBLE GO SW, HORIZ, 2 KM,
.1 VEL/RETURN TO SHIP

The bubble floated lazily away from him—and sure
enough, the tyrannosaurs veered to follow. Elliot grinned.
A minor victory, to be sure, but he had just saved two
seconds' worth of laser fire, and little things like that often
made the difference. Waiting until the animals were too
distant to notice him, Elliot checked his bearings and
began to walk.

He'd taken maybe ten steps when he heard a faint
whistle. He froze, searching around him for the source of
the noise. Nothing was visible, so he risked a slow
turn . . . and spotted it. Or, rather, them.

In the southern sky, a mass of black specks had appeared.
They seemed to be closing, fast.

Elliot looked around him, but there wasn't a scrap of
cover anywhere within reach. The hills were still too far
away, and nothing higher than the cattails seemed to be
growing on the plain. The birds—or whatever—were close
enough now that he could estimate their numbers. There
were at least two hundred of them, far too many to pick off
with his laser. And he'd seen what these birds could do to
light armor like this.

He'd have to move fast. Running to a bare spot of
ground, he lay down—

LIE DOWN ON L SIDE, TUCK
LEGS CLOSE TO BODY, LH=
TORCH, RH=TORCH

—and drew in his legs, sheathing his laser and taking a
thermite torch in each hand. Waiting until the birds were
nearly on him, he—

IGNITE TORCHES, LH = SWEEP
HORIZ ABOVE LEGS, RH =
SWEEP HORIZ ABOVE TORSO
AND HEAD

—lit the torches and made them into a fast-moving shield
above him. On the TV screen, words began appearing,
telling him whenever a bird got through and how much
damage it did to his armor. Most of the birds seemed to be
blinded or burned before they could hurt him, however.
He kept at it grimly, even though the screen warned him
that he himself was suffering light burns from the torches'
heat.

As quickly as it had started, the attack was over, the
surviving birds resuming their northward course. Elliot
had sustained light damage to his armor, especially on the
arms, and had first-degree burns on arms and chest. Both
would be duly noted by the computer, and Elliot's defense
and attack capabilities appropriately adjusted. All in all,
though, it had been a very successful encounter.

Standing up, Elliot extinguished the remains of the
torches and stowed them away, again taking up his laser.
Looking around carefully, he set off again toward the hills.

*The data flow finally ceased, and the Sirrachat paused to
consider it, impressed in spite of himself. The Drymnu had
amassed a truly fantastic store of information on Earth and
its fragmented race, not only monitoring the various
broadcast media but also managing to tap into the more
private cable systems. And all this without dropping even a
hint of its own existence, as far as the Sirrachat could tell.
"You have done well," he told the other.*

*The Drymnu didn't even bother trying to hide his
pleasure at the compliment. "Thank you," he said. Then,
more seriously, "But now what of this race and its threat?"*

*"You have already mentioned the key to their behavior,"
the Sirrachat began slowly, part of his mind still busy
searching the newly acquired information. "Namely, competition. Fragmented races do not act together for their*

mutual good; indeed, they often cannot do so, any more than two animals can when there is one bit of food and both want it. Now, survival is often a matter of competition, and any race not possessing the desire to challenge and win soon vanishes from the universe. Obviously, both you and I possess such a desire. But—and here is the point—our battles were with our own worlds; their creatures and environments. Once we had mastered these, our inbred competitive spirits pushed us into space and, ultimately, to the stars. I say 'pushed' very deliberately, because space was the only major goal left to us, and a race without challenge soon withers away. But fragmented races are never without challenge, for they can always fight among their own members, something that is impossible for us to do. You see this happening below us at this very moment: competition among single members for their own gains, competition among huge groups of them for resources and honor, and everything in between. Is it any wonder the cultures of fragmented races are unstable?"

The Drymnu pondered. "I understand what you say. But there is evidence of cooperation as well, at least to some extent. Those large groups of members have survived for years without collapsing back to single-member size. Their orbiting colony is fairly new, but its group seems even more cooperative, at least so far. And much of the race's technological progress is stimulated by its internal conflict, as ours was by our desire to reach outward."

"That technology is also designed for the internal competition, however," the Sirrachat pointed out. "Eventually it will reach a level sufficient to destroy the race; and at that point it is only a matter of waiting for the triggering spark."

"I do not doubt they will ultimately destroy themselves. But . . . is it not possible that the race may discover the stardrive before that happens and send some of its members outward? If even a handful survive, it could be a serious matter."

"It will not happen," the Sirrachat said emphatically. "I will explain in a moment . . ." He paused, still searching

the Earth data. The idea he was about to present to the Drymnu would undoubtedly strike the latter as so bizarre that it would be best to have an example ready . . . and seconds later, he found one. "Please join me in observing this event, which is even now occurring," he invited the Drymnu, indicating the proper channel, "and I will explain the concept of games."

The hills were not particularly high, but they were craggy, and Elliot had been forced to settle for a slow walk in order to avoid repeated falls. He was less worried about his own safety than that of his equipment, especially since his right arm—which held the laser—could not be used to help break a dangerous fall. Still, he wished he could hurry. Several brands of unfriendly creatures lived in these hills and he was hoping to get off the treacherous terrain before he ran into one. That he hadn't already done so was merely an indication of Thorndyke's world-building skills. Inexperienced builders usually crowded their worlds with deadly animals and plants, only to discover that, all too often, they fell to attacking each other instead of the explorer. It was an effect that couldn't be postulated away; the *Deathworld* Game Committee required the ecology on every planet they accepted to be as sensible as the physics and chemistry. The best builders got around the problem by spacing out their predators so they wouldn't run into each other. It was small comfort to the explorers, of course.

Elliot was traversing a flat but rock-strewn section when a large creature came around a pile of boulders. At first glimpse it seemed to be a large turtle, complete with leathery head and neck, short legs, and a large, multifaceted carapace. The second glance showed the differences: the long neck and razor teeth, the scorpion tail . . . and the surprising speed.

Elliot backed away as the creature came toward him, surprise freezing all but reflex responses. It was one step up from *déjà vu:* he himself had *invented* this creature three years ago for one of his own deathworlds! It could not be coincidence; the shape of the carapace was too distinctive, too unique to Elliot's megatort. Consciously or otherwise, Thorndyke had clearly borrowed it.

The creature was still coming. Automatically, Elliot fired a burst from his laser—and then immediately cursed himself for wasting power. A megatort couldn't be killed easily by laser fire; its skin and shell were too tough. As a matter of fact, it couldn't be killed easily by *anything*, as near as Elliot could recall. Still backing off, he racked his brain. After all, he'd *created* the damn beast—he ought to know how to kill it.

The answer came, almost too late. Snatching a concussion grenade with his free hand—

```
LH = CONC GRENADE; ARM 2
SEC; THROW 5 DEG R, O DEG
        VERT, 4 MS
```

—he bounced it to just under the megatort's left side. With a deafening thunderclap it went off, rocking the creature onto its right side, where it balanced precariously, legs and tail thrashing furiously. Elliot didn't hang around to see what would happen next, but took off as fast as he safely could. The megatort would eventually right itself, and he had no intention of being in the neighborhood when it did so.

He had gone another two hundred meters when a six-legged wolverine-sized animal sprang at him from a camouflaged burrow. A single shot from the laser killed it, but not before it had chewed a hole in his left gauntlet down to the steel mesh. Elliot paid more attention to the ground after that, which probably saved his life a few minutes later when he nearly stepped onto a paper-thin sheet of rock that bridged a narrow and well-camouflaged chasm. Spotting it in time, he inflated his balloons and floated across, deflating them as soon as he was on the other side of the gorge. It was too bad, he reflected, that he couldn't simply float to his target. But trying would probably be fatal. He had seen at least two other flocks of birds since the group that had attacked him, and he didn't want to be off the ground if another group spotted him.

He emerged from the hills without further incident and found himself at the dark-blue area he had seen from the bubble. It was not, as he had supposed, a lake, but was a stretch of woods.

Elliot scowled, not liking it a bit. Forests were dangerous areas—lots of handy places for predators to lurk, and you could be attacked from any direction. But there was little he could do about it. The band of blue-leaved trees extended to the east and west as far as he could see, and it was too wide to risk flying over. Taking a deep breath, he typed in the proper commands, and the Orion Nomad went forward.

He wasn't a hundred meters into the woods when the first attack came, and it caught him flatflooted. Concentrating on the bushes and undergrowth around him, he didn't even notice the wide-meshed net hidden among the tree branches until it had fallen on him. The net, he noted in passing, seemed to be made of thick, dark-hued vines crudely fastened together. He had no time for further observation, though, for the woods around him had suddenly come alive with screaming creatures.

Elliot acted instinctively—

RH = ARMGUN; AIM THROUGH
NET AT CLOSE ANIMAL: FIRE/
SAME/ SAME/ SAME/ SAME

—firing through the mesh. The creatures were no larger than chimpanzees, but they were armed with what looked like flint knives and knew how to use them. Several got within range before he could shoot them, and without his armor he would have been thoroughly skewered.

They lost eight of their number to his laser before they seemed to realize they were losing and drew back from him. He killed three more and the rest fled, leaving him alone. Elliot let out his breath in a sigh of relief, feeling a slight shock as he noticed the living room around him. It was sometimes easy to forget that he wasn't really on an alien world. There was no time to waste, though—the arboreal creatures could regroup and come back at any time, and there were bound to be other nasties nearby. With his left hand he pulled out the remaining stub of a thermite torch . . . and hesitated. Something about the net seemed disturbingly familiar. Shifting his gaze to the part of the TV screen that listed sensory data, he skimmed through it—and there it was:

The net is coated with a very sticky substance.

Thorndyke had done it again: Elliot had used this same trick years ago. The sticky coating, ideal for trapping the creatures' victims, also happened to be highly flammable. Elliot had just come within an ace of incinerating himself.

Replacing the torch, he drew his hunting knife. One cut later, though, he realized this wasn't going to work. The knife sliced the vine, all right, but the tarry coating slowed it down drastically. It might take him an hour to cut himself free, and until then he was a sitting duck. Starting on the second vine, he kept a sharp eye on the surrounding woods and tried to think.

What kind of escape mechanism had he set up when he invented this net? He hadn't consciously made one, of course; he'd been the world-builder on that game, and getting *out* of the net had been everyone else's problem. But he must have had *some* ideas.

"Aha!" he yelled out loud, slapping the table that held his keyboard.

RH = HUNTING KNIFE, LH = HELI =
UM TANK; OPEN VALVE .2,
SPRAY FOR 2 SEC ON KNIFE
AND FRONT OF NET

It did the trick. The expanding jet of helium froze the targeted vines into brittle, nonsticky rods and protected the knife from any of the other vines it happened to touch. A little experimentation showed him that he could get away with just cooling the knife, and within five minutes he was free of the net. He'd emptied one helium tank in the process, but the other still held enough to inflate his balloons at least once more. A very fair trade, he decided.

Laser again in his right hand, and with one eye on the overhead branches, he continued on into the woods.

"I don't understand this at all," the Drymnu said, clearly bewildered. "Where is the world Doomheim that this simulation refers to? Is this journey part of the racial history, or is it a plan for the future?"

"It is neither," the Sirrachat answered, still watching Elliot's progress on the Drymnu's monitoring equipment. "This is what fragmented races call a game. It's a stylized form of competition engaged in between two or more members of the race. There is nothing corresponding to games in our own cultures, just as other forms of intraracial competition are absent. Each game has an object or a goal and a set of rules which mimic, after a fashion, the laws of nature. In fact, the game is a sort of simplified universe, limited in both space and time, where the members engage in combat of a specified mode."

"To what end? Why create a new universe when a real one already exists?"

"There are three reasons that I know of. First, it allows the members to engage in a safe conflict, one which threatens the life and health of neither member. Recall that the race is caught between two conflicting goals: the goal of each member to gain for himself, even at the expense of others; and the goal of the race as a whole to survive. Games help to channel the members' competitive drives."

"But that leaves less of this drive for the race to use for useful purposes," the Drymnu objected.

"You are beginning to understand," the Sirrachat said. "Its progress is thus much slower than it otherwise would be. The second reason is related to the first: Games allow the members to achieve a goal of success in a very short time."

"Are fragmented races so impatient, then? The stars hold

the promise of great successes to all who reach them. Even in this planetary system there are goals to be achieved."

"You are not thinking like a fragmented race," the Sirrachat reminded him gently. *"Many of the goals you have in mind would take longer than a given member's lifetime to accomplish. Bear in mind that each member feels the same desire for victory that we as complete races feel. You, I am sure, could feel only limited satisfaction in one of my victories, one which you yourself did not directly contribute to; in the same way, a fragmented race's victories do not wholly satisfy the needs of its members. Games help to fill this gap. And note an important side effect: Not only do games blunt the race's drive, but they absorb a great deal of its scientific and technological growth. Consider the work that has gone into the game we are watching, the time and resources that would otherwise have been used for other purposes. The members who designed the equipment and those who are the actual players all have skills of imagination and intelligence which would be vital to the development of the stardrive."*

"I see." The Drymnu paused again. *"You mentioned a third reason for games."*

"Yes, I did."

Slightly surprised he was still alive, Elliot stepped out from under the last tree and stood once more on a vast plain. The forest had been grueling. No fewer than eight attacks had been launched at him, some of them back to back. He'd won all of them, but at high cost. His weaponry had been reduced to ten seconds' worth of laser fire and two concussion grenades, plus his hunting knife. His armor was damaged in several places, his left arm was injured and could only be moved at half speed, and he was limping from a piece of one of his own fragmentation grenades in his ankle. The Orion Nomad was in bad shape, and there was still at least a kilometer to go.

Ahead of him, dotting the plain, were thirty or so large humpbacked creatures, apparently grazing. With his binoculars, Elliot took a moment to study their small heads, flat vegetarian teeth, and defense-oriented porcupinelike quills. Clearly, they were not predators, and chances were they wouldn't attack unless he spooked them. Taking a deep breath, and one more look into the woods behind him, he limped carefully forward.

Several of the creatures paused in their meal to glare as he passed slowly among them, but none of them made any move against him. He was about twenty meters past the last one, and beginning to breathe again, when a group of six tigers broke from the woods toward him.

They were not exactly Earth-type tigers, of course; Elliot had given them that name after a run-in with three of the species in the forest, a battle he'd barely survived. With his injuries and shrinking power supply, he knew he'd never win another fight. And to make matters worse, the quilled animals were also apparently afraid of the tigers, for they had abandoned their grazing and were running from the predators . . . running straight at Elliot. It was a toss-up whether they would trample him to death before the tigers could get to him.

There was no time for conscious thought. Elliot's next move was one of pure reflex. Snatching a concussion grenade, he armed it and tossed it to land directly in front of the lead quillback. The creature went down, stunned or killed by the blast, and its startled companions stopped abruptly, some even turning to run in the opposite direction. Seconds later, the tigers reached them.

And there was instant pandemonium. Elliot, completely forgotten in the clash, kept moving, making for the edge of the plain as fast as he could. The sounds of the battle were fading behind him as he topped a rise—and barely managed to stop in time. Just past the rise was a three-meter drop into a twenty-meter-wide gully running across his line of travel. A gully filled with literally millions of moving black spots.

Army ants, or their equivalent.

Elliot wiped a sudden layer of sweat off his forehead. For some reason forever lost in his past, masses of insects horrified him as even tigers couldn't do, and even seeing them on a TV screen was enough to make him feel shaky. But he couldn't stop now. Across a gray mud flat directly ahead of him, nestled among some stubby bushes and the ubiquitous cattail plants, was the squat egg-shape that was his lifter. Opening the stopcock of his remaining helium tank, he filled the balloons and floated to a height of a few centimeters. Taking a deep breath, he fired a short burst from his jets and drifted over the ants.

His progress was slow, due mainly to a mild headwind, and—largely to avoid looking at the ants—he found himself studying the gray ground ahead. The closer he got, the less it looked like a mud flat, and the more like quicksand. It was, at least, an easy theory to test. Taking his compass, he tossed it ahead of him into the middle of the flat area. It hit with a muffled *splat* and slowly sank from sight.

So Elliot would simply continue flying over it, instead of landing as he had originally planned. But even as he made that decision, a memory tugged at his mind. Normally, he would have ignored it . . . but this had already happened twice on Doomheim. He had best be ready.

He was past the ants now and at the edge of the quicksand. Pointing his laser downwards, he took his last concussion grenade in his left hand, set it for a five-second fuse, and waited.

A slight motion of the mire was his only warning, but he was ready; and even as the dripping tentacle snaked toward him he fired into it, simultaneously dropping the grenade. The tentacle writhed away, and he fired at three more that rose to meet him. And then the ground exploded, showering him with muck. Dropping limply as suddenly as they had emerged, the tentacles lay briefly on the quicksand before disappearing beneath its surface.

He reached solid ground moments later, deflating his balloons with a sigh of relief. Now all that remained was for him to walk the remaining fifty meters to the lifter, step into the open door, and press the "return" lever.

The *open* door? Elliot stopped, suddenly suspicious.

There was no reason for it to be open . . . unless it held a final present from Doomheim.

There were no stones nearby that Elliot could throw that distance, but his direction finder was the right size and weight. He arched it squarely through the door—and a cloud of angry insects exploded from inside the lifter, buzzing to within ten meters of him in search of their attacker. Resisting the urge to run or shoot, Elliot stood stock-still and waited for them to return to their appropriated metal nest. He didn't know whether or not they were dangerous, but he rather expected they were and certainly didn't want to find out the hard way. The problem now was to find a way, with what was left of his equipment, to get rid of them.

By the time the last of the insects had gone back into the lifter he had a plan. Moving as quietly as possible, he picked an armload of the cattail plants and carried them as close as he dared to the lifter door. The TV screen informed him that the breeze had shifted and was now at his back, a stroke of luck. Removing his balloons, he emptied the remainder of the steering-jet fuel onto the pile of plants. Another armload of cattails went on top, followed by a layer of wet plants from the edge of the quicksand. Then he backed off, and, crossing his fingers, ignited the mass with his laser.

It was all he could have hoped for. The pile burst into flame, sending a thick column of dense white smoke directly into the lifter. The insects never had a chance. Minutes later, respirator firmly in place, Elliot stepped through the door, crunching dazed insects underfoot, and pressed the proper lever.

The game was over. Elliot Burke—the Orion Nomad—had defeated Doomheim IV.

"The third reason for games," the Sirrachat said, "is one which I fear I may never truly understand. Virtually all fragmented races that have been studied obtain a particular emotional satisfaction from games, a satisfaction not

*only far out of proportion to the actual victory involved,
but possibly even unconnected to it. They generally refer to
this quality as 'fun.' It is this fact, I believe, which is the
most important factor in keeping fragmented races from
the stars until they finally destroy themselves. Creating a
stardrive is work, and as long as the race allows its
members an alternative source of activity which provides
both competition and fun, it will forever remain within its
system."*

"How wasteful," the Drymnu murmured. "How very
wasteful."

Elliot slumped in his chair, ignoring the congratulatory
messages appearing on his screen. He had won; he had
defeated Doomheim IV. He should be ecstatically happy.
But he wasn't . . . and he knew why.

No less than three times tonight he'd run into ideas lifted
directly from his own worlds. In a very real sense, he'd
actually wound up *fighting himself*.

It was a possibility that had never once occurred to him.
He'd begun playing *Deathworld* six years ago, confident
that he would always have the excitement of conquering
new worlds, as well as the joy of creating them. With the
ideas and resources of a million gamers to draw on, how
could it be otherwise? But the rapid and widespread
communication which the Net permitted had thrown him a
curve. His own ideas had been picked up, bounced around
by others, and then tossed back at him. There was no real
way to stop it from happening—the more good ideas he
came up with, the more he would find them staring back
at him on someone else's world. Conceited though it
sounded, he was apparently too good at this. Either he
would have to quit building worlds or he would have to
drop out of *Deathworld* completely. There was no joy in
battling his own reflection.

Only . . . what would he do then?

He could take up a new game; start from scratch at
Fantasy or *Star Empire*. But sooner or later he'd run into

the same problem. So what was the use? There were other types of games, of course, but the solitaire video ones that his parents had grown up with would probably drive him stir-crazy, and the old spectator sports like football were definitely out. And that was pretty much it, unless he wanted something like chess or Monopoly.

The result was clear. His gaming days were over.

Congratulations were still appearing on the screen. With a sudden flash of anger Elliot cut them off, and for a minute he stared at and through the screen. He'd never realized before just how much the games meant to him, how much they made the rest of his life tolerable. It was as bad as losing a girlfriend. Maybe worse.

Slowly his fingers moved, typing for the list of public lectures/conversations currently on the Net. Perhaps talking with someone would help take his mind off his loss, he decided, scanning the list. One of the lectures caught his eye: *Theory of Interstellar Travel: Lecture 1*. Not what he'd had in mind, really, but . . . Shrugging, he punched in the proper code.

"The theory was established in the nineties," a voice boomed out at him. Grabbing for the volume control, Elliot hastily turned it down from its usual game position. As he did so, words began to appear on the screen: someone in the audience making a comment. "But it's never been completely verified," he wrote. "And it contradicts Einstein in several places."

"Granted," the speaker returned. "But it agrees on all the points that *have* been tested experimentally."

"Excuse me," Elliot typed in, "but I've just joined in. Could you tell me what theory you're referring to? Reply to CET-4335T."

Another question for the speaker flowed across the center of the screen; at the same time, words began to crawl along the bottom. Someone was responding privately to Elliot's question. "Hi," the message said. "We're discussing Bobdonovitch's theory about the possible extension of tunnel diode effects to interstellar travel. Have you heard of Bobdonovitch?"

"No, but I'm familiar with tunnel diodes."

"OK. Well, Dr. Stanley Raymond here thinks there are ways to confirm the theory on a microscopic, electronic level, where it diverges slightly from quantum mechanics and relativity."

"I see—I think," Elliot typed. "Thanks."

"Sure," the other replied and disconnected from Elliot's line.

Turning his attention back to the main discussion, Elliot listened to the last half of the speaker's answer to someone's question on actual hyperspace travel. ". . . basic hardware is still at least a decade or two away. Probably more like a century, given the disinterest of the scientific community."

He paused, and a new voice spoke up. "That's as good a lead-in, I think, as any for our next speaker. Proving that Bobdonovitch was right is, of course, the key to getting other scientists interested in the whole idea of star travel. Dr. Hans Kruse, at Syracuse, will now discuss some possible ways to test the theory."

Elliot settled back comfortably in his chair as Dr. Kruse cleared his throat and began to speak.

"I see my fears were groundless. I have apparently wasted some time," said the Drymnu.

"Not wasted," the Sirrachat disagreed. *"All knowledge is valuable. And it was an easy mistake to make. Fragmented races look so powerful, sometimes."*

"Yes," the Drymnu agreed ruefully. *"A shame that they waste their energy on the idle pursuit of fun."*

"Their loss. But, ultimately, our protection."

"True."

Elliot worked late into the night, an electronics textbook propped up on his keyboard, a notepad balanced on his knees, and Bobdonovitch's paper displayed on his TV screen. Many of the concepts were new to him, but that was all right—it simply added to the challenge. He had the time it would take to learn the basics; the time and, thanks to the Net, the information. In its own way, this was a more exciting puzzle than any he'd met in *Deathworld*—and the possible rewards were infinitely greater. Elliot Burke might someday be hailed as the man who took humanity to the stars. Glancing out the window at the starlike lights of the city, he smiled.

This was going to be fun.

Afterword

"The Challenge" was one of the first stories I wrote after going pro in 1980, and I'm reasonably sure it predates most of the crush of game-oriented stories that have appeared since then. If a leader is defined as one who sees which direction the crowd is going and gets in front of them, then I suppose I could claim to have started a trend. But I wouldn't claim it very loudly.

For any of you sharp-eyed, perfect-memoried people who may have recognized the Drymnu as also having made an appearance in the 1982 *Analog* story "Final Solution": yes, they (it?) are (is) the same. Like "The Shadows of Evening," "The Challenge" was originally to be the first of a series which somehow got sidetracked. I've really *got* to stop doing that.

The Cassandra

It had been raining all morning the day Alban Javier left Aurora: a dull, cold, persistent drizzle out of a uniformly gray sky. Looking up from under the wide brim of his hat, Javier wished that the rain could have been accompanied at least by roiling thunderheads and crashing lightning—something that would have lent dignity to the event taking place. But perhaps it was more fitting this way, he told himself blackly. It was, after all, with a whimper instead of a bang that mankind was abandoning this world.

He had been scheduled to leave on the nine A.M. flight, but it was now nearly two and his part of the long line had barely made it past the landing field's inner gate. Behind him, outside the fence, the waiting crowd had abandoned any semblance of order and was pressing close to the mesh, taking advantage of the minuscule shelter offered by the fence's two-meter overhang. Javier glanced back at them from time to time, but always turned away quickly. Too many of the rain hats and poncho hoods had bits of pure-white hair poking from beneath them, and with the nearer ones Javier could see the emerald green of their eyes as well. It was something like looking in a multiple-image mirror, and it made him feel all the more uncomfortable.

Ahead of him, the line shuffled forward a half meter. Picking up his single travelbag—all that the colonists were permitted to bring—Javier moved up and focused on the building into which the line ultimately disappeared. A good hundred meters away yet. Still, a considerable number of the city's residents had left in the past week. Perhaps the inevitable trance would hold off long enough for him to escape finally into space.

It didn't. He had, in fact, covered barely five more meters when the familiar tingle rippled through his body, and as his muscles locked in place the gray rain faded from before him. . . .

A fireball becomes a river of flame racing through a dark, narrow corridor, erupting finally from a woodshored entrance to blacken the grassy knoll above. The screams from within fill the air, but even as swearing rescuers plunge into the mine they are fading into the silence of death. Those still alive are brought out first, their agony muted by drugs. The rescuers who carry out the dead are no longer swearing. All are grim-faced; some are crying. The blackened bodies pass closely enough to touch. . . .

And Javier was back on Aurora, standing in the rain with knotted muscles and a throat full of nausea. Behind him someone—a younger teen, probably—was sobbing with reaction. Ahead of him, the people had bunched together a bit more closely, leaving a small bubble of space around him, as if he were the carrier of some loathsome disease. He didn't bother to turn around; he knew that his own inner horror was mirrored in a hundred pairs of green eyes, and he had no desire to see it. Even misery could get tired of company.

With a shuddering sigh he slid a wet hand under his collar and massaged the taut neck muscles there. One final going-away present, he thought dully; with love, from Aurora.

* * *

The cubicle euphemistically referred to as the kitchen manager's office was about the size of a king-sized coffin, Javier decided as he stood silently in the half-meter of space between the front wall and the cluttered desk. Wedged into a chair across the mound of paper was a man so fat that it was hard to understand how he had ever gotten into such a limited area. Unbidden, an irreverent thought flickered through Javier's sense of futility: that Hugo Schultz had been placed behind the desk as a child and allowed to grow into his current position.

Schultz looked up from the application he'd been reading and fixed Javier with a pig-eyed stare. "You didn't put down what job you wanted," he said, his voice just loud enough to cut through the sounds of the hotel kitchen that the cubicle's walls made only token effort to keep out.

"I'll take anything that's open," Javier said simply, matching the other's volume.

Schultz nodded. "Uh-huh. I see you've got Earth citizenship. You born here?"

A lie would be so easy—and so useless. Javier's entire public information file was available via a single phone call, should Schultz choose to check on it. Besides, to anyone who had followed the events at the frontier over the past few years, his hair and eyes were a dead giveaway. "No, I was born on Aurora."

"Thought so," Schultz grunted. "You're a Cassandra, then?"

Javier winced at the term, but its use was far too widespread these days to be avoided. "Yes."

Schultz grunted again and studied the application some more. "A master's degree, no less. You get that on Earth?"

"No, on Aurora."

"I thought all the schools went when the rest of the planet fell apart."

"They did. But I was one of the first of my generation—the first generation of Cassandras. The society didn't begin its collapse until we entered the labor force, and by then I had my degree." He shuddered slightly at the memories.

"I stayed on Aurora to try and help. Six months later Earth ordered the planet evacuated."

"At Aurora's request." The words were heavy with accusation.

"Yes," Javier acknowledged, making no effort to defend Aurora's leaders or their decision. On some worlds of the Colonia, he'd discovered, the stigma of being from a failed colony was almost as bad as that associated with his Cassandra visions, and he had long since tired of both fights.

Schultz's expression didn't change, but his voice softened a shade. "Why? What were you running from?"

"Ourselves. Each other. The visions." Javier shook his head. "You can't understand what it's like, Mr. Schultz. Never anything but people dying—usually on a massive scale, and always so close you can practically smell them."

"But they don't come true, do they? That's what I heard, anyway."

"Enough do," Javier said. "A few percent, I suppose. But that doesn't really help. All it does is add uncertainty to the whole thing, like watching a laser being aimed at someone and not knowing whether it's charged or not."

"Did leaving Aurora help?"

There it was at last: the question that, in one form or another, everyone eventually got around to. *Have the trances stopped coming?* Again, the temptation was to lie; again, he knew it would be useless. "Not really. Scattering us around the Colonia eliminated the group trances, but that's about all."

"Those are the ones where someone had a seizure and half the Cassandras in the city joined in?"

"Sort of," Javier said carefully. They were treading on dangerous ground here. He would have to watch what he said.

"The story goes that every time the dust cleared from one of those you had a bunch of dead people and a mess of wrecked equipment." Schultz's steady gaze had challenge in it.

Javier understood; it was a roundabout way of asking

another familiar question. "The deaths came about mainly when people driving or working heavy machinery weren't able to stop before the trance began. But we always get a couple seconds' warning, so for most jobs there really isn't any danger, either to ourselves or anyone else."

"You were pretty stupid to let Cassandras do that sort of work."

Javier shrugged. "We didn't have much choice. The entire third generation had the curse, and the work force desperately needed us. Anyway, the deaths and damage weren't all that devastating in themselves. It was the panic and fear that went with all of it."

Schultz held his gaze for a moment and then dropped his eyes to the application again. Javier waited silently, listening to the muted clatter of dishes around him and trying to ignite at least a spark of hope. The effort was futile. Schultz was far too smart not to have realized that someone with Javier's education wouldn't be looking for work in a hotel kitchen unless he was desperate. Bracing himself, Javier waited for the inevitable turndown.

"All right," Schultz grunted abruptly. "You can start on dishwasher and cleanup duties. Our stuff's not very fancy— sonic washers and brooms—but it's not likely to get away from you, either. If you're carrying a stack of dishes or something and it happens, put them down, pronto. And don't tell any of the other kitchen staff where you're from. They're not too bright, most of them," he added, anticipating Javier's obvious question, "and probably won't connect the hair and eyes to Aurora."

"I . . . yes, sir. Thank you, sir," Javier said, thrown off balance by the unexpected response.

"Sure. One other thing." Again the pig-eyes bored into Javier's face. "How often do you get these trances of yours?"

"Two or three times a week, usually, in a big city; maybe once a month in a less populated area."

"What's your accuracy rate?"

"About five percent. All the ones that do come true seem to happen within twenty-four hours of the vision."

"One in twenty. Not too good, is it? So okay, here's the

deal. You get a vision, you keep it to yourself. I don't want to hear about it, and I don't want the staff to hear about it. Life in New York is hectic enough without doomsayings that probably won't happen. Got that?"

"Yes, sir."

"Good." Abruptly, Schultz raised his voice in a shout that made Javier jump. *"Wonky!"*

A moment later the door at Javier's right popped open and a thin, weasellike face peered in. "Yeah, boss?"

"This is Javier; he's on cleanup duty. Show him around and get him started."

"Sure." Wonky tossed a broken-toothed grin at Javier. "Let's go, kid."

"You like the boss, Javier? Huh?" Wonky asked as they left the cubicle.

"He seems very fair," Javier answered cautiously.

Wonky nodded vigorously. "Yeah, sure is. Friend of mine, good friend. Knew him in Jersey, couple years ago. He told me if I ever needed a job just come to him. So I did."

Javier nodded. Wonky was a thin youth with darting eyes and quick movements. He had probably grown up on the city's streets, his scars and missing teeth the dues of survival. Such people hadn't existed on Aurora, but Javier had met many in the old cities of Earth. None of the younger worlds of the Colonia, he had once heard, had been in existence long enough to develop the vast social and economic disparities of the mother world. Give them time, though, and the slums would come.

He shook off the mood. It was probably natural—maybe even inevitable—for a Cassandra to lean toward morbid thoughts. But such borderline self-pity should not be overdone, especially on a day like today. He had a job!

Now if only he could keep it.

The first few days went well. The work itself was, of course, childishly simple, and Javier quickly learned all that Wonky could tell him about the kitchen and its operation. Of the hotel served by the dining facilities he learned nothing. Wonky's duties as busboy ended at the edge of the dining room; so, effectively, did his world.

Javier threw himself into his job with a will and efficiency that caused many puzzled looks and—inevitably—snide comments from his fellow workers. The strange coloring of his hair and eyes probably also slowed their acceptance of him, but if anyone actually identified the newcomer as a Cassandra he kept that knowledge to himself.

Strangely enough, Wonky seemed immune to the general aloofness and would often hang around Javier during slow times. His conversational range was limited, but Javier learned many helpful tips about living in the big city from him. He was grateful, too, for the company.

Luck was with him in another guise, as well: his first three visions occurred outside of working hours, away from the hotel. Two happened in the tiny run-down room he had rented a few blocks away, the other as he was walking home one afternoon. As always, they were images of disasters: an aircar crash, an earthquake, and a flash flood. And as usual, they did not come true, at least not as far as a check of the news media could establish. Years ago, Javier had believed he would get used to the visions, as one could get used to nightmares or scenes of violence on the evening news. Now, though, he knew differently. There was an overpowering immediacy to the disasters he was forced to witness, an accuracy of sensory detail that made them as real to him as anything else in the world. To deny the visions at any level would require similar denial of all reality, and Javier wasn't yet desperate enough to yield to insanity.

He'd been at work for almost a week when Wonky came in from the dining room with a load of dishes and the look of a kid with a secret. "Hey, Javier, guess what I just saw in the dining room."

"What?" Javier asked. His eyes and most of his attention were on the sonic washer, which had a tendency to drift off its proper frequency and rattle the dishes.

"There's a girl out there who looks just like you," the other grinned.

The washer was sudenly forgotten. "What do you mean?"

"You know—got the same hair as you. Same green eyes, too. I saw her up close."

Another Cassandra? *Here?* "Show me, will you?"

Wonky led the way to the swinging doors that opened into the dining room. Opening one of them a crack, he gestured beyond it. "Next to the wall."

Javier squinted through the opening. Details were hard to see at that distance, but he was almost sure—

She turned in his general direction for a second and he stiffened. Pulling off his apron, he tossed it to Wonky. "I'm going to talk to her. Cover for me, okay?"

"Hey, wait, you're not supposed—" The rest of Wonky's protest was cut off by the closing door. Feeling horribly conspicuous, Javier threaded his way through the maze of tables. "Excuse me," he said as he reached the girl's side. "Are you Melynn Uhland?"

She glanced up, then took a longer look. "Yes. Do I know you?"

"I doubt it. My name's Alban Javier. I went to Aurora Northern, too, but I was a year behind you. Mainly, I know your picture from news reports of your work with Dr. Rayburn."

"What can I do for you?" she asked coolly.

"Uh—may I sit down?" This wasn't going quite as Javier had expected it to and he was beginning to get flustered.

She hesitated, then nodded curtly. He sank gratefully into the seat at her right. "I—well, I just wanted to find out what's happening in your work," he told her. "The articles I've read don't really say much."

"The final report won't, either," she said, her voice strangely flat. "At least, it won't say what you want to hear."

"What do you mean?"

"I mean we haven't found a way to stop the visions." Javier froze. "But . . . you said *final report.*"

"That's right. We're quitting."

He started to speak, but no sound came out of his suddenly dry mouth. He tried again. "You can't *do* that. I mean—look, we've been living with this for fifteen *years,* some of us. We've had friends die and other friends go permanently psychotic. We can't stop until we find a cure."

"What do you mean, *we*?" Melynn snapped, green eyes blazing. "*I'm* the one who's been living in Rayburn's hellhole, not you." She glared at him for a moment as he sat there, speechless. Then, lowering her gaze, she passed her hand across her forehead; and when she again raised her eyes the anger was gone. "Alban," she said quietly, "I know what you're going through. Just because I was working with Dr. Rayburn doesn't mean I didn't get my share of the fear and misunderstanding everyone dumps on us. I did. And the job . . . it was ten times worse than Aurora. The staff spent half their time trying to learn what triggers the trances, and the other half looking for a way to suppress them." She shook her head. "Nothing worked, but they tried everything. I had to live through changes in diet, environment, biorhythm—I don't remember all of them. Some of them—a lot of them—made either the vision or side effects worse. I've lost ten kilograms since we started, and been on the brink of a nervous breakdown twice. Others of us weren't that lucky—two of our original eighteen are dead, and another four might as well be. I've been Dr. Rayburn's only test subject for three months now; everyone else had to drop out. Alban, I want to find out how to stop the trances; I want it so badly I dream about it. But I can't do any more. I've paid my pound of flesh. It's up to someone else now."

"I'm sorry," he said. Dimly, he was aware of how inadequate the words were, but at the moment another, more urgent thought was uppermost in his mind. "Tell me," he asked carefully, "*did* they ever figure out what triggers the visions?"

It was as if a thin glaze of ice had dropped over the emerald of her eyes; and in that moment Javier knew that she, too, knew the truth. "No," she said in a low voice. "And I doubt they ever will."

He nodded, trying to dislodge the lump that had formed in his throat. "You could have made it easier on yourself, you know, if you'd just told them."

Her smile was bitter. "You don't find enough hatred directed toward you, Alban? You want to try living among people who know how your visions come to you?"

"No." Javier glanced at the people sitting nearby, but if they were listening they gave no sign of it. "I'm sorry; it was a stupid comment."

"That's all right." She touched his arm. "I'm sorry, too—I didn't need to be sarcastic. I'm just very burned out right now."

"Any way I can help?"

She shook her head. "Thanks, but no. I'm just passing through, actually—I'm heading up to the most desolate part of northern Newfoundland I can afford to get to." She smiled faintly. "My first choice was central Australia, but Dr. Rayburn's budget couldn't stretch that far."

Javier nodded. "I guess I'd better get back," he said. "Thanks for talking to me."

She caught his wrist as he started to get up. "Look, Alban, I'm sorry I—well, I know how much you and everyone else has been counting on us. And we *did* turn up one bright spot: the virus that linked into our parents' chromosomes apparently requires a naked protein from the Auroran biosphere to make its linkage properly, and the pseudogene it forms is highly recessive besides. That means that unless you marry another Cassandra your children won't have it; and even if you do the pseudogene will probably break off and disappear before your grand-children can inherit it."

He swallowed, unsaid, the first words that came to mind. If she wanted to see that as a bright spot it wasn't his place to burst her bubble. "Well, that's something," he said instead. "I—good luck with your trip, Melynn; I hope it helps you."

"Thanks. Good-bye, and good luck to you, too."

He made his way back to the kitchen through the sea of covertly staring eyes and returned to work, feeling a familiar numbness settling over his brain. Somewhere deep inside him, he knew, part of the drive that kept him going had died. He had never honestly admitted to himself just how much hope he had been putting in Dr. Rayburn's work; the true quantity was now painfully clear. Rayburn was the last major researcher still working on the Cassandra trances. If he was giving up, then that was it. The visions would be with Javier now until his death, ending forever any chance he might have had to live a normal life. A wife and children . . . he almost wished Melynn would be able to keep such a naïve hope. But outside Rayburn's lab it was unlikely to last. The real world was a sobering experience for social outcasts.

Somehow Javier managed to make it through the day, and by evening his bitterness and frustration had abated somewhat. Many people throughout history, he told himself as he walked home, had survived without hope; he could, if necessary, do likewise. Besides, he seemed to be lucky these days. Maybe luck would serve him where hope had failed.

Two days later, his luck ran out.

He was sweeping the kitchen floor when the two-second warning came, and he had just time to step close to a wall before his muscles locked in place and the world faded away. . . .

Lying on its side is the tangled wreckage of a tube train, squeezed between the tracks and the tunnel wall. Smoke and fire are everywhere, the crackling of flames mingling with the screams of the injured and the shouts of rescue workers. From outside the tunnel comes a barely audible roll of thunder, the sound strangely incongruous in the midst of the carnage. An eddy in the air currents momentarily clears the smoke from one car's number plate: 1404. From somewhere inside a scream goes on and on. . . .

"Hey, Javier! Hey!"

The voice came from far away, scared and insistent. Gradually, the train wreck faded from sight. The usual wave of nausea rose into Javier's throat, and he screwed his eyes shut as he fought it down. His muscles trembled with tension and adrenaline shock, and his head ached fiercely. Opening his eyes carefully, he found himself looking into

Wonky's anxious face. "I'm okay, Wonky," he croaked through dry lips. "Don't worry."

The weasel face relaxed only fractionally. "What happened, kid? You looked like you were seeing a ghost."

"I saw a train wreck," Javier said. The headache and nausea were beginning to recede now. A violent shiver swept through his body, scooping up tension and leaving weakness in its wake. "It's okay, though," he added as Wonky's eyes widened, "it happens to me a lot. The trance only lasts a few seconds."

"Gardam! You one of them whatchyasay—fortune-tellers? What'd you see?"

Javier's hands ached, and he suddenly realized he was still squeezing the broom handle. "I'm not a fortune-teller. I just see these things sometimes. Look, I'm not supposed to talk about it."

"What'd you see?" Wonky persisted.

Javier sighed, but he lacked the emotional energy to argue. Haltingly, he described the vision in as much detail as he could stand. "Now please don't tell anyone else about me, okay?" he said when he had finished. "Mr. Shultz told me not to—"

He was cut off by a sudden grip on his arm. "Hey! The fourteen-hundred cars are always on the Paterson train— that's the one Mr. Schultz goes home in!" Wonky flicked a glance at the wall clock. "Gardam, he's gone already. C'mon, we got to stop him!"

"Wait a sec," Javier protested, but it was too late. Wonky's wiry body was a lot stronger than it looked, and before Javier could break loose he found himself outside in the hot, muggy air.

"Hold it," he tried again. "Mr. Schultz told me not to tell him about any visions I saw."

"You just gonna let him die?" Wonky snorted. He took off through the late-afternoon crowd of pedestrians, moving like a combination jackrabbit and bulldozer. Javier ran after him, and managed to catch up again two blocks later.

"Wait, Wonky, hold on," he said, trying not to pant.

"Look, it may not come true. Probably won't, actually. Hey, remember it thundered in the vision? Look, no thunder!"

It was no use. Wonky had gotten it into his head that his boss/friend was in danger and no one was going to stop him from delivering a warning. Groaning inwardly, Javier followed, wondering what he was going to do.

They reached the tube station minutes later and Wonky, who obviously was familiar with the layout, headed off to the left. Shivering as sweaty skin met the air-conditioning, Javier plunged through the crowd after him. A low rumble made him glance back at the entrance before he'd gone very far. He shivered again, this time not from the cool air, and hurried on. Outside, it was starting to rain.

Hugo Schultz was easy to spot, his huge girth making him stand out among the other commuters. Javier hesitated, but Wonky showed no signs of uncertainty. He caught up to Schultz just as the latter was about to step into a waiting train. Pulling him out of line—no mean feat—Wonky launched into an animated monologue. From his position Javier couldn't hear what was being said, but Schultz's face quickly clouded over with anger. Twice he tried to pull from Wonky's grip, but the little man hung on grimly, letting go only when the train began to move down the tunnel. As it passed, Javier noted the number on one of its cars: 1404.

He looked back to see Schultz bearing down on him, face livid with rage, with a relieved but puzzled-looking Wonky in his wake. "Javier!" the fat man bellowed. "I thought I told you to keep your damned tricks to yourself. Now you've made me miss my train, and you've got Wonky all in a lather—"

"Boss, he saved your life," Wonky said.

"Mr. Schultz, believe me, I tried to tell him—" Javier began.

"Shut up! You're fired. *Both* of you—got that, Wonky?"

Wonky's jaw dropped, and he started to protest.

The words never came. From down the tunnel came a hideous crash.

Someone in the crowd screamed and someone else

began shouting something, but Javier didn't really hear them. Turning, he started off through the crowd, hoping desperately to reach a wall or doorway where he'd be safe. But it was too late; and even as he took his first few steps his body went stiff. Through the vision of an exploding starship that danced before his eyes, he dimly felt the jostling of the crowd pushing him off balance. An instant later, the universe went black.

He woke up—or, more properly, returned to a state of relative consciousness—four or five times in the next few hours, as nearly as he could later piece events together. It was a foggy sort of awareness, distinguished from sleep mainly by the throbbing pain in arms, chest, and head. Occasionally he heard voices, indicating there were others in the room with him. Sometimes all he could hear was groaning.

It was the periods between those times that nearly drove him insane.

Only once before in his life had he ever had even two visions come one right after the other; now, they were coming in strings.

Two aircars collide violently just short of a rooftop landing pad, obvious victims of a guidance computer malfunction. One slides over the edge and falls two hundred stories. . . .

An explosive decompression aboard an orbiting space colony. Three are killed instantly, seven others suffocate before help can reach them. . . .

Screams in an unknown language are swallowed up by the roar of an erupting volcano. The rain of ash and flowing lava cut through a jungle village, obliterating it completely. . . .

A fleet of unidentifiable starships fights a short but violent battle with a planetary defense force, destroying it to the last ship. . . .

The starship battle was the worst of the visions, its intrinsic horror stretched agonizingly by its sheer persistence. Again and again Javier was pulled back to the scene, forced to watch as the victors, apparently not satisfied with the deaths they had already caused, proceeded with cold-blooded efficiency to burn off the world they had defeated. From space the expanding rings of nuclear flame were clearly visible; at ground level they were the height of redwoods and the brightness of the noonday sun. For once, no one screamed in pain. No one had time.

Finally—finally—the hurricane of death subsided. With an effort, Javier swam his way back to consciousness. The first thing he saw when his eyes opened was Wonky's face.

"Where am I?" he whispered, his throat very dry.

"Hospital," Wonky told him. "Ward two. How you feel?"

"Terrible. You've got to help me get out of here."

"You're not well enough," Wonky protested. "You got kinda trampled when you fainted at the station. You should wait till morning, anyway—it's pretty late."

"I don't care. If it starts up again I'll go crazy. Never mind," he added, seeing Wonky's puzzled expression. "My clothes must be here somewhere. Find them, and then hunt up a doctor. I'll sign any release they want. But I have to get out."

For a long minute Wonky stared at him, brows tight with thought. Then he nodded once, curtly, and began to search among the ward's lockers. He found Javier's clothing, and after being assured that Javier could get into them alone, went in search of a doctor. Javier dressed slowly, his body aching with every movement. A radio was playing softly at the nurses' station at the end of the room, and he paused once to listen as a report of interstellar news came on. The doctor Wonky dragged back with him proved stubborn, but in the end was persuaded to produce the necessary papers, and a few minutes later Javier was out on the street. Supported by Wonky, he headed toward his apartment building. They just made it.

Javier slept for nearly ten hours; a deep sleep, untroubled by visions. When he awoke he lay quietly, staring at the ceiling and thinking about what he'd seen and heard. After a while, he slept again.

By the time he woke up he had made his decision. He showered, ate the last of the packaged food he had in the room, and wrote a long letter. Then he began packing.

Wonky arrived before he had finished. "Hi, kid, how you feeling?" he asked as Javier offered him the room's only chair.

"Better," Javier said, sitting on the edge of the bed. "Thanks for helping me home last night."

Wonky shrugged. "Yeah . . . look, Mr. Schultz sent me to see you."

"He was going to let me come back, but then changed his mind. Right?"

Wonky seemed taken aback. "How'd you know?"

"I expected it. Word of my vision got around the kitchen, probably, and the people don't want to work with me. Happens all the time."

"It ain't that they don't like you, you know. They're just kinda scared."

"I know." Javier looked at him thoughtfully. "What about you, Wonky?"

"You saved the boss's life. That was a good thing to do. I don't think it's right to fire you just 'cause some of the others are scared. I told him so."

"Thanks for backing me up. Did you get your own job back?"

"Oh, sure. Mr. Schultz doesn't mean it when he fires me. He told me to give you this." He fished a bulky envelope from his pocket and handed it over. "He said it was all he could do."

Inside the envelope, in well-worn bills, was about three hundred dollars. "That was very kind of him," Javier said, surprised by the gift. "Please thank him for me."

Wonky glanced at the travelbags. "You leaving town?"

"Yes. I'm getting as far away from people as I can. Northern Maine, maybe." Thoughts of central Australia flashed briefly through his mind.

"How come?"

Javier hesitated. This was not the time nor the place, he told himself. But the secret had been bottled up within him for too long. "Wonky, have you wondered how it is I can get these visions, wondered what it is that causes them?"

"Naw, not really. Mr. Schultz said it's a kinda curse."

"It is indeed. But it's a curse with a very simple basis." He closed his eyes briefly. "Death."

Wonky's eyes narrowed. "I don't get it."

"It's painfully simple. Someone fairly nearby dies, and that event triggers a vision. That's what happened at the station—the train wreck started a trance, and I got trampled. At the hospital, with crash victims and others dying all around me, I got visions strung together like previews of Armageddon."

He stood up and went to the window. "It was the group trances on Aurora that finally tipped me off," he said, as much to himself as to Wonky. If felt good to finally let it all out. "Always there was one death in the obit list that wasn't connected to the accidents—that was the death that started the whole thing. A few Cassandras would be affected; one, maybe, would be driving a car and would run down a pedestrian. Another death, more trances. With enough Cassandras doing dangerous things it could have gone on forever." He sighed. "I think the old philosophers must have been right. Human life—maybe sentient life in general—is more important to the universe than we like to think these days. Somehow, the two instances of death— the triggering one and the ones in the vision—seem to form a link through time and space, a bridge that we Cassandras can somehow travel. Maybe because death takes the person out of time, so that all deaths are in some way congruent— I don't know. All I know is that it happens. The philosophers can play games with the semantics."

Wonky had been listening silently—probably, Javier thought, not really understanding. But now he spoke up. "Wait a minute. Mr. Schultz and you both said that most of the things you see don't ever happen. So what's this bridge thing you're talking about?"

Javier didn't turn around. He didn't want Wonky to see his face. "Mr. Schultz is wrong, like the rest of us have been. Maybe we didn't want to believe it . . . but it's the only way this can possibly make sense. You see, just because a vision isn't fulfilled nearby doesn't mean it isn't fulfilled *somewhere*. We just never— I mean, there are just too many *worlds* out there that we don't hear much from." He bit his lip. "As I was getting dressed at the hospital I heard a report that had come in from Centauri, saying somebody important had been killed in an aircar crash. They gave enough details that . . . well, I saw the crash, Wonky, saw it almost a week ago. But if that VIP hadn't been in it, I'd still think the vision hadn't come true."

He turned back to face Wonky. "No, Wonky. Every one of those damnable visions must come true. Maybe some of them haven't, yet. But they will."

He stopped; not necessarily waiting for a response, but simply out of words. "I don't get it all," Wonky said slowly. "But I guess you know what you're talking about. You're a lot smarter than me, anyway." He hesitated, then stood up and held out his hand. "Good luck."

A few minutes later Javier was back on the street, trudging toward the tube with his travelbags. He walked mechanically, only dimly aware of his surroundings, his mind numbed by emotional fatigue. On the way he dropped his letter in a mailbox; Dr. Rayburn would receive it in a day or two.

Wonky hadn't understood, of course. How could he? To know someone had died each time you were awarded the dubious privilege of watching someone else die—it was too far out of his experience. And he probably wouldn't have been able to live with the idea if he *had* understood it.

For Javier, though, there was no escape, either from the knowledge or its consequences. He could leave the city now, but he knew he'd have to return. Even if Dr. Rayburn believed him, experiments and massive data searches would have to be performed to prove it to the rest of humanity. And that would be only the beginning, because the ultimate goal was still to control the trances and their side effects. More experiments would have to be done, experiments like the ones that had nearly destroyed Melynn Uhland and her friends. It would require more volunteer Cassandras . . . and Javier knew who the first of those would have to be.

Himself.

The thought of it was terrifying—his hospital experience multiplied by a hundred. But he had no choice. The truth had to be told; the Cassandras *had* to learn, at whatever cost, how to use their curse.

Because Earth was going to need all the resources she could muster. Glancing involuntarily at the sky, Javier shivered as he remembered that terrible hospital vision. Somewhere out there, sometime in the future, a war fleet powerful enough and vicious enough to burn off an entire planet was going to win a great victory. If the race that owned that fleet was expanding their own empire into space, they would someday reach the Colonia . . . perhaps very soon.

And if the cost of developing the Cassandra ability into a weapon against that threat was enhanced public hatred and the loss of a few lives, then so be it. It would, Javier knew, be worth such a price.

Even if one of those lives was his own.

Afterword

"The Cassandra" was one of those stories that I simply couldn't let go of, no matter how many rejection slips it collected. From 1979 to 1983 it underwent two complete rewrites and quite a bit of incidental fiddling on top of that. Eventually, the persistence paid off.

Why I pushed the thing so hard is a little more difficult to explain. Certainly it's not a particularly upbeat story (and if you've made it this far you've surely noticed my fondness for upbeat stories); in fact, it almost qualifies as a tragedy. And, unlike the case in many of my stories, I would emphatically NOT want to be in the protagonist's shoes.

All I can suggest is that it was the story's underlying philosophy that had a grip on me. In an era where mankind too often considers itself to be a meaningless accident of nature, perhaps I needed to remind people that that wasn't necessarily so. We *could* just as easily be important—even vital—to the universe at large; and until and unless that's proven wrong, I intend to keep on believing it. You can't very well care about people, after all, unless you feel those people are ultimately worth the effort.

I wax overly philosophical. Let's get to the next story.

Dragon Pax

Scholars and doomsayers had been predicting the Great War for almost a century beforehand, and when it finally came it was brief and furious, erupting like a fusion bomb among the sixty worlds of the Empire. The more strategic planets were fought over by as many as seven separate factions, and were often reduced to rubble in the process. Other planets—the poor or unimportant ones—were largely neglected by the starfleets, and were left to their individual fates as space travel all but disappeared.

Power, not the destruction of civilization, was the goal of those in the struggle; but, too late, they realized they were in over their heads. For although each faction had carefully calculated its strength and chances before making its move, none had anticipated the wild-card effect of the Dragon-masters who had suddenly appeared from nowhere onto the scene. These twelve men—virtual unknowns, all of them—had no warships and only minimal troops. But the powerful nightmare shapes that were their dragons evened the odds tremendously. Huge, virtually indestructible, appearing and vanishing on command, the dragons wreaked havoc on any ground forces that opposed their masters, crushing soldier and armored treader with equal ease.

Their size and sheer impossibility inspired almost universal fear and hatred, but it also prompted new alliances and betrayals among the warring factions as each tried to guess who the ultimate victor would be. But the forces unleashed were too destructive and the scramble for power quickly became a fight for survival. For many, even this goal was not to be achieved.

One of the few planets untouched by the war was Troas, and this was due more to luck than good planning. Rosette, the western end of Troas's single continental land mass, was the summer home of the Emperor and a resort area for members of the Imperial Court. Had anybody of importance been there when hostilities broke out, Rosette would undoubtedly have been burned to a cinder. But the Emperor was back on the capital, and the relative handful of Imperial troops were quickly withdrawn from Rosette for more important duties.

Royd Varian was three years old when the war began; he was five when Dragonmaster Harun Grail arrived at Troas and declared himself absolute dictator. At his age, Royd knew nothing of the politics of the situation. All he knew was that, later that year, his father was taken away to fight against the Easterlings from the other end of the continent, a war from which he never returned. Lying awake night after night, tears streaming down his cheeks, Royd listened to his mother's muffled sobs in the next room and resolved that, someday, he would kill the Dragonmaster.

His mother died barely a year later, and Royd—with no close relatives at hand—spent the rest of his childhood in a state-run orphanage. Though with the passage of the years the fire of his hatred waned, his resolve remained firm, and as he grew up all aspects of his life began to shape themselves toward his goal.

He studied history and political science in school, the better to know his enemy. On his own he learned military science and the use of weapons, and he worked at building up his physical strength and stamina. He sent letters asking about the chances of working on the household staff at either of the Dragonmaster's two estates, and landed a temporary job as mason's assistant; at about the same time he made his first delicate contacts with the outlawed Rosette Freedom Party. He rose through the ranks upon both sides, his single-minded determination driving him over all obstacles.

And finally, at age twenty-four, he considered himself ready.

Royd hefted the little four-shot dart gun doubtfully. "I don't know, Phelan," he told the tower of muscle standing beside him in the backroom darkness. "This doesn't pack much punch."

Phelan Hapspur shrugged. "You want something with punch or something you can hide? We've only got a limited arsenal, you know."

"Yeah." Royd frowned, then stuck the gun into his waistband, pulling his tunic down to conceal it. "All right, I guess this'll have to do. I'd better go now; the loading should be finished out front."

"Good luck." Phelan slapped him on the shoulder. "We'll be watching for your signal."

Royd nodded and slipped out the door into the meat market's main room. A burly man in a bloodstained apron came up and handed him a piece of paper. "All loaded, sir," he said. "If you'll sign here . . ."

Royd glanced through the store window in time to see one of the butcher's boys closing the doors on the cold-truck outside. As one of the food buyers for the Dragon-master's city palace it was Royd's responsibility to personally check all the meat as it was loaded; but he knew Temmic could be trusted. Taking the paper, he glanced over it and then signed.

"Thanks, Mr. Varian," Temmic nodded. "See you next week?"

Probably not. "Sure, Temmic. So long."

Stepping out into the afternoon sunlight, Royd paused for a moment to listen. Above the normal city sounds

around him, he could just make out the low roar of many
vehicles. Grail's convoy, returning from the Dragonmaster's
country retreat as scheduled. Royd squinted off in the
proper direction—sometimes Grail had the smaller of his
two dragons lead his convoys—but nothing could be seen.
No matter; the Dragonmaster would soon be home.

Climbing into the cab of his cold-truck, Royd started the
engine and headed toward the palace, threading through
the mixture of pedestrian, animal, and motorized vehicle
traffic with practiced skill. Within a few minutes he was at
the outer wall of the palace grounds. The gate guard passed
him through with a nod, and he drove another two
kilometers through sculped lawns and gardens to the huge
building itself.

Entering one of the service bays, he helped the kitchen
workers unload the cold-truck and then chatted with one of
the cooks for a few minutes before returning to his bed in
the number two servants' dorm. He was now off duty until
later in the evening. Then, by prearrangement with one of
the other servants, he would help clear the dishes from
Civil Affairs Director Marwitz's customary late-evening
supper . . . a task that would bring him to within fifty
meters of Grail's own office suite.

Lying back on his bunk, Royd closed his eyes and pre-
tended to be asleep. Curiously, despite the nervous tension
slowly building within him, he felt no elation or pride in
what he was about to do. Assassinating Dragonmaster Grail
had long ago ceased to be just a matter of personal
vengeance. It was something he had to do for the people of
Rosette, for while Grail and his dragons lived there could
be no freedom. And if it cost Royd his life—as it probably
would—it was still a fair bargain.

At seven-thirty he got up, changed clothes—making sure
no one saw the gun—and reported to the majordomo for
work. With three other boys he was sent up to the palace's
fifth floor.

Civil Affairs Director Clars Marwitz was a short, dark-
eyed man with a perpetual scowl and an acrid personality.
Royd had disliked him from the first, and that opinion had

been going steadily downhill ever since. His power over the lives of Rosette's people was absolute, and he used it ruthlessly to crush any dissention that he found. Next to Grail himself, Marwitz was the most hated man in Rosette. Still, Royd managed to give him a vacuous servant's smile as they collected the Director's dishes.

Back in the hall, Royd took a deep breath. This was it. "You go on ahead," he told the other three servants. "I'm going to check down the hall and see if there's anything to pick up in the Dragonmaster's office."

Picking up an empty tray, he turned and started walking, not giving them the chance to warn him that no one could enter Grail's suite without an invitation. The hall was very long, and Royd's throat was very dry by the time he reached the Dragonmaster's door.

Two men wearing hard faces and the gray uniforms of Grail's personal bodyguard flanked the portal; their laser-sighted automatic rifles pointed a centimeter or so to either side of him. "That's close enough, kid," one of them growled as Royd came to within three meters. "State your business."

"Hey, I'm just a waiter," Royd said, staring with suitable nervousness at the guns. He'd been holding the tray vertically in front of him, concealing the dart pistol clutched in his right hand; now he lifted the tray to a waist-high horizontal position, bringing the gun invisibly to bear on one of the guards. "I just came by to pick up any dishes that Dragonmaster Grail might need washed."

"Anyone send for you? No? Then scram."

"Yes, sir." Gently, Royd squeezed the trigger, turning the tray and gun slightly. The drug was supposed to act almost instantly to paralyze the nervous system—if the darts penetrated the guards' clothing, that is. He fired again. "I just thought—"

Without a word, the first man crumpled to the ground. The other wasted his last second gaping in bewilderment, then he too collapsed.

Royd dropped the tray and snatched up one of the rifles, shoving his dart gun back in his waistband. He tried the

door; it was locked. Stepping back, he raised the rifle and
gave the lock a full second on automatic. The wood and
metal shattered, and a single kick sent it swinging inward.
Royd charged in as the hall behind him filled up with the
raucous clang of alarm bells.

The room he had entered was an anteroom of sorts, with
three other doors heading inward from it. A saucer-eyed
woman sat frozen at a desk by one of the doors, her fingers
still poised over her scriber. Keeping his gun pointed
toward the doors, Royd snapped, "Where is he?"

She might have been carved from stone. Cursing under
his breath, Royd studied the doors. Barely visible under
the leftmost was a thin line of light. He strode to it,
wrenched it open, and stepped in, rifle at the ready.

Sitting at a desk in the center of a luxuriously furnished
office, his eyebrows raised quizzically, was Dragonmaster
Harun Grail.

Royd raised his rifle. "Don't move, Grail."

The Dragonmaster's gaze never faltered. "You've got
exactly one second to put that gun down before I call out
my dragon," he said with icy calmness.

"Don't waste your breath on bluffs; I know better.
Neither of your dragons is small enough to fit in a room this
size. You're all alone now."

"All right." Grail's tone hadn't changed. "What do you
want?"

"Your life."

"Why?"

He was stalling for time, Royd knew; waiting for
reinforcements to arrive. "Ask the devil," he retorted.

"You can't escape," Grail pointed out. "Soldiers are on
their way right now."

"That doesn't matter. What matters is that Rosette will
be free again once you're dead."

"You're a fool if you believe that."

Royd opened his mouth to reply, but just then he heard
the sound of running feet out in the hall. He aimed the
rifle—

And with a miniature thunderclap of displaced air a five-meter-long black creature appeared, its serpentine neck arching high over Grail's desk, its wings spread in defense of its master. Fiery red eyes glared balefully at Royd; taloned paws rose against him. Reflexively, Royd pulled the trigger; for all their effect, the steel-jacketed slugs might have been confetti. At least two of the ricochets came close enough to hear.

"You see," Grail's voice came from behind the outstretched wings as the echoes died away, "I have *three* dragons, not two."

"Damn," Royd breathed—and just then a half-dozen soldiers stormed through the door behind him.

Wrenching his gaze from the dragon, he spun around, rifle ready. But these weren't Grail's professional bullies; they were just common soldiers, many of them draftees— the sort of people whom he was trying to free. Besides, killing them wouldn't buy him more than a few minutes at most. Taking his finger off the trigger, he lowered the weapon and prepared to die.

"Don't kill him!" Grail's voice snapped from behind him. Royd half-turned, a bitter curse ready for delivery . . . and then the soldiers were swarming over him. Something wet and aromatic hit his face and the world went black.

He awoke slowly, by degrees, as if his head had gone on a long journey and had to be coaxed back. Something was pressing against his back; only slowly did he realize he was lying face-up on a cot of some sort. With a supreme act of will, he managed to force his eyes open.

"How do you feel?" a gruff voice behind him asked.

"All—all right." Gritting his teeth, Royd sat up, fighting paroxysms of dizziness and nausea. Carefully, he turned around.

Dragonmaster Grail was sitting on a chair, watching him.

Royd gazed back, wondering briefly if this was a dream. "What are you doing here?" he croaked, his throat strangely dry.

"I want to talk with you."

Frowning, Royd looked around him. The room he was in, though small and plain, was clean and airy. The two chairs looked comfortable; the cot he was sitting on was soft and had clean sheets and blankets. Whatever this was, it was no ordinary cell.

Grail interpreted Royd's inspection correctly. "No, you're not in my dungeon. This is a sort of guest room I've had set up for you."

"Why bother? You're going to shoot me anyway. Or do you want me in good shape for the torture?"

"There will be no torture, and perhaps no shooting either. Tell me, why did you try to kill me?"

"That again? What difference does it make?"

"It matters a great deal to me." Grail's voice was low, but strangely intense.

Royd looked at him, seeing for perhaps the first time the wrinkles in the dictator's face, the slight stiffness in his movements. How old *was* Grail, anyway? Royd suddenly realized he didn't know. "I wanted to kill you because you've turned Rosette into a repressive, regimented society where individuals have no rights and no purpose except to serve you. You've had hundreds of your opponents jailed or murdered and started at least three wars with Easterland since you took over."

"You sound like the Rosette Freedom Party's recruiting speech," Grail said dryly, "but I can see you really believe it. Oh, don't worry, you won't have to answer any questions about your friends—I already know everything worth knowing about them.

"You're right, of course; I've done most everything you mentioned. But have you taken note of the *good* things I've done for Rosette? When the Great War started and all the Imperial troops and technicians were pulled out, Rosette went right to the brink of total collapse. Most of your food and machinery had been imported from offworld, you know, and those supplies were diverted pretty damn quick to more vital fronts.

"Now Rosette's own food production is way up; in the last four years we've actually had crop surpluses. We're now making our own machinery and vehicles, and have two new power plants well into the design stage. And those 'wars' you mentioned were attempts by the Easterlings to invade Rosette. We successfully fought them off—"

"Fought them off!" Royd spat. "Slaughtered them, you mean, with your machine guns, artillery, and those damn dragons—"

Abruptly, Grail stood up. "Look, you young idiot," he snapped, "without the dragons all of Rosette would have been overrun by hordes of Easterlings and trampled into the dust."

"Damn it, all they wanted was food. There are people *starving* over there!"

"You want to starve with them?" Without warning, Grail was seized by a coughing fit. He sat back down, and Royd briefly considered jumping him. But the older man's eyes were alert . . . and the room was large enough to hold the dragon he had seen earlier. Royd stayed where he was.

Grail finished coughing and took a couple of deep breaths. "Look, Varian," he said quietly, using Royd's name for the first time. "There are twenty million people in Rosette and just over a billion in Easterland. Even at the current rate of food production here we can't possibly relieve their annual crop shortfalls. In five or ten years we may be able to do it, but until then there's just no way. Their only hope is to leave us alone and to let us put our full energy into developing our economy and our land— Rosette's got the richest soil on the planet, though a lot of it's still tied up uselessly in the old Imperial estates. It's a long-term hope, sure, but it's the best we can offer them."

"It's hard to be patient when you're starving," Royd muttered. Something was off-key here; Grail's speeches and official pronouncements had always painted Easterland as a deadly enemy whose destruction was vital to Rosette's security. What was this talk about supplying them with food?

Grail smiled faintly when Royd put the question to him. "The 'Easterland threat' campaign was put together by Clars Marwitz, my Civil Affairs Director, to try and unite

Rosette behind me. Marwitz is shrewd—damn shrewd—
but he's power-hungry and completely amoral. Bears close
watching. . . . Anyway, I went along with the plan because I'd rather have all you dissidents working to help
build up Rosette's potential than inciting riots and forcing
me to put you in prison. Most of you are smart and
educated, and Rosette needs all the help you can give her."

A frown had been growing steadily across Royd's forehead, in direct proportion to his confusion. "What's going
on? Why are you telling me all this?"

Grail's eyes bored into Royd's. "I want you to take over as
head of state when I die."

For a long moment there was dead silence in the room.
"*What?*" Royd whispered at last.

"You heard me. Rosette's developed about as far as it can
under an absolute dictatorship. It needs to be nudged
toward something more decentralized—a constitutional
monarchy, perhaps, as a first step. But I can't do that."

"Why not? There's no one to stop you."

Grail sighed. "All right. Suppose I announced I was
reorganizing the government and wanted the Rosette
Freedom Party to share power with me. Would your
leaders be willing to drop by the palace and discuss the
issue?"

"Not likely," Royd admitted. "They'd think it was a trap."

"You see the problem, then. I'm known as a dictator, and
there's no way I can easily change that image."

"But you could abdicate. Go into retirement."

"I could," Grail nodded. "Of course, there would
probably be a bloody power struggle, possibly even a civil
war. Rosette was on the brink of one when I arrived
nineteen years ago, as a matter of fact, though you're too
young to remember it. But assume for the moment I can
find a way to block that. Who's going to defend Rosette
from another Easterling attack?"

"Uh . . ." Royd hesitated; it sounded like a trick
question. "I gather the army's not strong enough?"

"Not now. It could be, by drafting every single man from
age seventeen on up. But then the economy would go

straight to hell." Grail shook his head. "No, Easterland is held back mainly by fear—fear of the dragons. Rosette needs a Dragonmaster, at least for a few more years, and it's up to me to make sure the wrong man doesn't get that kind of power."

There were a lot of implications in Grail's statement, not the least of which the suggestion that the dragons could be transferred to a new owner. But for Royd one question overrode all the others. "Why me?"

Grail shrugged. "You care about the people of Rosette."

"How do you figure that? Just because I tried to kill you?"

"Because you were willing to spend many years of study and even give your life to gain freedom for them. And, maybe more important, because you didn't fire on the common soldiers who came to arrest you." Grail ran a gnarled hand through his graying hair.

"And besides, I haven't got enough time to go out searching for more likely candidates. The doctors tell me I've only got six to eight months left. All my instincts tell me you can handle the job of putting this country—and eventually the whole planet—back on its feet. If you're willing, the job's yours. I can start your Dragonmaster training tomorrow. What'll it be?"

Royd's head was spinning. This couldn't possibly be what it seemed; it *had* to be some sort of trick. And yet, what did he have to lose? He'd been prepared to die—had *expected* to die—and there was nothing worse Grail could do to him. As long as he was careful not to betray his comrades, it would probably be best for him to play along. Whatever Grail's plan was, perhaps he could turn it to his advantage. "All right," he said slowly. "I can't make any promises yet about succeeding you, but I'm willing to give it a try."

"Good." Grail got to his feet, rapped twice on the door. "I'll come for you in the morning. Sleep well."

The door opened, giving Royd a glimpse of gray uniforms in the hallway. Without another word the Dragonmaster strode out, and the door was slammed firmly behind him.

* * *

The emotional drain of the day's events made for a deep
sleep, and Royd would probably have kept at it through
much of the morning had Grail not awakened him at the
stroke of seven. No guards were in sight; in fact, Royd saw
no one else at all as the Dragonmaster led the way down
two dimly lit corridors and up a narrow staircase.

"Where is everyone?" he asked, fighting the urge to
whisper.

"These hallways are seldom used," Grail answered. "I'm
sure you understand the need for secrecy. In here."

The room they entered was large and high-ceilinged, its
furnishings those of a conference room. The view through
the diamond-patterned windows told Royd he was on the
east side of the palace and about four or five floors up—
somewhere in Grail's private section, he guessed. On the
carved rock-ebony table were four suitcase-sized boxes and
a covered tray. The odors from the latter made Royd's
stomach growl.

"Sit down," Grail said, indicating the chair closest to the
tray. "We'll want to get started as soon as possible, but I can
fill in some of the background for you while you eat."

Royd removed the lid and did a quick survey. Chopped
phorlax meat mixed with nuts; two twelve-centimeter surf-
skimmers, finned and roasted whole; a four-fruit salad cup;
and a steaming cup of ch'a. His opinion of Grail went up a
notch—anyone who would serve a meal like this to a
prisoner couldn't be all bad. Another thought crowded in
on the tail of the first: that that might be precisely what
Grail wanted him to think. In a somewhat more subdued
state of mind, he sat down and began to eat. "You and your
dragons have already had breakfast?" he asked.

"I have; the dragons haven't," Grail said. "That's the first
popular misconception you'll have to unlearn. The dragons
aren't alive; they're just machines."

Royd blinked. Like everyone else, he'd always assumed
that the dragons were living pets of their Dragonmaster.
The idea that they were mechanical was actually harder to
believe. "Machines?"

"Yes." With a pop, the small dragon appeared a few meters off to the side. "Take a look yourself. Go on, it won't hurt you."

Swallowing hard, Royd got up and approached warily. The creature sat motionless on its haunches, its talons glinting in the thick purple carpet, its red eyes following Royd's every movement. "Look at the outer skin, the eyes, and the talons," Grail instructed. "And inside the mouth; you'll see there is no saliva."

The monster opened its mouth. Gingerly, Royd looked in, then glanced briefly at the other points Grail had mentioned. "Doesn't look like any machine I've ever seen, but I'll take your word for it," he said, backing away. "You build them yourself?"

"Oh, hell, no. They're way beyond human technology. They were built by some extinct race out in the Castor stars millennia ago. My guess is that they were used as body-guards." Another pop and the dragon was gone.

"That vanishing act is a good trick," Royd said as casually as he could, determined not to be overawed. "How does that work?"

"Look here." Reaching into his tunic, Grail pulled out a small gemlike object hung around his neck by a thin gold chain. He handed it to Royd. "This is the key. Somehow, the dragons are kept—well, not *inside*, of course, but sort of *next* to it. That's bad wording; what I mean is that there's some sort of dimensional pocket associated with the amulet, where the three dragons are kept. A kind of limited subspace, I expect, similar to the one starships travel in, except more localized."

Royd examined the amulet. A deep, brilliant red in color, it was roughly teardrop-shaped and shimmered in a way that made it look like he wasn't actually touching its surface. It was warm to the touch, and when he squeezed it he could feel . . . not a vibration, exactly, but something that didn't belong in a normal rock, either.

"The sensation you're feeling isn't physical," Grail said. "At least, I've never been able to detect it with any kind of sensor. It's strictly a psychic effect."

Royd nodded abstractedly. The key to Grail's power, and he was holding it in his hand. For a moment he was tempted . . . but Grail wasn't stupid. He wouldn't have deliberately disarmed himself. Reaching across the table, Royd dropped the amulet back into Grail's outstretched hand.

"I can call the dragons out to any distance from the amulet I choose, up to a few kilometers," the Dragonmaster went on, slipping the chain around his neck again. "And, of course, I don't have to be touching the amulet at the time."

"Of course," Royd repeated, a slight shiver running down his back. The old dictator was definitely not a safe man to underestimate. If Royd had yielded to the temptation to grab the amulet and run . . .

He resumed eating. Grail busied himself with the boxes of equipment, and by the time Royd had finished breakfast there were three sets of electronic displays arranged in a semicircle on the table in front of him.

Grail glanced at the empty tray. "Finished? Good. Get up, and put that tray somewhere."

Royd did so, and Grail slipped into his vacated chair, flipping a handful of switches and putting on a bulky headset. At once the displays came to life, showing a variety of squiggly curves. "What you're seeing are the shapes of some of the electrical waves in my brain," Grail explained. "Watch what happens to the patterns when I call one of the dragons."

Subtly, but noticeably, the curves changed, and an instant later the dragon stood beside them.

"And they'll change a bit more as I give it commands," Grail continued. "Watch."

The dragon turned and sprang to the window in a single twelve-meter leap, hissed once, and then did a little shadowboxing with its front paws. Then it vanished, and the displayed curves resumed their original shapes.

Grail looked up at Royd. "You're going to have to learn how to control your own brain waves so as to match the ones you just saw. For starters"—he pointed out a relatively high peak on one of the curves—"you can try to flatten this to about half its size." He demonstrated, then stood up and handed the headset to Royd. Automatically, Royd took it and put it on. "But how do I do that?" he asked, bewildered.

"You'll have to figure that out for yourself," the dictator answered, making a slight adjustment in the helmet's position and all but pushing Royd down into the chair. "Try flexing some muscles, or thinking different thoughts, or whatever else works for you. Keep your eyes on the trace. When it shrinks even a little go back and try what you were just doing again."

He pointed across the room. "That door leads to a bathroom; the dumbwaiter over there will bring you lunch at noon. I'll be by sometime in the afternoon, and I'll want to see some progress here." He tapped the proper peak on the display and, without another word, strode from the room.

Royd stared after him a moment, then turned back to the displays. Somewhere in all of this window dressing, he knew, Grail was planning some sort of trickery. But he couldn't for the life of him see the trap; and until he did he had no choice but to play along. Sighing, he set to work.

It was more like early evening when Grail finally returned. "Let's see how you've done," was his only greeting.

Gritting his teeth against the throbbing headache which had developed in the past hour, Royd made the high peak flatten a bit. A dismal showing, he thought, but Grail nodded in apparent satisfaction. "Not bad for the first day. How do you feel?"

"I've got a headache. Otherwise okay."

"I expected as much." The Dragonmaster dug a small bottle from his pocket and tossed it to Royd. "Two of these will take care of your head."

"Thanks," Royd said, grudgingly. "What's happening in the outside world today?"

"Not too much." Grail pulled out one of the chairs and

sank into it. He looked tired. "A hailstorm in the northwest destroyed a good deal of Androc District's corn; we're trying to decide if we've got time to replant or whether we should try to put in a different crop, one with a shorter growing season." He looked keenly at Royd. "You know much about agriculture?"

"Not a thing."

"I'll get you some books to read. Efficient farming is the key to lasting peace on this planet. I also had a long talk with some Easterland envoys this afternoon. They're threatening war if Rosette doesn't give them more food and industrial assistance. Oh, and your Rosette Freedom Party friends have added your name to the list of those 'murdered by the brutal son of Satan.' That's me."

"What did you tell them—the Easterlings, I mean?"

"Oh, I told them we couldn't spare any more than we were already giving them, and that if they didn't like it, that was their problem."

"But they're talking *war*."

"Sure, but that's all it is: talk. True, their army outnumbers ours by at least ten to one, but they know they can't order an all-out attack. The dragons are too powerful a deterrent." Grail shook his head. "They know that, but they still insist on making high-voltage threats. That'll hurt them, too, in the long run, because it then looks like they keep backing down. Keep that in mind, Varian—never make a threat you can't follow through on."

"That's at least twice now you've implied your dragons keep Easterland off our backs." Royd's headache was nearly gone, but he was still feeling grouchy. "How do you figure that? There are at least three hundred kilometers of land border and five or six times that much coastline. You and your dragons can't possibly defend all that from a really serious assault."

"Of course not. But it's the *psychological* effect that does it. How would you feel about going to war if you knew you'd eventually have to face being torn apart by an indestructible monster that's as tall as this palace?"

He shook his head wearily. "I call it *dragon pax*—or

more correctly *pax dracontea,* I suppose: a peace imposed by the dragon. But it's based upon fear, and that kind of peace can't last." He fixed Royd with a sudden glare. "And that's why you have to move Troas toward something else, something more stable."

Royd swallowed the retort that came to mind as Grail leaned over and turned off the power to the displays. "That's enough of this for now," the dictator said. "You can stay here tonight; there's an adjoining room I've had set up for you to sleep in. In the meantime, I brought something for you to read." The small dragon appeared beside him, its gaping mouth holding a stack of perhaps a dozen books. Setting them down on the table, the creature vanished.

"It's easier than carrying them myself," Grail grunted. "These cover some of the basics of politics, diplomacy, and psychology. Read as much as you can tonight, then go back to your mind-conditioning exercises in the morning. Your meals will be delivered as before, and there's spare clothing in the other room. I may or may not see you tomorrow, but I think you've got enough to keep you busy for a while." He stood up and nodded. "Good evening, Varian."

Royd didn't see Grail the next day, nor the day after. Late the third evening, however, the Dragonmaster returned. "How are you doing with your exercises?" he asked, sinking into a chair.

Royd put down the book he'd been reading and reached for the headset. "Not too bad. Let me show you."

A minute later, Grail concurred. "Very good. It's still not completely down, but that'll come with time. Here's your next task." He touched a jagged trace on a second display. "This should become more like a sine wave: smoother curves and with the peaks spaced farther apart. I found this step easier than the last one when I was learning, if that makes you feel any better."

Royd felt his ears prick up. "You learned to control the dragons this way, too? Who did you learn from?"

Grail ignored the question, nodding instead toward the

book on the table. "I see you're reading Iviza. What do you think of his theories?"

"I don't like them," Royd told him, switching mental gears with somewhat less ease. "He doesn't seem to even allow for the existence of morality in politics. I think he's wrong."

Smiling slightly, Grail settled himself more comfortably in his chair. "Tell me why," he challenged.

The two men talked long into the night, discussing politics and related subjects. At times Royd almost forgot who he was talking to; the Dragonmaster's political views— or at least the ones he was admitting to—were much closer to Royd's than the latter would ever have expected. It was a wrench sometimes to remember that this was the man who had sent Royd's father to his death. The man Royd had sworn to kill.

The days stretched into weeks, and Royd's life settled into a reasonably comfortable routine. He worked several hours daily on the mind-conditioning equipment; ate, slept, and exercised on a rigid schedule; and spent the rest of his time reading. Every few days Grail would stop by, usually in the evenings, to check on Royd's progress and to bring him new books.

He also kept Royd informed on current events, both general news and the more private details of governmental business and infighting. His candor in speaking about his subordinates was sometimes surprising, and gradually Royd began to see that the Dragonmaster was less an omnipotent ruler than simply a powerful man in the midst of a machine not entirely under his control.

Almost against his will, Royd frequently found himself in sympathy with the dictator's goals, and at such times he had to sharply remind himself to watch for traps, verbal and otherwise. If there *were* any traps, though, he never spotted them.

Oddly enough, as Royd's feelings toward Grail began to soften, he noticed his own confinement was being eased. His door was no longer locked, and he was allowed to move freely among the half-dozen rooms of his section of the palace, though he was still forbidden to enter the more public areas where people might see him.

More than once he considered escaping and rejoining the Rosette Freedom Party's underground, where his new knowledge of Grail, the government, and the dragons could be put to good use. Each time, though, he chose to stay. The more he learned, he told himself, the better their chances of ultimately bringing down the regime—he no longer thought of it in terms of Grail alone—and of restoring freedom to Rosette.

It never occurred to him that he might be staying simply because doing otherwise would be betraying Grail's trust.

But Grail was not the type to let his subordinates have secrets, even from themselves, and eventually he forced the issue in his characteristically blunt way.

It was in Royd's eighth week of captivity when Grail showed up unexpectedly as the youth was beginning his mind-conditioning work. "Turn that off and get your coat," the Dragonmaster ordered. "We're going on a little trip today."

Royd blinked his astonishment. "What? Where are we going?"

"To see *dragon pax* in action. Come on."

He led the way to the palace roof, where one of Rosette's three VTOL gunships was waiting for them. The craft was designed to carry up to thirty troops: on this trip, Royd and Grail were its only passengers. They strapped in, and Grail used the intercom to give the pilot his orders.

"Where exactly are we going?" Royd asked as they lifted silently into the sky.

"The Rosette-Easterland border," Grail answered. "Louys Pass, about six kilometers southeast of Hagston. Our patrols say that there's a new Easterling base being set up there. I want to walk One past it, just to remind them what they'll have to face on this side of the line."

One. It was the first time Royd had ever heard Grail refer to any of his dragons by any sort of name. "'One' is your biggest dragon, I take it?"

Grail nodded. "One, Two, and Three, in decreasing order of size."

"Not terribly original."

The Dragonmaster stared out a window. "I originally called them Alecto, Magaera, and Tisiphone—the three Furies from ancient Earth mythology, who pursued and punished evildoers in terrible ways. But . . . I suppose after the fracture-bombing of Solfa it seemed to me that I had no business calling the dragons by cute names. They're fearsome, deadly weapons and shouldn't be treated like pets."

Royd shivered. For the Furies to be considered 'cute names' . . . "It must have been pretty bad. Solfa, I mean."

"The entire world was destroyed. I mean that literally; what the bombs themselves didn't get the tectonic upheavals that followed did." Grail's jaw muscles tightened visibly. "Three billion people killed, for the sole purpose of trying to destroy two Dragonmasters. That shows you how much the Emperor fears us."

Royd digested that. "How'd you escape?"

"I was already in space when the attack started. My ship took some damage, but I got away. That's when I came here." Grail spoke almost mechanically; from the look in his eyes it was clear his thoughts were still with the slagged surface of Solfa. His breathing seemed to have quickened, and Royd noted with some uneasiness that he was beginning to wheeze.

"Maybe we'd better stop talking for a while," he said. "You don't want to go into one of your coughing fits."

"You're right." Grail sank back in his seat and smiled wanly. "It *has* been getting worse, hasn't it?"

"Yeah. What are the doctors doing for you?"

"Not much they *can* do. My lungs are slowly filling up with scar tissue. It's something I picked up forty years ago out on Agave. Not contagious, by the way."

"Glad to hear it. Now shut up and get some rest."

Grail smiled again. "Yes, Doctor," he murmured, closing his eyes.

The aircraft reached its destination—one of Rosette's border outposts—an hour or so later. Grail, seemingly recovered from his earlier discomfort, obtained two horses, and he and Royd rode off into the low mountains that formed a natural barrier between Rosette and Easterland. No one at the base asked Royd's name or position; Grail did not volunteer that information.

The mountains were not particularly high, but they were steep and treacherous in places. Clearly, though, Grail had taken this path before, and he led them skillfully up the slope. After perhaps an hour he reined in. "We go on foot from here," he told Royd. "I want to get a little closer before I release One."

They made their way through the trees and underbrush for half a kilometer to a small clearing where, without warning, the forty-meter dragon appeared. Shifting its bulk with surprising grace, it moved off between the trees. "Glad we found this clearing," Grail grunted. "If you bring One out in the woods you usually knock down a tree or two in the process. Makes a hell of a noise." He looked at Royd. "Did you feel anything when I released it?"

Royd hadn't even thought to try applying his mind-conditioning work. "Uh—"

"Forgot to, huh? Never mind; get ready and I'll bring out Three."

And this time Royd *did* sense something. A presence of sorts, but cold and faintly menacing.

Grail nodded when Royd tried to describe it. "That's the dragon, all right. Scared hell out of me when I first contacted it, too. I'm going to put Three through its paces; watch how the feeling changes with each movement." The dragon turned and leaped into the lower branches of the nearest tree.

"Shouldn't you stick with one dragon at a time?" Royd asked, glancing in the direction that One had taken.

"No problem. I can handle all three at once." He smiled crookedly. "And no more than three—which is why there are twelve Dragonmasters instead of just one."

"Oh?" Royd said with forced casualness. Grail had never

given him more than tantalizing hints about how the older man had become a Dragonmaster, and Royd didn't want to scare the story back underground by seeming too eager.

"Yeah. The man who found the first amulet out at Castor was able to use it to find the other eleven. It had taken him nine years of trial and error to figure out how to call and control his first set of dragons, but he found out that there was simply no way for him to control two amulets at once— I suspect they were deliberately designed that way. So he called in a bunch of his cronies and taught us how to be Dragonmasters. We had it easy; with his knowledge the process only took a few weeks."

Royd shook his head. "Nine years. The man had a lot of patience."

"He didn't have much else to do," Grail replied bluntly. "He was in hiding. If he'd stuck his nose out of the Castor system the Imperial Patrols would have shot it off."

"What do you mean?"

"He was a pirate. So was I."

For a moment the two men looked at each other in silence. Then, slowly, Royd shook his head. "I don't beleive it."

"Why not?"

"You don't *talk* like a pirate, for one thing. And you're too well educated."

From the other side of the mountains came the sound of gunfire. "Just the Easterlings shooting at One," Grail explained as Royd, startled, turned to face the sound. "Don't worry; it's not going to kill any of them today. You know, you can't be stupid and be a pirate these days— running a starship takes brains." He sighed. "But you're partly right: I didn't start life as a pirate. For several years I taught microelectrical engineering on Goldstone."

Royd looked at the dictator's lined face. "What happened?"

Grail shrugged awkwardly. "I'm not really sure. Academic life was just too frustrating, I suppose. There were many improvements that needed to be made in the university, but no one would listen to my ideas. As low man in the pecking order I couldn't accomplish anything except irritating those in charge.

"When they finally tossed me out, I drifted around industry for a while—no other college would hire me—and when Damrosch offered me a job on one of his ships, I took it. I didn't know then that he was a pirate, and when I found out . . . I don't know; I suppose I've always been a better follower than a leader. That's probably why he gave me one of the amulets—he figured I could be trusted to back him up."

"Did you?"

"More or less. Even when most of the other Dragonmasters deserted him during the Great War to try and set up their own kingdoms, I stayed with him. His plan was to capture one planet, build it up over a period of several years, and then use it as a base of operations to take over the whole Empire."

"Is that when you left him?"

"Soon afterward. The planet he chose was Solfa."

"Oh." Royd was silent for a moment. "For a born follower you sure picked up the trade of dictator pretty fast."

Grail took a step toward him, face contorted with sudden anger. "I had no *choice*, damn it!" he shouted. "This place was coming apart at the seams. Can't you get that through your head? I was the *only* one who could hold it together." He broke off in a fit of coughing, clutching his sides and sinking to his knees in the brush. "My inhaler," he managed to get out. "It's with the horse."

Royd glanced at Three as the dragon crouched motionless, temporarily bereft of guidance. "The dragon would be faster," he said.

"Scares the horses," Grail gasped, shaking his head. "You go. Hurry."

Royd sprinted the half kilometer back to where they had tied the animals. There was a pouch tied to one of the pommels; opening it, he found a small gas cylinder with an attached mouthpiece. He had it in his hand, and had actually taken the first few steps back toward Grail, when the realization of what he was doing crashed in on him and brought him to an abrupt halt.

Grail was the *Dragonmaster*, the ruthless dictator Royd had sworn to kill . . . and Royd was about to try and save his life.

For a brief moment he wavered; but the proper course was unfortunately clear. No end could ever be divorced from its means, and to allow an old, sick man to choke to death would be to sink to Marwitz's level. A government that gained power in that way would have proved itself merely a successor, not an alternative, to the Dragonmaster's—how then could it ask for the people's trust? And besides, Grail had *asked* him for help. To betray that trust would be the act of a Judas . . . and Royd did not wish such a bloodstain on his conscience.

The coughing had stopped, but Grail was still wheezing badly when Royd reached him. His hands trembling, the old man took the cylinder, turned a valve, and held it to his mouth. Within a few seconds his breathing had eased.

"You okay?" Royd asked, himself still somewhat out of breath from the return sprint.

Grail nodded and got carefully to his feet. His eyes swept across Royd's face, a strangely knowing expression in them . . . and Royd felt his face reddening.

"You *bastard*!" he exploded. "That was a test, wasn't it? Damn it—and you *knew* I'd come back, didn't you?"

Grail held up a hand. "I really *did* need the inhaler," he said. "And no, I wasn't sure you would return. But I thought it likely."

"Does that thing let you read minds, too?" Royd asked bitterly, nodding at the amulet.

"No, not at all. But the state of mind you've been learning gives you a sort of sense for danger." His eyes looked deep into Royd's. "You still want to kill me, don't you?"

Royd returned the gaze. "Yes," he said harshly. "And someday I'll find a way to do it."

"I'm sure you will. But wait until you learn to control the dragons." Grail glanced toward Three, and the dragon vanished. "Come, it's time to return to the outpost. We'll take a short air tour of the border and be back at the palace by nightfall. I've called One back; I think we've given the Easterlings enough to think about for a while. I trust a short tour is all right with you?"

"Whatever you want," Royd said curtly. "You're the boss here."

"Yes," Grail agreed. "I am. Shall we go?"

Back in his room again, Royd slumped into a chair and glared at the mind-conditioning equipment, his stomach still churning with anger and shame. Wait until he could control the dragons, indeed: Sound advice—and an obvious trap, for Grail had made it a point to keep himself familiar with Royd's progress. He would know exactly when Royd had the necessary skill. And when that point was reached . . . what? Royd still didn't know what the old dictator's ultimate plan for him was.

But that was almost irrelevant. A swift, unexpected attack was the only way to kill the Dragonmaster. Royd had had that chance and had blown it. His sense of justice and honor had played him false, he realized; there was no honorable way to commit murder. The next time, he told himself firmly, he would ignore the prickings of conscience . . . if there was a next time.

Across the room, the door opened. Royd looked up, expecting to see Grail; but it wasn't the Dragonmaster who entered the room.

It was Civil Affairs Director Marwitz. And two of his uniformed bullies.

Marwitz stopped abruptly; clearly, he hadn't expected the room to be occupied. "Who are you? What are you doing here?"

Royd opened his mouth, then closed it again. There was no reason he should tell Marwitz anything, "Who are *you*, and what gives you the right to disturb my privacy?" he countered.

Marwitz murmured something, then walked farther into the room. The guards followed, closing the door behind them. Their guns were drawn; their expressions were not pleasant.

Royd felt sweat breaking out on his forehead. "I warn you, Dragonmaster Grail will be furious when he hears you've disturbed me."

"Will he, now." Recognition flickered across the Director's face. "And why would he be upset for me to find a failed assassin in his own palace?" The voice hardened. "What's going on?"

Royd remained silent. "Waverly!" Marwitz snapped.

One of the guards stepped forward, yanked Royd to his feet, and backhanded him hard across the mouth. Knocked off balance, Royd tripped over his chair and fell heavily to the floor. "What's going on?" Marwitz repeated. "I warn you—tonight of all nights I have no time to waste on false valor. Talk fast or I guarantee you'll soon wish you had."

Royd wiped blood from the corner of his mouth, shook his head. "The Dragonmaster will roast you over one of your own fires for this," he said with as much bravado as he could muster.

"Svoda." Marwitz turned to the other guard. "Go call Quebbe and tell him to set up his equipment; I'm sending him a new test subject. You'll be leaving by the south service road; pull all but one guard off the gate there, and make sure he's one of mine. Then quietly collect four or five other men you can trust and bring them back here."

The guard saluted and left. Marwitz turned back to Royd. "It will be a few minutes before you'll be leaving. You have just that long to change your mind." He pulled out one of the chairs and sat down, the guard Waverly standing by his side.

Royd felt the first prickings of panic inside his throat. He'd heard rumors of Marwitz's torturers, stories that had made his blood turn to ice water. And unless he could somehow alert Grail as to what was happening, he was going to find out firsthand if the rumors were true. He had to escape before the other guard returned. But how? He was still sprawled on the floor, his every twitch the object of close scrutiny. And he had no weapons at all . . . or did he?

It was his only chance. Carefully taking a deep breath, he began to concentrate.

The first few steps were easy: convolutions of the mind that he had already mastered. But his training was not yet complete, and he found himself in the position of a thief who knows all but the last two numbers of a combination lock. Desperately, he visualized the wave patterns he had seen so many times before; brought back the sensations he'd felt near Louys Pass that morning; tried to remember how the amulet itself had felt . . . and suddenly it all seemed to click. Opening his eyes—he hadn't remembered closing them—he focused on a spot a few meters behind Marwitz and Waverly. . . .

And the small dragon was there.

The two men spun around, Waverly with his gun raised. There were many ways for Three to attack, but Royd knew instinctively that he didn't have enough control yet to order them. Instead, he tried a simple command, visualizing both the words and the action: *Pivot around quickly on your hind legs.*

Three whipped around in a one-hundred-eighty-degree turn—and its tail lashed Waverly and Marwitz, slamming them hard into the edge of the rock-ebony table. They crumpled to the floor and stayed there.

Royd crawled over to them, the effort of holding Three making him a little light-headed. Waverly was dead; Marwitz only unconscious. Retrieving the gun, Royd got to his feet and let his control relax, sending Three back to the amulet around Grail's neck.

He staggered to the door, but just as he reached it he heard footsteps in the hall. There was barely enough time for him to leap behind the door before it swung open. Svoda and four other guards strode into the room.

The first time, Royd discovered, was the hardest. The guards had barely time to recover from the sight in front of them and to reach for their weapons before Three was once again in the room. Royd repeated the tail-swinging technique, and within seconds the guards were sprawled across the room in various degrees of injury and unconsciousness.

The dragon vanished, and Royd drew a shuddering breath. For an instant a wave of nausea swept over him, both from the effort of controlling Three and from the destruction he had so easily unleashed. But there was no time to lose. Either Marwitz was up to something especially devious or deadly—"tonight of all nights," he had said—or, more unlikely, this was a test Grail had cooked up for him. In either case, however, his course was clear: he had to get out, and fast. And if Marwitz had really left the south service road clear . . . then it was time to strike.

Stuffing Waverly's pistol into his belt, Royd left the room, locking the door behind him.

He found Phelan Hapspur in one of the Rosette Freedom Party's secret meeting places, and the two men greeted each other like long-lost cousins.

"Damn, but I thought we'd never see you again," Phelan grinned. "How'd you escape?"

"Never mind that now," Royd said. "I can get us into the palace if you can be ready in half an hour or so."

"What?" Phelan stared wide-eyed at Royd; for the first time he seemed to notice the latter's clothing and physical condition. He drew back slightly, his eyes narrowing. "Just where were you being held, Varian?"

"That's not important—"

"Yes, it is. You haven't been tortured; you haven't even gone hungry. What do you think that looks like to us?"

Royd was suddenly aware that there was a ring of people around them. Many were armed and dressed in black nightsuits; not all looked friendly.

"Look," he said, keeping his voice calm, "I can get you inside the palace—*inside*, not out in the grounds where they can pick us off one by one. You going to pass up a chance like this?"

"How you gonna do that?" a voice from the crowd challenged.

"Director Marwitz was going to take me out for some

unauthorized torture. He cleared all but one guard off the south service gate to avoid having unnecessary witnesses to my departure. I escaped and clobbered that guard on my way out. But he'll be found when the next shift goes on duty in an hour or so. I see you're set up for some kind of raid anyway—damn it, you'll never have this chance again."

There was a moment of silence. "All right," Phelan said slowly. "There's a lot here you're not telling us. But you're right; this is worth taking a chance on. But if you're lying—if it's a trap—you'll be the first to die."

"Understood. Now, we have to work fast. Give me some paper and I'll sketch our route. Oh, and there are some people we absolutely *have* to hit . . ."

Far away the sounds of sporadic gunfire could be heard as Royd sprinted down the deserted hallway toward Dragonmaster Grail's office suite. He'd left Phelan's squad minutes earlier to find Marwitz, to make sure the Director didn't escape. But Phelan had moved faster than Royd had expected, and the group had already entered Grail's office. He'd heard firing from that direction as he came up the stairs, but now there was only an ominous silence.

Running through the bullet-chipped outer doorway, between the crumpled bodies of the guards, he skidded to a halt in Grail's office.

The tableau before him was a potent mix of surrealism and *déjà vu*, and for an instant Royd flashed back to his own invasion of this sanctum a short eternity ago. In the dim light and harsh shadows thrown by Grail's desk lamp, Phelan and his five men stood or crouched motionlessly, their automatic rifles half-lowered in a gesture of uselessness.

Facing them across the room, Grail stood by his desk, the black figure of Three between him and the rifles. Grail had been speaking; he broke off as Royd entered.

"So this is your doing, is it?" he said. "I should have known. You deserved death for trying to kill me, but instead I treated you humanely—and this is the thanks I get."

The words of the Dragonmaster were bitter, but, strangely, the tone was not. Royd frowned, searching Grail's face for clues to his feelings.

"Varian, did you get Marwitz?" Phelan asked, his eyes still on Grail.

"No. Someone beat me to him."

"Damn! According to Grail here most of the soldiers we've been killing were Marwitz's men, in the middle of their own coup attempt. But maybe it's not too late to join forces. Whip over to the communications section—north side, third floor—and tell McDodd to call for a parley."

"Join forces with Marwitz's butchers? Are you crazy? They'd stab us in the back first chance they got."

"I didn't ask your opinion," Phelan snapped. "Get moving. We can use their help."

Grail laughed, a short bark that sounded almost like a cough. "Such shortsighted naïveté—and you really believe you can govern Rosette? You're a fool."

"The *people* will govern Rosette," Phelan corrected.

"The people aren't ready," Grail said flatly. "Democracy isn't something you learn overnight. And even if it were, even if you had every man in Rosette behind you, you couldn't keep the Easterlings from immediately pulling the whole thing out from under you. Only the dragons—and their master—have enough power to protect Rosette. Or haven't you been listening?"

"Damn you!" Phelan's temper was very near the breaking point. "Your damn dragons and your damn *dragon pax* don't mean a single thing to me. You're no different from anyone else, and if *you* can control those animals, then so can I."

"As I said, a fool." Grail's voice fairly dripped with contempt. Reaching up, he pulled the amulet from around his neck and tossed it to Phelan, who automatically reached out and caught it. "There—that's the key to controlling my dragons. Go ahead. See what good it does you."

Phelan stared at Grail, opened his mouth and closed it

again, and then peered down at the amulet in his hand. For a minute he squinted hard at it. Finally, he looked up.

"You see?" Grail said. "You have no more chance of controlling my pets than you have of swimming around Troas. Any of the rest of you want to try it? Go ahead, try it. The sooner you're convinced Rosette's survival depends on me, the sooner you'll surrender and we can put an end to this nonsense."

"Don't listen to him," Phelan said grimly. "He's bluffing."

"Yeah, maybe," someone muttered. "But what if he's not?"

"Shut up!"

"And you would have controlled my dragons," Grail scoffed. "You can't even control your own men. Look, even Varian ignores you."

Phelan glanced over in surprise. "Varian? I gave you an order, damn it. Get moving."

"No." Royd took a deep breath. "*I* can command the dragon."

All eyes turned to him. "What?" Phelan asked.

"You heard me." Royd's eyes were locked onto Grail's. "I learned while I was a prisoner here. The . . . dragons . . . took a liking to me. All of them will obey me."

Grail's face was unreadable. "Prove it," he said flatly.

Royd nodded slowly. He began to concentrate . . . and he had contact. But there was something else there, a presence he'd not felt the last time: Grail's own control, undoubtedly. He set his teeth—and suddenly, with absurd ease, the presence fell away. The dragon was his.

Royd held out his hand and tried an order. Without hesitation, Three walked forward.

There was a gasp from Phelan's group. Royd glanced at them. They still held their guns, but, curiously, seemed to have forgotten them. It was up to Royd then; and the long-forgotten debt was finally going to be paid. He turned his attention back to the dictator and ordered Three to turn and prepare to jump . . .

And hesitated.

He couldn't do it. He couldn't kill Grail.

The realization was a shock that even the incident at Louys Pass hadn't prepared him for, and it hit him like a hot needle in the gut. It wasn't just that he couldn't kill Grail dishonorably—he simply couldn't kill the dictator at all. The old reasons for his hatred still existed; but in the past few weeks he'd found the reasons were not always justified.

But even that was almost irrelevant, for all intellectual arguments paled before Royd's emotional response. He suddenly realized he *liked* Grail; liked him and sympathized with his attempts to handle the job he hadn't really wanted. And with new clarity he saw that, in many ways, he had come to consider the Dragonmaster his friend.

For a long moment he stood amidst the turmoil of truth crumbling in self-delusion. And then, suddenly, it was too late; for even as Royd's internal battle raged, he felt control of Three being wrenched from him.

Once more the chance to kill the dictator had come and gone—and looking into Grail's eyes, he finally realized that this was the trap the Dragonmaster had been patiently planning all these weeks.

He had tricked Royd into exposing the Rosette Freedom Party's hierarchy in this futile attack, secure in the knowledge that Royd himself could not throw his full loyalty to his old friends. Even the exquisite timing—pitting the underground against Marwitz's attempted coup—had probably been part of the plan. Grail had been toying with them, and now the game was over . . . and they were all about to die.

From its crouch, the dragon leaped—

And Grail screamed as it slammed into him.

The competing presence vanished; automatically, Royd took control of Three once more, his own mind a maelstrom of stunned disbelief. What had just happened was completely incomprehensible. He stared at the torn figure that had been Grail, half-expecting it to get up again. Nausea rose into his throat, blistering it, and for a moment he thought he would faint.

Someone had moved to his side. Phelan. "Good job,

Royd," he said huskily. "I guess this is yours now." He held out the amulet to Royd, who numbly took it. "Uh, we'd better get going—we've still got to clear out the rest of the palace. Are you and him"—he nodded carefully toward Three—"going to help us?"

Royd automatically started to nod . . . and suddenly realized it had been a question, not an order. He looked at Phelan with some surprise, and slowly the realities of the situation began to penetrate his numbed mind. He, Royd, was Dragonmaster of Troas now. Whatever else happened today, whether Phelan or someone else came out on top, Royd was ultimately the pivotal figure of Rosette's ruling structure. He had the final say here . . . and the final responsibility.

He cleared his throat. "Yes, I'll come along. Instruct the men to kill only soldiers who are shooting at them; all civilians and surrendering guards should be taken alive. There's no need for a bloodbath; a lot of them will be willing to work with us, and the rest can be taken care of later. Understood?"

Phelan threw one last glance at the dragon. "Understood," he growled.

It was nearly one in the morning, but the lights in Grail's old study were still blazing. Hunched over the desk, a pot of ch'a by his elbow, Royd felt like he could sleep for a week. But, tired or not, there was work here that only the Dragonmaster could do. Leaning back in his chair, Royd reflected half-bitterly that Grail had chosen his successor well—Royd's own sense of responsibility held him to his desk as effectively as chains.

Someday, he hoped, he'd be able to tell the people of Rosette—or maybe the people of a united Troas—the other side of their former tyrant: the Grail who had worked quietly and thanklessly in their behalf. Even now, six months after Grail's death, Royd felt hot shame at the ways he had often misjudged Grail, right up to the Dragonmaster's final, cold-blooded sacrifice.

It hadn't made any sense at the time; but now, Royd

could see how the swift transfer of power and reputation had effectively short-circuited any possibility of a civil war. Grail's ruthless type of nobility had run deeper in the man than even Royd had realized; and although the people were not yet ready to accept that, Royd knew there was still one way he could build a proper and lasting monument to the late dictator's efforts.

Gazing down, he frowned at the papers on his desk. Even his first, tentative steps toward a constitutional monarchy had caused uneasiness among some of his more powerful supporters, and these new proposals would have to be carefully worded if he was to avoid more grumbling. Still, if it came to a political fight, Royd had the power to force the changes, and everyone knew it. *Dragon pax*, he was learning, had many aspects.

Taking a sip of ch'a, Royd got back to work.

Afterword

How does a hard-SF-oriented writer work dragons—traditionally fantasy denizens—into a story? Now you know.

For many of you "Dragon Pax" will be a new story . . . which in a way is sort of a pity. The story was originally published in *Rigel* magazine, a quarterly edited by Eric Vinicoff which lasted two years before folding. I was consistently impressed by the quality of the stories Eric printed, and I've often wished more people had been able to find *Rigel* while it was around. Each loss of an SF magazine means one less market for short fiction; and if you like short fiction, as I do, these losses eventually start to hurt. So get out there and support your local SF magazine!

Ahem. Enough from the soapbox, already. And now, in the words of Monty Python, for something completely different. . . .

Job Inaction

The Monday-morning commuter into Baltimore was exactly on time for a change, and with an unexpected half hour on his hands Charley Addison decided to walk the six blocks to his office instead of fighting the crowds for one of the golf cart–sized electric cars lined up in the station's lot. It would save his blood pressure and the shine on his shoes, and the medicomputer at the clinic had been nagging him to get more exercise, anyway.

It was a beautiful spring day, but Charley hardly noticed as he concentrated instead on plotting out his morning's work. Checking over the programming on the new chip for GM should come first, but his subordinates were good at their jobs and he didn't expect this final check to turn up any major problems. After that he'd take another shot at the submic processor that he'd been fighting with last Thursday afternoon. It was one of the toughest jobs he'd seen in his thirty-five years at Key Data Services, but it would crack eventually—they all did. Grinning in anticipation, he bounded up the outside steps of the KDS building, bade farewell to the sunshine, and went inside.

And then the universe crashed in on him.

His first indication came when he tried to call up the morning's mail on his desk terminal. Instead of the usual sender headings, the screen lit up with a terse, red-bordered message:

ACCESS DENIED
CHARLES DOUGLAS ADDISON
8497-46-6604
IS NO LONGER EMPLOYED BY KDS.

Charley stared at the screen in disbelief for several seconds, then tried again. The same message came back. Turning the terminal off and on, he tried in succession for his last work file, the weekly cafeteria menu, and the interoffice memo file. Nothing worked. Frowning, he flipped the machine off again and headed for his boss's office.

Will Whitney, president of KDS, was on the phone when Charley walked in, a respectable frown creasing his own forehead. "Look, this may be a minor aberration to you, but it's at the catastrophe level for us," Whitney was saying as he waved Charley to a chair. "Isn't there *something* . . . ? I know, I know, but . . . Yeah, well, thanks."

Dropping the phone into its cradle, Whitney looked over at Charley. "I know why you're here, Charley. I just found out about it myself thirty minutes ago—and it doesn't look like there's anything I can do."

"Why not? Isn't this just some sort of computer glitch?"

"Of course it is—"

"Well, then, get it fixed and let me get back to work."

"—but the problem is that the report's already been transmitted to the National Employment Office. As far as they're concerned you've been legitimately fired."

Charley thought about that. "That's crazy, but even so I don't see the problem. Just hire me back."

Whitney gave him an odd look. "You haven't paid much attention to the country's employment policies lately, have you?"

"Well . . ." Charley wasn't all *that* ignorant. "I know how the unemployment system's been turned over to the private sector and all. But there's supposed to be a grace period after someone's fired before that goes into effect—something like ten days."

"It used to be ten days," Whitney nodded heavily. "But as the system's been improved and errors like this have become less and less frequent the grace period's been shortened—it's down to twenty-four hours now. Apparently this order went through over the weekend and . . . well, it's too late to rescind it."

A cold feeling was working its way into Charley's stomach. "Are you telling me I really *am* fired? You can't let this happen, damn it!"

Whitney spread his hands helplessly. "There's nothing I can *do*. I've talked to our lawyer and to the Employment Office people here in town—there just aren't any loopholes I can squeeze you through. If I let you on the payroll without going through the job lottery it'd be worth a felony-two fine."

Charley rubbed his hand across his forehead. "Yeah, I know. I sure wouldn't want you to wreck KDS over this—you know that. I'm just—it's not something I was expecting."

"Sure." Whitney's voice was sympathetic. "Look, we're not licked yet—maybe someone in Washington will listen to me. But . . . in case I can't get anywhere, maybe you'd better go sign up with the lottery."

Charley made a face. "I don't want to work anywhere else."

"You think *I* want you to?" was the dry response. "Aside from the fact that you know far too much about our stuff, you're just too good a man to lose. But I have to be honest about your chances here . . . and you can't live off your savings forever."

Charley stared at the floor for a moment, then sighed and got to his feet. "Yeah, you're right. I guess I'd better. I'll check back with you later."

"Yes, please do." Whitney came around from behind his desk and gave Charley a warm handshake. "Good luck."

The world seemed darker when Charley emerged onto the sidewalk. He paused for a moment, feeling a mild disorientation that seemed part of the numbness in his brain, and then turned east and began walking. He still couldn't believe this was really happening to him, that a lifetime of conscientious work could be threatened by something as meaningless as a burp in a bubble-memory somewhere.

Walking in a private fog, he almost passed right by the Baltimore branch of the National Employment Office, a modern building he'd seen often from the commuter but never entered. Steeling himself, he joined the stream of people at one of the revolving doors and made his way inside.

It was unlike anything he'd ever seen, and for a moment he stood rooted in place, taking it all in. The entire first floor seemed devoted to rows and rows of computer terminals. Each machine had a line of people waiting in front of it; around these relatively stable promontories swirled a sea of people traveling to or from other terminals or the huge display boards that lined the walls. In the center of the floor ran a pair of escalators; through their openings he could see that the second floor seemed laid out like the first, and was just as crowded. To his right, on the wall by the entrance, was a building directory, and Charley worked his way across the stream of people until he was close enough to read it. COMPLAINT DEPT. was listed as Room 702. Spotting a bank of elevators, he pushed his way into the crowd. Minutes later, he was on the seventh floor.

Room 702 had nothing of the wide-open spaces of the ground floor, consisting instead of eight boxed-off cubicles with strategically placed upright panels directing the flow of traffic. There were about sixty people ahead of him, so Charley chose one of the shorter lines and settled down to wait. Surprisingly enough, the lines moved quickly, and within a half hour of his arrival he was sitting down across from a tired-looking middle-aged man with frown lines stamped across his face. "Good day, Mr. Ryon—" Charley began, glancing at the desk nameplate.

"Name, number, and previous job category?" the other snapped, fingers resting on his terminal keyboard.

Charley gave them. "What happened, you see, was that I was fired accidentally—"

"Just a minute," Ryon interrupted peevishly. "Your file's not on yet."

Charley subsided. He should have expected a delay; after being at the same job for so long, his records were probably on one of the "low-use" tapes in Washington's master files, and an operator would have to be sent to get it. The way things were going, of course, his file would probably be moved to a more accessible tape on the next adjustment run.

"Says here you were terminated as of Friday, 8 May 2009, from Key Data Services, Baltimore," Ryon said at last. "That true?"

"Yes, but it was an accident—computer malfunction or human error or something."

"Should've corrected it last Saturday. Way too late now. Next!"

"Hold on! That's not fair—no one goes into work on weekends. We should be allowed one *business* day."

Ryon's frown lines deepened a bit. "The book says 'twenty-four hours.' If your boss is too lazy to pull a ten-minute computer overview on weekends, it's not our fault. *Next!*"

Charley didn't budge. "I want to see your superior."

"Forget it. I said you haven't got a case." His finger hovered over a button. "You gonna leave quietly or do we do this the hard way?"

Swallowing, Charley took the easy way.

He got off the elevator on the second floor which, as he'd surmised, was laid out like the first. For a long moment he hesitated, distaste and apprehension holding him back. But Whitney had been right; it only made sense to sign up. Picking a line at random, Charley took his place at the end.

Again, the line moved quickly. Watching the men and women at the keyboard, Charley could tell they were all familiar with this routine. Not only were they fast, but they all invariably skipped past the pages of instructions. Fidgeting uncomfortably, Charley tried to remember everything he'd ever read about the lottery.

Finally, it was his turn. Stepping up to the console, he pushed the "start" button.

TYPE YOUR NAME, NUMBER, AND PREVIOUS JOB CATEGORY, the machine instructed him.

Charley complied. CATEGORY/REGION? it asked.

COMPUTER PROGRAMMER/BALTIMORE, Charley typed carefully.

RANGE?

Range? What did *that* mean? Punching for the first page of instructions, Charley skimmed it and discovered the machine was asking the outer limit of his job interest. 20KM, he typed, picking a distance at random.

The machine answered with a screen full of company names, arranged alphabetically, each one followed by a string of incomprehensible numbers. NUMBER OF JOBS BEING APPLIED FOR IN THIS CATEGORY? appeared at the bottom.

Charley seemed to remember that the limit was ten. 10, he typed.

The computer's response was swift. DISALLOWED. MAXIMUM IS THREE (3).

Charley blinked. *Three?* Had they changed the law? Or was he—or programming in general—a special case? Gritting his teeth, he again called up the instructions.

The impatient rumbling behind him was growing stronger. "Hey, come on, would ja?" someone growled. "We ain't got all month."

"Put it in 'park,'" Charley shot back, tension adding snap to his tone. "I'm working as fast as I can."

"So put in new batteries, huh?" a different voice suggested. "Sign up and let someone else have a turn."

"I'll be happy to, as soon as I figure out how."

There was a loud groan. "Aw, c'mon, friend: you hitting senility early to avoid the crowds?"

Charley felt his face reddening. *"Look—"*

"If you don't know what you're doing, go up to fourth floor and get some help," someone else put in.

Charley hadn't realized help was available. "Yeah, okay," he muttered. Pushing the "cancel" button, he stepped away, the next man in line shouldering past with a growled profanity. Too embarrassed to even turn around, Charley pushed hurriedly through the crowd toward the elevators.

Surprisingly, the fourth floor was practically deserted. Several dozen cubicles like those he'd seen three floors up lined the walls, most of them darkened and apparently empty. Of the handful that were open for business, only about half were being used. The rest of Baltimore's citizenry, Charley reflected, must have learned the ins and outs of the lottery years ago. The thought made him feel old and a little bit silly. Choosing a cubicle with a sympathetic-looking older woman, he hesitantly approached. "Uh . . . excuse me?"

She looked up, folding up the portable thin-screen she'd been watching. "Can I help you?"

"I hope so." He sat down. "I was accidentally fired this weekend, and while my boss tries to get me reinstated I thought I'd sign up for the lottery—just to tide myself over. But I'm afraid I don't understand exactly how to go about it."

"What do you mean?" She frowned. "Are you trying to find a new category or something?"

"No, it's just that I've never had to use the lottery before."

Her eyes widened. "You're kidding. Never?"

"I like my job." He shrugged self-consciously. "I've been there for the past thirty-five years."

That awed look was still there, and Charley felt more than ever like a revived fossil. "Wow!" she breathed. "I didn't think there was *anyone* who hadn't gone through the lottery at least once." She seemed suddenly to realize she was staring and dropped her eyes. "Well, let's see what we can do for you," she continued in a more professional tone, swiveling the terminal screen so that they could both see it. "Could you give me your name, number, and previous job, please?"

He did so. She pushed a few keys, and Charley was faced with the third page of lottery instructions.

"Right, now, first let's figure out how many jobs you can sign up for," she said, tapping a paragraph with her pen. "The longer you've been unemployed, the more job lotteries you can be in. Since you've been out of work less than a week, you can only sign up on three lists. Anything over six months and you can be on twenty of them.

"Each job list is open for sign-up for a minimum of twenty-four hours. Once it's closed, all the names on the list are put in random order by the computer and the company in question hires the first person on it for, usually, at least one four-day week."

"After interviews, you mean?"

The woman blinked. "There aren't any interviews, Mr. Addison. This is an equal opportunity system; we don't allow discrimination over educational advantages any more than over race or religion."

"But—" Charley floundered.

"It really *does* work," she assured him. "Maybe a bit slower than the old methods, but it spreads the jobs and wealth around more evenly and eliminates the need for a welfare system. And *that* saves all of us money."

She was repeating the same arguments that the developers of the system's precursor had used twenty years ago—the arguments, he remembered now, that had originally induced him to vote for it back then. It had seemed like a good idea at the time . . . but now he wasn't quite so sure. "I'll take your word for it," he told her. "What do I do next?"

"Sign up for your three jobs. Let's see . . ." She punched some keys, scanning the displays that flicked across the screen at the touch of a button. "Accounting looks pretty good today—here's a firm that has only thirty people signed up. Here's one with twenty-six."

"Wait a second—I don't know anything about accounting."

She frowned at him. "So? If they get down to your number the law says they *will* hire you for at least a week. Qualifications are irrelevant—equal opportunity, remember?"

"But what if, say, thirty short-order cooks and only one accountant sign up for the job. How is the company going to get the one they need before mid-August?"

"Oh, the law allows concurrent employment if all parties are willing. If the accountant they want is number nine in the lottery, they'd just hire him plus the eight people ahead of him. Those eight would get their week's salary and could leave right away; the accountant would begin work in his new job at the same time. See?"

"Very convenient." Also very expensive if the right person didn't make the top ten. No wonder Whitney always looked so harried when KDS was hiring. "How on Earth do small companies survive a financial shock like that?"

"The smallest companies are exempt from the lottery." She pressed a button and a different page of the lottery instructions appeared. "And there's an intermediate range where the company can hire applicants for only one, two, or three days instead of a full week." She pointed out the appropriate numbers, then turned back to the job listing she'd had on earlier. "You ready to try your luck now?"

"Well . . . I guess so. You really think I should try for that accounting job?"

"Absolutely." She scanned the listing. "The one's up to thirty-two people; the other's hit thirty now. Only six hours to go for each one, too—unless a bunch of people notice how empty they are you should have a good shot at making some money on either one."

"How do you know about that six hours?" Charley asked, squinting at the screen.

She tapped a number with her pen. "Here's the closing date and time: May 8, 1700 hours. This column gives the opening date and time; this one's the job ID number; this one's the yearly salary; and here's the current number of people on the list. Now, what'll it be—one or both?"

Charley pursed his lips. After all, he *was* just looking for something to tide him over until he could get back with KDS. "I guess I'll sign up just on the shorter list."

"Okay." She showed him how to line up the display pointer on the proper job and then how to officially get on the list. "You've got two more chances coming to you. Any preferences?"

He chose two computer programming jobs that would also close at five that evening, ignoring her warning that with three hundred people already signed up for each one he had little hope of making any money from either of them. When he had finished, she showed him how to confirm he was properly registered by calling up his Secure Government Personal File and checking his newly acquired job list. "You can drop out of contention for any of the jobs at any time, by using the display pointer and 'cancel' key. And don't forget, once you've been out of work one to three weeks you can be on five lists at a time."

"Right." Charley made a mental note to find a quiet corner at the library later and read over all these regulations more carefully. "What do I do now?"

"Go home and wait, I guess," she shrugged. "If you've got a computer tie-in on your phone you'll be able to find out your standing on the lottery lists as soon as they close; otherwise, you can find out on the terminals downstairs. If you're high enough, the company'll contact you. If you're really low on the lists, you might as well drop out and sign up on a new list; you'll be automatically dropped as soon as the job is permanently filled, anyway. Any other questions?"

"Well . . . I guess not. Thanks for your help."

"Oh, no problem." She smiled brightly, shaking her head. "Imagine—thirty-five whole years in the same job."

She was still clucking with amazement as she opened up her thin-screen again and settled back to watch.

* * *

It was almost lunchtime when Charley left the National Employment Office building, feeling something like a worn-out paper towel. Not really hungry yet, he decided it would be a good time to do some research on the lottery. A municipal lot was right around the corner, with a handful of the little in-town cars still available. Presenting his driver's-credit card to the attendant, he watched to make sure it was logged correctly into the computer and then drove out of the lot, heading for the nearest branch of the venerable Enoch Pratt Library. Traffic was brisk, but with the city-wide ban on internal combustion engines finally in effect, fighting the crowds was at least no longer a suffocatingly noisy task. Remembering the city of his youth, Charley's irritation at the government eased somewhat. Occasionally, their schemes made life a bit easier.

He emerged from the library about two hours later, slightly boggled at the number of laws and regulations the lottery had generated over the years and completely discouraged as to his chances of finding a loophole he could use. His one half-formed idea—that of setting himself up as a one-man "consulting firm" which KDS could exclusively retain—was scotched early in his reading, and he hadn't been able to come up with anything else that offered even a spark of hope. The National Employment Office had had two decades to close the loopholes, and they'd done a good job. Squinting up at the early-afternoon sun, Charley flipped a mental coin. Lunch lost; climbing into his car, he headed back to KDS.

Will Whitney was off somewhere when Charley arrived, but was expected back momentarily. "I'll wait," Charley told Whitney's secretary. "I haven't got much else to do."

"I heard," she said sympathetically. "We're all pretty upset about it. I hear the people in Programming are missing you already."

"Thanks," Charley grunted. "It's nice to be needed."

Whitney barreled through about ten minutes later. "Charley, hi; come on in," he called as he passed.

"I just stopped by to see if you had anything new," Charley said as he sat down across from Whitney's desk.

"Afraid not," Whitney said distractedly, shuffling through a mound of papers on his desk. "Damn GM chip's got a glitch in it Sanders can't find. Did you give me the preliminary stat sheet yet?"

"Last week," Charley told him. "Look, why don't I go and give Sanders a hand with the debugging?"

"Great. No—wait." Whitney looked up, frowning. "No, you'd better not. I mean, you're no longer on the payroll. . . ." He trailed off.

"You don't need to pay me," Charley assured him. "Come on, Will—I want to help. Consider it a public service to keep my brain from atrophying."

"Believe me, I wish I could let you. But . . . I don't think we can risk it. If someone found out—I mean, there's no way we could prove I wasn't going to pay you under the table."

Charley sighed. "Yeah; and then blam goes a big government fine. I suppose you're right." He stood up awkwardly. "Well, then, I guess I might as well go on home."

"Okay." Whitney had found the paper he wanted. Clutching it, he headed for the door, his free hand sweeping Charley along with him. "Look, I'm still trying to get you back, so keep in touch, okay?"

"Right." Standing in the corridor, Charley watched his boss—his ex-boss—hurry away. Feeling vaguely as if he'd just lost part of his family, Charley turned and trudged toward the exit. A short time later, having turned in his car to the lot at the train station, he was on his way home.

At exactly 5:01 that evening he keyed his phone's computer tie-in and, holding his breath, checked his standings. The list for the accounting position had swelled to one hundred seventy-six since he'd signed up; the computer job rosters hovered near the five-hundred mark. On none of them had he even made it above a hundred.

The next few days settled easily—too easily—into a dull routine. Each morning Charley headed into the city— cursing the fact that the job lottery wasn't accessible from home tie-ins—and fought the crowds at the National Employment Office building. After a few disappointing experiences with the high-paying jobs that attracted lots of applicants, he became adept at flipping through page after page of job listings, scanning for medium-paying ones that were being largely ignored. As a matter of pride, though, he made sure he was always listed for at least one computer-oriented job, even though they were generally long shots. Once signed up, his "work" was done for the day. At first he spent his new free time constructively: catching up on all the journals he'd been promising himself to read, working out at the fleeball courts, and carrying out needed maintenance on his condo. But as the days went by he found himself drifting from self-improvement toward self-indulgence. The trend didn't worry him particularly; sitting in front of his wall thin-screen, he told himself that things would be all right again once he was back at work.

And exactly one week after losing his job, a break finally came. Not the one he'd hoped for, but a break nevertheless.

The receptionist at Dundalk Electronics looked up as Charley came in. "May I help you?" she asked pleasantly.

"My name's Charles Addison; I'm here about the programmer job."

"Down the hall, second door on the right," she said, her voice noticeably cooler.

"Thank you." Wondering what he'd said, Charley left the room and headed down the corridor.

The sign on the door said Employment Office, and the young man behind the anteroom desk had the busy look of a man clawing his way up the corporate ladder. "Yes?" he said as Charley stepped up. "Name, please?"

"Charles Addison. I was called yesterday—"

"Right." The junior exec took a piece of paper from a stack beside him and handed it over. "Sign it and you can have your chit."

Frowning, Charley took it and read the first paragraph. It was a contract stating that he was withdrawing from the lottery for job #442–0761–3228–764 in exchange for a cash payment. "I think there's been a mistake," he said. "I'm here about the programmer job."

The other looked up, mild irritation on his face. "And there's your release. Sign it and you'll get your money."

"But I don't want any money—I want the job."

The younger man stared up at him in disbelief. "What are you trying to pull?" he demanded.

"Nothing. But I'm number eight in the lottery and I'm qualified for the job, so I'd like to take a shot at it."

"But—" the other sputtered. "You can't; we've already hired the woman we wanted."

"Then why did you call me? Wait a minute. What was her lottery number?" Anger was beginning to grow in Charley's mind; anger and a conviction that someone was trying to cheat him. "Well?"

The junior exec hesitated, then took refuge in his intercom. "Mr. Girard; there's someone here I think you'd better see."

A moment later the inner door opened and a broad-faced man strode into the anteroom. "Yes? Is there some problem?"

"This man refuses to sign the lottery release," his subordinate said, pointing at Charley.

Girard's eyebrows rose fractionally. "Is that true, Mr.—?"

"Addison; Charles Addison. Yes, it is. I've worked in computers since I was twenty-three, and I want to take this job."

"I see. Would you step into my office, please?"

Charley followed him inside, sat down in the proffered seat. "Now, Mr. Addison," Girard said, perching on a corner of his desk, "I'm sure you understand the computer industry these days; how fast things are changing and all. I don't doubt that you're an excellent worker, but we need someone fresh from the leading edge of research in the field."

"Mr. Girard, you don't seem to understand. I'm not just someone who wandered in off the lottery—up till a week ago I was chief programmer at Key Data Services. I *know* I can do the job."

"Yes, I'm sure you could—with proper training. But we can't afford to take the time."

"Not even a week? I'm legally entitled to a week, you know."

Girard shrugged. "Quite frankly, Mr. Addison, you'd be wasting both your time and ours. The higher-ups have already decided who they want, and they would be the ones to decide whether or not your work had been satisfactory."

Charley stared at him. "And it wouldn't be, of course," he said bitterly.

The other spread his hands. "It's standard company policy, designed to speed up the employment process. I'm sorry, but there's nothing I can do."

Charley grimaced, a sour taste in his mouth. This was something his reading hadn't prepared him for, and he didn't know how to fight it. Suddenly realizing he was still clutching the release form, he raised it and began reading. A number caught his eye. "This says you're only going to pay me three hundred fifty to drop out of the list. A week's salary for a twenty-five-kay job should be five hundred, shouldn't it?"

"Oh, well, that's standard policy, too. You see, if you're actually hired for a job, even concurrently and only for a week, you lose your buildup of unemployed time. Most of the people we pay off are up to the twenty-listing level and don't want to start over again at three. They're willing to take less money to simply drop out of line and therefore maintain their status."

A status that apparently enabled them to avoid work entirely while still making money. The welfare system hadn't died, Charley realized; it had merely been given plastic surgery and sent out under a new name. "Cute. Probably legal, too."

"Of course." Girard reached into his pocket. "So if you'll just sign the agreement—"

"But I'm not one of your professional moochers," Charley interrupted him. "I prefer to work for my living, even if only for a week at a time."

Girard froze halfway through the motion of handing Charley a pen. "I . . . well, I suppose that would be all right. I guess your status doesn't matter much when you've only been out a week, eh? I'll just get a concurrent-employment agreement—"

"That's not good enough," Charley said calmly. The rules of this game, he was learning, were far different than he'd expected. It was time to find out if they would bend for *him*, too. "Maybe working here *would* be a waste of time—but I've got plenty to spare. If you and your new whiz kid don't want to sit around for a week, you'll have to make it worthwhile for me to drop out."

Girard's eyes narrowed. He was silent a long moment, searching Charley's face. "How much?" he said at last, some of the starch seeming to go out of his backbone with the words.

Pay dirt. Anticipating business as usual, Dundalk Electronics must have jumped the gun. Their new programmer was probably hard at work already—and Charley was suddenly in a strong position. Maybe. "I want two weeks' salary," he told the other, daring greatly. If Girard called his bluff and refused, Charley wasn't at all sure he could get official attention to the case—or even whether the government really prosecuted cases like this.

But Girard didn't refuse. "Wait here," he growled and left the room. Within two minutes he was back with an electronic transfer chit and a new form, both of which he thrust at Charley. Skimming the paper, Charley learned he had accepted a week's concurrent employment at a "special payment rate" of a thousand dollars. The chit was made out in the proper amount; pocketing it, Charley signed the agreement.

"Okay. Now get out," Girard growled as he took back the paper.

Charley stood up. "I don't want you to think I'm deliberately trying to cheat you," he said. "As far as I'm concerned, you're entitled to two weeks' worth of my services. I'm sure I could be of help around—"

"Forget it. And if you ever wind up on one of our lists again, don't think you'll be able to pull this trick twice. Troublemakers like you go onto our computer, and it carries grudges a long time."

"I'll keep that in mind. Good-bye, Mr. Girard."

It was a small victory, Charley realized as he walked outside, and not one he was particularly proud of. Still, getting paid for not working was the next best thing to actually having a job. He just hoped it wouldn't get to be a habit.

"Will, I'm rapidly going nuts. Isn't there *anyone* else you can try?"

Whitney's face, even given the limitations of telephone pictures, looked pretty haggard. "I tell you, Charley, I've gone the whole route. I've talked to everyone in the local Employment Office and half of the button-pushers in Washington. Apparently no one but the director himself can do anything at this point, and he's already refused to intercede. Ignores my letters and calls completely now."

"Maybe you should write to the president," Charley suggested, only half-jokingly.

"Of the United States? I already did. Also the Secretary of Labor. They each sent me back a form letter and list of the administration's accomplishments." Whitney shook his head tiredly. "Look, if you need to borrow some money or something—"

"Aw, no, it's not that," Charley assured him. "I'm making a little bit now and my savings account is still healthy. I just can't stand this business of collecting money for doing absolutely nothing. I thought I'd get used to it, but I'm not. How do people do this for years at a time? Five weeks and already I feel like a cross between a parasite and a professional gambler."

"Have you tried for any government jobs? They're mostly low-skill, low-pay types, but at least you'd be working for your income."

"I'd rather sweep floors for private industry, if it comes to that. Look, Will, if we're stuck, we're stuck. Let's open up the job, and I'll just take my chances with the lottery."

"Well . . ." Whitney seemed acutely embarrassed. "It doesn't look like we can afford to do that. The law limits how much internal shifting we can do when a position is vacated, and it turns out that the lowest job we'd be able to offer on the lottery would be that of level-two programmer. With the thirty-three-kay salary that goes with that we'd get hundreds of applicants, and we can't possibly afford to pay off even a fraction of them. We're just going to have to make do with one less programmer for a while."

Charley felt his jaw sag. "But if you don't even open the job up I won't have *any* chance of getting it back."

"I'm sorry, but we've got no choice. We'd give practically anything to have you back—you know that. But we can't go bankrupt in the process."

"Yeah. Yeah, I understand."

"Again, I'm sorry. If you can come up with any new ideas, I'm game to try them." Whitney glanced away as someone apparently came into his office. "I've got to go. Keep in touch, okay?"

"Sure. Good-bye."

For a minute after the connection was broken Charley remained where he was, staring through the blank screen. The hope of eventually getting his job back was all that had kept him going these past few weeks. He couldn't—*wouldn't*—give that up.

So the director of the National Employment Office wasn't answering calls and letters, eh? Well, there was always the direct approach. Flipping on his computer tie-in, Charley called up the Baltimore–Washington train schedule.

"Mr. Addison, there really isn't any point in waiting—really," the secretary said, her manner one of polite irritation. "Director Pines *never* sees anyone without an appointment."

"I understand," Charley told her from his seat by the

reception room door. "If you don't mind, I'll wait a bit longer. In case he changes his mind."

She sighed and returned to her typing as Charley buried his nose in his magazine again. It was clear that Pines's refusal to see him wasn't merely general policy; the secretary had been in and out of the inner office twice since Charley's arrival, and he had no doubt that the director knew of his presence and business. Equally clear was the fact that Pines wouldn't be coming out through the reception room as long as Charley was waiting to buttonhole him. But if Charley had judged things correctly the director had a private door into his office—a door just within view from Charley's carefully chosen seat. Trying to avoid him was the director's prerogative, of course—but it was almost noon, and Charley doubted Pines had his lunch in there with him. Pretending to read his magazine, Charley gave the private door his undivided attention.

And minutes later his diligence was rewarded as the door opened and a dignified-looking older man slipped out. Dropping his magazine, Charley charged out after him, catching up before the other had gone ten steps. "Dr. Pines? My name's Charles Addison."

Pines glanced at Charley with a look of extreme annoyance and increased his pace. Charley stayed with him. "Dr. Pines, this isn't a problem that'll just go away if you ignore it long enough. I've been cheated out of my job by your system, and I'm not going to give up until I've got it back. Now, are you going to discuss it with me, or am I going to have to follow you all over town?"

With the explosive sigh of barely restrained exasperation Pines stopped abruptly and faced Charley. "Mr. Addison, your complaint was brought to my attention weeks ago," he said, his words precise and clipped. "As I explained to your employer then, the law is *very* clear on the subject of error correction: twenty-four hours—no more—is the time limit. Period; end file; good day."

He started walking again. Charley hurried to catch up. "I don't think that's at all fair, Doctor," he said, "and for a system that bills itself as the first truly fair employment scheme in modern history something like this would be an ugly blot, wouldn't it? How would you feel if the news media got the story?"

Pines didn't even break stride. "To quote the Duke of Wellington, publish and be damned."

So Pines was the type to call bluffs . . . and Charley had already tried vainly to interest the media in his situation. "*Hell*," Charley exploded, his self-control finally breaking. "Look, I've worked and sweated for thirty-five years at a job and company I've really grown to like. I'm a good citizen, I pay my taxes on time, and I've had jury duty twice. Why the hell would it be such blasphemy to bend the rule *just once*?"

Pines stopped again. "Because it wouldn't *be* just once," he snapped. "If I let *you* bypass the rules there would be hundreds of people who'd demand the same privilege, whether their claims were justified or not. A flood like that would cost tremendous time and money, and ultimately hurt both the lottery system and the taxpayers and businesses that support it. It's not worth that kind of risk for *any* job, Mr. Addison—not yours, mine, or anyone else's. If you've been dealt with unfairly, I'm sorry—but I am *not* going to change anything. Understand? Good *day*."

He strode off down the hall with a snort. Charley watched him go, his mind numb with defeat. He'd gone to the very top . . . and come away with absolutely nothing.

The train ride back to Baltimore seemed very long.

He stayed in his condo the next three days, not even coming out to register with the lottery. A great deal of his time was spent staring out the window in deep thought: thought about his past and future, and the things various people had said lately about both.

Perhaps he should just give up and find a permanent job somewhere, even if it weren't in programming. Whitney's comment about the low demand for government jobs kept coming back to him, but the thought left him cold. Even if he couldn't work at KDS, he at least wanted a job in computers somewhere. But after his experience at Dundalk Electronics he wondered if *any* programming firm would hire him, or whether they all preferred fresh new college graduates. And to be honest, he was afraid to find out. In some ways it was infinitely safer to stay on the lottery's pseudowelfare.

Still, something inside him refused to give up . . . and when he woke on the fourth day he had the first faint glimmerings of an idea. Incomplete and even slightly crazy, it was nevertheless all he had left. Getting dressed, he took the next commuter into Baltimore.

It took him ten minutes at a terminal to locate and sign up for all the jobs he could in the proper class. All of them fizzled out by day's end; but the turnover was high, and there was a new crop of them waiting for him the next morning . . . and the next. Doggedly, he kept at it.

And within a week he was in. Job description: maintenance engineer, custodial; evening/weekend shift. Employer: U.S. government. Job location: National Employment Office Administration Building, Washington, D.C. Salary: not worth mentioning.

The National Employment Office had never had a new building designed for it, but had from its beginnings been housed in a century-old structure whose masonry and vaulted ceilings clashed curiously with the ultramodern computer equipment that had been more recently installed. Charley had noticed the contrast on his last visit here—but he hadn't expected the janitorial equipment to match the building's age. The sweepers, waxers, and one genuine monstrosity of a floor buffer were older than they had any right to be. Pushing them around every night was harder work than he would have guessed, and he quickly learned why these jobs changed hands so often.

The soreness generated in Charley's muscles by two nights on the job would be short-lived, though. His supervisor had already made it clear that Charley's first three-day weekend on the job would be his last. No reason aside from "unsatisfactory performance" was given, but Charley could see Director Pines's hand behind it. With the high turnover rate, Charley wouldn't have had to stick with the job more than a month or so to work his way up to field boss—a position that would give him keys to the private as well as public areas of the building. After their last encounter, Charley couldn't blame the director for not wanting that to happen. And that meant that Charley's move had to be made tonight.

"Hey, Addison," a voice came faintly over the floor buffer's roar, breaking into Charley's train of thought. Flipping the buffer off, he turned as Lanthrop, his field boss, sauntered up behind him "I hear this's your last night," Lanthrop continued when the machine's big motor had ground down far enough to permit normal conversation.

"Yep. Back on the lottery tomorrow, I guess," Charley said.

"Too bad. You're a better worker than we mostly get here. Haupt's crazy to send you back."

Charley shrugged. "That's life."

"Yeah. Hey, what say we all go out at break time; treat you to a bottle of the good stuff or something. You know, give you a proper send-off."

"Fine—but we won't have to go anywhere. I figured you guys've been such a big help to me that I owed you one. I won a bottle of the *really* good stuff in a bet the other day, and I brought it along tonight."

Lanthrop's eyes lit up. "Hey, that sounds great. Matter of fact, it sounds so great that I declare it to be break time right now. C'mon, let's get the others."

"I'll do that," Charley volunteered. "Why don't you go on and—um—make sure the stuff's up to your standards. It's in my locker."

With a wide grin, Lanthrop winked. "*Damn*, but I'm gonna hate to lose you."

Charley took his time collecting the other seven custodial workers, and when they arrived downstairs they discovered Lanthrop was well ahead of them. "*Great* stuff, Addison—got a real kick to it!" he called cheerfully, his speech already beginning to slur.

"Sure does," Charley agreed as they all sat down around the table. It ought to, he thought wryly; the bottle had been only two-thirds full of bourbon before he'd filled it up with straight ethanol.

The other workers joined into the spirit of the occasion with remarkable speed. Passing the bottle around the circle—a method that allowed Charley to keep his own consumption to practically zero—they were soon laughing and talking boisterously, wishing Charley good luck in the days ahead. Charley joined in the laughter, and kept the bottle moving.

Lanthrop had a reasonable capacity, but with his head start he was roaring drunk before anyone else was even close, and by the time someone suggested it was time to return upstairs he was sprawled in his chair, slumbering peacefully. Assuring the others he would take care of the boss, Charley waited until they had staggered out, and then set to work. Setting Lanthrop into a more comfortable position, he relieved the field boss of his master keys, replacing them with his own public-area set to keep the loss from being too obvious. His next task took him to the main file room, where the employment records and résumés of every worker in the nation were stored on huge reels of holo-magnetic tape. This was the riskiest part of his plan—the file room connected directly to the main computer room, and the dozen or so operators on duty had a fair chance of knowing that Charley wasn't authorized in there. Fortunately, the reels he wanted were "low-use" ones stored in the racks farthest from the computer itself, and he was able to pull the three he wanted without being seen. Back out in the hall, he hid the tapes in the bottom of the garbage container on his wheeled cleaning-supplies cart and, heart pounding painfully, pushed it down the hall as casually as his shaking knees would permit.

Now came the waiting. From conversations with others, he knew that Director Pines invariably arrived early on Monday mornings, usually before the night shift was due to check out. If Charley's luck held, this would be one of those mornings.

* * *

It was.

Pines was four steps into his office before he noticed Charley sitting quietly by the wall. "Who are you?" he asked, stopping abruptly, apparently too startled for the moment to be angry.

Charley remained seated. "I'm Charles Addison. We met a couple of weeks ago."

The mental wheels visibly clicked into place. "Why, you—you—" he sputtered. "Get the hell out of my office—you hear me? Now!" He stepped forward menacingly.

"Before you do anything drastic," Charley suggested, "you ought to take a look over there in the corner."

Pines came to an abrupt halt. "My tapes!" he exclaimed, the first hint of uneasiness creeping through his anger. "What are you doing with them?"

"Engaging in an old custom called blackmail," Charley told him, glancing at the pile. It *was* an unusual sight, he had to admit: three tape reels—minus their protective casings—stacked neatly beneath the old floor buffer. "Magnetic tapes have come a long way in fifty years, especially in storage density, but they still have an unavoidable weakness: they're susceptible to strong electromagnetic fields. That thing on top is an old electric floor buffer. It packs a huge electric motor."

Pines understood, all right. Already his eyes were flickering between the tapes and Charley, clearly wondering whether he could beat Charley to the buffer's switch. He was bracing himself to charge when Charley raised his hand, showing the director that he held the machine's plug. "The buffer's switched on already," he explained. "All I have to do is plug it in. You can't possibly reach either the tapes or me before they're ruined, so you might as well sit down and relax."

"You're insane," Pines muttered as he sank into a nearby chair. "You can get twenty years for sabotaging government property like this."

"So far nothing's been damaged," Charley assured him.

"You're right, of course, I'll be in big trouble if I plug this in. But have you considered what'll happen to you?"

"What do you mean?"

"Your security's gotten pretty lax. I got into the file room without any trouble, picked up these tapes, and just walked out with them. That's going to make your department look pretty bad."

"You couldn't have taken them out of the building, though—there's an alarm-trigger built into each of the reels."

"Oh? I didn't know that. But that hasn't prevented me from threatening them here in the building itself. I wonder what your bosses at the Labor Department are going to say."

Pines was beginning to look worried, but he still had plenty of fight left in him. "They won't say much. The tapes you've got can be reconstructed, surely. No security system is perfect—they know that. You're the one in trouble, not me."

"I'm sure most tapes *would* be easy to reconstruct," Charley nodded. "With the job market shifting so often, I imagine ninety percent of your master tapes are duplicated at any given time in the thousands of temporary bubble storages you've got in the local offices around the country. But I'll bet that some of the files on *these* three aren't. Don't you want to know which tapes I've got here?"

Pines's eyes flickered to the pile. "All right—tell me."

"They're the complete records of some people who haven't gone through the lottery for a few years now: the President, Cabinet, Supreme Court, most of Congress, and the top people in the Foreign Service, military, and federal judiciary. If I plug this in, you'll have to go to every single one of those people and ask for access to their Secure Personal Files to get the information back. Still think your bosses won't say anything?"

Pines went white. "No!" he hissed. "You wouldn't!"

"That's entirely up to you. You get me my job back at Key Data Services and no one will ever hear about this from me. I'll walk out that door and you'll never see me again."

"At least until you start demanding money," Pines said bitterly.

"With a twenty-year jail sentence hanging over my head? Don't be absurd. Besides, what would I blackmail you with—the use of your legitimate authority to correct an error?" Charley shook his head.

"But the rules—"

"—aren't in charge here: you are. And you're here *because* the rules don't adapt to these unexpected changes, to things that *shouldn't* have happened but did anyway. If they could—if computers could balance justice and mercy—you wouldn't be needed. As it is, a system like the National Employment Office couldn't exist without you—it would have been torn apart years ago."

For a moment Pines gazed into space. Then, with just a glance at the tapes, he stepped over to his desk terminal. "What was the name of that company again?"

And Charley knew he'd won.

"Frankly, Charley, I never expected to see you at this desk again—but I'm damn glad I was wrong," Will Whitney said, smiling like his face was going to split.

"Me, neither," Charley agreed, savoring the feel of his old chair as he gazed at the piles of work on his desk. "I'm glad to see you can still use me. I was half afraid Sanders would've completely taken over by now."

"You kidding? He's happier to have you back than I am." Whitney shook his head. "I'd never realized before how indispensable you are to KDS. I'm glad you found someone in Washington who agreed."

Charley grinned. "That's the whole secret of success, Will. You can accomplish a lot when someone thinks you're irreplaceable." And even more, he thought wryly, when he thinks that of himself.

Afterword

This was my first real foray into the world of business and finance; and as far as I'm concerned, those already in the field can *have* it. I'll take wading through lunar maps and the physics of black holes any day.

The job lottery idea itself came out of a long discussion of such matters with a friend, after which I sat down and hammered at the logic, cash flow, and loopholes until I got to the system you've just read about.

Would it work? I don't know. Though I don't see any flaws, of course (or I would have corrected them before sending the story out in the first place), I've never had an expert in such arcana take it apart for me. Even if it would work, I suspect it would be impossible to actually *get* there from here.

For which—I'm sure—we can all bow our heads in silent thanks.

Teamwork

The hospital bed was uncomfortably hard, with a lump that poked into his lower back no matter how much he squirmed. Not that he could squirm far, of course; the straps across his chest and legs were quite adequate to their task. Staring at the ceiling, tracing imaginary patterns among the holes in the acoustic tile there, he tried to shut out the gurgling sounds from the next bed. The gurgling he hated even more than the crying and laughing.

"Mr. Charles Bissey?"

New voices weren't common here. Lowering his gaze, he focused on the two men at the foot of his bed. One was Dr. Housman, who often appeared in his nightmares these days. The other, standing rather stiffly, was a stranger in a military-type uniform. "Yes," he acknowledged. "Who are you?"

"My name is Colonel Lee, Charles," the stranger said. "We need your help."

Charles glanced at Dr. Housman and sighed. "Sure you do. What is this, Doctor, another of your tests?"

"It's no test, Charles," Housman shook his head. "Please listen to the colonel. This is deadly serious."

"Charles," Lee said, "have you ever heard of the San Bernadino Dome?"

"I'm allowed to read newspapers," Charles told him mildly. "It showed up one night a week ago in a shopping center parking lot. The newspapers think it may be the start of a space invasion."

"Right, although the invasion angle is pure speculation at this point." Lee seemed to be relaxing a bit now. Doubtless he was relieved to find Charles wasn't a raving madman. "But we believe the dome to be a threat in other ways. We'd like you to help us destroy it."

"Suicide mission?" Charles asked. Not that it really mattered.

Lee shook his head. "We hope not. But it *will* be dangerous."

"Why should I help you? What do I get out of this?"

He was prepared for a lecture on patriotism, and Housman's words were therefore a surprise. "Perhaps," the doctor said quietly, "you'll have your dream."

Charles stared hard at him. So many times he'd hoped . . . so many times had watched it all crumble. But he had little else to live for. "I accept," he said.

The preliminary psychomedical work took two days. Charles was in hypnotic sleep a good portion of that time, but it was a strangely exhausting sleep, and he hoped he'd have a chance to rest after it was over. But Colonel Lee was apparently in a hurry, and within an hour he had called a mission orientation meeting.

"Good day to you all," Lee nodded as he strode into the room. "I know you're tired, so I'll make this brief." He touched a switch on the console next to his chair and a picture of a huge gray hemisphere appeared on the room's screen. Behind it could be seen a long building with several different business signs, as well as a section of a city street, all looking like it had been in a war. No people were in sight anywhere.

"The San Bernadino Dome," Lee said. "Thirty meters high at the center, ninety meters across at the base.

Completely impervious to everything we've tried against it. Even the best antitank missiles don't do so much as scratch the surface."

"How about atomic weapons?" Arthur asked.

"We haven't tried anything that drastic yet, but all the extrapolations indicate that even that wouldn't do any good from the outside. From the *inside*, though . . . possibly."

"Wait a minute," Frank growled. "You're not gonna send us into that thing, are ya?"

"We could get hurt!" Dennis piped up.

"Hold it, hold it," Lee said, raising a hand for order. "Getting into the dome shouldn't be physically dangerous. There are already nearly a hundred people inside, by our estimates."

"What do you mean, not *physically* dangerous?" Susan asked in her prim alto. "What kind of dangerous *is* it?"

Lee took a deep breath. "Well . . . it seems that the dome is surrounded by a sort of . . . *effect*, I guess you could call it. Everyone who's gone inside a certain distance drops whatever else he's doing and heads straight for this door." He indicated a black triangle on the dome. "We've tried sending people just over the edge of the effect and then hauling them back with ropes, and once they're back outside they're okay again. They report a tremendous compulsion to get into the dome, but no idea why they were wanted. Our experts say the effect resembles a strong hypnosis, but they have no idea how the order was implanted. What happens inside is anyone's guess; all we know is that the agents we sent in with bombs apparently never triggered them. Yes, Charles?"

Charles spoke up hesitantly, still shy in the presence of the others. He'd met them barely three hours earlier, and his natural bashfulness with strangers made his tongue feel awkward. "I take it, Colonel, that you think we can get past this conditioning?"

"Of *course* he thinks that, dummy," Arthur snapped. "Why else would we be here?"

"Actually, we *don't* expect all of you to get through untouched," Lee said quickly, perhaps seeing Charles's blush. "Frankly, we'll be happy if any one of you can get in with enough control left to carry out the mission. We really don't know what will happen to you since—well—"

"Since everyone else who's gone in has been perfectly sane?" Charles suggested.

"Now, Charles, don't pick on the colonel," Susan admonished.

Lee spread his hands in a gesture of helplessness. "I know it sounds cruel and manipulative, but yes, that's precisely why we recruited you. The hypnosis isn't perfect; it has limitations—"

"How do you know?" Arthur spoke up quickly.

"Because on that first morning people were dribbling into the dome in ones and twos until we set off the sirens; after that there was a general rush. From that we gather the hypnosis wasn't strong enough to wake people up or make people walk in their sleep. People like you, we hope, will also be outside the thing's capabilities. The experimental technique that set you up with your new pseudotelepathic intercommunication may help, too—spread the effect around or something."

"Or maybe it won't," Frank said. "If y'ask me, this is a whole lotta work for nothin'. The door to the thing's open, right? So toss in a nuke and get it over with."

"Frank!" Susan was aghast. "There are a hundred *people* in there. Not to mention whoever was there to begin with."

"So what?"

"Actually," Lee said, "we couldn't do that even if the dome were empty. There's an airlock sort of arrangement that seems to be made of the same material as the dome. As an absolute last resort, we might try sending in a volunteer with an activated time bomb. But even if that worked—which isn't at all certain—it would mean sacrificing anybody who may still be alive in there." He shrugged, looking uncomfortable. "Anyway, the high-level decision was made to give you a chance first."

"That's all well and good, Colonel," Susan said, "but I, for one, want to know why you want so badly to destroy this artifact. It doesn't seem to be doing anything threatening, so as long as you keep people away from it, what's the trouble? Death and destruction are easy, I suppose, but they're so *final*."

"The trouble," Lee answered, "is that, whatever the owners of the dome want with the people they've grabbed, they've decided they want more . . . and since we've evacuated the whole area they can't get them. So they're expanding their compulsion-effect field. The thing's pushed another hundred meters out in the past four days and shows no signs of stopping."

There was a long moment of silence. "Well," Lee said at last, "if there are no more questions or comments, I'll let you get some rest. You'll start a couple of days of saboteur training tomorrow morning. Good-bye for now."

The next two days were frantic, filled with intensive studies. Charles had always envied people who could assimilate knowledge quickly, and was more than a little surprised that he was actually able to keep up. He became adept at putting together the tiny nuclear bomb the team would be taking into the dome, and discovered that he had a distinct aptitude for solving logic problems. Though little time had been specifically set aside for the members of the team to get to know each other, Charles found himself becoming more relaxed in their company as they worked and learned together. He didn't consider them friends, of course—true friendships had been few and far between for him—but he no longer feared them as enemies, either. On the whole, that was already more than he'd hoped for.

All too soon, it was time. A midnight plane ride—with Dennis gurgling excitedly at the stars overhead—and a short drive brought the team to a line of grim-faced soldiers patrolling the deserted San Bernadino streets. A major pointed the way and offered good luck.

The first twenty steps were the hardest, at least for Charles. He felt as if he were walking through a mine field: never knowing when it would happen; wondering if it would hurt or not; almost hurrying so as to get it over with. Compulsively, he found himself counting the steps: nineteen, twenty, twenty-*one*—

And with the suddenness of a light switch a red haze seemed to drop over his vision, and all thoughts fled before the overpowering desire to get into the dome. He broke into a run, dimly aware of the others but incapable of taking the slightest interest in them. The buildings around him were gray fog; but as he rounded one last corner a burst of color assaulted his senses. It was the dome, as bright and eye-catching as the finest sunset he'd ever seen and utterly irresistible. The triangular entrance beckoned; lowering his head he increased his speed. Ninety seconds later, he was inside.

"Well," Arthur said aloud, his words coming in short bursts as his wind slowly returned, "that was . . . quite a race. Everyone . . . okay?"

"Yeah," Frank said.

"I feel fine," Susan replied. "Dennis?"

"Wow! These roofs are really high," Dennis chirped, oblivious to the others' conversation. "Can we go up there?"

"*Ceilings*, kid, not *roofs*," Frank growled. "Let's get movin' before someone comes along, huh?"

"Can we go up there?" Dennis repeated, more insistent this time.

"Not just now," Arthur said. The catwalks twenty feet above them were far too high for his taste. "Maybe later." He looked back down quickly and glanced around the room they'd wound up in. The walls were lined with pipes and strangely shaped machinery, but he could see what looked like a pair of doors in the far wall. "Looks like that's the way deeper in," he said.

"Wait a minute," Susan cut in. "Charles? Charles, are you okay?"

"I . . . I think they got me," Charles murmured. "I'm sorry."

"Damn!" Frank growled.

"Okay, relax," Arthur said, trying to keep his excitement from showing. He could be leader now! "Are you going to be fighting us, Charles, or are you just going to be deadweight from now on?"

"I don't know. I don't feel like shouting out the truth or anything. I just feel like doing what . . . I guess it's what they told me to do when we came in."

"Well, that'll do for now, I suppose. If it changes, let me know fast and we'll either sit on you or try to work around your conditioning. Now, what exactly—"

"Wait a second," Frank cut in. "Who died and left *you* in charge?"

"This is the pecking order Lee gave us, remember?" Arthur said. "Charles first, then me. *Then* you."

"Yeah, but—"

"Then it's settled. Dennis, stop that whimpering."

"Is Charles sick?" Dennis asked anxiously, his voice trembling.

"Oh, for— Susan, explain it to him, will you? We've got to get moving. Charles, what exactly did they tell you to do?"

"I'm supposed to go through the left door up there, down a corridor, right at the second cross-corridor—"

"Hold it," Arthur interrupted. "Does all this take us further in or just around the edge of the dome?"

"Uh . . . I think all the way to the center."

"Then let's just go. What happens when we get to the center?"

"I'll be helping to put together some kind of machine."

The door opened into a narrow corridor. Glancing up, Arthur noted that the catwalks from the room extended over the corridor as well, passing through the six-foot gap between the tops of the walls and the arched ceiling. Would there be guards posted up there?

"This doesn't make any sense at all," Susan complained as they started down the corridor. "Why should the creatures who live in here need people to help build their machines?"

"Maybe they don't know how," Dennis suggested.

"Then how's Charles supposed to figure it out?" Frank snorted. "More likely they're all dead."

"Dead?" Susan sounded appalled.

"Or else never here," Arthur mused. "I didn't notice any effort to filter the air at the entrance. What kind of alien would be stupid enough to risk breathing our germs?"

"Then who's running this thing?" Frank argued. "Some kind of computer?"

"Why not?"

"Because whoever built it should have made sure it could repair itself," Susan said.

"Damn it, Susan, lemme handle my own fights," Frank snapped.

"Don't you swear at *me*," she returned icily.

"All right, everyone, take it easy," Arthur put in, desperately trying to hold things together. "Looks like we're coming into a main room up here. Everybody stay alert and look for a good place to plant the bomb."

The final door opened, and the sight behind it silenced even Frank. The room was *huge*—covering perhaps a quarter of the dome's floor area—and stocked with a bewildering collection of machines and what could only be the aliens' equivalent of electronic equipment. The other trapped humans were there, too, working at various tasks with a diligence uncomfortably reminiscent of ants. There was no talking or other obvious communication; it wasn't even clear whether the laborers were aware of each other's presence. And in the center of the room—

A miniature version of the dome itself.

Dennis was the first to say anything. "Wow! This is *neat!*"

"What the hell *is* this?" Frank asked, bewilderment in his voice. "Some kinda Chinese puzzle box?"

"You're thinking of Russian dolls, I think," Arthur corrected absently. "I don't think there are more than just these two, though—that little one's barely twenty feet tall; I'd guess."

"They're certainly paying a lot of attention to it," Susan pointed out.

Even as she spoke, a group of five people left one of the machines carrying a small device they had apparently been building there. Maneuvering it carefully, they worked it through the outsized triangular door of the smaller dome and disappeared inside.

"Wonder what that was," Arthur muttered.

"One of *those*," Dennis piped up, pointing to one of the machines lining the room's walls.

"Shut up," Frank growled.

"No, wait—he's right," Susan said. "See? It was a smaller version of that machine; same shape and color pattern." Abruptly, she caught her breath. "They're making a *baby dome*."

"Uh, excuse me," Charles spoke up into the silence, "but I'm supposed to help with something over across the room."

"Okay," Arthur said, making a quick decision. "Let's do it. You just go ahead and take the lead."

"*What?*" Frank snapped. "The hell with this. Let's just drop the bomb someplace and get outta here."

"What about the other people?" Susan asked.

"Hell with 'em."

"Absolutely not." Susan's voice left no room for argument. "They're not here of their own free will. We aren't just going to leave them to die."

"Besides which," Arthur said, overriding Frank's comeback, "we've got another little problem here. If that dome's made of the same stuff as the big one, we're going to have to put a bomb inside it if we want to be sure of knocking it out."

"So?"

"Don't be stupider than you have to, Frank," Arthur snapped, suddenly tired of him. "We *also* need a bomb out here . . . and we only have *one*. So until we come up with an idea, we've got to stay as inconspicuous as possible."

They reached the target machine a minute later, and their first close look at the human workers elicited gasps from Susan and Dennis and a curse from Frank. Two of the four people working over the machine looked like refugees of the Nazi starvation camps: gaunt and pallid, with thin arms and sunken cheeks. The other two weren't in much better shape.

"Colonel Lee said some of the people had been in here since the dome appeared," Susan said in a choked voice. "That's nearly twelve *days* ago."

"Maybe the dome doesn't know enough to feed them," Arthur suggested, feeling slightly sickened. "Still . . . I suppose that's good, in a way. It means the dome can't read minds."

"Arthur, we've got to get this over with as soon as possible," Susan said. "These people need medical attention right away."

"If you can suggest a way to make one bomb into two," Arthur grunted, "I'd be happy to do so."

"Well, why don't you just find one of the agents Colonel Lee said had come in and take *his* bomb?"

There was a short pause. "That's easy to say," Frank grumbled, sounding impressed in spite of himself. "But how are we gonna find any of 'em in this crowd?"

"He'll be wearing street clothing, for one thing," Susan pointed out. "At least half these people are in pajamas and nightgowns. We could just . . . well, frisk all the possibilities."

"Let's try just *looking* at their clothing to start with," Arthur suggested. "Everyone here's lost a lot of weight, and their clothes are hanging unnaturally. Check for any extra bulges or the kind of wrinkle lines you get with something heavy in your pocket."

The casual stroll around the room took several minutes, and it was Dennis who spotted it first. "Over there!" he bubbled excitedly. "Under his arm—see? I found him!"

"Looks like it, awright," Frank said. "Lemme get it—he might put up a fight."

"Frank!" Susan snapped. "Don't you *dare*—"

"He'll do what he has to, Susan," Arthur cut in brusquely. "Frank has a job to do here, just like the rest of us. Let's *do* it." Without waiting for comments he headed toward the other man, pleased with his last speech. All good leaders, he knew, should know how to be eloquent when necessary.

As it turned out, both his speech and Susan's fears were for nothing. The agent kept at his job, offering no resistance as Frank lifted his coat and relieved him of the innocent-looking black box.

"Half-hour delay," Frank muttered, peering at the lettering by the uncrimped metal tube that held the bomb's chemical fuse. "Not any better than ours."

"Yeah," Arthur agreed. "Well . . . let's get ours put together. Then we'll figure out how to get one into the little dome—yes, Charles, what *is* it?"

"I've got to get back," Charles said, a hint of desperation sounding clearly in his voice. "I've got *work* to do—back at my machine—"

"Hey, hey, hey—don't go nuts on us now." Arthur thought quickly. "Frank, give me a hand here—we've got to hang onto him. Susan, get that bomb assembled, pronto. Charles, you just try to relax—or struggle, if that makes you feel any better."

"I'm . . . trying . . . to fight it," Charles whispered. "It's . . . *strong*. . . ."

"Susan!" Arthur snapped. "Hurry up."

"Almost done," Susan said, an island of calm in the tension. "We still haven't figured out how we're going to get these people out of here, though."

"Forget . . . 'em," Frank managed.

"Is Charles sick again?" Dennis spoke up timidly.

"He'll be all right," Susan soothed. "The machines in the dome are trying to make him do something he doesn't want to do."

"Can't you make them stop?"

"I'm afraid— Dennis, that's it!" Susan interrupted herself abruptly. "Arthur—all we have to do is to find and shut off whatever machine's doing this to Charles and the others. In fact, we don't really have to destroy anything else."

"The hell we don't." Without warning, Frank snatched a nutcrackerlike tool from a man at a nearby machine. Before any of the others could act, he'd crimped the fuses on both bombs.

"Frank!" Arthur all but bellowed. "Why did you do that?"

"'Cause we can't hold onto Charles forever," the other snarled. "What if he gets loose and gets all of us killed? I sure as hell wanna take this damn dome with me when I go."

"Frank, *when* are you going to stop thinking with your fists?" Susan groaned, her anger already turned to resignation. "Why must you *always* put things in terms of fighting?"

"Are we gonna plant these or not?" Frank asked impatiently, ignoring her.

"Of course we are," Arthur said. "There—that group heading toward the little dome. We'll put one of the bombs on top of that console they're carrying and make sure none of them tosses it off. The other one can be put down anywhere out here."

If the group of workers so much as noticed Frank adding the flat box to their burden, they gave no sign. Disappearing into the small dome, they emerged a few minutes later empty-handed. Frank didn't wait for further instructions, but simply shoved the second bomb under the nearest machine.

"Now," Arthur said, trying not to show his tension, "we've got just twenty-five minutes to find that hypnosis machine and get out of here." He took a long, sweeping look around the room, and for the first time the enormity of that task hit him. There were literally hundreds of instruments lining the walls, not even counting the freestanding ones scattered around.

How were they going to find the right one?

"This is ridiculous," Frank said. "What're we supposed to do, smash everything in sight?"

"No," Charles gasped. "It's easier than that."

"What is it, Charles?" Arthur asked, suddenly alert. Charles, after all, had a sort of inside track here. "You know which one it is?"

"No. But—" He halted, as if having to fight out the words. "The people here . . . building and . . . and fixing things. We're not . . . working like we're . . . supposed to."

And suddenly Arthur understood. "*Aha!* Got it!" He scanned the room again, and this time he saw it. "Over there, on the wall—that gadget with eight people working on it. Let's go."

"But how do you know that's the right one?" Susan asked.

"Because no one was working over there when we first came in."

"Huh?" Frank asked.

"It's really very simple." Arthur grinned tightly. "We're not doing what we're supposed to; therefore, the hypnosis gadget must have developed a fault—and therefore, the dome's started getting people over there to try and fix it."

The workers had the instrument's cover off by the time Frank began shoving through the group. For the first time there was resistance to his advance, as if the dome had belatedly recognized the magnitude of the threat and was trying to counter it. But long starvation had left far too little strength to the men, and Frank brushed them aside as if they were children. Seizing the heaviest tool within reach, he began flailing about at the exposed circuitry. His first three blows seemed to have no effect; but at the fourth—

"That's it!" Charles shouted.

And all around the room activity suddenly ceased, replaced by an equally abrupt babble as all the frustration and terror of the past days found release in newly loosened tongues. But Charles was ready, and before the noise had time to reach panic levels, he filled his lungs and bellowed, "Everybody get out of here *now!* This dome will blow up in less than twenty minutes. The door's in that direction; *move!*"

Perhaps the time under hypnosis had left a residual susceptibility to orders, or perhaps getting out simply struck them all as the smart thing to do. But whatever the reason, they obeyed without question or complaint. It wasn't easy—in the absence of artificial compulsion, the physical drain of their ordeal abruptly appeared. But with a lot of mutual support, they kept moving.

"I don't suppose there's any way to disarm the bombs," Susan said wistfully. "I mean, now that there's no reason to destroy all of this . . ."

"No reason, my eye," Charles snorted. "You never felt how *strong* that hypnosis machine was. If anyone got ahold of it and figured out how to make it work again—"

"Would it hurt people?" Dennis asked.

"Very much," Susan sighed. "You're probably right, Charles. Let's just get out of here, then."

There was less than a minute to go on the fuses when they reached the first row of buildings, the point at which Charles had earlier gotten his first glimpse of the dome. "It was a lot more colorful before," he commented to no one in particular as he turned for one final look. "Must have been part of the hypnosis."

"Can we stay here and watch the bang?" Dennis asked eagerly.

"Probably won't be much to see," Charles told him. "The dome will contain most of the explosion, and anything that leaks out the door probably won't be very bright."

"Aw, what the hell," Frank said, to everyone's surprise. "Let's let the kid have a look."

"I thought you didn't like Dennis, Frank," Susan said.

"Naw, he's okay. And—look, he did his share, right?"

"Sure," Charles said. "Okay, we'll stay."

The seconds ticked by. "Even if we don't see anything, we ought to feel the ground shake when they go off," Arthur remarked, talking to cover up his nervousness. He had led them through the critical part of the mission; he alone was responsible for success or failure. And if— somehow—this didn't work, no one would ever let him be a leader again.

"Oh, I'm sure we'll see *some*thing," Susan assured him.

As it turned out, she and Charles had both rather underestimated things.

This hospital, he decided early on, was much nicer than the other one. Not only was the bed more comfortable, with no lumps or straps, but the nurses were friendlier and more attentive. His eyes still hurt a little beneath their bandages and the perpetual darkness was sometimes scary, but Dr. Housman and the others assured him he would be all right. Best of all, there were none of the horrible sounds of the other hospital here; no one laughed or cried or gurgled. He slept a great deal now, and nightmares were no longer commonplace.

"Charles?" a familiar voice asked softly. "Are you awake?"

"Hello, Colonel Lee," he said. "I didn't hear you come in."

There was the sound of a chair being pulled over to his bed. "I thought I'd drop by and let you know that all of the people you got out of the dome are off the critical list now, though most are still pretty weak."

"Glad to hear it. You ever figure out what went wrong that the dome needed them?"

"Only indirectly—you didn't leave us a whole lot to study, you know. But a couple of the others told us they saw a bunch of things that looked like robots lying around one of the outer corridors. Best guess is that the dome had an accident and lost control of its automated workers. Whether recruitment of native help was already programmed in or whether the dome was smart enough to develop the hypnosis field from scratch we'll probably never know."

"So it really wasn't a threat, after all."

Lee must have heard the regret in his voice. "We don't *know* that. It's quite possible that it intended to cover the whole globe with copies of itself. And even if it wasn't deliberately threatening us, the people inside would have started dying very soon. Who knows how big the field would have become, or how many people would have been sucked in to die? No, Charles, you did the right thing. Now, I'm going to leave and let you rest, but I want you to hurry up and get well. The president is anxious to meet you—" he paused dramatically—"at the White House ceremony where you'll be getting the Medal of Freedom."

Charles tried to find the right words; finally gave up. "Thank you," he said.

"You earned it. All of you did." A hand briefly gripped his shoulder. "I'll drop back in next week, after the bandages are off your eyes. Good-bye for now."

Charles heard him walk to the door and open it. Another voice greeted Colonel Lee as he stepped into the corridor: Dr. Housman's, Charles recognized it. For a moment the two men talked by the open door; and while the conversation was obviously meant to be private, Charles had always had exceptional hearing.

"How's he doing?" Lee asked.

"Better than our best predictions, I'm delighted to say. That new hypnotic technique for intrapsyche communication was very helpful, but I personally think the success of his mission played a bigger role. Low self-esteem, you see, is often at the root of these really chronic cases. Eliminate that problem and you're halfway home."

"So who did I just talk to? I mean, who's where now?"

"The Susan and Dennis fragments have been completely integrated into the main Charles personality. Arthur and Frank are still separate—especially Frank; Charles still has a great deal of suppressed anger within him—but both are moving toward integration. I give them a month, maybe less. If you've got a few minutes I can show you the progress charts."

The voices faded as the two men moved away down the hall. "A month," Charles whispered to himself, savoring the sound of the words. One month . . . and he would have his dream.

He would be whole.

Afterword

This was another story whose original (unsalable) version refused to stay banished in my reject files—not for any particular philosophical reasons, but because it was such a *neat* little sinking curve ball to throw at the unsuspecting reader. The nicest thing about it was that every bit of dialogue was perfectly fair and legal, owing entirely to the often annoying fact that in English "you" can be either singular or plural.

And yet, even in what's essentially a gimmick story, I find myself growing to like my characters. I hope Charles made it; he certainly deserved to.

The Final Report on the Lifeline Experiment

It has been less than a month now since the sealed personal files of the late Daniel Staley have been opened, but already the rumors are beginning to be heard: rumors that explosive new information concerning the Lifeline Experiment has been uncovered. Though these rumors contain a grain of truth, they are for the most part the products of prejudice and hysteria, and it is in an effort to separate the truth from the lies that I have consented to write this report. Since, too, I find that even after twenty years a great number of popular misconceptions still surround the experiment itself, I feel it is necessary for me to begin with a full recounting of those controversial events of 1994.

I suppose I should first say a word about my credentials. I became Dr. Staley's private secretary in 1989 and continued in this role full-time until his tragic death. My usefulness to him stemmed from my eidetic memory which, especially when coupled with his telepathic abilities, made me a sort of walking information retrieval system for him. It is also the reason I can claim perfect accuracy for my memories of the events and conversations I am about to describe.

The popular press usually credits Dr. Staley with coming up with the Lifeline Experiment idea on his own, but the original suggestion actually came from the Reverend Ron Brady in mid-January of 1994. Brady, a good friend of Dan's, was driving us back to San Francisco from a seminar on bioethics at USC and the conversation, almost inevitably, turned to the subject of abortion.

"You realize last week's decision makes the third time the Supreme Court's reversed itself in the last twenty years," Brady commented. "I think that must be some kind of record."

"I wasn't keeping score, myself," Dan replied, stretching his legs as far as the seat permitted. It had been a hard weekend for him, I knew; though it had been over two years at that point since the National Academy of Sciences had officially certified his telepathic ability, there were still a few die-hard skeptics around determined to prove he was a fraud. From the number of handshakes I'd seen him wince over I gathered most of the doubters must have converged on USC for the weekend, and he was only now beginning to relax.

"It's crazy." Brady shook his head. "The legality of something like that shouldn't change every time a new administration sets up shop in Washington. It makes for emotional and legal chaos all around and gives the impression that there are no absolute standards of morality at all."

Dan shrugged. "You know me, Ron. I believe in letting people do what they like in this life, on the theory that whatever they do wrong will catch up with them in the next."

Brady smiled lopsidedly. "The laissez-faire moralist. But don't we have an obligation to help our fellow men minimize the problems they'll have in the next life? That seems to me a perfectly good rationale for the inclusion of morality in law."

Dan reached a hand back over the seat toward me. "Iris: a devastating quotation to put this fellow in his place, if you please."

I made no move to take his hand. "I'm sorry, Dr. Staley," I said primly, "but it would be unethical for me to help you in your arguments. Especially against a man of the cloth."

He chuckled, threw me a wink, and withdrew his hand. "Seriously, though, I don't see how you can expect anything but political flip-flopping when you have an issue that's so long on emotion and so short on real scientific fact. A human fetus is alive, certainly; but so are mosquitoes and inflamed tonsils. *When* a fetus becomes a human being and entitled to society's protection is something we may never know."

"True." Brady glanced at Dan. "Maybe you ought to try contacting a fetus telepathically someday; see if *you* can figure it out."

"Sure," Dan deadpanned. "I could go in claiming to be womb service or something."

Brady came back with a pun of his own, and the conversation shifted to the topic of microcurrent therapy for certain brain disorders, where it remained for the rest of the drive. But even though Dan didn't say anything about it for four months, it is clear in retrospect that Brady's not-quite-serious comment had taken root in his imagination. Even for somebody as phlegmatic as Dan, the possibility that he could take a swing at such a persistent controversy must have been an intriguing idea, especially after the weekend he'd just gone through. Unfortunately, it also is abundantly clear that he started things in motion without any real understanding of what he was getting himself into.

It was just before five o'clock on May 23, and I was preparing to go home when Dan called me into his office. "Iris, didn't I meet a couple of professors in the Child

Development Department of Cal State Hayward down at USC last January? What were their names?"

"Dr. Eliot Jordan and Dr. Pamela Halladay," I supplied promptly. "Do you want the conversation, too?"

He pursed his lips, then nodded. "I'd better. I'm pretty foggy on what they were like."

I sat down next to him and took his hand in mine. Even now there are many people who don't realize that Dan's telepathy required some form of physical contact with his subject. They envision him tapping into the secrets of government or industry from his San Mateo home. In reality a moderately thick shirt would block his reception completely.

The conversation hadn't been very long to begin with, and playing it back took only a few seconds. When I'd finished, Dan let go and frowned off into space for a moment, while I played the conversation back again for myself, wondering what he was looking for. "They both seemed pretty reasonable people to you, didn't they?" he asked, breaking into my thoughts. "Competent scientists, honest, no particular axes at the grindstone?"

"I suppose so." I shrugged. "It might help if you told me what you had in mind."

He grinned. "I'll show you. What's the phone number over there?"

I gave him the college's number, and within a few minutes he'd been routed to the proper department. "Of course I remember you, Dr. Staley," Dr. Jordan said after Dan had identified himself and mentioned their brief USC meeting. Even coming out of a tiny phone speaker grille, his voice sounded as full and hearty as it had in person. "It would be very hard to forget meeting such a distinguished person as yourself. What can I do for you?"

"How would you like to help me with an experiment that might possibly put the lid on the abortion debate once and for all?"

There was a long moment of silence. "That sounds very interesting," Jordan said, somewhat cautiously. "Would you care to explain?"

Dan leaned his chair back a notch and began to stroke his cheek idly with the end of his pencil. "It seems to me, Doctor, that the issue boils down to the question of when, exactly, the fetus becomes a human being. I believe that, with a little bit of practice, I might be able to telepathically follow a fetus through its entire development. With luck, I may be able to pin down that magic moment. At worst, I may be able to show that a fetus *isn't* human during the entire first month or trimester or whatever. Either way, an experiment like that should inject some new scientific facts into the issue."

"Yes," Jordan said slowly, "depending on whether your findings would be considered 'scientific' by any given group, of course." He paused. "I agree that it's at least worth some discussion. Can you come to Hayward any time this week to talk about it?"

"How about tomorrow afternoon?"

"Tomorrow's Tuesday . . . yes, my last class is over at two."

"Good. I'll see you about two, then. Good-bye."

"Good-bye."

Dan hung up the phone and looked at me. "Does that answer your question?"

It took me a moment to find my voice. "Dan, you're crazy. How exactly do you propose to read a fetus's mind without climbing into the embryonic sac with it?"

"Via the mother's nervous system, of course. There must be neural pathways through the placenta and umbilical cord I can use to reach the fetus's brain."

"With the mother blasting away and drowning out whatever the fetus may be putting out?"

"Well, yes, I suppose that might be a problem," he admitted.

"*And,* even if you do manage to touch the baby's mind, are you even going to know it?" I persisted. "This isn't going to be like the colic studies you did with Sam Sheeler, you know—those babies were at least being exposed to a normal range of stimuli. What on Earth has a fetus got to think about?"

He grinned suddenly. "I *said* it might take some practice." He stood up. "Look, there's no sense dithering over these questions now. We'll go see Jordan tomorrow and hash it all out then. Okay?"

"All right," I said. "After all, if it doesn't work out, no one will ever have to know we came up with such a crazy idea."

"That's what I like about you, Iris: your confidence in me. See you tomorrow."

We arrived on the Hayward campus at two o'clock sharp the next day—and it took only ten minutes for my hopes of keeping this idea under wraps to be completely destroyed.

They were waiting for us outside the door to Jordan's office: a man and woman, both dressed in conservative business suits. I recognized them from TV news shorts of the previous year, but before I could clue Dan in they had stepped forward to intercept us. "Dr. Staley?" the man said. "My name's John Cooper; this is Helen Reese. I wonder if we might have a word with you?" He gestured down the hall to where the door of a small lounge was visible.

"We have an appointment with Dr. Jordan," I put in.

"He's not back from class yet," Mrs. Reese said. "This will only take a few minutes, if you don't mind."

Dan shrugged. "All right," he said agreeably.

The others remained silent until we were seated in a small circle in a corner of the otherwise deserted lounge. "Dr. Staley, we understand you're planning some sort of experiment with Dr. Jordan to determine when life begins," Cooper said, leaning forward slightly in his chair. "We'd like to ask you a few questions about this, if we may."

Dan cocked an eyebrow. "I fail, first of all, to see how you learned about my private conversation with Dr. Jordan," he said calmly, "and, secondly, to understand what business it is of yours."

"Mr. Cooper is the Bay Area president of the Family Alliance," I told him. "Mrs. Reese is their chief antiabortion advocate."

They both looked at me with surprise. "I see," Dan

nodded. "Well, that explains the second part of my question. You folks want to take a crack at the first part now?"

"How we heard about it is unimportant," Mrs. Reese said. "What *is* important is that we find out how you stand on the abortion issue."

Dan blinked. "Why?"

"Surely, Doctor, you understand the highly subjective nature of the experiment you're planning," she said. "Naturally, we need to know what your own beliefs are concerning when life arises."

"My telepathic ability is *not* subjective," Dan said, a bit stiffly. "It's as scientific and accurate as anything you'd care to name. Whatever my beliefs happen to be, I can assure you they do *not* interfere with either my perception or interpretation."

"Beliefs *always* affect interpretation, to one degree or another," Cooper said. "Now, you yourself said you could prove the fetus wasn't human until the second trimester of pregnancy. It seems to us that, with such an attitude, you would be very likely to interpret any brain activity before that point as 'nonhuman,' whether it is or not."

Dan looked at me. "Iris?" he invited.

I nodded. "The exact quote, Dr. Cooper, was as follows: 'At worst, I may be able to show that a fetus *isn't* human during the entire first month or trimester or whatever.' End quote. Dr. Staley made no assumptions in that statement. I suggest you ask your spies to be more accurate in the future."

Reese bristled. "We weren't spying on anyone, Miss Marx; the information relayed to us was obtained quite legitimately."

"I'm sure it was," Dan said, getting to his feet. "Now if you'll excuse us, Dr. Jordan is expecting us."

The rest of us stood, as well. "We haven't finished our conversation, though——" Cooper began.

"Yes, we have," Dan interrupted him. "If—*if*, mind you—I do this experiment it'll be because I'm convinced it can be done objectively and accurately. If you have any suggestions or comments you're welcome to write them up and send them to my office. Good day."

Threading between them, we left the lounge.

Jordan and Dr. Pamela Halladay were waiting for us when we arrived back at Jordan's office. "Sorry we're late," Dan told them after quick handshakes all around, "but we ran into the local ethics committee. Any idea how the Family Alliance might have overheard our conversation, Dr. Jordan?"

The two of them exchanged glances, then Jordan grimaced. "My secretary, probably," he said. "I called Pam right after I talked to you, and the door to her office was open. I'm sorry; it never occurred to me that she'd go off and tell anyone."

"No harm done," Dan shrugged. "Let's forget it and get down to business, shall we?"

"Your idea sounds very interesting, Dr. Staley," Halladay said, "but I think there are one or two technical points that need clearing up. First of all, would you be following a single fetus from conception to term, or would you try to reach a group of fetuses at various stages of growth?"

"I hadn't really thought that much about it," Dan said slowly. "I suppose the second method would be faster."

"It would give better statistics, too," Jordan said. "What do you think, Pam—would a hundred be enough?"

"A hundred subjects?" Dan said, looking a little taken aback.

"Well, sure. If you want this to have scientific validity you'll need a reasonable sample. Why?—did you have a smaller number in mind?"

"Yeah. About ten." Dan frowned. "Maybe we could compromise at twenty-five or so."

"You cut the sample too small and it won't be scientific enough to satisfy the skeptics," Jordan warned.

"Whether it'll be scientific enough anyway was my second question," Halladay put in.

We all looked at her. "What do you mean?" Jordan asked.

"Oh, come on now, Eliot—the heart of the scientific method is the reproducibility of an experiment. With only one proven telepath on Earth, this one is inherently unrepeatable. Whatever Dr. Staley concludes we'll have to take on faith."

"Are you suggesting I might lie?" Dan asked quietly.

"No—I'm suggesting you might misinterpret what you hear. How are you going to know, say, whether the differences you see are human versus nonhuman or simply four months versus two months?"

Dan nodded. "I see. I wondered why you hadn't told Dr. Jordan you'd seen Cooper and Mrs. Reese loitering out in the hall earlier. You called them down on us, didn't you?"

Halladay's face reddened. "No, I . . . uh . . . look, I didn't expect anyone to come out here and ambush you like that. I just wanted to know whether you were pro- or antiabortion; if you'd ever taken a public stand on the issue. I mean, they keep files on that sort of thing."

Jordan was looking at his co-worker as if she'd just shown a KGB membership card. "Pam! What on *earth*—"

"It's all right, Dr. Jordan. As I said before, no harm done." Dan turned to Halladay, and there was a glint in his eye I didn't often see. "I'll tell you what I told your friends: I'm not doing this to push anyone's opinions, and that includes any *I* might have. If you have to pigeonhole me anywhere, put me down as 'protruth.' I won't wear any other labels, understand?"

"Yes. I'm sorry, Doctor." She smiled wanly. "I guess I'm not immune to the emotions the whole subject generates. I'll keep my feelings to myself from now on—I promise."

"Will you prove your sincerity?" Dan leaned forward and offered his hand.

She frowned at it for a second before understanding flickered across her face. Then, visibly steeling herself, she reached out and gingerly took his hand. They held the position for nearly twenty seconds before Dan released his grip and sat back. "Thank you," he said. "I'm sure you'll be a great help to us." Turning to Jordan, he nodded. "Now then, are we ready to begin working out some of the details?"

The discussion took nearly an hour, and the experimental

design arrived at was essentially the one that was actually used later that year. Several important problems still remained, however, notably the question of masking the mother's thoughts while Dan tried to touch those of the fetus. From past experience we knew that a deep, sedative-induced sleep would probably do the trick, but Jordan was understandably opposed to giving large dosages of such drugs to pregnant women. The question of whether or not Dan could recognize humanness in a fetal mind at all also remained unanswered.

During the drive back to San Francisco, I asked Dan if Halladay could be trusted.

"I think so," he said. "I didn't see any evidence of duplicity when I touched her. And she *was* genuinely upset to find the Family Alliance people lying in wait for us."

"What about them? Do you think they'll make trouble?"

"How could they? Denouncing the experiment before it even takes place would make them look silly—especially since a check with Halladay will show them that the design still has some pretty basic problems. Saying this far in advance that they reject the results will leave them wide open to a charge that they're afraid of the truth."

Something in his voice caught my attention. "You sound less optimistic than you did yesterday," I said. "You thinking of calling it off?"

He was silent a long moment. "No, not really. It's just that the whole thing is getting more complicated than I'd envisioned it."

I shrugged. "True—but don't forget that it's *your* experiment. If you don't want to do things Jordan's way, all you have to do is say so."

"I know. But he's unfortunately got a good point: that if we don't at least take a stab at doing things rigorously, all we're going to do is throw more gasoline at the emotional bonfire." He paused. "Tell me, do you have any relatives or close friends who are pregnant?"

I blinked at the abrupt change of subject. "Yes—four to nine, depending on how close a friend you need."

"Let me have a fast rundown, will you?"

I drove one-handed for a while as I gave him a brief personality sketch of each of the nine women. Afterward he sat silently for several minutes, digesting it all. "What do you think Kathy would say if I asked to be present at her delivery?" he said at last.

"I don't know," I said. "But I know the right person to ask."

We called Kathy as soon as we got back to Dan's office. Though clearly surprised by the request, she agreed to act as Dan's guinea pig, provided her husband didn't object. I got the most recent estimate of her due date—another month—and extracted a promise of secrecy before hanging up. "You going to tell Jordan and Halladay about this?" I asked Dan.

He shook his head. "No, I don't think so. A slip of the tongue could have the entire Fresno chapter of the Family Alliance descending on Kathy's birthing room, and I have no intention of putting the Ausberrys through that."

"Besides which, if you find you can't even read the mind of a baby that's only hours from birth, you don't want anyone to know?" I hazarded.

His slightly pained smile was my only answer.

But the Family Alliance was subtler than we'd expected, and neither of us was prepared for the page-twenty story in the *Chronicle* the next morning.

"I don't *believe* this," I fumed, stomping around Dan's office with a copy of the paper gripped tightly in my hand. "How can they print something like this without at least contacting you first?"

"'The Lifeline Experiment,'" Dan quoted, reading at his desk. "Gack. Why do newspeople always have to come up with cutesy titles for everything? Contact me? Of course they should have. Obviously, some fine upstanding citizen or group of same convinced them that the story didn't need checking."

"Someone like our Family Alliance friends?"

"Undoubtedly. You'll notice they don't include any of the details we discussed yesterday, which implies Halladay has dried up as an information source for them. I guess that's something."

"*How* can you sit there and take it so calmly?" I snapped, slapping my newspaper down on the desktop for emphasis. "Look: there it is for the whole damn world to see."

He looked up at me. "Simmer down, Iris—the first client's due in ten minutes and the last thing he'll want is to have his head taken off by my secretary. I'm mad, too, but there's nothing we can do now except make sure the experiment comes off as planned."

I was only listening with half an ear. "But *why?* What did they expect to gain by leaking the story? It's not even particularly slanted."

"Sure it is," Dan contradicted me. "Sixth paragraph, fourth and fifth sentences."

"'In addition to his private psychiatric practice, Staley does volunteer counseling once a week at the Rappaport Mental Health Clinic of San Mateo County, which he helped found. He also works frequently with the public defender's office and has worked with the Greenpeace Save-the-Whales Project.'" I rattled off. "So?"

"So someone realized that this was going to be a very difficult experiment to do. So difficult, in fact, that we conceivably might have to give it up—and that someone wanted to make sure I was established in the public mind as a liberal right from the start. A liberal and, by implication, proabortion."

"I still don't see—oh. Sure. If the experiment turns out to be unworkable they'll claim you learned something in the initial stages that clashed with your liberal views on the issue, won't they, and that you backed out because of it."

"Bull's-eye. Or so I'm guessing."

I sat down, my anger replaced by a sudden chill. "Who exactly are we up against here—the Family Alliance or the CIA covert operations group?"

"We're up against people who've been up to their necks in politics for at least a decade," he told me, laying his own paper on top of mine. "Along the way they've probably picked up all the standard political tricks one can employ against an opponent—which is almost funny, since the experiment has just as much chance of supporting their point of view as it has of opposing it."

"One would think they haven't much faith in their beliefs, wouldn't one?" I suggested.

"I think that's a self-contradictory sentence, but you've got the right idea," Dan said, smiling. "And you might remember that any group that size is a mixed bag. Some of the members would probably be madder than you are if they knew what was being tried here." He tapped the newspaper.

Just then there was a knock on the outer office door. "Mr. Raymond's early," I commented, heading out to unlock it.

"No problem," Dan called after me. "You can send him right in."

But it wasn't Raymond, or any of Dan's other clients. It was, instead, a committee of four people.

"We'd like to see Dr. Staley for a moment, if he isn't too busy," their spokeswoman, a young woman with a recognizable face, said briskly. Without waiting for a reply she started forward.

Out in Hayward I'd been taken by surprise, but here in my own office I had better control of things. I remained standing in the doorway, and the woman had to pull up sharply to keep from running into me. "I'm sorry, Ms. McClain, but Dr. Staley is expecting a client," I said firmly. "If you'd like to make an appointment he has an hour available a week from Friday."

It was abundantly clear from her expression that she hadn't expected to be put off like that, but she recovered quickly. "Perhaps Dr. Staley will be able to squeeze us in between appointments later this morning," she said. "Would you tell him Jackie McClain and other representatives of the National Institute for Freedom and Equality are here? We'll wait until he's free."

I couldn't legitimately deny them waiting-room space, so I let them in, hoping that what I knew would be a long wait would discourage them. Three of them did eventually get up and leave, the last one about one o'clock, with whispered apologies to their leader. But McClain stayed all the way until Dan's last client left at five-thirty, a persistence I had to admire. I consulted briefly with Dan and he agreed to see her.

"I'm sorry you had to wait so long, Ms. McClain," he said as we all sat down in his office. "But, as Iris said, this was a particularly long day."

"She's a very efficient secretary," McClain said ambiguously. "I'll get right to the point, Dr. Staley: this so-called Lifeline Experiment. We'd like to know exactly what it is you intend to prove."

Dan frowned. "I'm not out to *prove* anything, really. I'm simply trying to find where in its development a fetus becomes a human being."

"In what sense? Medical, moral, legal—there are several ways to define *human,* and they don't necessarily correspond."

"I'm not sure I understand the question," Dan said, frowning a bit.

"Suppose you discover that, in your opinion, human life begins during the third month of pregnancy," McClain said. "The Supreme Court earlier this year stated that abortions through the sixth month are legal, which implies that a fetus is not *legally* human through that point."

"In that case the law would have to be changed, obviously," I told her.

"Obviously, you've never been pregnant with a child you didn't want," she said, a bit tartly. "A law like that would condemn thousands of women to either the trauma of an unwanted pregnancy and labor or to the danger of an illegal abortion. It would necessarily put the rights of a fetus over those of her mother—a mother whose rights, I'll point out, *are* clearly and definitely guaranteed by the Constitution."

"I understand all that," Dan said, "but I don't really know what to do about it. I'm not trying to make a legal or political statement with this, though I'm sure others will probably do so. But, then again, shouldn't the law reflect medical realities wherever possible?"

"Yes—but you're talking metaphysics, not medicine,"

McClain returned. "And as far as the law goes, what right do you or any other man have to tell women what we can or cannot do with our own bodies?"

"Just a second," I put in before Dan could reply. "Aren't we jumping the gun just a little bit here? Dr. Staley hasn't even *done* the experiment yet and already you're complaining about the results. It's entirely possible that the whole thing will be a boost to your point of view."

"You're right, of course," McClain admitted, cooling down a bit. "I'm sorry, Doctor; I guess I forgot that working with Pamela Halladay didn't automatically mean you were against us."

Dan waved a hand. "That's all right," he said, clearly thankful the argument had been temporarily defused. "I was unaware when we started that Dr. Halladay had strong feelings on the subject, but I'm convinced she'll be able to keep her feelings under wraps."

"I hope so." McClain paused. "I wonder, Doctor, if you would consider allowing a member of NIFE to participate in the planning of your experiment. We have quite a few doctors and other bioscience people who would be qualified to understand and assist in your work."

"Actually, I don't think we really need any help at the moment," Dan said slowly. "There are only a couple of problems to be dealt with, and I'm sure we can find solutions reasonably quickly. If not, I'll keep NIFE in mind."

"Will we at least be permitted to have an observer present during the main part of the experiment?" McClain persisted.

"If it'll make you feel better, sure," Dan said tiredly. "Give Iris your phone number and we'll do our best to keep you informed."

She gave me the number and then stood up, her expression that of someone who's gotten more or less what she hoped for. "Thank you for your time, Doctor. I hope this Lifeline Experiment of yours will prove to be something we can wholeheartedly support."

I saw her out and returned to Dan's office. "Is it my

imagination," I asked, "or is this project starting to get just a little out of hand?"

He shook his head. "I can't believe it. First the Family Alliance and now NIFE—people are practically standing in line for a chance to complain about the experiment. Is the opportunity to find out the truth really so frightening?"

"I thought all psychologists were cynics," I said. "Of *course* nobody wants to hear facts that'll contradict their long-held beliefs. And organizations are even worse than individuals."

"*I'd* rather know what the truth is," he countered. "So would you. Are we the only intellectually honest people around?" He held up a hand. "Skip it. I'm just tired. Let's go somewhere quiet where we won't run into a hit squad from the PTA and get some dinner."

Sometime that evening both the wire services and the major networks picked up on the story, and by the next morning the entire country was hearing about the Lifeline Experiment—the name, unfortunately, having been picked up as well. Commentaries, both pro and con, appeared soon after. Though the publicity was stifling to Dan's everyday work, I think he found a grim sort of amusement in watching the creative ways various organizations phrased their statements so as to condemn the experiment without actually saying they would reject its results. Only the most fanatical were willing—or clumsy enough—to burn such a potentially useful bridge behind them.

The reporters who began hanging around Dan's home and office were more of a nuisance, but Dan had years ago mastered the art of giving newspeople enough to keep them satisfied without unduly encouraging them to keep coming. Fortunately, though, as the initial excitement passed and the experiment itself still seemed far in the nebulous future, the media's interest waned, and within ten days of the story's initial release the reporters' physical presence was replaced by periodic phone calls asking if anything was new. I, at least, was relieved by this procedural change; my friend Kathy would be calling any day now, and I preferred sneaking away from telephones than from people.

Late one evening in the last week of June the call came, and Dan and I drove down to Fresno for the birth of Kathy's third daughter.

It was the first birth I'd ever seen, but even so I gave the main operation scant attention; I was far more interested in what Dan was doing. The obstetrician, a close family friend, had been clued in, but I could still sense his professional uneasiness each time Dan's ungloved hand probed gently into the birth canal. What was visible of Dan's expression above his mask indicated a frown of intense concentration that remained even when his hand had been withdrawn, a look that silenced the questions I was dying to ask. He reached into the canal four times during the labor, and in addition had a hand on the baby's head from its first appearance to the moment when the crying child was laid across her mother's breast.

"What did you find out?" I asked him a few minutes later, after our tactful withdrawal from the birthing room. "Can you reach the baby through its mother's nervous system?"

"Yes," he said, absently picking at a bloodstain he hadn't quite managed to get off his finger. "Once I knew what I was looking for I could find it even with the loud interference from Kathy's mind. I wouldn't want to try it with a baby much farther from term, though—we're still going to have to find a safe way to knock out the mothers."

I nodded. "How about . . . humanness?"

"No doubt," he said promptly. "Those people who want to believe the first breath is the dividing line are fooling themselves. Elizabeth Anne's mind was as human as ours in there."

"'Elizabeth Anne'?"

He smiled sheepishly. "Well, that's the name they were planning for a girl. I sort of picked that up along the way." The smile vanished. "Picked it up through a *lot* of real trauma. I don't think I ever realized before how much it *hurts* to have a baby—I'm exhausted, and I only got it secondhand."

"Why do you think they call it labor?" I asked, only half humorously. He grimaced, and I quickly changed the subject. "So what does a baby think about in there? I mean, she couldn't have all that much sensory experience to draw on and certainly wouldn't have what we'd consider abstract thoughts."

"Oh, there really was a fair amount of sensory input— tactile and auditory mostly, but taste and even vision also got used some." He shook his head thoughtfully, his forehead corrugated with concentration. "But it wasn't the use of her senses, or even the way that such information was processed that made her a human being. It was—oh, I don't know: a feeling of *kinship,* I guess I'd have to say. Something familiar in the mental patterns, though I'll be damned if I can describe it."

"Whatever it was didn't change at the actual birth?"

"Not really. There was a sudden sensory overload, of course, but if anything it heightened the feeling . . ." He trailed off, then abruptly snapped his fingers. "*That's* what it was. On some very deep level the baby felt herself to be an *individual,* distinct in some way from the rest of the universe."

"I didn't think even young children understood that," I said.

"On a conscious level, no—but that part of the mind seems to be the last to develop, long after the more instinctive levels are firmly in place. Now that I think about it, I've picked up this sense of distinctness in babies before—even in the Kilogram Kids I worked with at Stanford last year—but just never bothered to put a label on it."

I pondered that for a moment. "Is that the yardstick you're going to use, then?"

He shrugged uncomfortably. "Unless I can come up with something better, I guess I'll have to. I know it sounds like pretty flimsy evidence, but it really seems to be an easy characteristic to pick up. And I'm sure I've never felt it in any of the other mammals I've touched."

"Um. It still sounds awfully mystical for an experiment that purports to be scientific."

"I'm sorry," he said with a touch of asperity. "It's the best I can do. If you don't think it's worth anything we can quit right now."

I took his arm, realizing for the first time how heavily the national controversy was weighing on him. "It'll be all right," I soothed him. "As long as people know exactly what you're testing for, no one will be able to claim you misrepresented either yourself or the experiment."

"Yeah." He sighed and looked at his watch. "Two-thirty. No wonder I'm dead tired. Come on, Iris; let's go say good-bye to your friends and get out of here."

For a wonder, the news of our unofficial test run didn't leak to the media at that time, and so Dan was spared the extra attention such a revelation would have generated. As it was, public interest—which had remained at a low level for the past two or three weeks—began to rise again as the procedural problems began to be worked out and Jordan announced a tentative date of July 25 for the experiment to take place.

In light of the recently discovered papers, there is one conversation from that period that I feel must be included in this report.

It took place on the evening of July 12 at the home of Ron Brady and his wife Susan. It had been only the previous day that Halladay's idea of using electrical sleep stimulation had been proved adequate for Dan's needs, removing the final obstacle still holding things up.

"So the Lifeline Experiment's going to come off after all," Ron said after the dinner dishes had been cleared and the four of us had settled down in the living room.

Dan nodded. "Looks that way. Eliot and Pam are lining up volunteers now; they expect to have that finished in ten days at the most." He cocked an eyebrow. "You seem disapproving, somehow."

Ron and his wife exchanged glances. "It's not disapproval, exactly," Ron said hesitantly, "and it's certainly not aimed at you. But we *are* a little worried about the potential influence this one experiment is going to have on the way people think about abortion and human life in general, both here and in other countries."

Dan shrugged. "I'm just trying to inject some facts into the situation. Is influencing people to use rational thought instead of emotion a bad thing?"

"No, of course not," Susan said. "But what you're doing and what the public *perceives* you as doing are not necessarily the same. You're searching for the place where a fetus's mind becomes human; but a person is more than just his mind. Will the Lifeline Experiment show where the child's soul and spirit enter him? I'm not at all sure it will."

"That almost sounds like quibbling," I pointed out. "If Dan can detect a unique humanness in the mind, isn't that basically the same thing as the soul?"

"I don't know," Susan said frankly. "What's more, I haven't the foggiest idea of how you'd even begin to test that kind of assumption. It's just the fact that the assumption *is* being made that concerns me."

"The problem we see," Ron put in, "is that the media isn't bothering with this—to us, at least—very important point, but is preparing the public to expect a clear-cut answer to come out of the experiment. What's worse, every organized group that sees support for their point of view will immediately jump on the bandwagon, reinforcing the media's oversimplification. Do you see what I'm getting at?"

"Yes." Dan pulled at his lower lip. "Iris, have I been clear enough with the media as to exactly what the Lifeline Experiment will and won't show?"

Dan had talked to reporters over a hundred times since the story's first appearance; quickly, I played back the relevant parts. "I think so," I said slowly. "Especially since our trip to Fresno."

"The media's not picking up on it," Ron insisted.

I nodded. "He's right, Dan. I haven't seen any major newspaper or TV report even mention questions like Susan's, let alone seriously discuss them."

Dan pondered a moment. "Well, what do you think I should do about it? I could yell a little louder, I suppose, but evidence to date indicates that won't do a lot of good."

"I tend to agree," Ron said. "You've been something of a folk hero since you fought the National Academy of Sciences and won, but the extremists—on both sides—have louder voices. I'm afraid yours would probably get lost amid the postexperiment gloatings and denunciations."

"Do you think I should cancel the whole thing, then?" Dan asked bluntly.

For a moment there was silence. Then Susan shook her head. "I almost wish you could, or at least that you could postpone it for a while. But at this late date canceling would probably just start fresh rumors, with each faction trying to persuade people that you'd quit because you'd learned something that supported their particular point of view and conflicted with your own."

Dan's own words the morning the story appeared in the *Chronicle* came back to me; from the look on his face I knew he was remembering them, too. "Yeah," he said slowly. "Yeah, I guess you're right."

I think we all heard the pain in his voice. Susan was the first one to respond to it. "I'm sorry, Dan—we didn't mean to add to the pressure. We're not blaming you for what other people are doing with your words."

"I know," Dan said. "Don't worry about it—the pressure was there long before tonight." He sighed. "I really wasn't expecting it to be so intense, somehow. It wasn't nearly this bad when I was trying to prove my telepathic ability, not even when they were calling me a criminal fraud on network TV. I must be getting soft in my old age."

"I doubt it," Ron said. "The problem is more likely that last time *you* were the only one under the hatchet, so to speak, whereas this time your actions are going to be affecting the lives of others. You're suffering because, whatever happens, the Lifeline Experiment is likely to

hurt some group of people. That's an infinitely heavier
burden for someone like you than watching your own name
dragged through the mud."

Dan nodded. "I wish I'd thought about that two months
ago. If I'd known how I'd react, I'd never have started this
whole thing in motion."

"Well, if it makes you feel any better," Susan said gently,
"it's only *because* you're so sensitive that Ron and I aren't
more worried about the experiment. We can trust you, at
least, to be as honest and fair-minded in what you report as
is humanly possible."

"Thanks." Dan took a deep breath, let it out slowly. "Let's
change the subject, shall we?"

There are films of the Lifeline Experiment itself, of
course, films that have been shown endless times over the
past twenty years. I have seen them all and do not deny
that they adequately portray the physical events that took
place on July 25, 1994. But there was more than just a
scientific test taking place that day. There was a battle
taking place in Dan's own mind, a battle between what his
senses told him and what his reason could accept; and it
was this unresolved conflict, I know now, that ultimately
led to the secret study whose results have only now come
to light.

Dan and I arrived at the small lecture room where the
experiment was to take place just before one o'clock. The
TV and film cameras had long since been set up, and the
spectators' gallery was crammed with nearly fifty reporters
and representatives of interested groups. I glimpsed Eve
Unger, NIFE's handpicked representative, and John Cooper of the Family Alliance sitting several rows apart. Near
the front, in seats Dan had had reserved for them, were
Ron and Susan Brady.

The front of the room looked uncomfortably like a
morgue. Laid out in neat rows were thirty waist-high
gurneys, each bearing the form of a sleeping woman. From
the neck down each was covered by a pup-tent sort of
arrangement designed to give Dan limited access to the

area near the uterus while minimizing physical cues that might otherwise influence him. A number was sewn onto each tent, corresponding to a numbered envelope containing the woman's name and length of time she'd been pregnant. At a raised table at one end of the floor sat Jordan, Halladay, and John Cottingham of the Associated Press, who held the stack of envelopes.

"We're all set here, Dan," Jordan said as we reached the table. "You can begin whenever you want."

Dan nodded, and as I slid into my own front-row seat he stepped to the nearest gurney. With a single glance at the cameras, he reached into the tent's access tunnel. Almost immediately he withdrew his hand and silently picked up the number card lying on the gurney beside her. Marking one of the squares on the card, he stepped carefully over the sleep-stimulator wires and walked to the table, placing the card face down in front of Cottingham so that only its number showed. "Is it a boy or a girl, Dr. Staley?" the reporter quipped, sliding the card to one side without turning it over.

"I'm not even going to try to guess, Mr. Cottingham," Dan said. A slightly nervous chuckle rippled through the spectators; but I could see that Dan hadn't meant the comment to be funny. Not even a hint of a smile made it to his face as he walked back to the next gurney. He held the contact a little longer this time, but there was no hesitation I could detect as he picked up her card and marked it. Cottingham didn't try any jokes this time, and Dan went on to the third woman.

All the reports I've ever seen refer to the tension in the room that afternoon; what they don't usually mention is the strangely uneven quality the experimental setup imposed on it. Dan had expected—correctly, as it turned out—that the younger the fetus, the harder it would be to make both the initial contact and the determination of its humanness. But with the random order and the camouflaging tents it was impossible for anyone watching to tell how far along a given mother was. With some, the spectators would barely have settled into a watchful silence before Dan was walking

away with the card; but with others, he would stand
motionlessly for minutes at a time as the tension slowly
grew more and more oppressive. At those times, his
movement toward the card was like a lifting of Medusa's
curse, and there would be a brief flurry of noise as people
shifted in their seats and whispered comments to each
other. The reprieve would last until Dan started his next
contact, and the tension would then begin its slow rise
again.

The first forty-five minutes went smoothly enough, both
Dan and the spectators quickly growing more or less
accustomed to the emotional roller coaster ride we were
on. Dan made decisions on seventeen fetuses during that
time, and while he was clearly not having fun up there, I
could tell from his face that he was holding up reasonably
well against the pressure.

The eighteenth subject changed all that.

Dan stood by her for nearly five minutes, his face rigid
with concentration and something else. Finally, leaving her
card untouched on the gurney, he stepped over to the
table. "There's something wrong," he said, his voice low
but audible from where I was sitting. "I can't find any life at
all in there. I think the fetus must be dead. I . . . please
don't release the moth— the woman's name. It's going to be
hard enough on her as it is."

Jordan tapped Cottingham's arm and muttered something. The reporter grimaced slightly, but gamely shuffled
out the proper envelope and opened it. His frown vanished
as he read the contents and he smiled wryly. "Number
twenty-eight. Linda Smith; not pregnant. Control."

There was a collective sigh of released tension. An
unreadable expression flickered across Dan's face as he
glanced at Jordan and Halladay. Then, clamping his jaw
tightly, he walked back to the gurneys. To others in the
room he may have simply looked determined—but I knew
better. He was flustered, and flustered badly. He'd coun-
seled several women in the past who'd given birth to
stillborn children, and dropping the memory of that trauma
into the middle of an already emotional experience must

have been like a kick in the head. The fact that he obviously hadn't even considered the possibility of a control was clear evidence of his overwrought state. I wondered briefly if he would call for a break, but I already knew that he wouldn't permit himself that luxury. He had fought hard these past few weeks to portray himself as a calm, dispassionate scientist who could make the Lifeline Experiment a genuinely impartial search for truth, and he would turn his stomach into a massive ulcer before he would undermine that effort with even a suggestion of weakness.

From that point on, Dan's face was a granite mask, and for the next forty minutes I sat helplessly by, grinding my fingernails into my palms.

The silence in the room as Dan handed Cottingham the last card was so complete that I could clearly hear the ticking of Jordan's antique wristwatch. Picking up the first of his envelopes, Cottingham opened it. "Number twenty-three," he read into the microphone, enunciating his words carefully. "Alice Grant; nine months pregnant." Reaching to the line of cards in front of him, he turned the corresponding one over. "Human," he read. Card and envelope went to one side, and as he opened the second envelope I shifted my attention to Dan. He had stepped back among the gurneys and was watching Cottingham, his expression calm but with a strange, brittle quality to it that sent a sudden shiver up my back. "Number one. Vicki Thuma; eight and a half months pregnant," Cottingham read. Pause. "Human."

One by one he worked his way down the stack, finishing with the third-trimester mothers and starting on those in their second three months . . . and as each card he picked up identified the child as fully human, the silence began to give way to a buzz of unsure conversation. Cottingham read on; and as he reached the first-trimester women the buzz took on edges of both triumphant and angry disbelief. No one, I sensed, had really expected the result that was unfolding.

He reached the last envelope, and as he tore it open the room suddenly became quiet again. "Number fourteen.

Barbara Remington: five weeks pregnant." His hand was trembling just slightly as he turned over the final card. "Human. Human," he repeated, as if not quite believing it.

"That's impossible!" Eve Unger's clear voice cut through the silence, a fraction of a second before the whole room exploded into pandemonium. "A fetus's brain has hardly *started* development at five weeks," she shouted over the din. "It's a fraud—Staley's been bought by the Family Alliance!"

Dan didn't reply, though anything he said would have been inaudible anyway through the accusations, claims, and counterclaims filling the air like opposing mortar barrages. He just stood there, looking up at the NIFE representative, his expression still calm. He knew what he'd seen and would not be moved from his testimony. And yet, as I look back on his face now, I can see the faintest hint of the uneasiness—the knowledge that what she said made sense—that I now know must have haunted the last fifteen years of his life.

Of the aftermath there is little that isn't common knowledge. Though the Lifeline Experiment carried no legal weight whatsoever, it was very clearly the rallying point for the final successful drive that established the Fetal Rights Amendment in the Constitution. But the bitter struggle that surrounded the issue made it a Pyrrhic victory at best, threatening at times to tear the country apart as had no issue since the Vietnam War. It was too much for Dan to bear at close range, and for eight years after the experiment he remained outside the country, living in self-imposed seclusion in Australia. I think that the only thing that got him through that period was the knowledge that he *had* seen humanity in those tiny bits of new life, and that whatever the cost he had done the right thing. Eventually things settled down, the proabortion forces gradually losing strength as grudging acceptance of the new law grew, until they became the vocal but powerless minority of the present day. And I wish with all my heart the controversy could be left alone to continue its slow death.

But it can't.

* * *

I enclose the following excerpt from Dan's papers with a feeling of dread, remembering the agony of the past two decades as few others remember it and knowing that my action is likely to rekindle the fires again. But above all other things Dan prized his reputation for honesty, and it is solely because of this that I quote here the last entry from his private journal, made just two days before the car accident that took his life. I believe that, given the time, he would have come to the same conclusion.

October 18, 2009: I have been sitting here since the sky first began to show the colors of sunset, wondering how to write this. The stars now shine brightly where I watched the sun go down, and I am no nearer to finding a way to ease the shock of what my seven-year study has shown me . . . to finding a less brutal way to confess what I have unwittingly done to all the people who trusted me.

There can be no further doubt as to what I have done. Linda Grant, whose mother was nine months pregnant at the experiment, shows virtually none of the traits I myself showed as a teenager; at the other end of the scale Tom Remington, whose mother was only five weeks along, is so like me it is agonizing to watch him. Only today I learned that, while he has my passionate love of basketball, he does not intend to try out for the school team, despite his skill and height. There is no reason why he would not do well at the game . . . except that I was a mere five foot six at his age and convinced I could never play. All the rest of them fall somewhere between these two extremes, their individual degrees of mimicry directly correlated with their ages at the experiment . . . and for what I've done to these children alone I owe a debt I'll never be able to repay. What I've done to the country and the millions of women whose lives my naïveté had changed—I can't even comprehend the enormity of my crime.

My crime. The word is harsh, unforgiving. But I can't justify it as anything else. In my foolish arrogance I assumed the universe was simple, that its secrets were absolute and could be had for the asking. Worse yet, I assumed it would bend its own rules just for my convenience.

The experimenter influences his experiment. How long has that truth been known? Close to a hundred years, I'm sure, at least since the earliest beginnings of quantum mechanics. Such a simple thing . . . and yet neither I nor any of those I worked with ever even bothered to consider what it might mean to us.

The Lifeline Experiment was doomed from the very beginning. Young minds, their development barely started—how could they fail to be overwhelmed as I touched them with what must have been the delicacy of an elephant? That flicker of humanness I saw in each fetus—how much of that was innate and how much merely my own imposed reflection? I'll never know. No one ever will. My very presence obliterated the line I was trying to find.

And in the meantime I have helped to force what is essentially an arbitrary decision on the country. What should I do with this knowledge? Do I keep it to myself and allow the lie to continue, or do I speak out and risk tearing the society apart once again?

I wish I knew the answer.

Afterword

The abortion issue is one of a growing list of topics these days in which middle ground is increasingly hard to find. Both extremes are vocal, organized, and often—in my opinion—inconsistent in their overall world views, and I had little doubt that "Lifeline" would generate a minor avalanche of hate mail from both ends of the target range.

And I was wrong. I got a couple of letters, *Analog* printed a couple more, and all of them were polite enough as they springboarded off the story to state their own views on the topic.

Heartening? Certainly. It may imply that SF readers tend to be, by and large, reasonable people; less inclined than the average American, perhaps, to let emotions or national spokespersons define their thoughts for them. But then again, people who like idea-oriented literature *are*, almost by definition, more likely to try and treat abortion as an intellectual problem. An intellectual problem, with an intellectual solution.

So did I default on my own responsibility as a writer of idea-oriented fiction by, in effect, straddling the fence? I don't think so. The abortion issue simply has too much of a philosophical, religious nature embedded in it to yield to a simple, logical solution, much as I might wish otherwise.

Cascade Point

In retrospect, I suppose I should have realized my number
had come up on the universe's list right from the very
start, right from the moment it became clear that I was
going to be stuck with the job of welcoming the *Aura
Dancer's* latest batch of passengers aboard. Still, I suppose
it's just as well it was me and not Tobbar who let Rik
Bradley and his psychiatrist onto my ship. There are some
things that a captain should have no one to blame for but
himself, and this was definitely in that category.

Right away I suppose that generates a lot of false
impressions. A star liner captain, resplendent in white and
gold, smiling toothily at elegantly dressed men and women
as the ramp carries them through the polished entry
portal—forget all of that. A tramp starmer isn't polished
anywhere it doesn't absolutely have to be, the captain is
lucky if he's got a clean jumpsuit—let alone some pseudo-
military Christmas tree frippery—and the passengers we
get are the steerage of the star-traveling community. And
look it.

Don't get me wrong; I have nothing against passengers
aboard my ship. As a matter of fact, putting extra cabins in

the *Dancer* had been my idea to start with, and they'd all too often made the difference between profit and loss in our always marginal business. But one of the reasons I had gone into space in the first place was to avoid having to make small talk with strangers, and I would rather solo through four cascade points in a row than spend those agonizing minutes at the entry portal. In this case, though, I had no choice. Tobbar, our master of drivel—and thus the man unofficially in charge of civilian small talk—was up to his elbows in grease and balky hydraulics; and my second choice, Alana Keal, had finally gotten through to an equally balky tower controller who wanted to bump us ten ships back in the lift pattern. Which left exactly one person— me—because there was no one else I'd trust with giving a good first impression of my ship to paying customers. And so I was the one standing on the ramp when Bradley and his eleven fellow passengers hoved into sight.

They ranged from semiscruffy to respectable-but-not-rich—about par for the *Dancer*—but even in such a diverse group Bradley stood out like a red light on the status board. He was reasonably good-looking, reasonably average in height and build; but there was something in the way he walked that immediately caught my attention. Sort of a cross between nervous fear and something I couldn't help but identify as swagger. The mix was so good that it was several seconds before it occurred to me how mutually contradictory the two impressions were, and the realization left me feeling more uncomfortable than I already did.

Bradley was eighth in line, with the result that my first seven greetings were carried out without a lot of attention from my conscious mind—which I'm sure only helped. Even standing still, I quickly discovered, Bradley's strangeness made itself apparent, both in his posture and also in his face and eyes. Especially his eyes.

Finally it was his turn at the head of the line. "Good morning, sir," I said, shaking his hand. "I'm Captain Pall Durriken. Welcome aboard."

"Thank you." His voice was bravely uncertain, the sort my mother used to describe as mousy. His eyes flicked the length of the *Dancer*, darted once into the portal, and returned to my face. "How often do ships like this crash?" he asked.

I hadn't expected any questions quite so blunt, but the fact that it was outside the realm of small talk made it easy to handle. "Hardly ever," I told him. "The last published figures showed a death rate of less than one per million passengers. You're more likely to be hit by a chunk of roof tile off the tower over there."

He actually cringed, turning halfway around to look at the tower. I hadn't dreamed he would take my comment so seriously, but before I could get my mouth working the man behind Bradley clapped a reassuring hand on his shoulder. "It's all right, Rik—nothing's going to hurt you. Really. This is a good ship, and we're going to be perfectly safe aboard her."

Bradley slowly straightened, and the other man shifted his attention to me. "I'm Dr. Hammerfeld Lanton, Captain," he said, extending his hand. "This is Rik Bradley. We're traveling in adjoining cabins."

"Of course," I said, nodding as if I'd already known that. In reality I hadn't had time to check out the passenger lists and assignments, but I could trust Leeds to have set things up properly. "Are you a doctor of medicine, sir?"

"In a way," Lanton said. "I'm a psychiatrist."

"Ah," I said, and managed two or three equally brilliant conversational gems before the two of them moved on. The last three passengers I dispatched with similar polish, and when everyone was inside I sealed the portal and headed for the bridge.

Alana had finished dickering with the tower and was running the prelift computer check when I arrived. "What's the verdict?" I asked as I slid into my chair and keyed for helm check.

"We've still got our lift slot," she said. "That's conditional on Matope getting the elevon system working within the next half hour, of course."

"Idiots," I muttered. The elevons wouldn't be needed until we arrived at Taimyr some six weeks from now, and

Matope could practically rebuild them from scratch in that amount of time. To insist they be in prime condition before we could lift was unreasonable even for bureaucrats.

"Oh, there's no problem—Tobbar reported they were closing things up a few minutes ago. They'll put it through its paces, it'll work perfectly, they'll transmit the readout, and that'll be that." She cleared her throat. "Incidentally . . . are you aware we've got a skull-diver and his patient aboard?"

"Yes; I met—*patient?*" I interrupted myself as the last part of her sentence registered. "Who?"

"Name's Bradley," she said. "No further data on him, but apparently he and this Lanton character had a fair amount of electronic and medical stuff delivered to their cabins."

A small shiver ran up my back as I remembered Bradley's face. No wonder he'd struck me as strange. "No mention at all of what's wrong—of why Bradley needs a psychiatrist?"

"Nothing. But it can't be anything serious." The test board bleeped, and Alana paused to peer at the results. Apparently satisfied, she keyed in the next test on the check list. "The Swedish Psychiatric Institute seems to be funding the trip, and they presumably know the regulations about notifying us of potential health risks."

"Um." On the other hand, a small voice whispered in my ear, if there was some problem with Bradley that made him marginal for space certification, they were more likely to get away with slipping him aboard a tramp than on a liner. "Maybe I should give them a call, anyway. Unless you'd like to?"

I glanced over in time to see her face go stony. "No, thank you," she said firmly.

"Right." I felt ashamed of the comment, not really having meant it the way it had come out. All of us had our own reasons for being where we were; Alana's was an overdose of third-degree emotional burns. She was the type who'd seemingly been born to nurse broken wings and bruised souls, the type who by necessity kept her own heart in full view of both friends and passersby. Eventually, I gathered, one too many of her mended souls had torn out the emotional IVs she'd set up and flown off without so much as a backward glance, and she had renounced the whole business and run off to space. Ice to Europa, I'd thought once; there were enough broken wings out here for a whole shipload of Florence Nightingales. But what I'd expected to be a short vacation for her had become four years' worth of armor plate over her emotions, until I wasn't sure she even knew anymore how to care for people. The last thing in the universe she would be interested in doing would be getting involved in any way with Bradley's problems. "Is all the cargo aboard now?" I asked, to change the subject.

"Yes, and Wilkinson certifies it's properly stowed."

"Good." I got to my feet. "I guess I'll make a quick spot survey of the ship, if you can handle things here."

"Go ahead," she said, not bothering to look up. Nodding anyway, I left.

I stopped first at the service shafts where Matope and Tobbar were just starting their elevon tests, staying long enough to satisfy myself the resulting data were adequate to please even the tower's bit-pickers. Then it was to each of the cargo holds to double-check Wilkinson's stowing arrangement, to the passenger area to make sure all their luggage had been properly brought on board, to the computer room to look into a reported malfunction—a false alarm, fortunately—and finally back to the bridge for the lift itself. Somehow, in all the running around, I never got around to calling Sweden. Not, as I found out later, that it would have done me any good.

We lifted right on schedule, shifting from the launch field's grav booster to ramjet at ten kilometers and kicking in the fusion drive as soon as it was legal to do so. Six hours later we were past Luna's orbit and ready for the first cascade maneuver.

Leeds checked in first, reporting officially that the proper number of dosages had been drawn from the sleeper cabinet and were being distributed to the passengers. Pascal gave the okay from the computer room, Matope from the engine room, and Sarojis from the small chamber housing the field generator itself. I had just pulled a hard copy of the computer's course instructions when Leeds called back. "Captain, I'm in Dr. Lanton's cabin," he said without preamble. "Both he and Mr. Bradley refuse to take their sleepers."

Alana turned at that, and I could read my own thought in her face: Lanton and Bradley had to be nuts. "Has Dr. Epstein explained the reasons behind the procedure?" I asked carefully, mindful of both my responsibilities and my limits here.

"Yes, I have," Kate Epstein's clear soprano came. "Dr. Lanton says that his work requires both of them to stay awake through the cascade point."

"Work? What sort of work?"

A pause, and Lanton's voice replaced Kate's. "Captain, this is Dr. Lanton. Rik and I are involved in an experimental type of therapy here. The personal details are confidential, but I assure you that it presents no danger either to us or to you."

Therapy. Great. I could feel anger starting to churn in my gut at Lanton's casual arrogance in neglecting to inform me ahead of time that he had more than transport in mind for my ship. By all rights I should freeze the countdown and sit Lanton down in a corner somewhere until *I* was convinced everything was as safe as he said. But time was money in this business; and if Lanton was glossing things over he could probably do so in finer detail than I could catch him on, anyway. "Mr. Bradley?" I called. "You agree to pass up your sleeper, as well?"

"Yes, sir," came the mousy voice.

"All right. Dr. Epstein, you and Mr. Leeds can go ahead and finish your rounds."

"Well," Alana said as I flipped off the intercom, "at least if something goes wrong the record will clear us of any fault at the inquest."

"You're a genuine ray of sunshine," I told her sourly. "What else could I have done?"

"Raked Lanton over the coals for some information. We're at least entitled to know what's going on."

"Oh, we'll find out, all right. As soon as we're through the point I'm going to haul Lanton up here for a long, cozy chat." I checked the readouts. cascade point in seventeen minutes. "Look, you might as well go to your cabin and hit the sack. I know it's your turn, but you were up late with that spare parts delivery and you're due some downtime."

She hesitated; wanting to accept, no doubt, but slowed by considerations of duty. "Well . . . all right. I'm taking the next one, then. I don't know, though; maybe you shouldn't be up here alone. In case Lanton's miscalculated."

"You mean if Bradley goes berserk or something?" That thought had been lurking in my mind, too, though it sounded rather ridiculous when spoken out loud. Still . . . "I can lower the pressure in the passenger deck corridor to half an atmosphere. That'll be enough to lock the doors without triggering any vacuum alarms."

"Leaves Lanton on his own in case of trouble . . . but I suppose that's okay."

"He's the one who's so sure it's safe. Go on, now—get out of here."

She nodded and headed for the door. She paused there, though, her hand resting on the release. "Don't just haul Lanton away from Bradley when you want to talk to him," she called back over her shoulder. "Try to run into him in the lounge or somewhere instead when he's already alone. It might be hard on Bradley to know you two were off somewhere together talking about him." She slapped the release, almost viciously, and was gone.

I stared after her for a long minute, wondering if I'd actually seen a crack in that heavy armor plate. The bleep of the intercom brought me back to the task at hand, Kate telling me the passengers were all down and that she, Leeds, and Wilkinson had taken their own sleepers. One by one the other six crewers also checked in. Within ten minutes they would be asleep, and I would be in sole charge of my ship.

Twelve minutes to go. Even with the *Dancer*'s old manual setup there was little that needed to be done. I laid the hard copy of the computer's instructions where it would be legible but not in the way, shut down all the external sensors and control surfaces, and put the computer and other electronic equipment into neutral/standby mode. The artificial gravity I left on; I'd tried a cascade point without it once and would never do so again. Then I waited, trying not to think of what was coming . . . and at the appropriate time I lifted the safety cover and twisted the field generator control knob.

And suddenly there were five of us in the room.

I will never understand how the first person to test the Colloton Drive ever made it past this point. The images silently surrounding me a bare arm's length away were life-size, lifelike, and—at first glance, anyway—as solid as the panels and chairs they seemed to have displaced. It took a careful look to realize they were actually slightly transparent, like some kind of colored glass, and a little experimentation at that point would show they had less substance than air. They were nothing but ghosts, specters straight out of childhood's scariest stories. Which merely added to the discomfort . . . because all of them were me.

Five seconds later the second set of images appeared, perfectly aligned with the first. After that they came more and more quickly, as the spacing between them similarly decreased, forming an ever-expanding horizontal cross with me at the center. I watched—forced myself to watch—knew I *had* to watch—as the lines continued to lengthen, watched until they were so long that I could no longer discern whether any more were being added.

I took a long, shuddering breath—peripherally aware that the images nearest me were doing the same—and wiped a shaking hand across my forehead. *You don't have to look*, I told myself, eyes rigidly fixed on the back of the image in front of me. *You've seen it all before. What's the point?* But I'd fought this fight before, and I knew in advance I would lose. There was indeed no more point to it than there was to pressing a bruise, but it held an equal degree of compulsion. Bracing myself, I turned my head and gazed down the line of images strung out to my left.

The armchair philosophers may still quibble over what the cascade point images "really" are, but those of us who fly the small ships figured it out long ago. The Colloton field puts us into a different type of space, possibly an entire universe worth of it—that much is established fact. Somehow this space links us into a set of alternate realities, universes that might have been if things had gone differently . . . and what I was therefore seeing around me were images of what I would be doing in each of those universes.

Sure, the theory has problems. Obviously, I should generate a separate pseudoreality every time I choose ham instead of turkey for lunch, and just as obviously such trivial changes don't make it into the pattern. Only the four images closest to me are ever exactly my doubles; even the next ones in line are noticeably if subtly different. But it's not a matter of subconscious suggestion, either. Too many of the images are . . . unexpected . . . for that.

It was no great feat to locate the images I particularly needed to see: the white-and-gold liner captain's uniforms stood out brilliantly among the more dingy jumpsuits and coveralls on either side. Liner captain. In charge of a fully equipped, fully modernized ship; treated with the respect and admiration such a position brought. It could have been—*should* have been. And to make things worse, I knew the precise decision that had lost it to me.

It had been eight years now since the uniforms had appeared among my cascade images; ten since the day I'd thrown Lord Hendrik's son off the bridge of the training ship and simultaneously guaranteed myself a blackballing with every major company in the business. Could I have handled the situation differently? Probably. Should I have? Given the state of the art then, no. A man who, after three training missions, still went borderline claustrophobic every time he had to stay awake through a cascade point had no business aboard a ship, let alone on its bridge. Hendrik might have forgiven me once he thought things through. The kid, who was forced into a ground position with the firm, never did. Eventually, of course, he took over the business.

I had no way of knowing that four years later the Aker-Ming Autotorque would eliminate the need for *anyone* to stay awake through cascade maneuvers. I doubt seriously the kid appreciated the irony of it all.

In the eight years since the liner captain uniforms had appeared they had been gradually moving away from me along all four arms of the cross. Five more years, I estimated, and they would be far enough down the line to disappear into the mass of images crowded together out there. Whether my reaction to that event would be relief or sadness I didn't yet know, but there was no doubt in my mind that it would in some way be the end of a chapter in my life. I gazed at the figures for another minute . . . and then, with my ritual squeezing of the bruise accomplished, I let my eyes drift up and down the rest of the line.

They were unremarkable, for the most part: minor variations in my appearance or clothing. The handful that had once showed me in some nonspacing job had long since vanished toward infinity; I'd been out here a long time. Perhaps too long . . . a thought the half-dozen or so gaps in each arm of the pattern underlined with unnecessary force. I'd told Bradley that ships like the *Dancer* rarely crashed, a perfectly true statement; but what I hadn't mentioned was that the chances of simply disappearing en route were something rather higher. None of us liked to think about that, especially during critical operations like cascade point maneuvers. But the gaps in the image pattern were a continual reminder that people still died in space. In six possible realities, apparently, I'd made a decision that killed me.

Taking another deep breath, I forced all of that as far from my mind as I could and activated the *Dancer's* flywheel.

Even on the bridge the hum was audible as the massive chunk of metal began to spin. A minute later it had reached its top speed . . . and the entire ship's counterrotation began to register on the gyroscope set behind glass in the ceiling above my head. The device looked out of place, a decided anachronism among the modern instruments, control circuits, and readouts filling the bridge. But using it was the only way a ship our size could find its way safely through a cascade point. The enhanced electron tunneling effect that fouled up electronic instrument performance was well understood; what was still needed was a way to predict the precise effect a given cascade point rotation would generate. Without such predictability, readings couldn't even be given adjustment factors. Cascade navigation thus had to fall back on gross electrical and purely mechanical systems: flywheel, physical gyroscope, simple on-off controls, and a nonelectronic decision maker. Me.

Slowly, the long needle above me crept around its dial. I watched its reflection carefully in the magnifying mirror, a system that allowed me to see the indicator without having to break my neck looking up over my shoulder. Around me, the cascade images did their own slow dance, a strange kaleidoscopic thing that moved the images and gaps around within each branch of the cross, while the branches themselves remained stationary relative to me. The effect was unexplained; but then, Colloton field theory left a lot of things unexplained. Mathematically, the basic idea was relatively straightforward: the space we were in right now could be described by a type of bilinear conformal mapping—specifically, a conjugate inversion that maps lines into circles. From that point it was all downhill, the details tangling into a soup of singularities, branch points, and confluent Riemann surfaces; but what it all eventually boiled down to was that a yaw rotation of the ship here would become a linear translation when I shut down the field generator and we reentered normal space. The *Dancer's* rotation was coming up on two degrees now, which for the particular configuration we were in meant we were already about half a light-year closer to our destination. Another—I checked the printout—one point three six and I would shut down the flywheel, letting the *Dancer's* momentum carry her an extra point two degree for a grand total of eight light-years.

The needle crept to the mark, and I threw the flywheel switch, simultaneously giving my full attention over to the gyro. Theoretically, over- or undershooting the mark could be corrected during the next cascade point—or by fiddling the flywheel back and forth now—but it was simpler not to have to correct at all. The need to make sure we were stationary was another matter entirely; if the *Dancer* were still rotating when I threw the field swtich we would wind up strung out along a million kilometers or more of space. I thought of the gaps in my cascade image pattern and shivered.

But that was all the closer death was going to get to me, at least this time. The delicately balanced spin lock worked exactly as it was supposed to, freezing the field switch in place until the ship's rotation was as close to zero as made no difference. I shut off the field and watched my duplicates disappear in reverse order, waiting until the last four vanished before confirming the stars were once again visible through the bridge's tiny viewport. I sighed; and fighting the black depression that always seized me at this point, I turned the *Dancer*'s systems back on and set the computer to figuring our exact position. Someday, I thought, I'd be able to afford to buy Aker-Ming Autotorques and never, *never* have to go through this again.

And someday I'd swim the Pacific Ocean, too.

Slumping back in my chair, I waited for the computer to finish its job and allowed the tears to flow.

Crying, for me, has always been the simplest and fastest way of draining off tension, and I've always felt a little sorry for men who weren't able to appreciate its advantages. This time was no exception, and I was feeling almost back to normal by the time the computer produced its location figures. I was still poring over them twenty minutes later when Alana returned to the bridge. "Another cascade point successfully hurdled, I see," she commented tiredly. "Hurray for our side."

"I thought you were supposed to be taking a real nap, not just a sleeper's worth," I growled at her over my shoulder.

"I woke up and decided to take a walk," she answered, her voice suddenly businesslike. "What's wrong?"

I handed her a printout, pointed to the underlined numbers. "The gyroscope reading says we're theoretically dead on position. The stars say we're short."

"Wumph!" Frowning intently at the paper, she kicked around the other chair and sat down. "Twenty light-days. That's what, twice the expected error for this point? Great. You double-checked everything, of course?"

"Triple-checked. The computer confirmed the gyro reading, and the astrogate program's got positive ident on twenty stars. Margin of error's no greater than ten light-minutes on either of those."

"Yeah." She eyed me over the pages. "Anything funny in the cargo?"

I gestured to the manifest in front of me. "We've got three boxes of technical equipment that include Ming metal," I said. "All three are in the shield. I checked that before we lifted."

"Maybe the shield's sprung a leak," she suggested doubtfully.

"It's supposed to take a hell of a break before the stuff inside can affect cascade point configuration."

"I can go check if you'd like."

"No, don't bother. There's no rush now, and Wilkinson's had more experience with shield boxes. He can take a look when he wakes up. I'd rather you stay here and help me do a complete programming check. Unless you'd like to obey orders and go back to bed."

She smiled faintly. "No, thanks; I'll stay. Um . . . I could even start things alone if you'd like to go to the lounge for a while."

"I'm fine," I growled, irritated by the suggestion.

"I know," she said. "But Lanton was down there alone when I passed by on my way here."

I'd completely forgotten about Lanton and Bradley, and it took a couple of beats for me to catch on. Cross-examining a man in the middle of cascade depression wasn't a terrifically nice thing to do, but I wasn't feeling terrifically nice at the moment. "Start with the astrogate program," I told Alana, getting to my feet. "Give me a shout if you find anything."

Lanton was still alone in the lounge when I arrived. "Doctor," I nodded to him as I sat down in the chair across from his. "How are you feeling?" The question was more for politeness than information; the four empty glasses on the end table beside him and the half-full one in his hand showed how he'd chosen to deal with his depression. I'd learned long ago that crying was easier on the liver.

He managed a weak smile. "Better, Captain; much better. I was starting to think I was the only one left on the ship."

"You're not even the only one awake," I said. "The other passengers will be wandering in shortly—you people get a higher-dose sleeper than the crew takes."

He shook his head. "Lord, but that was weird. No wonder you want everyone to sleep through it. I can't remember the last time I felt this rotten."

"It'll pass," I assured him. "How did Mr. Bradley take it?"

"Oh, fine. Much better than I did, though he fell apart just as badly when it was over. I gave him a sedative—the coward's way out, but I wasn't up to more demanding therapy at the moment."

So Bradley wasn't going to be walking in on us any time soon. Good. "Speaking of therapy, Doctor, I think you owe me a little more information about what you're doing."

He nodded and took a swallow from his glass. "Beginning, I suppose, with what exactly Rik is suffering from?"

"That would be nice," I said, vaguely surprised at how civil I was being. Somehow, the sight of Lanton huddled miserably with his liquor had taken all the starch out of my fire-and-brimstone mood. Alana was clearly having a bad effect on me.

"Okay. Well, first and foremost, he is *not* in any way dangerous, either to himself or other people. He has no tendencies even remotely suicidal or homicidal. He's simply . . . permanently disoriented, I suppose, is one way to think of it. His personality seems to slide around in strange ways, generating odd fluctuations in behavior and perception."

Explaining psychiatric concepts in layman's terms obviously wasn't Lanton's forte. "You mean he's schizophrenic? Or paranoid?" I added, remembering our launch-field conversation.

"Yes and no. He shows some of the symptoms of both—along with those of five or six other maladies—but he doesn't demonstrate the proper biochemical syndrome for any known mental disease. He's a fascinating, scientifically annoying anomaly. I've got whole bubble-packs of data on him, taken over the past five years, and I'm convinced I'm teetering on the edge of a breakthrough. But I've already exhausted all the standard ways of probing a patient's subconscious, and I had to come up with something new." He gestured around him. "This is it."

"This is what? A new form of shock therapy?"

"No, no—you're missing the point. I'm studying Rik's cascade images."

I stared at him for a long moment. Then, getting to my feet, I went to the autobar and drew myself a lager. "With all due respect," I said as I sat down again, "I think you're out of your mind. First of all, the images aren't a product of the deep subconscious or whatever; they're reflections of universes that might have been."

"Perhaps. There *is* some argument about that." He held up a hand as I started to object. "But either way, you have to admit that your conscious or unconscious mind *must* have an influence on them. Invariably, the images that appear show the results of *major* decisions or events in one's life; never the plethora of insignificant choices we all make. Whether the subconscious is choosing among actual images or generating them by itself, it *is* involved with them and therefore can be studied through them."

He seemed to settle slightly in his chair, and I got the feeling this wasn't the first time he'd made that speech.

"Even if I grant you all that," I said, "which I'm not sure I do, I think you're running an incredibly stupid risk that the cascade point effects will give Bradley a shove right over the edge. They're hard enough on those of us who *haven't* got psychological problems—what am I telling you this for? *You* saw what it was like, damn it. The last thing I want on my ship is someone who's going to need either complete sedation or a restraint couch all the way to Taimyr!"

I stopped short, suddenly aware that my volume had been steadily increasing. "Sorry," I muttered, draining half of my lager. "Like I said, cascade points are hard on all of us."

He frowned. "What do you mean? You were asleep with everyone else, weren't you?"

"Somebody's got to be awake to handle the maneuver," I said.

"But . . . I thought there were autopilots for cascade points now."

"Sure—the Aker-Ming Autotorque. But they cost nearly twenty-two thousand apiece and have to be replaced every hundred cascade points or so. The big liners and freighters can afford luxuries like that; tramp starmers can't."

"I'm sorry—I didn't know." His expression suggested he was also sorry he hadn't investigated the matter more thoroughly before booking aboard the *Dancer*.

I'd seen that look on people before, and I always hated it. "Don't worry; you're perfectly safe. The manual method's been used for nearly two centuries, and my crew and I know what we're doing."

His mind was obviously still a half kilometer back. "But how can it be that expensive? I mean, Ming metal's an exotic alloy, sure, but it's only selenium with a little bit of rhenium, after all. You can buy psy-test equipment with Ming-metal parts for a fraction of the cost you quoted."

"And we've got an entire box made of the stuff in our number one cargo hold," I countered. "But making a consistent-property rotation gauge is a good deal harder than rolling sheets or whatever. Anyway, you're evading my question. What are you going to do if Bradley can't take the strain?"

He shrugged, but I could see he didn't take the possibility seriously. "If worst comes to worst, I suppose I could let him sleep while I stayed awake to observe his images. They *do* show up even in your sleep, don't they?"

"So I've heard." I didn't add that I'd feel like a voyeur doing something like that. Psychiatrists, accustomed to poking into other people's minds, clearly had different standards than I did.

"Good. Though that would add another variable," he added thoughtfully. "Well . . . I think Rik can handle it. We'll do it conscious as long as we can."

"And what's going to be your clue that he's *not* handling it? The first time he tries to strangle one of his images? Or maybe when he goes catatonic?"

He gave me an irritated look. "Captain, I *am* a psychiatrist. I'm perfectly capable of reading my patient and picking up any signs of trouble before they become serious. Rik is going to be all right; let's just leave it at that."

I had no intention of leaving it at that; but just then two more of the passengers wandered into the lounge, so I nodded to Lanton and left. We had five days before the next cascade point, and there would be other opportunities in that time to discuss the issue. If necessary, I would manufacture them.

Alana had only negatives for me when I got back to the bridge. "The astrogate's clean," she told me. "I've pulled a hard copy of the program to check, but the odds that a glitch developed that just happened to look reasonable enough to fool the diagnostic are essentially nil." She waved at the long gyroscope needle above us. "Computer further says the vacuum in the gyro chamber stayed hard throughout the maneuver and that there was no malfunction of the mag-bearing fields."

So the gyroscope hadn't been jinxed by friction into giving a false reading. Combined with the results on the astrogate program, that left damn few places to look. "Has Wilkinson checked in?"

"Yes, and I've got him testing the shield for breaks."

"Good. I'll go down and give him a hand. Have you had time to check out our current course?"

"Not in detail, but the settings look all right to me."

"They did to me, too, but if there's any chance the computer's developed problems we can't take anything for granted. I don't want to be in the wrong position when it's time for the next point."

"Yeah. Well, Pascal's due up here in ten minutes. I guess the astrogate deep-check can wait until then. What did you find out from Lanton?"

With an effort I switched gears. "According to him, Bradley's not going to be any trouble. He sounds more neurotic than psychotic, from Lanton's description, at least at the moment. Unfortunately, Lanton's got this great plan to use cascade images as a research tool, and intends to keep Bradley awake through every point between here and Taimyr."

"He *what?* I don't suppose he's bothered to consider what that might do to Bradley's problems?"

"That's what *I* wanted to know. I never did get an acceptable answer." I moved to the bridge door, poked the release. "Don't worry, we'll pound some sense into him before the next point. See you later."

Wilkinson and Sarojis were both in the number one hold when I arrived, Sarojis offering minor assistance and lots of suggestions as Wilkinson crawled over the shimmery metal box that took up the forward third of the narrow space. Looking down at me as I threaded my way between the other boxes cramming the hold, he shook his head. "Nothing wrong here, Cap'n," he said. "The shield's structurally sound; there's no way the Ming metal inside could affect our configuration."

"No chance of hairline cracks?" I asked.

He held up the detector he'd been using. "I'm checking, but nothing that small would do anything."

I nodded acknowledgement and spent a moment frowning at the box. Ming metal had a number of unique properties inside cascade points, properties that made it both a blessing and a curse to those of us who had to fly with it. Its unique blessing, of course, was that its electrical, magnetic, and thermodynamic properties were affected only by the absolute angle the ship rotated through, and not by any of the hundred or so other variables in a given cascade maneuver. It was this predictability that finally had made it possible for a cascade point autodrive mechanism to be developed. Of more concern to smaller ships like mine, though, was that Ming metal drastically changed a ship's "configuration"—the size, shape, velocity profile, and so on from which the relation between rotation angle and distance traveled on a given maneuver could be computed. Fortunately, the effect was somewhat analgous to air resistance, in that if one piece of Ming metal were completely enclosed in another, only the outer container's shape, size, and mass would affect the configuration. Hence, the shield. But if it hadn't been breached, then the cargo inside it couldn't have fouled us up. . . . "What are the chances," I asked Wilkinson, "that one of these other boxes contains Ming metal?"

"Without listing it on the manifest?" Sarojis piped up indignantly. He was a dark, intense little man who always seemed loudly astonished whenever anyone did anything either unjust or stupid. Most everyone on the *Dancer* OD'd periodically on his chatter and spent every third day or so avoiding him. Alana and Wilkinson were the only exceptions I knew of, and even Alana got tired of him every so often. "They couldn't do that," Sarojis continued before I could respond. "We could sue them into bankruptcy."

"Only if we make it to Taimyr," I said briefly, my eyes on Wilkinson.

"One way to find out," he returned. Dropping lightly off the shield, he replaced his detector in the open tool box lying on the deck and withdrew a wandlike gadget.

It took two hours to run the wand over every crate in the *Dancer's* three holds, and we came up with precisely nothing. "Maybe one of the passengers brought some aboard," Sarojis suggested.

"You've got to be richer than any of *our* customers to buy cases with Ming-metal buckles." Wilkinson shook his head.

"Cap'n, it's got to be a computer fault, or else something in the gyro."

"Um," I said noncommittally. I hadn't yet told them that I'd checked with Alana midway through all the cargo testing and that she and Pascal had found nothing wrong in their deep-checks of both systems. There was no point in worrying them more than necessary.

I returned to the bridge to find Pascal there alone, slouching in the helm chair and gazing at the displays with a dreamy sort of expression on his face. "Where's Alana?" I asked him, dropping into the other chair and eyeing the pile of diagnostic printouts they'd thoughtfully left for me. "Finally gone to bed?"

"She said she was going to stop by the dining room first and have some dinner," Pascal said, the dreamy expression fading somewhat. "Something about meeting the passengers."

I glanced at my watch, realizing with a start that it was indeed dinnertime. "Maybe I'll go on down, too. Any problems here, first?"

He shook his head. "I have a theory about the cascade point error," he said, lowering his voice conspiratorially. "I'd rather not say what it is, though, until I've had more time to think about it."

"Sure," I said, and left. Pascal fancied himself a great scientific detective and was always coming up with complex and wholly unrealistic theories in areas far outside his field, with predictable results. Still, nothing he'd ever come up with had been actually dangerous, and there was always the chance he would someday hit on something useful. I hoped this would be the day.

The *Dancer's* compact dining room was surprisingly crowded for so soon after the first cascade point, but a quick scan of the faces showed me why. Only nine of our twelve passengers had made it out of bed after their first experience with sleepers, but their absence was more than made up for by the six crewers who had opted to eat here tonight instead of in the duty mess. The entire off-duty contingent . . . and it wasn't hard to figure out why.

Bradley, seated between Lanton and Tobbar at one of the two tables, was speaking earnestly as I slipped through the door. ". . . less symbolic than it was an attempt to portray the world from a truly alien viewpoint, a viewpoint he would change every few years. Thus *A Midsummer Wedding* has both the slight fish-eye distortion *and* the color shifts you might get from a water-dwelling creature; also the subtleties of posture and expression that such an alien wouldn't understand and might therefore not get right."

"But isn't strange sensory expression one of the basic foundations of art?" That was Tobbar—so glib on any topic that you were never quite sure whether he actually knew anything about it or not. "Drawing both eyes on one side of the head, putting nudes at otherwise normal picnics—that sort of thing."

"True, but you mustn't confuse weirdness for its own sake with the consistent, scientifically accurate variations Meyerhäus used."

There was more, but just then Alana caught my eye from her place at the other table and indicated the empty seat next to her. I went over and sat down, losing the train of Bradley's monologue in the process. "Anything?" she whispered to me.

"A very flat zero," I told her.

She nodded once but didn't say anything, and I noticed her gaze drift back to Bradley. "Knows a lot about art, I see," I commented, oddly irritated by her shift in attention.

"You missed his talk on history," she said. "He got quite a discussion going over there—that mathematician, Dr. Chileogu, also seems to be a history buff. First time I've ever seen Tobbar completely frozen out of a discussion. He certainly seems normal enough."

"Tobbar?"

"Bradley."

"Oh." I looked over at Bradley, who was now listening intently to someone holding forth from the other end of his table. *Permanently disoriented*, Lanton had described him. Was he envisioning himself a professor of art or something right now? Or were his delusions that complete? I didn't know; and at the moment I didn't care. "Well, good for him. Now if you'd care to bring your mind back to ship's business, we still have a problem on our hands."

Alana turned back to me, a slight furrow across her forehead. "I'm open to suggestions," she said. "I was under the impression that we were stuck for the moment."

I clenched my jaw tightly over the retort that wanted to come out. We *were* stuck; and until someone else came up with an idea there really wasn't any reason why Alana shouldn't be down here relaxing. "Yeah," I growled, getting to my feet. "Well, keep thinking about it."

"Aren't you going to eat?"

"I'll get something later in the duty mess," I said.

I paused at the door and glanced back. Already her attention was back on Bradley. Heading back upstairs to the duty mess, I programmed myself an unimaginative meal that went down like so much wet cardboard. Afterwards, I went back to my cabin and pulled a tape on cascade point theory.

I was still paging through it two hours later when I fell asleep.

I tried several times in the next five days to run into Lanton on his own, but it seemed that every time I saw him Bradley was tagging along like a well-behaved cocker spaniel. Eventually, I was forced to accept Alana's suggestion that she and Tobbar offer Bradley a tour of the ship, giving me a chance to waylay Lanton in the corridor outside his cabin. The psychiatrist seemed preoccupied and a little annoyed at being so accosted, but I didn't let it bother me.

"No, of course there's no progress yet," he said in response to my question. "I also didn't expect any. The first cascade point observations were my baseline. I'll be asking questions during the next one, and after that I'll start introducing various treatment techniques and observing Rik's reactions to them."

He started to slide past me, but I moved to block him. "Treatment? You never said anything about treatment."

"I didn't think I had to. I *am* legally authorized to administer drugs and such, after all."

"Maybe on the ground," I told him stiffly. "But out here the ship's doctor is the final medical authority. You will *not* give Bradley any drugs or electronic treatment without first clearing it with Dr. Epstein." Something tugged at my mind, but I couldn't be bothered with tracking it down. "As a matter of fact, I want you to give her a complete list of all the drugs you've brought aboard before the next cascade point. Anything addictive or potentially dangerous is to be turned over to her for storage in the sleeper cabinet. Understand?"

Lanton's expression stuck somewhere between irritated and stunned. "Oh, come on, Captain, be reasonable—practically every medicine in the book can be dangerous if taken in excessive doses." His face seemed to recover, settling into a bland sort of neutral as his voice similarly adjusted to match it. "Why do you object so strongly to what I'm trying to do for Rik?"

"I'd hurry with that list, Doctor—the next point's scheduled for tomorrow. Good day." Spinning on my heel, I turned and stalked away.

I called back Kate Epstein as soon as I reached my cabin and told her about the list Lanton would be delivering to her. I got the impression that she, too, thought I was overreacting, but she nevertheless agreed to cooperate. I extracted a promise to keep me informed on what Lanton's work involved, then signed off and returned once more to the Colloton theory tapes that had occupied the bulk of my time the past four days.

But despite the urgency I was feeling—we had less than twenty hours to the next cascade point—the words on my reader screen refused to coalesce into anything that made sense. I gritted my teeth and kept at it until I discovered myself reading the same paragraph for the fourth time and still not getting a word of it. Snapping off my reader in disgust, I stretched out on my bed and tried to track down the source of my distraction.

Obviously, my irritation at Lanton was a good fraction of it. Along with the high-handed way he treated the whole business of Bradley, he'd now added the insult of talking to me in a tone of voice that implied I needed his professional services—and for nothing worse than insisting on my rights as captain of the *Dancer*. I wished to hell I'd paid more attention to the passenger manifest before I'd let the two of them aboard. Next time I'd know better.

Still . . . I had to admit that maybe I *had* overreacted a bit. But it wasn't as if I was being short-tempered without reason. I had plenty of reasons to be worried; Lanton's game of cascade image tag and its possible effects on Bradley, the still-unexplained discrepancy in the last point's maneuvers, the changes I was seeing in Alana—

Alana. Up until that moment I hadn't consciously admitted to myself that she was behaving any differently than usual. But I hadn't flown with her for four years without knowing all of her moods and tendencies, and it was abundantly clear to me that she was slowly getting involved with Bradley.

My anger over such an unexpected turn of events was not in any way motivated by jealousy. Alana was her own woman, and any part of her life not directly related to her duties was none of my business. But I knew that, in this case, her involvement was more than likely her old affinity for broken wings, rising like the phoenix—except that the burning would come afterwards instead of beforehand. I didn't want to see Alana go through that again, especially with someone whose presence I felt responsible for. There was, of course, little I could do directly without risking Alana's notice and probable anger; but I could let Lanton know how I felt by continuing to make things as difficult as possible. And I would.

And with that settled, I managed to push it aside and return to my studies. It is, I suppose, revealing that it never occurred to me at the time how inconsistent my conclusion and proposed course of action really were. After all, the faster Lanton cured Bradley, the faster the broken-wing attraction would disappear and—presumably—the easier Alana would be able to extricate herself. Perhaps, even then, I was secretly starting to wonder if her attraction to him was something more than altruistic.

"Two minutes," Alana said crisply from my right, her tone almost but not quite covering the tension I knew she must be feeling. "Gyro checks out perfectly."

I made a minor adjustment in my mirror, confirmed that the long needle was set dead on zero. Behind the mirror, the displays stared blankly at me from the control board, their systems having long since been shut down. I looked at the computer's printout, the field generator control cover, my own hands—anything to keep from looking at Alana. Like me, she was unaccustomed to company during a cascade point, and I was determined to give her what little privacy I could.

"One minute," she said. "You sure we made up enough distance for this to be safe?"

"Positive. The only possible trouble could have come from Epsilon Eridani, and we've made up enough lateral distance to put it the requisite six degrees off our path."

"Do you suppose that could have been the trouble last time? Could we have come too close to something—a black dwarf, maybe, that drifted into our corridor?"

I shrugged, eyes on the clock. "Not according to the charts. Ships have been going to Taimyr a long time, you know, and the whole route's been pretty thoroughly checked out. Even black dwarfs have to come *from* somewhere." Gritting my teeth, I flipped the cover off the knob. "Brace yourself; here we go."

Doing a cascade point alone invites introspection, memories of times long past, and melancholy. Doing it with someone else adds instant vertigo and claustrophobia to the list. Alana's images and mine still appeared in the usual horizontal cross shape, but since we weren't seated facing exactly the same direction, they didn't overlap. The result was a suffocatingly crowded bridge—crowded, to make things worse, with images that were no longer tied to your own motions, but would twitch and jerk apparently on their own.

For me, the disadvantages far outweighed the single benefit of having someone there to talk to, but in this case I had had little choice. Alana had steadfastly refused to let me take over from her on two points in a row, and I'd been equally insistent on being awake to watch the proceedings. It was a lousy compromise, but I'd known better than to order Alana off the bridge. She had her pride too.

"Activating flywheel."

Alana's voice brought my mind back to business. I checked the printout one last time, then turned my full attention to the gyro needle. A moment later it began its slow creep, and the dual set of cascade images started into their own convoluted dances. Swallowing hard, I gave my stomach stern orders and held on.

It seemed at times to be lasting forever, but finally it was over. The *Dancer* had been rotated, had been brought to a stop, and had successfully made the transition to real space. I slumped in my seat, feeling a mixture of cascade depression and only marginally decreased tension. The astrogate program's verdict, after all, was still to come.

But I was spared the ordeal of waiting with twiddled thumbs for the computer. Alana had barely gotten the ship's systems going again when the intercom bleeped at me. "Bridge," I answered.

"This is Dr. Lanton," the tight response came. "There's something very wrong with the power supply to my cabin—one of my instruments just burned out on me."

"Is it on fire?" I asked sharply, eyes flicking to the status display. Nothing there indicated any problem.

"Oh, no—there was just a little smoke and that's gone now. But the thing's ruined."

"Well, I'm sorry, Doctor," I said, trying to sound like I meant it. "But I can't be responsible for damage to electronics that are left running through a cascade point. Even something as simple as an AC power line can show small voltage fluc—*oh, damn it!*"

Alana jerked at my exclamation. "What—"

"Lanton!" I snapped, already halfway out of my seat. "Stay put and *don't touch anything*. I'm coming down."

His reply was more question than acknowledgment, but I ignored it. "Alana," I called to her, "call Wilkinson and have him meet me at Lanton's cabin—and tell him to bring a Ming-metal detector."

I caught just a glimpse of her suddenly horrified expression before the door slid shut and I went running down the corridor. There was no reason to run, but I did so anyway.

It was there, of course: a nice, neat Ming-metal dual crossover coil, smack in the center of the ruined neural tracer. At least it *had* been neat; now it was stained with a sticky goo that had dripped onto it from the blackened circuit board above. "Make sure none of it melted off onto something else," I told Wilkinson as he carefully removed the coil. "If it has we'll either have to gut the machine or find a way to squeeze it inside the shield." He nodded and I stepped over to where Lanton was sitting, the white-hot anger inside me completely overriding my usual depression. "What the *hell* did you think you were doing, bringing that damn thing aboard?" I thundered, dimly aware that the freshly sedated Bradley might hear me from the next cabin but not giving a damn.

His voice, when he answered, was low and artificially calm—whether in stunned reaction to my rage or simply a reflexive habit I didn't know. "I'm very sorry, Captain, but I swear I didn't know the tracer had any Ming metal in it."

"Why not? You told me yourself you could buy things with Ming-metal parts." And I'd let that fact sail blithely by me, a blunder on my part that was probably fueling ninety percent of my anger.

"But I never see the manufacturing specs on anything I use," he said. "It all comes through the Institute's receiving department, and all I get are the operating manuals and such." His eyes flicked to his machine as if he were going to object to Wilkinson's manhandling of it. "I guess they must have removed any identification tags, as well."

"I guess they must have," I ground out. Wilkinson had the coil out now, and I watched as he laid it aside and picked up the detector wand again. A minute later he shook his head.

"Clean, Cap'n," he told me, picking up the coil again. "I'll take this one to One Hold and put it away."

I nodded and he left. Gesturing to the other gadgets spread around the room, I asked, "Is this all you've got, or is there more in Bradley's cabin?"

"No, this is it," Lanton assured me.

"What about your stereovision camera? I know some of those have Ming metal in them."

He frowned. "I don't have any cameras. Who told you I did?"

"I—" I frowned in turn. "You said you were studying Bradley's cascade images."

"Yes, but you can't take pictures of them. They don't register on any kind of film."

I opened my mouth, closed it again. I was sure I'd known that once, but after years of watching the images I'd apparently clean forgotten it. They were so lifelike . . . and I was perhaps getting old. "I assumed someone had come up with a technique that worked," I said stiffly, acutely aware that my attempt to save face wasn't fooling either of us. "How *do* you do it, then?"

"I memorize all of it, of course. Psychiatrists have to have good memories, you know, and there are several drugs that can enhance one's basic abilities."

I'd heard of mnemonic drugs. They were safe, extremely effective, and cost a small fortune. "Do you have any of them with you? If so, I'm going to insist they be locked away."

He shook his head. "I was given a six-month treatment at the Institute before we left. That's the main reason we're on your ship, by the way, instead of something specially chartered. Mnemonic drugs play havoc with otherwise reasonable budgets."

He was making a joke, of course, but it was an exceedingly tasteless one, and the anger that had been draining out of me reversed its flow. No one needed to remind me that the *Dancer* wasn't up to the Cunard line's standards. "My sympathies to your budget," I said briefly. Turning away, I strode to the door.

"Wait a minute," he called after me. "What are my chances of getting that neural tracer fixed?"

I glanced back over my shoulder. "That probably depends on how good you are with a screwdriver and solder gun," I said, and left.

Alana was over her own cascade depression by the time I returned to the bridge. "I was right," I said as I dropped into my seat. "One of the damned black boxes had a Ming-metal coil."

"I know; Wilkinson called from One Hold." She glanced sideways at me. "I hope you didn't chew Lanton out in front of Bradley."

"Why not?"

"Did you?"

"As it happens, no. Lanton sedated him right after the point again. Why does it matter?"

"Well . . ." She seemed embarrassed. "It might . . . upset him to see you angry. You see, he sort of looks up to you—captain of a star ship and all—"

"Captain of a struggling tramp," I corrected her more harshly than was necessary. "Or didn't you bother to tell him that we're the absolute bottom of the line?"

"I told him," she said steadily. "But he doesn't see things that way. Even in five days aboard he's had a glimpse of how demanding this kind of life is. He's never been able to hold down a good job himself for very long, and that adds to the awe he feels for all of us."

"I can tell he's got a lot to learn about the universe," I snorted. For some reason the conversation was making me nervous, and I hurried to bring it back to safer regions. "Did your concern for Bradley's idealism leave you enough time to run the astrogate?"

She actually blushed, the first time in years I'd seen her do that. "Yes," she said stiffly. "We're about thirty-two light-days short this time."

"Damn." I hammered the edge of the control board once with my clenched fist, and then began punching computer keys.

"I've already checked that," Alana spoke up. "We'll dig pretty deep into our fuel reserve if we try to make it up through normal space."

I nodded, my fingers coming to a halt. My insistence on maintaining a high fuel reserve was one of the last remnants of Lord Hendrik's training that I still held onto, and despite occasional ribbing from other freighter captains I felt it was a safety precaution worth taking. The alternative to using it, though, wasn't especially pleasant. "All right," I sighed. "Let's clear out enough room for the computer to refigure our course profile. If possible, I'd like to tack the extra fifty light-days onto one of the existing points instead of adding a new one."

She nodded and started typing away at her console as I called down to the engine room to alert Matope. It was a semimajor pain, but the *Dancer*'s computer didn't have enough memory space to handle the horribly complex Colloton calculations we needed while all the standard operations programming was in place. We would need to shift all but the most critical functions to Matope's manual control, replacing the erased programs later from Pascal's set of master tapes.

It took nearly an hour to get the results, but they turned out to be worth the wait. Not only could we make up our shortfall without an extra point, but with the slightly different stellar configuration we faced now it was going to be possible to actually shorten the duration of one of the points further down the line. That was good news from both practical and psychological considerations. Though I've never been able to prove it, I've long believed that the deepest depressions follow the longest points.

I didn't see any more of Lanton that day, though I heard later that he and Bradley had mingled with the passengers as they always did, Lanton behaving as if nothing at all had happened. Though I knew my crew wasn't likely to go around blabbing about Lanton's Ming-metal blunder, I issued an order anyway to keep the whole matter quiet. It wasn't to save Lanton any embarrassment—that much I was certain of—but beyond that my motives became uncomfortably fuzzy. I finally decided I was doing it for Alana, to keep her from having to explain to Bradley what an idiot his therapist was.

The next point, six days later, went flawlessly, and life aboard ship finally settled into the usual deep-space routine. Alana, Pascal, and I each took eight-hour shifts on the bridge; Matope, Tobbar, and Sarojis did the same back in the engine room; and Kate Epstein, Leeds, and Wilkinson took turns catering to the occasional whims of our passengers. Off duty, most of the crewers also made an effort to spend at least a little time in the passenger lounge, recognizing the need to be friendly in the part of our business that was mainly word of mouth. Since that first night, though, the exaggerated interest in Bradley the Mental Patient had pretty well evaporated, leaving him as just another passenger in nearly everyone's eyes.

The exception, of course, was Alana.

In some ways, watching her during those weeks was roughly akin to watching a baby bird hacking its way out of its shell. Alana's bridge shift followed mine, and I was often more or less forced to hang around for an hour or so listening to her talk about her day. *Forced* is perhaps the wrong word; obviously, no one was nailing me to my chair. And yet, in another sense, I really *did* have no choice. To the best of my knowledge, I was Alana's only real confidant aboard the *Dancer*, and to have refused to listen would have deprived her of her only verbal sounding board. And the more I listened, the more I realized how vital my participation really was . . . because along with the usual rolls, pitches, and yaws of every embryo relationship, this one had an extra complication: Bradley's personality was beginning to change.

Lanton had said he was on the verge of a breakthrough, but it had never occurred to me that he might be able to begin genuine treatment aboard ship, let alone that any of its effects would show up en route. But even to me, who saw Bradley for maybe ten minutes at a time three times a week, the changes were obvious. All the conflicting signals in posture and expression that had bothered me so much at our first meeting diminished steadily until they were virtually gone, showing up only on brief occasions. At the same time, his self-confidence began to increase, and a heretofore unnoticed—by me, at least—sense of humor began to manifest itself. The latter effect bothered me, until Alana explained that a proper sense of humor required both a sense of dignity and an ability to take oneself less than seriously, neither of which Bradley had ever had before. I was duly pleased for her at the progress this showed; privately, I sought out Lanton to find out exactly what he was doing to his patient and the possible hazards thereof. The interview was easy to obtain—Bradley was soloing quite a bit these days—but relatively uninformative. Lanton tossed around a lot of stuff about synaptic fixing and duplicate messenger chemistry, but with visions of a Nobel Prize almost visibly orbiting his head he was in no mood to worry about dangerous side effects. He assured me that nothing he was using was in the slightest way experimental, and that I should go back to flying the *Dancer* and let him worry about Bradley. Or words to that effect.

I really *was* happy for Bradley, of course, but the fact remained that his rapid improvement was playing havoc with Alana's feelings. After years away from the wing-mending business she felt herself painfully rusty at it; and as Bradley continued to get better despite that, she began to wonder out loud whether she was doing any good, and if not, what right she had to continue hanging around him. At first I thought this was just an effort to hide the growth of other feelings from me, but gradually I began to realize that she was as confused as she sounded about what was happening. Never before in her life, I gathered, had romantic feelings come to her without the framework of a broken-wing operation to both build on and help disguise, and with that scaffolding falling apart around her she was either unable or unwilling to admit to herself what was really going on.

I felt pretty rotten having to sit around watching her flounder, but until she was able to recognize for herself what was happening there wasn't much I could do except listen. I wasn't about to offer any suggestions, especially since I didn't believe in love at first sight in the first place. My only consolation was that Bradley and Lanton were riding round trip with us, which meant that Alana wouldn't have to deal with any sort of separation crisis until we were back on Earth. I'd never had much sympathy for people who expected time to solve all their problems for them, but in this case I couldn't think of anything better to do.

And so matters stood as we went through our eighth and final point and emerged barely eight hundred thousand kilometers from the thriving colony world Taimyr . . . and found it deserted.

"Still nothing," Alana said tightly, her voice reflecting both the remnants of cascade depression and the shock of our impossible discovery. "No response to our call; nothing on any frequency I can pick up. I can't even find the comm satellites' lock signal."

I nodded, my eyes on the scope screen as the *Dancer*'s telescope slowly scanned Taimyr's dark side. No lights showed anywhere. Shifting the aim, I began searching for the nine comm and nav satellites that should be circling the planet. "Alana, call up the astrogate again and find out what it's giving as position uncertainty."

"If you're thinking we're in the wrong system, forget it," she said as she tapped keys.

"Just checking all possibilities," I muttered. The satellites, too, were gone. I leaned back in my seat and bit at my lip.

"Yeah. Well, from eighteen positively identified stars we've got an error of no more than half a light-hour." She swiveled to face me and I saw the fear starting to grow behind her eyes. "Pall, what is going *on* here? Two hundred million people can't just disappear without a trace."

I shrugged helplessly. "A nuclear war could do it, I suppose, and might account for the satellites being gone as well. But there's no reason why anyone on Taimyr should *have* any nuclear weapons." Leaning forward again, I activated the helm. "A better view might help. If there's been some kind of war the major cities should now be big craters surrounded by rubble. I'm going to take us in and see what the day side looks like from high orbit."

"Do you think that's safe? I mean—" She hesitated. "Suppose the attack came from outside Taimyr?"

"What, you mean like an invasion?" I shook my head. "Even if there are alien intelligences somewhere who would want to invade us, we stand just as good a chance of getting away from orbit as we do from here."

"All right," she sighed. "But I'm setting up a cascade point maneuver, just in case. Do you think we should alert everybody yet?"

"Crewers, yes; passengers, no. I don't want any silly questions until I'm ready to answer them."

We took our time approaching Taimyr, but caution turned out to be unnecessary. No ships, human or otherwise, waited in orbit for us; no one hailed or shot at us; and as I turned the telescope planetward I saw no signs of warfare.

Nor did I see any cities, farmland, factories, or vehicles. It was as if Taimyr the colony had never existed.

"It doesn't make any sense," Matope said after I'd explained things over the crew intercom hookup. "How could a whole colony disappear?"

"I've looked up the records we've got on Taimyr," Pascal spoke up. "Some of the tropical vegetation is pretty fierce in the growth department. If everyone down there was killed by a plague or something, it's possible the plants have overgrown everything."

"Except that most of the cities are in temperate regions," I said shortly, "and two are smack in the middle of deserts. I can't find any of those, either."

"Hmm," Pascal said and fell silent, probably already hard at work on a new theory.

"Captain, you don't intend to land, do you?" Sarojis asked. "If launch facilities are gone and not merely covered over we'd be unable to lift again to orbit."

"I'm aware of that, and I have no intention of landing," I assured him. "But something's happened down there, and I'd like to get back to Earth with at least *some* idea of what."

"Maybe nothing's happened to the colony," Wilkinson said slowly. "Maybe something's happened to *us*."

"Such as?"

"Well . . . this may sound strange, but suppose we've somehow gone back in time, back to before the colony was started."

"That's crazy," Sarojis scoffed before I could say anything. "How could we possibly do something like that?"

"Malfunction of the field generator, maybe?" Wilkinson suggested. "There's a lot we don't know about Colloton space."

"It *doesn't* send ships back in—"

"All right, ease up," I told Sarojis. Beside me Alana snorted suddenly and reached for her keyboard. "I agree the idea sounds crazy, but whole cities don't just walk off, either," I continued. "It's not like there's a calendar we can look at out here, either. If we *were* a hundred years in the past, how would we know it?"

"Check the star positions," Matope offered.

"No good; the astrogate program would have noticed if anything was too far out of place. But I expect that still leaves us a possible century or more to rattle around in."

"No, it doesn't." Alana turned back to me with a grimly satisfied look on her face. "I've just taken signals from three pulsars. Compensating for our distance from Earth gives the proper rates for all three."

"Any comments on that?" I asked, not expecting any. Pulsar signals occasionally break their normal pattern and suddenly increase their pulse frequency, but it was unlikely to have happened in three of the beasts simultaneously; and in the absence of such a glitch the steady decrease in frequency was as good a calendar as we could expect to find.

There was a short pause; then Tobbar spoke up. "Captain, I think maybe it's time to bring the passengers in on this. We can't hide the fact that we're in Taimyr system, so they're bound to figure out sooner or later that something's wrong. And I think they'll be more cooperative if we volunteer the information rather than making them demand it."

"What do we need *their* cooperation for?" Sarojis snorted.

"If you bothered to listen as much as you talked," Tobbar returned, a bit tartly, "you'd know that Chuck Raines is an advanced student in astrophysics and Dr. Chileogu has done a fair amount of work on Colloton field mathematics. I'd say chances are good that we're going to need help from one or both of them before this is all over."

I looked at Alana, raised my eyebrows questioningly. She hesitated, then nodded. "All right," I said. "Matope, you'll stay on duty down there; Alana will be in command here. Everyone else will assemble in the dining room. The meeting will begin in ten minutes."

I waited for their acknowledgments and then flipped off the intercom. "I'd like to be there," Alana said.

"I know," I said, raising my palms helplessly. "But I *have* to be there, and someone's got to keep an eye on things outside."

"Pascal or Sarojis could do it."

"True—and under normal circumstances I'd let them. But we're facing an unknown and potentially dangerous situation, and I need someone here whose judgment I trust."

She took a deep breath, exhaled loudly. "Yeah. Well . . . at least let me listen in by intercom, okay?"

"I'd planned to," I nodded. Reaching over, I touched her shoulder. "Don't worry; Bradley can handle the news."

"I know," she said, with a vehemence that told me she wasn't anywhere near that certain.

Sighing, I flipped the PA switch and made the announcement.

They took the news considerably better than I'd expected them to—possibly, I suspected, because the emotional kick hadn't hit them yet.

"But this is absolutely unbelievable, Captain Durriken," Lissa Steadman said when I'd finished. She was a rising young business-administration type who I half-expected to call for a committee to study the problem. "How could a whole colony simply vanish?"

"My question exactly," I told her. "We don't know yet, but we're going to try and find out before we head back to Earth."

"We're just going to leave?" Mr. Eklund asked timidly from the far end of the table. His hand, on top of the table, gripped his wife's tightly, and I belatedly remembered they'd been going to Taimyr to see a daughter who'd emigrated some thirty years earlier. Of all aboard, they had lost the most when the colony vanished.

"I'm sorry," I told him, "but there's no way we could land and take off again, not if we want to make Earth again on the fuel we have left."

Eklund nodded silently. Beside them, Chuck Raines cleared his throat. "Has anybody considered the possibility that *we're* the ones something has happened to? After all, it's the *Aura Dancer*, not Taimyr, that's been dipping in and out of normal space for the last six weeks. Maybe during all that activity something went wrong."

"The floor is open for suggestions," I said.

"Well . . . I presume you've confirmed we *are* in the Taimyr system. Could we be—oh—out of phase or something with the real universe?"

"Highly poetic," Tobbar spoke up from his corner. "But what does *out of phase* physically mean in this case?"

"Something like a parallel universe, or maybe an alternate time line," Raines suggested. "Some replica of our universe where humans never colonized Taimyr. After all, cascade images are supposed to be views of alternate universes, aren't they? Maybe cascade points are somehow where all the possible paths intersect."

"You've been reading too much science fiction," I told him. "Cascade images are at least partly psychological, and they certainly have no visible substance. Besides, if you had to trace the proper path through a hundred universes every time you went through a cascade point, you'd lose ninety-nine ships out of every hundred that tried it."

"Actually, Mr. Raines is not being all *that* far out," Dr. Chileogu put in quietly. "It's occasionally been speculated that the branch cuts and Riemann surfaces that show up in Colloton theory represent distinct universes. If so, it would be theoretically possible to cross between them." He smiled slightly. "But it's extremely unlikely that a responsible captain would put his ship through the sort of maneuver that would be necessary to do such a thing."

"What sort of maneuver would it take?" I asked.

"Basically, a large-angle rotation within the cascade point. Say, eight degrees or more."

I shook my head, feeling relieved and at the same time vaguely disappointed that a possible lead had evaporated. "Our largest angle was just under four point five degrees."

He shrugged. "As I said."

I glanced around the table, wondering what avenue to try next. But Wilkinson wasn't ready to abandon this one yet. "I don't understand what the ship's rotation has to do with it, Dr. Chileogu," he said. "I thought the farther you rotated, the farther you went in real space, and that was all."

"Well . . . it would be easier if I could show you the curves involved. Basically, you're right about the distance-angle relation as long as you stay below that eight degrees I mentioned. But above that point there's a discontinuity, similar to what you get in the curve of the ordinary tangent function at ninety degrees; though unlike the tangent the next arm doesn't start at minus infinity." Chileogu glanced around the room, and I could see him revising the level of his explanation downward. "Anyway, the point is that the first arm of the curve—real rotations of zero to eight point six degrees—gives the complete range of translation distance from zero to infinity, and so that's all a star ship ever uses. If the ship rotates *past* that discontinuity, mathematical theory would say it had gone off the edge of the universe and started over again on a different Riemann surface. What that means physically I don't think anyone knows; but as Captain Durriken pointed out, all our real rotations have been well below the discontinuity."

Wilkinson nodded, apparently satisfied; but the term "real rotation" had now set off a warning bell deep in my own mind. It was an expression I hadn't heard—much less thought about—in years, but I vaguely remembered now that it had concealed a seven-liter can of worms. "Doctor, when you speak of a 'real' rotation, you're referring to a mathematical entity, as opposed to an actual, physical one," I said slowly. "Correct?"

He shrugged. "Correct, but with a ship such as this one the two are for all practical purposes identical. The *Aura Dancer* is a long, perfectly symmetrical craft, with both the Colloton-field generator and Ming-metal cargo shield along the center line. It's only when you start working with the fancier liners, with their towers and blister lounges and all, that you get a serious divergence."

I nodded carefully and looked around the room. Pascal had already gotten it, from the expression on his face; Wilkinson and Tobbar were starting to. "Could an extra piece of Ming metal, placed several meters off the ship's center line, cause such a divergence?" I asked Chileogu.

"Possibly." He frowned. "Very possibly."

I shifted my gaze to Lanton. His face had gone white. "I think," I said, "I've located the problem."

Seated at the main terminal in Pascal's cramped computer room, Chileogu turned the Ming-metal coil over in his hands and shook his head. "I'm sorry, Captain, but it simply can't be done. A dual crossover winding is one of the most complex shapes in existence, and there's no way I can calculate its effect with a computer this small."

I glanced over his head at Pascal and Lanton, the latter

having tagged along after I cut short the meeting and hustled the mathematician down here. "Can't you even get us an estimate?" I asked.

"Certainly. But the estimate could be anywhere up to a factor of three off, which would be worse than useless to you."

I nodded, pursing my lips tightly. "Well, then, how about going on from here? With that coil back in the shield, the real and physical rotations coincide again. Is there some way we can get back to our universe; say, by taking a long step out from Taimyr and two short ones back?"

Chileogu pondered that one for a long minute. "I would say that it depends on how many universes we're actually dealing with," he said at last. "If there are just two—ours and this one—then rotating past any one discontinuity should do it. But if there are more than two, you'd wind up just going one deeper into the stack if you crossed the wrong line."

"Ouch," Pascal murmured. "And if there are an infinite number, I presume, we'd never get back out?"

The mathematician shrugged uncomfortably. "Very likely."

"But don't the mathematics show how many universes there are?" Lanton spoke up.

"They show how many Riemann surfaces there are," Chileogu corrected. "But physical reality is never obliged to correspond with our theories and constructs. Experimental checks are always required, and to the best of my knowledge no one has ever tried this one."

I thought of all the ships that had simply disappeared, and shivered slightly. "In other words, trying to find the Taimyr colony is out. All right, then. What about the principle of reversibility? Will that let us go back the way we came?"

"Back to Earth?" Chileogu hesitated. "Ye-e-s, I think that would apply here. But to go back don't you need to know . . . ?"

"The real rotations we used to get here," I nodded

heavily. "Yeah." We looked at each other, and I saw that he, too, recognized the implications of that requirement.

Lanton, though, was still light-years behind us. "You act like there's still a problem," he said, looking back and forth between us. "Don't you have records of the rotations we made at each point?"

I was suddenly tired of the psychiatrist. "Pascal, would you explain things to Dr. Lanton—on your way back to the passenger area?"

"Sure." Pascal stepped to Lanton's side and took his arm. "This way, Doctor."

"But—" Lanton's protests were cut off by the closing door.

I sat down carefully on a corner of the console, staring back at the Korusyn 630 that took up most of the room's space. "I take it," Chileogu said quietly, "that you can't get the return-trip parameters?"

"We can get all but the last two points we'd need," I told him. "The ship's basic configuration was normal for all of those, and the Korusyn there can handle them." I shook my head. "But even for those the parameters will be totally different—a two-degree rotation one way might become a one or three on the return trip. It depends on our relation to the galactic magnetic field and angular momentum vectors, closest-approach distance to large masses, and a half-dozen other parameters. Even if we *had* a mathematical expression for the influence Lanton's damn coil had on our first two points, I wouldn't know how to reprogram the machine to take that into account."

Chileogu was silent for a moment. Then, straightening up in his seat, he flexed his fingers. "Well, I suppose we have to start somewhere. Can you clear me a section of memory?"

"Easily. What are you going to do?"

He picked up the coil again. "I can't do a complete calculation, but there are several approximation methods that occasionally work pretty well; they're scattered throughout my technical tapes if your library doesn't have a list. If they give widely varying results—as they probably

will, I'm afraid—then we're back where we started. But if
they happen to show a close agreement, we can probably
use the result with reasonable confidence." He smiled
slightly. "*Then* we get to worry about programming it in."

"Yeah. Well, first things first. Alana, have you been
listening in?"

"Yes," her voice came promptly through the intercom.
"I'm clearing the computer now."

Chileogu left a moment later to fetch his tapes. Pascal
returned while he was gone, and I filled him in on what we
were going to try. Together, he and Alana had the computer
ready by the time Chileogu returned. I considered staying
to watch, but common sense told me I would just be in the
way, so instead I went up to the bridge and relieved Alana.
It wasn't really my shift, but I didn't feel like mixing with
the passengers, and I could think and brood as well on the
bridge as I could in my cabin. Besides, I had a feeling Alana
would like to check up on Bradley.

I'd been sitting there staring at Taimyr for about an hour
when the intercom bleeped. "Captain," Alana's voice said,
"can you come down to the dining room right away? Dr.
Lanton's come up with an idea I think you'll want to hear."

I resisted my reflexive urge to tell her what Lanton could
do with his ideas; her use of my title meant she wasn't
alone. "All right," I sighed. "I'll get Sarojis to take over
here and be down in a few minutes."

"I think Dr. Chileogu and Pascal should be here, too."

Something frosty went skittering down my back. Alana
knew the importance of what those two were doing.
Whatever Lanton's brainstorm was, she must genuinely
think it worth listening to. "All right. We'll be there
shortly."

They were all waiting quietly around one of the tables
when I arrived. Bradley, not surprisingly, was there too,
seated next to Alana and across from Lanton. Only the six
of us were present; the other passengers, I guessed, were
keeping the autobar in the lounge busy. "Okay, let's have
it," I said without preamble as I sat down.

"Yes, sir," Lanton said, throwing a quick glance in

Pascal's direction. "If I understood Mr. Pascal's earlier explanation correctly, we're basically stuck because there's no way to calibrate the *Aura Dancer*'s instruments to take the, uh, extra Ming metal into account."

"Close enough," I grunted. "So?"

"So, it occurred to me that this 'real' rotation you were talking about ought to have some external manifestations, the same way a gyro needle shows the ship's physical rotation."

"You mean like something outside the viewports?" I frowned.

"No; something inside. I'm referring to the cascade images."

I opened my mouth, closed it again. My first thought was that it was the world's dumbest idea, but my second was *why not?* "You're saying, what, that the image-shuffling that occurs while we rotate is tied to the real rotation, each shift being a hundredth of a radian or something?"

"Right"—he nodded—"although I don't know whether that kind of calibration would be possible."

I looked at Chileogu. "Doctor?"

The mathematician brought his gaze back from infinity. "I'm not sure what to say. The basic idea is actually not new—Colloton himself showed such a manifestation ought to be present, and several others have suggested the cascade images were it. But I've never heard of any actual test being made of the hypothesis; and from what I've heard of the images, I suspect there are grave practical problems besides. The pattern doesn't change in any mathematically predictable way, so I don't know how you would keep track of the shifts."

"I wouldn't have to," Lanton said. "I've been observing Rik's cascade images throughout the trip. I remember what the pattern looked like at both the beginning and ending of each rotation."

I looked at Bradley, suddenly understanding. His eyes met mine and he nodded fractionally.

"The only problem," Lanton continued, "is that I'm not

sure we could set up at either end to do the reverse rotation."

"Chances are good we can," I said absently, my eyes still on Bradley. His expression was strangely hard for someone who was supposedly seeing the way out of permanent exile. Alana, if possible, looked even less happy. "All rotations are supposed to begin at zero, and since we always go 'forward' we always rotate the same direction."

I glanced back at Lanton to see his eyes go flat, as if he were watching a private movie. "You're right; it *is* the same starting pattern each time. I hadn't really noticed that before, with the changes and all."

"It should be easy enough to check, Captain," Pascal spoke up. "We can compute the physical rotations for the first six points we'll be going through. The real rotations should be the same as on the outbound leg, though, so if Dr. Lanton's right the images will wind up in the same pattern they did before."

"But how—?" Chileogu broke off suddenly. "Ah. You've had a mnemonic treatment?"

Lanton nodded and then looked at me. "I think Mr. Pascal's idea is a good one, Captain, and I don't see any purpose in hanging around here any longer than necessary. Whenever you want to start back—"

"I have a few questions to ask first," I interrupted mildly. I glanced at Bradley, decided to tackle the easier ones first. "Dr. Chileogu, what's the status of your project?"

"The approximations? We've just finished programming the first one; it'll take another hour or so to collect enough data for a plot. I agree with Dr. Lanton, though—we can do the calculations between cascade points as easily as we can do them in orbit here."

"Thank you. Dr. Lanton, you mentioned something about *changes* a minute ago. What exactly did you mean?"

Lanton's eyes flicked to Bradley for an instant. "Well . . . as I told you several weeks ago, a person's mind has a certain effect on the cascade image pattern. Some of the medicines Rik's been taking have slightly altered the—oh, I guess you could call it the *texture* of the pattern."

"Altered it how much?"

"In some cases, fairly extensively." He hesitated, just a bit too long. "But nothing I've done is absolutely irreversible. I should be able to re-create the original conditions before each cascade point."

Deliberately, I leaned back in my chair. "All right. Now let's hear what the problem is."

"I beg your pardon?"

"You heard me." I waved at Bradley and Alana. "Your patient and my first officer look like they're about to leave for a funeral. I want to know why."

Lanton's cheek twitched. "I don't think this is the time or the place to discuss—"

"The problem, Captain," Bradley interrupted quietly, "is that the reversing of the treatments may turn out to be permanent."

It took a moment for that to sink in. When it did I turned my eyes back on Lanton. "Explain."

The psychiatrist took a deep breath. "The day after the second point I used ultrasound to perform a type of minor neurosurgery called synapse fixing. It applies heat to selected regions of the brain to correct a tendency of the nerves to misfire. The effects *can* be reversed . . . but the procedure's been done only rarely, and usually involves unavoidable peripheral damage."

I felt my gaze hardening into an icy stare. "In other words," I bit out, "not only will the progress he's made lately be reversed, but he'll likely wind up worse off than he started. Is that it?"

Lanton squirmed uncomfortably, avoiding my eyes. "I don't *know* that he will. Now that I've found a treatment—"

"You're about to give him a brand-new disorder," I snapped. "*Damn* it all, Lanton, you are the most cold-blooded—"

"Captain."

Bradley's single word cut off my flow of invective faster than anything but hard vacuum could have. "What?" I said.

"Captain, I understand how you feel." His voice was quiet but firm; and though the tightness remained in his expression, it had been joined by an odd sort of determination. "But Dr. Lanton wasn't really trying to maneuver you into supporting something unethical. For the record, I've already agreed to work with him on this; I'll put that on tape if you'd like." He smiled slightly. "And before you bring it up, I *am* recognized as legally responsible for my actions, so as long as Dr. Lanton and I agree on a course of treatment your agreement is not required."

"That's not entirely true," I ground out. "As a ship's captain in deep space, I have full legal power here. If I say he can't do something to you, he can't. Period."

Bradley's face never changed. "Perhaps. But unless you can find another way to get us back to Earth, I don't see that you have any other choice."

I stared into those eyes for a couple of heartbeats. Then, slowly, my gaze swept the table, touching in turn all the others as they sat watching me, awaiting my decision. The thought of deliberately sending Bradley back to his permanent disorientation—*really* permanent, this time—left a taste in my mouth that was practically gagging in its intensity. But Bradley was right . . . and at the moment I didn't have any better ideas.

"Pascal," I said, "you and Dr. Chileogu will first of all get some output on that program of yours. Alana, as soon as they're finished you'll take the computer back and calculate the parameters for our first point. *You* two"—I glared in turn at Bradley and Lanton—"will be ready to test this image theory of yours. You'll do the observations in your cabin as usual, and tell me afterwards whether we duplicated the rotation exactly or came out short or long. Questions? All right; dismissed."

After all, I thought amid the general scraping of chairs, *for the first six points all Bradley will need to do is cut back on medicines. That means twenty-eight days or so before any irreversible surgery is done.*

I had just that long to come up with another answer.

We left orbit three hours later, pushing outward on low drive to conserve fuel. That plus the course I'd chosen meant another ten hours until we were in position for the first point, but none of that time was wasted. Pascal and Chileogu were able to program and run two more approximation schemes; the results, unfortunately, were not encouraging. Any two of the three plots had a fair chance of agreeing over ranges of half a degree or so, but there was no consistency at all over the larger angles we would need to use. Chileogu refused to throw in the towel, pointing out that he had another six methods to try and making vague noises about statistical curve-fitting schemes. I promised him all the computer time he needed between point maneuvers, but privately I conceded defeat. Lanton's method now seemed our only chance . . . if it worked.

I handled the first point myself, double-checking all parameters beforehand and taking special pains to run the gyro needle as close to the proper angle as I could. As with any such hand operation, of course, perfection was not quite possible, and I ran the *Dancer* something under a hundredth of a degree long. I'm not sure what I was expecting from this first test, but I *was* more than a little surprised when Lanton accurately reported that we'd slightly overshot the mark.

"It looks like it'll work," Alana commented from her cabin when I relayed the news. She didn't sound too enthusiastic.

"Maybe," I said, feeling somehow the need to be as skeptical as possible. "We'll see what happens when he starts taking Bradley off the drugs. I find it hard to believe that the man's mental state can be played like a yo-yo, and if it can't be we'll have to go with whatever statistical magic Chileogu can put together."

Alana gave a little snort that she'd probably meant to be a laugh. "Hard to know which way to hope, isn't it?"

"Yeah." I hesitated for a second, running the duty arrangements over in my mind. "Look, why don't you take the next few days off, at least until the next point. Sarojis can take your shift up here."

"That's all right," she sighed. "I—if it's all the same with

you, I'd rather save any offtime until later. Rik will . . .
need my help more then."

"Okay," I told her. "Just let me know when you want it
and the time's yours."

We continued on our slow way, and with each cascade
point I became more and more convinced that Lanton
really would be able to guide us through those last two
critical points. His accuracy for the first four maneuvers
was a solid hundred percent, and on the fifth maneuver we
got to within point zero two percent of the computer's
previous reading by deliberately jockeying the *Dancer*
back and forth until Bradley's image pattern was exactly as
Lanton remembered it. After that even Matope was willing
to be cautiously optimistic; and if it hadn't been for one
small cloud hanging over my head I probably would have
been as happy as the rest of the passengers had become.

The cloud, of course, being Bradley.

I'd been wrong about how much his improvement had
been due to the drugs Lanton had been giving him, and
every time I saw him that ill-considered line about playing
his mind like a yo-yo came back to haunt me. Slowly, but
very steadily, Bradley was regressing toward his original
mental state. His face went first, his expressions beginning
to crowd each other again as if he were unable to decide
which of several moods should be expressed at any given
moment. His eyes took on that shining, nervous look I
hated so much: just occasionally at first, but gradually
becoming more and more frequent, until it seemed to be
almost his norm. And yet, even though he certainly saw
what was happening to him, not once did I hear him say
anything that could be taken as resentment or complaint. It
was as if the chance to save twenty other lives was so
important to him that it was worth any sacrifice. I thought
occasionally about Alana's comment that he'd never before
had a sense of dignity, and wondered if he would lose it
again to his illness. But I didn't wonder about it all that
much; I was too busy worrying about Alana.

I hadn't expected her to take Bradley's regression well, of
course—to someone with Alana's wing-mending instincts a

backsliding patient would be both insult *and* injury. What I wasn't prepared for was her abrupt withdrawal into a shell of silence on the issue which no amount of gentle probing could crack open. I tried to be patient with her, figuring that eventually the need to talk would overcome her reticence; but as the day for what Lanton described as "minor surgery" approached, I finally decided I couldn't wait any longer. On the day after our sixth cascade point, I quit being subtle and forced the issue.

"Whatever I'm feeling, it isn't any concern of yours," she said, her fingers playing across the bridge controls as she prepared to take over from me. Her hands belied the calmness in her voice: I knew her usual checkout routine as well as my own, and she lost the sequence no fewer than three times while I watched.

"I think it is," I told her. "Aside from questions of friendship, you're a member of my crew, and anything that might interfere with your efficiency is my concern."

She snorted. "I've been under worse strains than this without falling apart."

"I know. But you've never buried yourself this deeply before, and it worries me."

"I know. I'm . . . sorry. If I could put it into words—" She shrugged helplessly.

"Are you worried about Bradley?" I prompted. "Don't forget that, whatever Lanton has to do here, he'll have all the resources of the Swedish Psychiatric Institute available to undo it."

"I know. But . . . he's going to come out of it a different person. Even Lanton has to admit that."

"Well . . . maybe it'll wind up being a change for the better."

It was a stupid remark, and her scornful look didn't make me feel any better about having made it. "Oh, come *on*. Have you *ever* heard of an injury that did any real good? Because that's what it's going to be—an injury."

And suddenly I understood. "You're afraid you won't like him afterwards, aren't you? At least not the way you do now?"

"Why should that be so unreasonable?" she snapped. "I'm a damn fussy person, you know—I don't like an awful lot of people. I can't afford to . . . to lose any of them." She turned her back on me abruptly, and I saw her shoulders shake once.

I waited a decent interval before speaking. "Look, Alana, you're not in any shape to stay up here alone. Why don't you go down to your cabin and pull yourself together, and then go and spend some time with Bradley."

"I'm all right," she mumbled. "I can take my shift."

"I know. But . . . at the moment I imagine Rik needs you more than I do. Go on, get below."

She resisted for a few more minutes, but eventually I bent her sense of duty far enough and she left. For a long time afterwards I just sat and stared at the stars, my thoughts whistling around my head in tight orbit. What *would* the effect of the new Bradley be on Alana? She'd been right—whatever happened, it wasn't likely to be an improvement. If her interest was really only in wing-mending, Lanton's work would provide her with a brand-new challenge. But I didn't think even Alana was able to fool herself like that anymore. She cared about him, for sure, and if he changed too much that feeling might well die.

And I wouldn't lose her when we landed.

I thought about it long and hard, examining it and the rest of our situation from several angles. Finally, I leaned forward and keyed the intercom. Wilkinson was off duty in his cabin; from the time it took him to answer he must have been asleep as well. "Wilkinson, you got a good look at the damage in Lanton's neural whatsis machine. How hard would it be to fix?"

"Uh . . . well, that's hard to say. The thing that spit goop all over the Ming-metal coil was a standard voltage regulator board—we're bound to have spares aboard. But there may be other damage, too. I'd have to run an analyzer over it to find out if anything else is dead. Whether we would have replacements is another question."

"Okay. Starting right now, you're relieved of all other duty until you've got that thing running again. Use anything you need from ship's spares—" I hesitated—"and you can even pirate from our cargo if necessary."

"Yes, sir." He was wide awake now. "I gather there's a deadline?"

"Lanton's going to be doing some ultrasound work on Bradley in fifty-eight hours. You need to be done before that. Oh, and you'll need to work in Lanton's cabin—I don't want the machine moved at all."

"Got it. If you'll clear it with Lanton, I can be up there in twenty minutes."

Lanton wasn't all that enthusiastic about letting Wilkinson set up shop in his cabin, especially when I wouldn't explain my reasons to him, but eventually he gave in. I alerted Kate Epstein that she would have to do without Wilkinson for a while, and then called Matope to confirm the project's access to tools and spares.

And then, for the time being, it was all over but the waiting. I resumed my examination of the viewport, wondering if I were being smart or just pipe-dreaming.

Two days later—barely eight hours before Bradley's operation was due to begin—Wilkinson finally reported that the neural tracer was once again operational.

"This better be important," Lanton fumed as he took his place at the dining-room table. "I'm already behind schedule in my equipment setup as it is."

I glanced around at the others before replying. Pascal and Chileogu, fresh from their latest attempt at making sense from their assortment of plots, seemed tired and irritated by this interruption. Bradley and Alana, holding hands tightly under the table, looked more resigned than anything else. Everyone seemed a little gaunt, but that was probably my imagination—certainly we weren't on anything approaching starvation rations yet. "Actually, Doctor," I said, looking back at Lanton, "you're not in nearly the hurry you think. There's not going to be any operation."

That got everyone's full attention. "You've found another

way?" Alana breathed, a hint of life touching her eyes for the first time in days.

"I think so. Dr. Chileogu, I need to know first whether a current running through Ming metal would change its effect on the ship's real rotation."

He frowned, then shrugged. "Probably. I have no idea how, though."

A good thing I'd had the gadget fixed, then. "Doesn't matter. Dr. Lanton, can you tell me approximately when in the cascade point your neural tracer burned out?"

"I can tell you exactly. It was just as the images started disappearing, right at the end."

I nodded; I'd hoped it was either the turning on or off of the field generator that had done it. That would make the logistics a whole lot easier. "Good. Then we're all set. What we're going to do, you see, is reenact that particular maneuver."

"What good will *that* do?" Lanton asked, his tone more puzzled than belligerent.

"It should get us home." I waved toward the outer hull. "For the past two days we've been moving toward a position where the galactic field and other parameters are almost exactly the same as we had when we went through that point—providing your neural tracer is on and we're heading back toward Taimyr. In another two days we'll turn around and get our velocity vector lined up correctly. Then, with your tracer running, we're going to fire up the generator and rotate the same amount—by gyro reading— as we did then. *You*"—I leveled a finger at Lanton—"will be on the bridge during that operation, and you will note the exact configuration of your cascade images at that moment. Then, *without shutting off the generator,* we'll rotate *back* to zero; zero as defined by your cascade pattern, since it may be different from gyro zero. At that time, I'll take the Ming metal from your tracer, walk it to the number one hold, and stuff it into the cargo shield; and we'll rotate the ship again until we reach your memorized cascade pattern. Since the physical and real rotations are

identical in that configuration, that'll give us the real angle
we rotated through the last time—"

"And from *that* we can figure the angle we'll need to
make going the other direction!" Alana all but shouted.

I nodded. "Once we've rotated back to zero to regain our
starting point, of course." I looked around at them again.
Lanton and Bradley still seemed confused, though the
latter was starting to catch Alana's enthusiasm. Chileogu
was scribbling on a notepad, and Pascal just sat there with
his mouth slightly open. Probably astonished that he hadn't
come up with such a crazy idea himself. "That's all I have to
say," I told them. "If you have any comments later—"

"I have one now, Captain."

I looked at Bradley in some surprise. "Yes?"

He swallowed visibly. "It seems to me, sir, that what
you're going to need is a set of cascade images that vary a
lot, so that the pattern you're looking for is a distinctive
one. I don't think Dr. Lanton's are suitable for that."

"I see." Of course; while Lanton had been studying
Bradley's images, Bradley couldn't help but see his, as well.
"Lanton? How about it?"

The psychiatrist shrugged. "I admit they're a little
bland—I haven't had a very exciting life. But they'll do."

"I doubt it." Bradley looked back at me. "Captain, I'd
like to volunteer."

"You don't know what you're saying," I told him. "Each
rotation will take twice as long as the ones you've already
been through. *And* there'll be two of them back to back;
and the field won't be shut down between them, because I
want to know if the images drift while I'm moving the coil
around the ship. Multiply by about five what you've felt
afterwards and you'll get some idea what it'll be like." I
shook my head. "I'm grateful for your offer, but I can't let
more people than necessary go through that."

"I appreciate that. But I'm still going to do it."

We locked eyes for a long moment . . . and the word
dignity flashed through my mind. "In that case, I accept," I
said. "Other questions? Thank you for stopping by."

They got the message and began standing up . . . all

except Alana. Bradley whispered something to her, but she shook her head and whispered back. Reluctantly, he let go of her hand and followed the others out of the room.

"Question?" I asked Alana when we were alone, bracing for an argument over the role I was letting Bradley take.

"You're right about the extra stress staying in Colloton space that long will create," she said. "That probably goes double for anyone running around in it. I'd expect a lot more vertigo, for starters, and that could make movement dangerous."

"Would you rather Bradley had his brain scorched?"

She flinched, but stood her ground. "My objection isn't with the method—it's with who's going to be bouncing off the *Dancer's* walls."

"Oh. Well, before you get the idea you're being left out of things, let me point out that *you're* going to be handling bridge duties for the maneuver."

"Fine; but since I'm going to be up anyway I want the job of running the Ming metal back and forth instead."

I shook my head. "No. You're right about the unknowns involved with this, which is why *I'm* going to do it."

"I'm five years younger than you are," she said, ticking off fingers. "I also have a higher stress index, better balance, and I'm in better physical condition." She hesitated. "And I'm not haunted by white uniforms in my cascade images," she added gently.

Coming from anyone else, that last would have been like a knife in the gut. But from Alana, it somehow didn't even sting. "The assignments are nonnegotiable," I said, getting to my feet. "Now if you'll excuse me, I have to catch a little sleep before my next shift."

She didn't respond. When I left she was still sitting there, staring through the shiny surface of the table.

"Here we go. Good Luck," were the last words I heard Alana say before the intercom was shut down and I was alone in Lanton's cabin. Alone, but not for long: a moment later my first doubles appeared. Raising my wrist, I keyed my chrono to stopwatch mode and waited, ears tingling with the faint ululation of the Colloton field generator. The sound, inaudible from the bridge, reminded me of my trainee days, before the *Dancer* . . . before Lord Hendrik and his fool-headed kid. . . . Shaking my head sharply, I focused on the images, waiting for them to begin their one-dimensional allemande.

They did, and I started my timer. With the lines to the bridge dead I was going to have to rely on the image movements to let me know when the first part of the maneuver was over; moving the Ming metal around the ship while we were at the wrong end of our rotation or—worse—while we were still moving would probably end our chances of getting back for good. Mindful of the pranks cascade points could play on a person's time sense, I'd had Pascal calculate the approximate times each rotation would take. Depending on how accurate they turned out to be, they might simply let me limit how soon I started worrying.

It wasn't a pleasant wait. On the bridge, I had various duties to perform; here, I didn't have even that much distraction from the ghosts surrounding me. Sitting next to the humming neural tracer, I watched the images flicker in and out, white uniforms dos-à-dosing with the coveralls and the gaps.

Ghosts. *Haunted.* I'd never seriously thought of them like that before, but now I found I couldn't see them in any other way. I imagined I could see knowing smiles on the liner captains' faces, or feel a coldness from the gaps where I'd died. Pure autosuggestion, of course . . . and yet, it forced me for probably the first time to consider what exactly the images were doing to me.

They were making me chronically discontented with my life.

My first reaction to such an idea was to immediately justify my resentment. I'd been cheated out of the chance to be a success in my field; trapped at the bottom of the heap by idiots who ranked political weaselcraft higher than flying skill. I had a *right* to feel dumped on.

And yet . . .

My watch clicked at me: the first rotation should be about over. I reset it and waited, watching the images. With agonizing slowness they came to a stop . . . and then started moving again in what I could persuade myself was the opposite direction. I started my watch again and let my eyes defocus a bit. The next time the dance stopped, it would be time to move Lanton's damn coil to the hold and bring my ship back to normal.

My ship. I listened to the way the words echoed around my brain. *My ship.* No liner captain owned his own ship. He was an employee, like any other in the company; forever under the basilisk eye of those selfsame idiots who'd fired me once for doing my job. The space junk being sparser and all that aside, would I *really* have been happier in a job like that? Would I have enjoyed being caught between management on one hand and upper-crusty passengers on the other? Enjoyed, hell—would I have *survived* it? For the first time in ten years I began to wonder if perhaps Lord Hendrik had known what he was doing when he booted me out of his company.

Deliberately, I searched out the white uniforms far off to my left and watched as they popped in and out of different slots in the long line. Perhaps that was why there were so few of them, I thought suddenly; perhaps, even while I was pretending otherwise, I'd been smart enough to make decisions that had kept me out of the running for that particular treadmill. The picture that created made me smile: my subconscious chasing around with secret memos, hiding basic policy matters from my righteously indignant conscious mind.

The click of my watch made me jump. Taking a deep breath, I picked up a screwdriver from the tool pouch laid out beside the neural tracer and gave my full attention to the images. Slow . . . slower . . . stopped. I waited a full two minutes to make sure, then flipped off the tracer and got to work.

I'd had plenty of practice in the past two days, but it still took me nearly five minutes to extricate the coil from the maze of equipment surrounding it. That was no particular problem—we'd allowed seven minutes for the disassembly—but I was still starting to sweat as I got to my feet and headed for the door.

And promptly fell on my face.

Alana's reference to enhanced vertigo apart, I hadn't expected anything that strong quite so soon. Swallowing hard, I tried to ignore the feeling of lying on a steep hill and crawled toward the nearest wall. Using it as a support, I got to my feet, waited for the cabin to stop spinning, and shuffled over to the door. Fortunately, all the doors between me and One Hold had been locked open, so I didn't have to worry about getting to the release. Still shuffling, I maneuvered through the opening and started down the corridor, moving as quickly as I could. The trip—fifteen meters of corridor, a circular stairway down, five more meters of corridor, and squeezing through One Hold's cargo to get to the shield—normally took less than three minutes. We'd allowed ten; but already I could see that was going to be tight. I kept my eyes on the wall beside me and concentrated on moving my feet . . . which was probably why I was nearly to the stairway before I noticed the kaleidoscope dance my cascade images were doing.

While the ship was at rest.

I stopped short, the pattern shifts ceasing as I did so. The thing I had feared most about this whole trick was happening: moving the Ming metal was changing our real angle in Colloton space.

I don't know how long I leaned there with the sweat trickling down my forehead, but it was probably no more than a minute before I forced myself to get moving again. There were now exactly two responses Alana could make: go on to the endpoint Lanton had just memorized, or try and compensate somehow for the shift I was causing. The former course felt intuitively wrong, but the latter might well be impossible to do—and neither had any particular mathematical backing that Chileogu had been able to find. For me, the worst part of it was the fact that I was now completely out of the decision process. No matter how fast

I got the coil locked away, there was no way I was going to
make it back up two flights of stairs to the bridge. Like
everyone else on board, I was just going to have to trust
Alana's judgment.

I slammed into the edge of the stairway opening, nearly
starting my downward trip headfirst before I got a grip on
the railing. The coil, jarred from my sweaty hand, went on
ahead of me, clanging like a muffled bell as it bounced to
the deck below. I followed a good deal more slowly, the
writhing images around me adding to my vertigo. By now,
the rest of my body was also starting to react to the stress,
and I had to stop every few steps as a wave of nausea or
fatigue washed over me. It seemed forever before I finally
reached the bottom of the stairs. The coil had rolled to the
middle of the corridor; retrieving it on hands and knees, I
got back to the wall and hauled myself to my feet. I didn't
dare look at my watch.

The cargo hold was the worst part yet. The floor was
swaying freely by then, like an ocean vessel in heavy seas,
and through the reddish haze surrounding me, the stacks of
boxes I staggered between seemed ready to hurl themselves down upon my head. I don't remember how many
times I shied back from what appeared to be a breaking
wave of crates, only to slam into the stack behind me.
Finally, though, I made it to the open area in front of the
shield door. I was halfway across the gap, moving again on
hands and knees, when my watch sounded the one-minute
warning. With a desperate lunge, I pushed myself up and
forward, running full tilt into the Ming-metal wall. More
from good luck than anything else, my free hand caught the
handle; and as I fell backwards the door swung open. For a
moment I hung there, trying to get my trembling muscles
to respond. Then, slowly, I got my feet under me and stood
up. Reaching through the opening, I let go of the coil and
watched it drop into the gap between two boxes. The hold
was swaying more and more violently now; timing my
move carefully, I shoved on the handle and collapsed to the
deck. The door slammed shut with a thunderclap that tried

to take the top of my head with it. I hung on just long enough to see that the door was indeed closed, and then gave in to the darkness.

I'm told they found me sleeping with my back against the shield door, making sure it couldn't accidentally come open.

I was lying on my back when I came to, and the first thing I saw when I opened my eyes was Kate Epstein's face. "How do you feel?" she asked.

"Fine," I told her, frowning as I glanced around. This wasn't my cabin. . . . With a start I recognized the humming in my ear. "What the hell am I doing in Lanton's cabin?" I growled.

Kate shrugged and reached over my shoulder, shutting off the neural tracer. "We needed Dr. Lanton's neural equipment, and the tracer wasn't supposed to be moved. A variant of the mountain/Mohammed problem, I guess you could say."

I grunted. "How'd the point maneuver go? Was Alana able to figure out a correction factor?"

"It went perfectly well," Alana's voice came from my right. I turned my head, to find her sitting next to the door. "I think we're out of the woods now, Pall—that four-point-four physical rotation turned out to be more like nine point one once the coil was out of the way. If Chileogu's right about reversibility applying here, we should be back in our own universe now. I guess we won't know for sure until we go through the next point and reach Earth."

"Is that nine point one with or without a correction factor?" I asked, my stomach tightening in anticipation. We might not be out of the woods quite yet.

"No correction needed," she said. "The images on the bridge stayed rock-steady the whole time."

"But . . . I saw them shifting."

"Yes, you told us that. Our best guess—excuse me; Pascal's best guess—is that you were getting that because you were moving relative to the field generator, that if you'd made a complete loop around it you would've come back to the original cascade pattern again. Chileogu's trying to prove that mathematically, but I doubt he'll be able to until he gets to better facilities."

"Uh-huh." Something wasn't quite right here. "You say I *told* you about the images? When?"

Alana hesitated, looked at Kate. "Actually, Captain," the doctor said gently, "you've been conscious quite a bit during the past four days. The reason you don't remember any of it is that the connection between your short-term and long-term memories got a little scrambled—probably another effect of your jaunt across all those field lines. It looks like that part's healed itself, though, so you shouldn't have any more memory problems."

"Oh, great. What sort of problems *will* I have more of?"

"Nothing major. You might have balance difficulties for a while, and you'll likely have a mild migraine or two within the next couple of weeks. But indications are that all of it is very temporary."

I looked back at Alana. "Four days. We'll need to set up our last calibration run soon."

"All taken care of," she assured me. "We're turning around later today to get our velocity vector pointing back toward Taimyr again, and we'll be able to do the run tomorrow."

"Who's going to handle it?"

"Who do you think?" she snorted. "Rik, Lanton, and me, with maybe some help from Pascal."

I'd known that answer was coming, but it still made my mouth go dry. "No way," I told her, struggling to sit up. "You aren't going to go through this hell. I can manage—"

"Ease up, Pall," Alana interrupted me. "Weren't you paying attention? The real angle doesn't drift when the Ming metal is moved, and that means we can shut down the field generator while I'm taking the coil from here to One Hold again."

I sank back onto the bed, feeling foolish. "Oh. Right."

Getting to her feet, Alana came over to me and patted

my shoulder. "Don't worry," she said in a kinder tone. "We've got things under control. You've done the hard part; just relax and let us do the rest."

"Okay," I agreed, trying to hide my misgivings.

It was just as well that I did. Thirty-eight hours later Alana used our last gram of fuel in a flawless bit of flying that put us into a deep Earth orbit. The patrol boats that had responded to her emergency signal were waiting there, loaded with the fuel we would need to land.

Six hours after that, we were home.

They checked me into a hospital, just to be on the safe side, and the next four days were filled with a flurry of tests, medical interviews, and bumpy wheelchair rides. Surprisingly—to me, anyway—I was also nailed by two media types who wanted the more traditional type of interview. Apparently, the *Dancer's* trip to elsewhere and back was getting a fair amount of publicity. Just how widespread the coverage was, though, I didn't realize until my last day there, when an official-looking CompNote was delivered to my room.

It was from Lord Hendrik.

I snapped the sealer and unfolded the paper. The first couple of paragraphs—the greetings, congratulations on my safe return, and such—I skipped over quickly, my eyes zeroing in on the business portion of the letter:

As you may or may not know, I have recently come out of semiretirement to serve on the Board of Directors of TranStar Enterprises, headquartered here in Nairobi. With excellent contacts both in Africa and in the so-called Black Colony chain, our passenger load is expanding rapidly, and we are constantly on the search for experienced and resourceful pilots we can entrust them to. The news reports of your recent close call brought you to my mind again after all these years, and I thought you might be interested in discussing—

A knock on the door interrupted my reading. "Come in," I called, looking up.

It was Alana. "Hi, Pall, how are you doing?" she asked, walking over to the bed and giving me a brief once-over. In one hand she carried a slender plastic portfolio.

"Bored silly," I told her. "I think I'm about ready to check out—they've finished all the standard tests without finding anything, and I'm tired of lying around while they dream up new ones."

"What a shame," she said with mock sorrow. "And after I brought you all this reading material, too." She hefted the portfolio.

"What is it, your resignation?" I asked, trying to keep my voice light. There was no point making this any more painful for either of us than necessary.

But she just frowned. "Don't be silly. It's a whole batch of new contracts I've picked up for us in the past few days. Some really good ones, too, from name corporations. I think people are starting to see what a really good carrier we are."

I snorted. "Aside from the thirty-six or whatever penalty clauses we invoked on this trip?"

"Oh, that's all in here too. The Swedish Institute's not even going to put up a fight—they're paying off everything, including your hospital bills and the patrol's rescue fee. Probably figured Lanton's glitch was going to make them look bad enough without them trying to chisel us out of damages too." She hesitated, and an odd expression flickered across her face. "Were you really expecting me to jump ship?"

"I was about eighty percent sure," I said, fudging my estimate down about nineteen points. "After all, this is where Rik Bradley's going to be, and you . . . rather like him. Don't you?"

She shrugged. "I don't know *what* I feel for him, to be perfectly honest. I like him, sure—like him a lot. But my life's out there"—she gestured skyward—"and I don't think I can give that up for anyone. At least, not for him."

"You could take a leave of absence," I told her, feeling like a prize fool but determined to give her every possible option. "Maybe once you spend some real time on a planet, you'd find you like it."

"And maybe I wouldn't," she countered. "And when I decided I'd had enough, where would the *Dancer* be? Probably nowhere I'd ever be able to get to you." She looked me straight in the eye and all traces of levity vanished from her voice. "Like I told you once before, Pall, I can't afford to lose *any* of my friends."

I took a deep breath and carefully let it out. "Well. I guess that's all settled. Good. Now, if you'll be kind enough to tell the nurse out by the monitor station that I'm signing out, I'll get dressed and we'll get back to the ship."

"Great. It'll be good to have you back." Smiling, she disappeared out into the corridor.

Carefully, I got my clothes out of the closet and began putting them on, an odd mixture of victory and defeat settling into my stomach. Alana was staying with the *Dancer*, which was certainly what I'd wanted . . . and yet, I couldn't help but feel that in some ways her decision was more a default than a real, active choice. Was she coming back because she wanted to, or merely because we were a safer course than the set of unknowns that Bradley offered? If the latter, it was clear that her old burns weren't entirely healed; that she still had a ways—maybe a long ways—to go. But that was all right. I may not have the talent she did for healing bruised souls, but if time and distance were what she needed, the *Dancer* and I could supply her with both.

I was just sealing my boots when Alana returned. "Finished? Good. They're getting your release ready, so let's go. Don't forget your letter," she added, pointing at Lord Hendrik's CompNote.

"This? It's nothing," I told her, crumpling it up and tossing it toward the wastebasket. "Just some junk mail from an old admirer."

* * *

Six months later, on our third point out from Prima, a new image of myself in liner captain's white appeared in my cascade pattern. I looked at it long and hard . . . and then did something I'd never done before for such an image.

I wished it lots of luck.

Afterword

"Cascade Point" started out as a raw idea—the visual effects of the Colloton Drive—plus a simple statement of the story problem—the ship getting lost through some sort of malfunction. That was it; and for *me* that's not a heck of a lot to start with. It was one of the few stories I've done where I was willing to just jump in without any real idea of where it was going or even where it was ultimately going to end up. Somewhere along the line the details worked themselves out, and the characters fleshed themselves out, and the story found its proper conclusion . . . and apparently it was the *right* conclusion, because the fans at the 1984 World Science Fiction Convention in Los Angeles voted it a Hugo Award for best novella of the year. There is no greater reward for a writer than to know the readers enjoy his work; that reward, not the Hugo itself, is the memory this story will always hold for me.

And with that final bit of philosophy we find ourselves at the end of the book. From "The Dreamsender" to "Return to the Fold" you've seen five years of style development as I've slowly grown from semi-rank amateur to at least journeyman status in this field, and from wading through all these afterwords you've perhaps gotten some insight into the view *I* have of those same five years. I hope you've found both journeys worthwhile.

Here is an excerpt from IRON MASTER by Patrick Tilley, to be published in July 1987 by Baen Books. It is the third book in the "Amtrak Series," which also includes CLOUD WARRIOR and THE FIRST FAMILY.

PATRICK TILLEY
IRON MASTER

The five sleek craft, under the control of their newly-trained samurai pilots, lifted off the grass and thundered skywards, trailing thin blue ribbons of smoke from their solid-fuel rocket tubes. Levelling off at a thousand feet, they circled the field in a tight arrowhead formation, then dived and pulled up into a loop, rolling upright as they came down off the top to go into a second—the maneuver once known as the Immelmann turn.

There was a gasp from the crowd as the lines of blue smoke were suddenly severed from the diving aircraft. A tense, eerie silence descended. The first rocket boosters had reached the end of their brief lives. Time for the second burn. The machines continued their downward plunge—then, with a reassuring explosion of sound, a stabbing white-hot finger of flame appeared beneath the cockpit pod of the lead aircraft. Two, three, four—five!

The watching crowd of Iron Masters responded with a deep-throated roar of approval. Cadillac, who was positioned in front of the stand immediately below his patrons, Yama-Shita and Min-Ota, swelled with pride. These were the kind of people he could identify with. Harsh, forbidding, and cruel, with unbelieveably rigid social mores, they nevertheless appreciated and placed great value on beautiful objects, whether they be works of nature or some article fashioned by their craft-masters. Cadillac knew his flying machines appealed to the Iron Masters' aesthetic sensibilities. Like the proud horses of the domain lords, they were lithe and graceful, and the echoing thunder that marked their passage through the sky conveyed the same feeling of irresistible power as the hoofbeats of their galloping steeds. Here, in the Land of the Rising Sun, he had been taken seriously, had been given the opportunity to demonstrate his true capabilities, and had been accorded the praise and esteem Mr. Snow had always denied him. And his work here was only just beginning!

As the five aircraft nosed over the top of the second loop, leaving a blue curve of smoke behind them, their booster rockets exploded in rapid succession. Boooomm! Ba-ba-boom-boomm. Booom!

Cadillac, along with everyone else in the stand behind him, watched in speechless horror as each one was engulfed by a ball of flame. The slender silk-covered spruce wings were ripped to pieces and consumed. On the ground below, confusion reigned as the shower of burning debris spiralled down towards the packed review stand, preceded by the rag-doll bodies of the pilots.

Steve Brickman, gliding high above the lake some three miles to the south of the Heron Pool, saw the fireballs blossom and fall. It had worked. The rocket burn had ignited the explosive charge he, Jodi, and Kelso had packed with loving care into the second of the three canisters each aircraft carried beneath its belly. Now there could be no turning back. Steve caught himself invoking the name of Mo-Town— praying that everything would go according to plan.

General To-Shiba, seated on his left, was quite unaware of the disaster. Fascinated by the bird's-eye view of his large estate, the military governor's eyes were fixed on the small island in the middle of the lake two thousand feet below. It was here, in the summer house surrounded by trees and a beautiful rock garden, that Clearwater was held prisoner. The beautiful creature who was now his body-slave and who possessed that rarest of gifts—lustrous, sweet-smelling body hair. The thought of his next visit filled him with pleasurable anticipation. As a samurai, To-Shiba had no fear of death but, at that moment, he had no inkling his demise was now only minutes away. . . .

July 1987 • 416 pp. • 65338-5 • $3.95

TRAVIS SHELTON
LIKES BAEN BOOKS
BECAUSE THEY TASTE GOOD

Recently we received this letter from Travis Shelton of Dayton, Texas:

I have come to associate Baen Books with Del Monte. Now what is that supposed to mean? Well, if you're in a strange store with a lot of different labels, you pick Del Monte because the product will be consistent and will not disappoint.

Something I have noticed about Baen Books is that the stories are always fast-paced, exciting, action-filled and seem to be published because of content instead of who wrote the book. I now find myself glancing to see who published the book instead of reading the back or intro. If it's a Baen Book it's going to be good and exciting and will capture your spare reading moments.

Another discovery I have recently made is that I don't have any Baen Books in my unread stacks—and I read four to seven books a week, so that in itself is a meaningful statistic.

Why do you like Baen Books? Drop us a letter like Travis did. The person who best tells us what we're doing right—and where we could do better—will receive a Baen Books gift certificate worth $100. Entries must be received by December 31, 1987. Send to Baen Books, 260 Fifth Avenue, New York, N.Y. 10001. And ask for our free catalog!

"Everybody is asking: How do we knock out ICBM's? That's the wrong question. How do you design a system that allows a nation to defend itself, that can be used, even by accident, without destroying mankind, indeed, must be used every day, and is so effective that nuclear weapons cannot compete with it in the marketplace? That's the right question."

THE MOON GODDESS AND THE SON

DONALD KINGSBURY

The great illusion of the Nuclear Peace is that there will be no war as long as neither side wants war. We have neglected to find a defense against nuclear weaponry—but we cannot guarantee that a military accident will not happen. We argue that defense is impossible and disarmament the only solution— but we know no more about how to disarm than we know how to shoot down rocket-powered warheads.

Exploring these situations is what science fiction does best, and author Donald Kingsbury is one of its stricter players. Every detail is considered and every ramification explored. His first novel, *Courtship Rite*—set in the far future—received critical acclaim. His new novel takes place during the next thirty years.

In the 1990s the Soviets, building on their solid achievements in Earth orbit, surge into ascendancy by launching the space station Mir. Mir in time becomes Mirograd, a Russian "city" orbiting only a few hundred miles above North America. Now the U.S. plays desperate catch-up in the space race they are trailing.

THE MOON GODDESS AND THE SON is the story of the men and women who will make America great again. "Kingsbury interweaves [his] subplots with great skill, carrying his large cast of characters forward over 30-odd years. Neither his narrative and characterization nor his eye for the telling detail fall short. . . . An original mind and superior skill have combined to produce an excellent book."—*Chicago Sun-Times*

416 pp. • 55958-3 • $15.95